HUNTING AND HERBALISM

HUNTING AND HERBALISM

BOOK ONE

Leif Roder

aka Synonymoose

Podium

Published in 2024 by Podium Publishing
www.podiumentertainment.com

Podium

HUNTING AND HERBALISM

CHAPTER ONE

Snowy Valley

Zalia

Cold, sharp winds blew through a valley deep in the north of the world. There, a forest of towering trees stood coated in a thick gathering of snow, the surrounding lands silent except for the whispering of the winds.

Within this forest was a small log cabin. The cabin was not a well-appointed house like most in this world would live in, instead containing only the barest necessities required for survival. The cabin's owner was a short woman in her midthirties, her hair naturally grey with threads of white peeking through. Her eyes were a cold blue, and her face some would perhaps describe as too sharp for conventional beauty. This woman wasn't large but neither was she thin, simply having a healthy amount of muscle gained during the course of her daily life in these harsh northern lands.

Amongst other things, the woman was a hunter. Skilled in many ways, she knew how to create and set basic traps, track various animals, and, using a large hunting bow with broadhead arrows, hunt well enough to keep herself fed. The skill was a necessity in this inhospitable environment, especially taking into account that she lived alone. The woman was named Zalia.

These are definitely deer tracks, Zalia thought, smiling.

She had run out of meat from her last catch three days after she had fallen sick. Since then, she'd been living off various foraged berries, slowly recovering her health, and while they were enough for a short time, she was now starting to feel the ache of hunger quite painfully. Two days past, a snow storm had come through and wiped out any tracks, drastically reducing her chance to find any prey to hunt, but her bad luck over the past week turned to good as she found these new tracks.

Best get to work then, she thought, settling her mind in for a long hunt.

Three-quarters of an hour later, Zalia found the animal she was looking for. It was a black-tailed deer, the only type she'd seen and the only type that lived there, as far as she knew. It would make for a good catch if she could get off a decent shot.

Zalia was currently wearing a very thick snow jacket coloured in a mottled white and grey, with its hood up to keep out the cold, and a scarf wrapped over the lower half of her face. She also wore thick pants in a matching colour, and a pair of black, heavy-duty boots. In her hands was a longbow with a draw weight of thirty kilograms, very slight tension placed on the string as she aimed at the deer in front of her. It wasn't the most advanced weapon in this world, but it was definitely her preferred one.

Exhaling slightly, Zalia drew the bow and stood in a smooth, practiced motion that she held for but a moment before noticing something quite strange. It was like a warping of the air, as if the fabric of reality itself was moving and rippling into a small, hovering ball. The deer seemed to notice it in the same moment as three things happened all at once. She released the arrow, the deer dashed away in a sudden movement, and the warping ball expanded in a rush—enveloping her, the deer, and a large chunk of land.

Zalia watched this all unfold in an instant with only one thought in her mind:

Well, shit.

What followed was a confusing sensation of movement, rushing, and spinning. Her mind couldn't understand the feeling, but her body could tell they were in motion, making her feel incredibly sick. All she could see before her eyes clamped shut was a swirling blur of colours: white, dark green, black, and brown. The sensation stopped with a feeling of sudden deceleration and a sound akin to a drop of water falling onto a still pond, only magnified a hundredfold.

Zalia opened her eyes to see the same thirty metres of land she remembered, yet it was as if it had been dumped on top of another area within the snow-laden landscape. The trees were half-fallen, the land beneath them split to the sides as it settled. Some trees from the underlying area stuck out through the top of the strange phenomenon, half-buried beneath the new chunk of earth.

Zalia looked around to get her bearings. She couldn't identify any familiar landmarks, which was quite concerning, considering that she was apparently no longer in the valley.

"Well, fuck. What the ever-living-shit was that. Looked like some full-blown magic, maybe an explosive or something," Zalia muttered.

She quickly followed up her statement by throwing up on the ground, still sick from whatever had happened. She then checked and found her bow lying nearby, two arrows missing from the quiver at her hip. She still had her emergency bag, something she kept on herself at all times when leaving the cabin. Inside the thin backpack was a small assortment of her remaining nuts and berries, enough to last a day or two if she stretched it. Alongside the food was a lighter, a tightly compressed sleeping bag, and a light, water-resistant tarp. Hanging on the side were a few metres of rope, a single metal pan, and a small hand axe she could use to cut down saplings or branches.

Zalia identified where one of the missing arrows was, quickly finding the deer dead with a single arrow sticking out from its chest where its heart lay.

A lucky shot, she thought. *Must have flinched to the side when that strange . . . explosion went off.*

It was closing in on nighttime, which was odd to Zalia. She'd left her cabin in the morning and to her reckoning, it had only been about two hours since then.

Maybe I got knocked out? she considered.

As Zalia inspected the dead deer, however, she realised that was not the answer. The body was still warm as it had been in life, though cooling quickly now. With a frown, Zalia used her knife to retrieve the arrow, which was thankfully undamaged, having missed any bone. She quickly field dressed the deer and buried the organs before tying the legs together, wrapping the tarp around it as much as she could, and hauling the animal up over her back.

Zalia walked for about an hour in the direction her cabin should've been before accepting that no, she was no longer near her home. She backtracked ten minutes to a nice camp location she'd found earlier. A small burrow cutting under a large tree's root system, while not the most comfortable place in the world, would still provide a nice reprieve from the night's cold winds.

All of Zalia's equipment and clothing were designed to camouflage her in a snowy forest environment, so after covering the deer body with her tarp, and some snow over that, she rugged up in the sleeping bag, feeling a remote sense of safety as she began to rest.

Zalia woke to the sound of snow crunching and an animal sniffing. She immediately froze, breathing lightly and making as little sound as possible. She slowly opened her eyes.

What the fuck is that?

In the small clearing outside her cover stood what could be described as an extremely intimidating, white, monstrous bear. Though it had the shape and build of a bear, the creature varied a little in that it was twice as big as a normal brown bear, was razor-backed with spines, and had six legs. After her observation, a tiny message popped up in her line of sight, at the top right. As she paid attention to it, the message expanded to the centre of her vision.

Congratulations! You have closely observed both your

> surroundings and a creature beyond your understanding.
> You have learnt the passive skill 'Aura Observation.'
> Aura Observation - passive
> Tin - you are able to identify what rank a creature is by sight,
> unless it has a method of hiding that information.

What!? Zalia thought, confused and terrified at the same time. *What the hell kind of top secret military experiment have I been kidnapped into?*

Ignoring the message, she looked at the creature once more, now noticing a little box with text had appeared above its head.

> ? - Silver rank.

The creature was now looking around, Zalia realised, for the freshly dead deer she had hidden in the snow on the other side of the clearing. It must have been following the scent of blood the body left behind.

For five minutes or so, the creature walked around the clearing, smelling the air. At one point it came so close as to push its head over Zalia, down into the small burrow. She almost lost her shit in that moment but held it together by a thread. Thankfully, the creature moved away from the clearing, leaving Zalia frozen and waiting, hoping it wouldn't come back. She lay there for about half an hour before finally deciding to get up, pack up, and, seeing where the creature had left, make her way as quickly as possible in the opposite direction.

Immediately after leaving the clearing Zalia saw another message.

> Congratulations! You have been the hunter and became the
> hunted, yet survived as both. You have unlocked the class
> 'Hunter.' Would you like to make this one of your classes?

What the hell? she thought. *Um . . . sure? Yes.*

> Congratulations! Your first class has become 'Hunter.'
> You have one more class spot available.
> Hunter. You are a hunter of beasts, animals, and monsters.
> Through hard work, precise preparation, and an instinctive
> understanding of creatures, you hunt down and catch even the
> strongest of prey. At the same time, you know the ins and outs of
> hunting and know how to avoid becoming the hunted yourself.

> Congratulations! You have learnt the active skill 'Kill Shot.'
> Active 1 - Kill Shot - spell - targeted - execute.

Tin - Enhance an attack, go for the kill. This ability deals
a tiny amount of damage. The damage of this ability scales
exponentially with the target's missing health.
Mana - high
Cooldown - 30 seconds

Congratulations! You have learnt the active skill 'Hunter's Mark.'
Active 2 - Hunter's Mark - spell - targeted - channel.
Tin - Marked by the Hunter, there is no escape. This ability marks a
creature you can see. A marked creature takes a small amount of extra
damage when damaged by you. You know the general direction of
marked enemies. Marking a second creature removes the first mark.
Mana - very low/s
Cooldown - N/A

Congratulations! You have learnt the active skill 'Escape.'
Active 3 - Escape - spell - cleanse.
Tin - The Hunter has become the hunted. This ability removes
all slowing and restraining effects and prevents further
slowing and restraining effects for the next five seconds.
Mana - medium
Cooldown - 2 minutes

Congratulations! You have learnt the passive skill 'Hunter's Sight.'
Passive 1 - Hunter's Sight - passive - body enhancement.
Tin - The Hunter tracks their prey. You can track creatures more easily.
When tracking, you learn very basic information such as the number
of legs, number of creatures, and the general size of creatures.

Congratulations! You have learnt the passive skill 'Survivalist.'
Passive 2 - Survivalist - passive - body enhancement.
Tin - The body of a hunter shall not fail easily. Gain the passive
skills for Heat Resistance and Cold Resistance. They level alongside
this ability. You are able to survive with less nutrition.

Congratulations! You have learnt the passive skill 'Heat Resistance.'
Heat Resistance - passive.
Tin - You take reduced damage from high
temperatures and heat related magics.

Congratulations! You have learnt the passive skill 'Cold Resistance.'

> **Cold Resistance - passive.**
> **Tin - You take reduced damage from low**
> **temperatures and cold-related magics.**
> **Your Hunter class has linked itself with your Strength and Dexterity**
> **attributes. As your class advances, so too shall the linked attributes.**

Zalia mentally pushed aside the host of notifications building up in her vision, and they obligingly disappeared. She quickly started feeling a burning sensation in her body, not painful or uncomfortable in any way, just . . . odd.

Ok, ok, ok, ok. What the hell . . . what the hell!? Magic? I swear one of those messages said magic. I'm going to need to read through those once I'm in the clear, Zalia thought to herself as she moved away as fast as possible.

Zalia travelled for as long as she could withhold her curiosity: about one and a half hours. Then she found a tall tree that she pulled herself and her deer up into, the coating of snow on the branches providing an almost room-like feel to the large limb of the spruce.

Ok, let's go through this assuming I'm not losing my mind. Class? I didn't know I had a class or whatever. One more class spot remaining . . . Sure, why not. Hunter, yeah, I mean, I do go hunting a lot, I guess it makes sense. Wait, ok, I heard "magic" somewhere, do I have mana? Like in those games I played back when I was a kid?

As she was thinking, a message popped up in front of her.

> **Profile - Zalia Taori**
> **Health - Excellent**
> **Mana - Full**
> **Stamina - High**
> **Class one - Hunter - Tin 1**
> **Linked attributes - Strength, Dexterity**
> **Active Skills**
> **Kill Shot - Tin 1**
> **Hunter's Mark - Tin 1**
> **Escape - Tin 1**
> **Passive Skills**
> **Hunter's Sight - Tin 1**
> **Survivalist - Tin 1**
> **Class two - None**
> **Unity Class - None**
> **General Passives**
> **Aura Observation - Tin 1**
> **Heat Resistance - Tin 1**
> **Cold Resistance - Tin 1**

Oooook then. I have mana . . . and skills . . . aaand this is crazy. I'm on the floor in the snow having a seizure, for sure. This can't be real, she thought, shaking her head. *Strange way to live out your last minutes in your mind, Zalia, real strange.*

She started reading through her abilities.

"Kill Shot, edgy," she murmured.

As she tried to activate it by thinking really hard, she suddenly felt something click and then tried punching the tree.

Ow, goddamn it. You can't just punch trees, Zalia, it still hurts.

Despite her ingenious testing methodology—punching a tree—she did feel like it had an effect. She had the distinct impression of mana flowing out of her body and the ability being locked from use.

Alright, so it works . . . I guess. You know what, this is actually really fucking cool. Ignoring the horrible, alternate-reality-looking, monstrous bear, this could make my life out here much easier. Wherever "here" is, Zalia thought.

She tried using the Hunter's Mark on a small bird flying past her to land on a nearby tree.

? - Tin rank

As she applied the mark, she could instinctively feel the general direction of the bird.

Interesting, could come in real handy with tracking down a kill as it bleeds out if I don't get a lucky shot like that last one, Zalia thought, pondering her new abilities.

Alright, it's time to get back to reality. If I'm going to survive out here, I need shelter first. I have water aplenty around me and an alright supply of food for now. She stopped for a moment to consider her options. *I could build something, but right now I think some exploration is a better idea.*

With that, Zalia got herself and the deer out of her hiding spot in the tree and began exploring.

CHAPTER TWO

Herbs and Berries

Zalia

During her exploration Zalia started paying a little more attention to her surroundings. She found a few herbs and berries that she actually did recognise, which was good. However, she also found quite a number that she did not. Still, she took some interesting ones with her as she went, wondering about their possible uses. Once her small herb pouch was full, she looked at all the bits she had collected.

Lavender - Tin rank
Thyme - Tin rank
Rosemary - Tin rank
? - Iron rank
? - Iron rank
? - Bronze rank
? - Silver rank

Quite a haul, she thought

Zalia also took and ate the berries she recognised as she went, not really having anywhere to store them. While it did slow her progress down, it was worth it in the end to hold off starvation.

She decided to head towards the single landmark she could see above the trees, bushes, and snow: a large mountain reaching up into the sky, one she very much didn't recognise and would have certainly known about if it were near her home.

Along her way, Zalia saw a variety of tracks and prints from creatures walking through the snow. Testing her Hunter's Sight ability, and using her foundation in tracking, she could very easily determine the number of creatures passing by, as well as the creature's size and number of legs. Some of these were quite concerning to her. A pack of a dozen four-legged creatures had passed through one location—wolves, she would have thought, except they were ginormous. Much larger than they should have been, she estimated them standing almost twice her height. After a few times using the ability, a notification popped into her head.

> **Congratulations! Hunter's Sight has reached Tin 2.**

Oh cool, a rank up. With a visible and audible notification. I can see that getting addicting, the affirmation of progress, she thought.

Eventually, as Zalia was travelling, she arrived at what she would call the base of the mountain. At this point however, she heard a loud, resounding roar close behind her. She looked to see the giant monstrous bear creature charging in her direction from a few hundred metres away. The thing smashed through a tree, slowing only slightly at the impact, while the whole tree toppled over.

Zalia panicked. She put her Hunter's Mark on the creature, dropped the deer, and sprinted away as fast as she could manage. She had a relatively big lead on the creature, but it was huge and barely even hindered by the trees, let alone the snow. Her heart pounded in her chest as she ran, desperately looking for anything that could offer an escape from the beast. She didn't think climbing a tree would help.

Zalia ran for what felt like forever, hearing the groaning and crashing of toppling trees, and a pounding on the ground caused by the beast; a terrifying sound that nearly matched the pounding of her heart. She could sense the creature gaining on her as she ran through the spell she had cast. She flew out from between two trees into a sparsely vegetated area at the base of what was a small cliff face reaching up into the sky—the base of the mountain. Desperately looking around, she spotted a crack in the face of the stone wall that looked like it led inwards for at least some distance.

Zalia bolted for the crack and slammed her body sideways into it, pushing herself further in as quickly as she could. The bear creature slammed against the mountain face with a resounding boom. She found herself in a small cave-like space, the crack reaching upwards to the sky above her. There was barely enough room to stand, maybe a metre in each direction before the crack narrowed again further into the mountain. Deciding this was far enough in, she breathed hard as she watched the bear scrambling and crashing against the entrance. She realised with some concern that the creature was actually managing to rip apart the stone, digging further in.

After a few seconds of the creature's efforts, Zalia noticed a growing sound. The sound of rocks tumbling and falling. The damn thing had caused a landslide. Mere moments later, a veritable flood of stone, snow, and wood came crashing down on top of the creature, crushing it underneath. Dust and snow fell down the crack as the world went dark.

CHAPTER THREE

No Violence

Zalia

Zalia fumbled around with her bag for a moment before finding the small lighter that she kept with her. Flicking it on, she could see that the crack above her had been filled in with snow and debris. In front of her, the entrance had been completely blocked, with only the head of the creature sticking out of the snow.

Zalia moved towards the creature, looking at it through the flickering light of the flame. As she pushed through the crack, the thing's eyes opened, and it stared right at her.

"Well damn, you're still alive," she said.

The creature tried to get up, but failed under the weight of all the snow and debris atop it. Then it let out a sound akin to a whimper, still staring up at her.

"Don't worry, buddy. I'll put you out of your misery," she murmured, looking sympathetically at it.

She got out her knife and leaned down, activating her Kill Shot and Hunter's Mark abilities before slamming the knife into the creature's eye.

> **Congratulations! You have killed ? - Silver rank. You have received extra experience for killing a creature three ranks above your own.**
> **Congratulations! Kill Shot has gained six levels reaching Tin 7.**
> **Congratulations! Hunter's Mark has gained four levels reaching Tin 5.**
> **Congratulations! Escape has gained two levels reaching Tin 3.**
> **Congratulations! Hunter's Sight has reached Tin 3.**
> **Congratulations! Survivalist and associated skills have reached Tin 2.**

> **Congratulations! Hunter class has reached Tin 2.**
> **Your Strength and Dexterity have increased.**

Zalia could feel the increase in her strength and dexterity. It was a minor thing, she wasn't going to go around lifting mountains but being enough for her to feel meant it was at least an improvement.

"Speaking of mountains," she murmured, "I just happen to be trapped under one." *But what the hell am I going to do now? Killing that thing increased my levels by a lot but that isn't going to help me down here.*

Damn, bringing that deer with me was a stupid ass idea. Especially after this thing already tracked me once because of it, she thought to herself.

It was a stupid decision, yet she needed the meat that deer would have provided. Now she was stuck under a damn mountain, and eating was no longer her biggest problem.

"Guess I'll have to see if this goes deeper."

Zalia ripped a small piece of wood out from the snow and debris blocking the entrance and used her hand axe to cut it down to a rough torch shape. Pulling up her snow jacket and thick undercoat, she cut off a small section of her thermal undershirt. She then cut some of the razor-like fur from the top of the bear creature's head. Using the section of cloth, she bound the fur to the top of the wood and lit it up. It probably wasn't the smartest thing to do since it would eat up her air and create smoke, but without light she wouldn't be able to find an escape and would die here anyways. The smell from the burning fur was horrendous, but she soldiered on and pushed her way further into the cave.

For twenty minutes Zalia pushed through the tight tunnel before it widened up enough for her to walk properly. Some sections she had to almost crawl through sideways, they were so tight. Ignoring the panic and fear within herself, she pushed on. The fur had been enough of a starter to light the actual wood, which now burned with a low light. As she kept on, a notification popped up.

> **Congratulations! You have learnt the passive skill 'Low Light Vision.'**
> **Low Light Vision - passive.**
> **Tin - You see better in low light areas.**

Zalia's vision suddenly got better, and she could see clearly in the dark for a few more metres than before.

"Well, isn't that just fancy," she muttered.

As she travelled further into the cave, Zalia noticed that it was getting much warmer. Significantly so, much more than it should have from just being out of the winds. She stopped for a moment to take off her snow jacket and carefully fold it before mashing it into her backpack. She still had on her undercoat, a thick, black long-sleeved top, and a thermal shirt under that.

After another ten or so minutes, Zalia had to drop the stub that remained of the torch lest she burn herself on it. As she ground down the remains of the torch with her boots, she noticed a faint glow of light coming from the tunnel ahead. Moving slowly, she approached the light to find another tunnel, this one wider, intersecting her own. Peeking around the corner to where the source of light was, she saw a small round room with sparse stone furnishings, some covered with various hides. What drew her attention the most, however, was the centre of the room where three humanoid figures sat facing away from her on rough-hewn stone stumps. Above them floated small streams of lava as if by magic.

Zalia quickly drew back into the darkness, unslinging the bow from her back and stringing it. Nocking an arrow, she decided to figure out if the creatures were aggressive or not before she attacked. She stepped out of her side tunnel, prepared to draw the bow.

"Hey!" she called out.

The three humanoids burst into motion, standing up and spinning around before freezing at the sight of her weapon.

? - Iron rank
? - Tin rank
? - Tin rank

Now that Zalia could see them more clearly, she could identify that while humanoid, they were definitely not human. Standing at about 1.2 metres tall, they had sharp, angular faces, pointy teeth, disproportionally large eyes, and were quite lanky. They wore hide clothing with hoods, almost like a poncho.

The creatures started chattering, communicating in a language made up of many varieties of clicks. Just as Zalia was about to speak again, the centre creature's eyes started glowing a deep red as the lava streams floating around the room formed into a dozen or so small spheres. As this happened she pulled the bowstring back, holding it at full draw.

"STOP, NO VIOLENCE, NO VIOLENCE," a screeching voice called from behind her.

The voice was odd, the pronunciation seeming off to her. It did however accomplish its goal, which was to give pause to both her and the other three creatures.

Zalia watched as another creature similar to the three in front ran out from the tunnel's other direction to stand between the two groups.

? - Bronze rank

It said something to the three in their language before turning back to her.

"No, no, no, no, no. No violence here. Yes, no violence," it said, nodding along, quite thoroughly out of breath.

"If you want no violence, tell them to put down the freaky magic lava orbs," Zalia said, nodding towards the three.

The mediator turned to the other group, speaking before the one in the centre released its magic. The orbs turned back into flowing streams, still quite a terrifying sight. As the orbs slowly returned to this state, Zalia released the tension on the bowstring but left the arrow nocked.

"So, I've got a question," said Zalia, "where the hell am I?"

The creature mediating the conflict looked at her with too-large eyes for a good three seconds before responding, "Under the mountain, yes, yes. Very tall mountain, yes."

Right, yes, that explains everything, Zalia thought.

"Alright, well how about a name, do you have a name?" she asked.

"Yes, yes, a name. Humans use names, yes, Glemp!" Glemp replied. "And what name would be given to you, human?"

"Zalia," Zalia replied. "You know of humans?"

"Oh yes, yes, of course. Humans, yes, very tall. A few I have met, learnt. Glemp speaks your language, yes?" Glemp replied.

"Are they . . . nearby?" Zalia asked.

"No, no, no, not anymore. Not since many, many passings of the sun," Glemp responded.

"Well, ah, do you know where I could go to find them?" Zalia asked.

"Mmm, no, no. Yes. No. Yes, a direction but not how far, yes," Glemp said, nodding.

Zalia slowly put away her bow, trusting enough in the small creatures to not immediately attack at this point. The three who she had initially met were talking amongst themselves, still suspicious of her.

"You are from the outside, yes?" Glemp asked.

"Yes," Zalia replied.

"Oh good, oh good, very interesting, yes. Did you bring any plants, or maybe some pieces of rare creatures, yes?"

"I might have, why do you ask?"

"Oh, oh, well, Glemp does much research, yes, hmmm, in the language of humans, alchemy maybe, science?"

"Alchemy, hey, I might be interested in learning a little bit from you," Zalia said. "I did, in fact, bring some plants with me—maybe you could tell me how I can use them," she continued.

"Oh good, yes, Glemp can show, follow, follow," Glemp replied, before saying something to the other three nearby creatures and beginning to walk off.

"May I ask, what does your race call themselves?" asked Zalia.

"Oh yes, humans call us Goblins, yes, but we call ourselves . . . hmm, in your language, Those Born of Heat and Stone, maybe, yes," Glemp said.

Born of Heat and Stone—I guess that explains the lava thing that other one had going on, Zalia thought.

Glemp led Zalia out of the tunnel onto a large outcropping in a giant cavern. Stretching far up and down, the cavern had pools of lava at the bottom that were lighting up the large space, the heat of which she could feel even from far away. All along the sides of the cavern spread tunnels, bridges, and paths dug into and made of stone. Streams of lava could be seen floating through the space, following other goblins as they clambered up treacherous paths. Looking further up, Zalia saw a peak of sunlight coming through at an angle far, far above them, where the peak of the mountain opened to the outside world.

As she followed Glemp, none of the other denizens of the mountain gave her much trouble apart from various stares and mutters in their language. From what Glemp said, she wasn't the first human to have travelled to the cavernous city, however rare that was.

They eventually arrived at what Zalia assumed to be Glemp's home. Rough-hewn benches lined the walls of the circular room, covered in all sorts of instruments, plants, and most prominently, animal parts. A doorway at the far end led to what she thought was probably a sleeping space of some sort. Glemp's eyes started glowing a deep red as a stream of lava flowed into the space, lighting up the dark corners of the room.

"Welcome, welcome, Zalia of the humans, to my home, yes," Glemp said, spreading their arms to the side.

"Much like your other kin, I don't really get along well with humans, Glemp. Call me . . . Zalia of the snow," she responded. "It's a nice home you have here, and you weren't kidding about the research stuff. What is all this?"

"Tools and pieces, pieces and tools, yes. Much you would have to learn to understand, above your rank, yes," Glemp said. "Of the snow, you say. Do not the beings of ice attack you?"

"Beings of ice? Not that I'm aware of. I did get attacked by some big bear thing though, if that's what you mean."

"No, no, bear things, no. I do not know what a bear is. No, we of Heat and Stone are attacked by elements of ice come to life when we stray from our home, yes."

"Huh, never saw any of those while I was there."

Glemp looked at her for a few seconds before turning to some of the benches and clearing off space.

"Place the plants, yes?" Glemp asked.

Zalia started to set out all the plants she'd brought from outside, and watched as Glemp looked over them.

"Hmm, yes, yes, I know most of these, yes. Tin rank ones, not much magic, no, no. These two of Iron rank, Snow-leaf, very common, very. Good for many snow and ice magics, yes. The other, yes, Bitterbalm, can use for some rituals, yes, rituals to put curses on others, good for cooking, too. From what Glemp has heard, it is in many places of the world, yes," Glemp said, looking at the first five.

"Curse rituals?" Zalia asked.

"Shh, shh, yes. Let me finish before you begin your questions, yes," Glemp admonished. "Now, Bronze rank, yes. Quite rare, yes, very. Good for injuries, yes. Some call it Frozen Heart, yes, a good name. Good for rituals of healing, yes, and many potions, very good use. Will slow down bleeding, diseases, all kinds of ailments, yes. But this last one, oh no, yes. Silver rank I have not seen, must be very rare, unheard of," Glemp continued, looking up to Zalia.

> **Congratulations! You have picked various herbs and learnt of their uses. You have unlocked the class 'Herbalist.' Would you like to make this one of your classes?**

Oooh, that I can get behind. Later though, later, Zalia thought.

"I wonder, Zalia of the snow, would you hunt for Glemp?" asked Glemp.

"Hunt for you?" Zalia replied, answering the question with another.

"Yes, yes, Glemp needs many materials from creatures beyond the mountains, yes."

"Hmm, you know, I wouldn't be opposed to it, but what do I get out of it? How about you teach me what you know of herbs in this region?" Zalia asked.

Glemp thought for a moment before responding, "This can be a deal, yes."

"Anything in particular that you want me to hunt for you?" asked Zalia.

An unnerving gleam appeared in Glemp's eyes.

"Oh yes, yes indeed, but not yet. Zalia of the snow needs to become much stronger, yes much. For now, whatever you find, yes, it will do."

"Alright, Glemp, it sounds like we have an arrangement. Do you have any food?" asked Zalia.

"Yes, yes, food, we have much. May I ask to keep this Silver rank plant to . . . experiment with?"

"Only if you give me something in return. Do you have any, like . . . healing potions? Is that a thing?"

"Hmmm, yes indeed, yes," Glemp replied. "You may have one for this, agreed? It is very strong for someone of your power, Zalia of the snow. You must only use in an emergency, when you are safe from outside danger. Very likely make you pass out."

"Agreed," said Zalia.

Glemp went to fetch the potion, and Zalia packed away her other herbs and plants. Returning with a small vial, Glemp handed it to her and took the Silver rank herb before moving out the door into the cavern once more.

"Let us find you food, yes, food we shall," said Glemp.

CHAPTER FOUR

Herbalist and Healing

Zalia

Zalia looked at the healing potion as Glemp walked on, leading her further into the tunnel system.

> **Healing potion - Bronze rank.**

She placed it in her bag as she followed Glemp into a large hall-like room, where she could tell they were now midway between the city's peak and the lava pools far below. The room was filled with many small circles made of stone, each surrounded by hide mats. A few of the circles had artful displays of lava swirling around inside, the shape ever-changing. Most of those circles were occupied by other Born of Heat and Stone, some few empty as the occupants were busy gathering plates of food. Around the edges of the room stood stalls built into the walls, each displaying startling varieties of what looked like mushroom-based foods.

Glemp led Zalia to a circle, gesturing for her to sit down as they spoke a small chant. The stream of lava flowing above Glemp's head moved into the circle and started swirling around, much like the other circles in the room. As they moved away, Zalia looked again at the message that had played earlier in her mind.

> **Congratulations! You have picked various herbs and learnt
> of their uses. You have unlocked the class 'Herbalist.'
> Would you like to make this one of your classes?**

She gave a mental affirmation and felt the same odd sensation as when she first accepted her Hunter class.

Congratulations! Your second class has become 'Herbalist.'
You have no more class spots available.
Herbalist. You are a collector of various magical and non-magical herbs and other flora. You use these ingredients to perform rituals and create ointments to various effects. You are a collector of herbs, berries, and useful flora. Using your knowledge of plants, you identify and refine various flora to heal, poison, and feed yourself and others.

Congratulations! You have learnt the active skill 'Flora Identification.'
Active 1 - Flora Identification - spell - targeted
Tin - Poison, cure, or food, you'll know. You may identify whether targeted flora is poisonous, helpful, nutritious, or all of the above.
Mana - very, very low
Cooldown - n/a

Congratulations! You have learnt the active skill 'Preparation.'
Active 2 - Preparation - spell - targeted
Tin - The careful preparation of herbs, poisonous or healing, can enhance their effects. You may magically dry, cut, or otherwise prepare various foods, herbs, and other similar items that are plant-based.
Mana - very, very low
Cooldown - n/a

Congratulations! You have learnt the active skill 'Stasis.'
Active 3 - Stasis - spell - targeted
Tin - Can put a small amount of herbs into stasis.
Mana - low
Cooldown - n/a

Congratulations! You have learnt the passive skill 'Harvester.'
Passive 1 - Harvester - passive - skill enhancement
Tin - The Herbalist harvests herbs and other flora, with which they do what they will. You gain an instinctual understanding of how to harvest flora of your rank and lower. Harvested flora of your rank or lower has increased potency.

Congratulations! You have learnt the passive skill 'Herbal Magic.'
Passive 2 - Herbal Magic - passive - varied

Tin - Minor herbal-based rituals are a keystone of magical herbalists. You gain an instinctual understanding of herbal rituals of your rank or lower. Herbal Magic you use of your rank and lower has slightly increased potency.
Your 'Herbalist' class has linked itself with your 'Resilience' and 'Vitality' attributes. As your class advances so too shall the linked attributes.

Congratulations! You have activated both of your classes. Your two classes have combined to form the Unity class 'Druid.'
You are a protector of nature and the natural cycle of life and death. Through your instincts and knowledge you understand both the flora and fauna of the wild places of the world. You use this ability to preserve the balance as you see fit.

Congratulations! You have learnt the active skill 'Nature's Wrath.'
Active 1 - Nature's Wrath - spell - area
Tin - You invoke the wrath of nature. Nearby enemies are bound by vines, sinking sand or other area-related hazards. Enemies are also subjected to a damage-over-time effect relevant to the biome that lasts until the restraint has ended. The damage-over-time effect deals moderate damage per second.
Mana - extreme mana
Cooldown - 6 hours

Congratulations! You have learnt the active skill 'Protection of the Wilds.'
Active 2 - Protection of the Wilds - spell - area - counter execute
Tin - You call upon the Protection of the Wilds. You and nearby allies are protected by a biome-specific shield and are subjected to a moderate heal over time effect. The heal over time heals exponentially more based on how low the target's health is and remains until the shield is broken.
Mana - very high mana
Cooldown - 6 hours

Congratulations! You have learnt the passive skill 'Healing Presence.'
Passive 1 - Healing Presence - passive - aura
Tin - Your very presence grants life to all around you. You, nearby allies, and any flora and fauna you so choose within your aura are affected by a heal-over-time effect. The heal-over-time effect heals for low health every second.
Your 'Druid' Class has linked itself with your Wisdom and Intellect attributes. As your class advances, so too shall the linked attributes.

The strange warm sensation rose to a painful heat as the second class acted out its own changes too. The sensation eventually faded as Zalia struggled through, and she was left with a host of messages explaining her new abilities.

Alllright. Various abilities to identify, harvest, and prepare herbs, pretty much what I expected. Stasis . . . hmm, I'll have to test that one out, no idea what that means. Instinctive understanding of herbal rituals. But I don't feel like I have any understanding, maybe that'll come later when I try and do it? Oh, and a second class; explains the extra pain that time around. Druid. Looks like some extra strong abilities compared to the other two, maybe because it's talking about this 'Unity class.' Healing Presence . . . Zalia thought, reading over everything.

Now that she focused on it, Zalia could feel the faint healing permeating her body and the area around her.

Well, that's just super cool. Never knew I wanted an ability like this until now. I won't be bothered by small cuts, grazes . . . or mosquitos during summer. Now that's what I call overpowered. I wonder what level of injury it could bring me back from.

Zalia looked at the others around their separate circles of stone to see if any had noticed her class activations, but they didn't seem to have, or at least didn't care if they had. She pulled out her knife, and after a few seconds of hesitation, made a small cut on her finger. She watched in fascination as it slowly closed, a few drops of blood escaping from the slice.

"Wow, I don't need to worry about small injuries anymore. Like splinters, stubbed toes, paper cuts, and a hell of a lot more," Zalia muttered to herself.

Glemp soon came back with two small stone plates filled with various types of sautéed mushrooms covered in a sweet and spicy sauce. Zalia wolfed hers down with a voracious appetite before her little alchemist buddy was even partway through.

After they had eaten, Glemp led Zalia back down the cavern, closer to the level where she had come in. They showed her the main entrance to the cavern from the outside: two massive stone doors at the end of a long hallway, barred with three large obsidian beams. At a motion from Glemp, two nearby guards started chanting in unison, their eyes glowing the deep red Zalia now associated with lava magic. The three beams of obsidian melted, flowing away and reforming nearby before the two pushed open the doors.

"I might be a week or two, Glemp. I'm quite unfamiliar with these lands and don't know how long a hunt will take," said Zalia

"Yes, yes, as long as you will need, of course, yes. It is shocking one at such a level as you can survive at all out there, yes," replied Glemp.

"I appreciate the faith you have in me," said Zalia sarcastically, a smile on her face. "Oh, and hey, if you travel down that crack you first found me coming out of, you'll find a big creature you might have an interest in studying . . . Though, it's kind of trapped under a tonne of ice, snow, and rocks," she added.

She held out her fist to the small alchemist. Glemp looked at her with a confused expression.

"Like this," Zalia said, bumping one fist with the other before extending her arm again.

Glemp gave her a fist bump with their small three-fingered hand, their own face holding a sharp-toothed smile.

"Yes, I will look for this creature you speak of, yes, yes," Glemp said, before turning back and walking into the cavern as the two doors closed shut with a muffled boom.

She could barely see where the doors met, the opening having seamlessly disappeared into the rockface. She turned her back to the doors and looked out at the snow-laden land as a gust of cold wind blew, tousling her hair.

"Home sweet home," Zalia whispered to herself before putting on her snow jacket, wrapping her scarf around her lower face, and putting the hood up. With a smile, she set off.

Zalia returned to where the bear creature had first chased her into the mountain, finding that there was very little chance she would dig out that entrance any time soon. She followed the path of destruction back to where she had dropped the deer she caught during her first moments in this place. To her disappointment, she found that some creature had come by and feasted on the deer in her absence.

"Piece of shit, that was my catch," Zalia muttered, looking at the tracks surrounding her.

She collected her rope and slightly chewed tarp before properly checking out the tracks.

"Five creatures, about half my size, four legs—and the shits were here not too long ago," Zalia murmured.

Deciding against hunting them down immediately, she got out the few sprigs of lavender, thyme, and rosemary, and used her Preparation skill on them. She watched in awe as the leaves stripped off the hardy wood stems and dried immediately, neatly separating themselves into piles. Unlike most of her hunter abilities, this was a very visible effect and it really brought home the fact that yes, magic was real. She then pulled out some of the Bitterbalm she had and used Stasis on it. The herbs went eerily still, unaffected by the wind or her movement. She realised this would most likely keep the herbs fresh, which was more important for some uses than others, but definitely a good skill to have. She quickly used it on all her other herbs, keeping them as fresh as possible.

Congratulations! Stasis has reached Tin 2.

Damn, that's addictive, she thought, smiling a little.

She saw a bush with some of the berries she didn't recognise her first time through and went to go have a look.

> **? (Poisonous) - Tin rank**

Picking some and looking again, she read:

> **? (Poisonous) (Potent) - Tin rank**

Then, using Preparation on them, she watched as they were crushed, the husks peeled away before an almost slimy substance was left behind, which promptly plopped to the floor, as she didn't want to catch it. Looking down towards the discarded husk, she read the next message:

> **? (Poison)(Potent) - Tin rank**

She got a few more and this time held up her emptied quiver underneath them, letting the substance fall in. She pushed all her arrows into the quiver, then took one back out, and to her delight, poison coated the arrowhead.

"Oh, that's just cool."

Grabbing a few more berries, Zalia used Stasis and put them away in the small pouch at her side.

> **Congratulations! Preparation has reached Tin 2.**
> **Congratulations! Harvester has reached Tin 2.**
> **Congratulations! Aura Observation has reached Tin 2.**

Using her skills had ranked up these three abilities, and she quickly read the new information provided for her. Then she set off through the forest, trying out her skills as much as she could, and finding a few more berries that were edible. She must have left a fine trail of cut and dried herbs and berries as she went, as she didn't really have anywhere to store them.

As it got closer to midday, Zalia decided to set up a hunting blind. Less for its actual purpose, but more as a home base to come back to. Using three nicely spaced trees as posts, she spent most of the day cutting down lengths of wood and using the back of the hand axe to hammer them into place between the trees. She left space for an entrance and a small window on one side. She then found a nearby river and thoroughly washed her tarp before tying it to the top of her makeshift home as a roof, with a few pieces of wood to provide support underneath. She then piled snow on top and around the thing to camouflage it a bit. It was not very spacious but she didn't need much, just a somewhat safe place to sleep. She gathered a few more berries from nearby, eating them as she sat in the small blind in her sleeping bag. With her Harvester skill, they were much more filling than she would have thought, and she soon fell asleep on the ground, rugged up.

CHAPTER FIVE

Size Doesn't Necessarily Matter

Zalia

Zalia awoke to a message in her mind:

> **Congratulations! Survivalist and associated skills have reached Tin 3.**
> **Congratulations! Hunter class has reached Tin 3.**

She felt a very slight increase to her strength and dexterity as it happened. All it was, was a slight feeling of increased strength and how fast her body could react. While not much to speak about, she felt it would definitely have an impact over time. Now that she thought about it, Glemp, who was Bronze rank, moved quite fluidly. She hadn't thought about it at the time, but she put it down to their attributes being much higher. She would bet that the little fella was also a lot stronger than they showed as well.

Zalia felt good about where she was at this point. When she'd left her original home, the town she grew up in, to move far north and live in the snow and ice by herself, it was a much different story. The first few weeks had been one big icy hell on earth, each shortcoming or problem that happened snowballing into the next. It had taken her a while to come out even and stabilise in the cold north. Now, however, she had a new friend, magical powers, and a head start on all the vital skills that she very much didn't have last time around. While her situation still held an edge of improbability or insanity to it, she was actually quite happy with how her life was going.

Zalia decided to leave her sleeping bag in the small home she had made, opting to have more room for herbs and berries she found. Heading back out into the cold, frozen landscape, she started looking for tracks. She wanted to start off with something smaller and much less dangerous than a giant six-legged bear from ice hell.

After a few minutes of looking, Zalia found the tracks of a small creature that her abilities told her was probably something like a rabbit. She followed its tracks to a burrow down in the snow and set up nearby, bow strung and nocked. It wasn't long before a small head popped up above the burrow, before the rest of the body followed. The animal looked like a rabbit with big floppy ears, except its fur had an almost metallic sheen to it. Following her fluid motion born of years of hunting, she stood, exhaled, and drew at the same moment before shooting off an arrow at the thing. As the arrow flew, she noticed one additional detail:

> **? – Bronze rank**

Which meant that the creature was on a level similar to Glemp.

The arrow practically bounced off the creature, leaving only a small cut. The two looked at each other for a single moment before both burst into movement. Zalia dropped the bow and drew her small dagger, using Preparation to refine and apply some poison to it as she stepped backwards a few steps. The bunny, however, flew at her like a tiny, fluffy missile. It hit with much more force than it should have been able to with such a small body, bowling her over. It hit just a moment after she applied the poison, and she stabbed down at the creature as they fell backwards. But the knife glanced off its fur just as the arrow had, leaving only a small gash.

> **? (Poisoned) – Bronze rank**

Much to her relief, the poison had at least been applied. The bunny-like creature started smashing its head down into her chest as she kept stabbing. Zalia felt a rib break as she threw the creature off her and stood up. She then applied her Hunter's Mark and used both her Nature's Wrath and Protection of the Wilds abilities in tandem. She watched as spiked, icy roots and vines sprang from the ground, wrapping around the creature and constricting it. At the same time, a cocoon of ice formed around her, and she felt a warmth much stronger than her Healing Presence flow through her.

Zalia watched as the creature struggled and pushed against the ice holding it still, cracks slowly forming in the magical vines and roots. She felt her rib crack back into place and let out a pained scream as it did. The creature was visibly weakening as it struggled, but it was not completely subdued—it broke out of the vines and came flying at her once more. Within her cocoon, she quickly put away the knife before pulling out her hand axe, activating Kill Shot, and waiting.

The bunny hit the icy cocoon with a loud slam, creating cracks in its surface. Additional cracks appeared in the ice as it slammed its head a few more times into the protective shell. After a few moments, its head smashed through the ice, and Zalia swung down with as much force as she could muster, slamming the axe into the bunny's head and finally killing it.

> **Congratulations! You have killed ? (Poisoned) – Bronze rank. You have received extra experience for killing a creature two ranks above your own.**
> **Congratulations! Kill Shot has gained two levels, reaching Tin 9.**
> **Congratulations! Hunter's Mark has gained three levels, reaching Tin 8.**
> **Congratulations! Escape has reached Tin 4.**
> **Congratulations! Hunter's Sight has reached Tin 4.**
> **Congratulations! Survivalist and associated skills have gained two levels, reaching Tin 5.**
> **Congratulations! Hunter has reached Tin 4.**
> **Congratulations! Preparation has reached Tin 3.**
> **Congratulations! Herbal Magic has reached Tin 2.**
> **Congratulations! Nature's Wrath has gained three levels, reaching Tin 4.**
> **Congratulations! Protection of the Wilds has gained three levels, reaching Tin 4.**
> **Congratulations! Healing Presence has gained two levels, reaching Tin 3.**
> **Congratulations! Druid class has gained two levels, reaching Tin 3.**

"Holy fucking sh—" Zalia started, before coughing up a little bit of blood. *I really need to check my assumptions about small prey being weak or vulnerable or prey at all.* "Almost got my ass put six feet under by a fucking bunny." *Check rank before you attack, check rank before you attack, check rank before you attack,* she repeated over and over in her head.

She really hadn't expected the bunny to be at such a high level. She had no doubts in her mind that if it were a bigger creature at that level she would have been dead in moments. Luckily, it seemed that what you were born as provided a starting level of power. One rank higher and that bunny would have been her end; it didn't even have magic, just pure, raw bun strength.

Zalia cleaned off her knife and axe, retrieved her arrow, slung the bunny over her shoulder, and started her walk back.

CHAPTER SIX

Progress . . . To Who Knows What

Zalia

On her way back to her blind, Zalia again cut and stored as many herbs and plants as she could.

> **Congratulations! Flora Identification has reached Tin 2.**
> **Congratulations! Stasis has reached Tin 3.**
> **Congratulations! Herbalist has reached Tin 2.**

She found quite a few more bits of Bitterbalm and Snow-leaf but no more of the rare Bronze rank Frozen Heart, or the Silver rank one she had left with Glemp.

Reaching her blind, Zalia quickly set up a small fire, over which she put a spit for the skinned and field-dressed rabbit. Actually skinning the thing took a considerable amount of time because cutting through the metallic hide was quite difficult. While it cooked she added some of the thyme, rosemary, and Bitterbalm, sprinkling it on. It wouldn't be the best meal she'd ever had, but it would do. She wished she had a bit of salt somewhere, but out in the snow you do what you can with what you have.

Probably can't fight any creature above Iron, and especially not if I don't have my long cooldown abilities, Zalia thought. *Mmm, Glemp wasn't lying that the Bitterbalm is quite good for cooking . . . and I'm poisoning myself by eating this, but Healing Presence is countering it.*

Now that she didn't have the emergency backup of those two abilities for six hours, she was feeling a bit less comfortable going out for another hunt just yet. As such, she spent the rest of the day collecting herbs and trying out what she could do with them. Chewing on a bit of Frost-leaf, she found that it quite significantly cooled down her body temperature but didn't do much else. The Bitterbalm just tasted nice, speaking to its use in cooking. When she decided to eat a little bit of the Frozen Heart, she found that it did feel like it healed her a little. Though she couldn't speak to its ability to slow down any disease or bleeding, it could be useful in the right circumstance.

Zalia didn't have any experience in alchemy like Glemp did, and neither did she have any interest in learning it. She was more interested in very simple applications of what herbs could do quickly. She decided to fold up the hide of the bunny and give it to Glemp as a gift next time she went back that way.

The next week and a half were spent testing out and finding the limits of her newfound magical powers. Zalia also found a few more of the bunnies, all of an Iron rank, however, and relatively easy to take down without her use of the high cooldown abilities. Her bag was now packed with as many herbs as she could find, so she had taken to leaving it at her blind. She came across a few more pieces of the Frozen Heart and had to use some during one of her fights where a bunny had gotten in a particularly savage headbutt. Drawing closer to the week and a half mark, Zalia decided to hunt something a bit bigger. She was sticking to her Iron-rank-only rule, making sure not to attack anything higher than that and running from anything that decided to give chase. Before going on this final hunt, she checked her progress.

Congratulations! Kill Shot has gained five levels, reaching Tin 14.
Congratulations! Hunter's Mark has gained four levels, reaching Tin 12.
Congratulations! Escape has reached Tin 5.
Congratulations! Hunter's Sight has gained five levels, reaching Tin 9.
**Congratulations! Survivalist and associated skills
have gained five levels, reaching Tin 10.**
Congratulations! Hunter class has reached Tin 5.
**Congratulations! Flora Identification has
gained five levels, reaching Tin 7.**
Congratulations! Preparation has gained five levels, reaching Tin 8.
Congratulations! Stasis has gained three levels, reaching Tin 6.
Congratulations! Harvester has gained five levels, reaching Tin 7.
Congratulations! Herbal Magic has gained two levels, reaching Tin 4.
Congratulations! Herbalist class has gained two levels, reaching Tin 4.
Congratulations! Nature's Wrath has reached Tin 5.
Congratulations! Protection of the Wilds has reached Tin 5.
Congratulations! Healing Presence has gained four levels, reaching Tin 7.
Congratulations! Druid class has gained two levels, reaching Tin 5.
Congratulations! Low Light Vision has reached Tin 2.

She was quite happy with her progress, although Herbal Magic was falling behind a bit because she hadn't found any Tin rank herbs she could do rituals with. Nature's Wrath and Protection of the Wilds had the same issue: they weren't levelling as fast since she couldn't or didn't use them as often. It was evident they all gained at least some experience from each kill, thus levelling even when not in use. Some of the higher level skills were also slowing down a bit as they got higher and she got used to fighting what she had dubbed the Ironfur rabbits. Her Healing Presence, however, actually levelled from healing the slight poisoning she got from eating the animals she killed. Each fight had gotten easier as her abilities grew in strength too, dealing more damage, healing more, and having more of an effect in general. She also grew somewhat stronger and faster, and was able to take more punishment before a long cooldown ability needed to be used.

She didn't know why the bunnies were so violent, but she assumed it was part of why they grew to such great strength. She had a sneaking suspicion that they were also carnivorous and probably what had taken her deer in the first place. The last thing she discovered was that if she dried up, crushed, and mixed some of the Snow-leaf with the poisonous berry gel she had started calling Frost berries, the effect of the poison was heightened and caused whatever was poisoned to move a little slower.

Zalia's new target was whichever creature made the new set of tracks she'd found. A large, four-legged animal about her size, from what Hunter's Sight told her. It seemed to move by itself, not in a pack, which was good for her. At least, she thought it was. She had tracked it down to what could be called a den of some sorts. Not wanting to go in, she set a trap out in the front of the den, pushing a bunch of sharpened spikes into the hardened earth by the entrance and covering them again with snow. Then she waited with her bow strung. This time around she knew to have both her axe and dagger pre-poisoned just in case.

An hour later, Zalia caught sight of the creature. The creature was dog-like— four-legged, and looked like it could run plenty fast. It had two tentacle-like protrusions coming out from either shoulder and was quite thick-furred with cold, blue eyes. As it came out of the den, it sniffed at the air before looking in her direction.

? - Iron rank

Luckily for her, it was Iron rank. Exactly what she was looking for. It met her eyes as she stood, activated Hunter's Mark, and shot, the arrow lodging into the creature's shoulder. It yelped before looking her way again, this time with its eyes glowing. She felt herself slow down and freeze as the two tentacle-like limbs lifted up and three crackling ice spears grew between them. Just as the ice spears shot towards her, Zalia used her Escape ability and threw herself out of their way. She received just a scratch for her efforts, which quickly healed, allowing her to nock another arrow as the creature ran towards her. As it ran over her trap, it slowed, making angry growling sounds as its feet were stabbed by the poisoned spikes.

> **? (Poisoned) (Slowed) - Iron rank**

Zalia fired off another shot, hitting it in the leg before it went down at speed, tumbling towards her in a pile of limbs. She hopped out of the way once more, activating Kill Shot before delivering one more arrow to its head as it tried to get up.

> **Congratulations! You have killed ? (Poisoned) (Slowed)**
> **- Iron rank. You have received extra experience for**
> **killing a creature one rank above your own.**
> **Congratulations! Kill Shot has reached Tin 15.**
> **Congratulations! Hunter's Mark has reached Tin 13.**
> **Congratulations! Healing Presence has reached Tin 8.**

"Doesn't seem like there are many other Tin rankers out there," Zalia said. "Maybe other humans are closer to my rank, though this fight seemed easy enough since I dodged most of its magic with one ability."

She quickly removed her arrows, of which she had only six left of her original twelve. Many had broken on the Ironfur rabbits during her week and a half of hunting. This creature had actually used some magic, so she thought Glemp might take an interest in it. She could see the creature's veins discoloured from where her arrows and spikes had poisoned it. It turned out the constant damage amplified by her Hunter's Mark did significant harm, as did arrows to its head. Hauling the thing up onto her shoulders, she made her way towards the Goblin city.

CHAPTER SEVEN

Lava and Ice

Zalia

Zalia came around the mountain, arriving back at where she remembered the door to be. She immediately noticed something was wrong, as the door was cracked and had been smashed open. Dropping her kill and stringing her bow, she carefully approached as she nocked an arrow. The only tracks she could see were those of about fifteen goblins and nothing else, though she did see patches of icy frost marking the door and hallway beyond. Coming into view of the whole hallway, she could see a frozen figure.

Zalia quickly ran up to the small goblin and realised they were quite literally frozen still, now simply a sculpture of a running goblin, looking over its shoulder. *Some kind of ice magic*, she thought.

Moving further into the hallway, she could hear whispering sounds coming from beyond, occasionally overlaid with a shout of pain.

Running quickly towards the city, Zalia came out of the hallway to a terrifying sight. Floating in the middle of the huge space were three figures. Two smaller and one larger, though all held the same form: they were made of six disconnected pieces of sharp, crystalline ice roughly shaped into a humanoid figure. Each of the smaller ones were Silver rank and the large one, Gold rank—much to her dismay. There wasn't much she would be able to contribute to this fight.

What made it a terrifying sight, however, were the hundreds if not thousands of pinprick-like eyes glowing red all around the walls of the space. From each of them, a whispering chant emanated that filled the room with a nearly tangible sound. She knew what this was and had, in fact, previously seen two of the goblins working their lava magic in unison before. That had been to simply open the door, but she was excited to see what happened when an entire city worked their magic in unison like this.

Zalia watched as the three icy creatures shot out dozens of spikes, each exploding with an ear-piercing shattering sound. As they did so, dozens of eyes went dark, but the chant didn't stop. It came to a crescendo as what must have been an entire mountain of lava flowed from the floor of the mountain and surged up towards the creatures. The two Silver rank figures were almost immediately dissipated with the hissing of melting ice and an unworldly scream that sounded like an iceberg shattering. The third and highest ranked one lasted a bit longer, creating a shield of ice around itself as the lava melted ever inwards. It fired off some remaining ice bolts and managed to take one goblin with it before its shield shattered and it too hissed away, giving a final scream.

Zalia watched as a large number of the goblins passed out immediately, with a few others bending down as if to catch their breath. The large majority of them seemed fine, though, so she wasn't worried. Unstringing her bow, she made her way back to pick up her kill, and started quickly heading towards Glemp's home. She hoped he hadn't suffered an icy death at those creatures' hands. Along the way she did notice that the goblins passed out were all of Iron rank, except for the singular Tin rank she saw.

Well, at least I'm not the only one, thought Zalia. *Probably the only one at my age, though.*

She received a few more hostile stares on her way to Glemp's home. Arriving, she popped her head around the corner to find Glemp leaning over a counter muttering to themself.

"Oh, thank god," she said upon seeing Glemp safe and sound.

"Yes, which one?" Glemp replied, looking up.

Zalia simply smiled, not quite ready to get into that topic just yet. "So, I brought you something, Glemp!" she said, and dumped the dead creature on their floor. She pointed at it, looking at Glemp proudly. "Look!"

Glemp scampered over quickly, inspecting the body.

"Yes, yes, very dead, good job, Zalia of the snow. What is this poison I see in its veins? Very potent yes, very," asked Glemp, looking up at her.

"Why, one of my very own make, of course. Got some berries, got some leaves, mashed them together and bam, poison," she replied.

Glemp looked at her, dumbfounded.

"No, no, no, no. That is not how research works, not how alchemy works!" Glemp said, looking back down at the creature, a little angry, or frustrated perhaps.

"It's how it works for me, my instincts told me so," Zalia stated.

Appearing ever more frustrated, Glemp looked back up at her once more. "No, no, no, have you been eating those you hunt like this?" Glemp asked.

"Sure have," she said.

"No, you are a ghost, not alive, not alive. Resistant to poisons?" Glemp asked.

"Nope," she said as she sat on one of Glemp's benches, getting out a few berries to eat.

Glemp gave her a real odd look; Zalia had no idea why.

"I have an ability that means I have to eat less. I think it slows down my metabolism and feeds my body with magic, or something? That plus a healing ability means the poison is neutralised before or as my body absorbs it... I think," Zalia said, after a few seconds of silence.

"Ah, yes, yes. Explains much. You should try some of this poison on yourself, yes indeed," Glemp said before getting back to what they were doing.

"Huh," Zalia said under her breath.

She popped the last berry in her mouth before getting out one of the poisoned arrows. She hesitated for a moment before cutting into her arm. Immediately, she felt a cold burning sensation running through her veins. The feeling when something is so hot it feels cold. She groaned before falling to her knees on the floor.

"Oh, holy shit," she moaned.

Getting out a little bit of Frozen Heart, she started chewing it. She could feel the poison slow down and relaxed a little bit, letting her healing do its work. She only relaxed for a moment however, before the poison reached her heart and was promptly pushed throughout her entire body. She let out a pained scream as her entire body lit on fire, and caught sight of a single message before she passed out:

> **Congratulations! You have learned the passive skill 'Poison Resistance.' Tin - take reduced damage from poisons and poison based magics.**

CHAPTER EIGHT

Poison and Pleasantries

Zalia

Zalia woke to the sight of two large eyes staring down at her.

"Uhhh, g— off mmm," Zalia slurred.

"Yes, yes, very alive," Glemp said before nodding and moving away.

Zalia sat up groggily, looking at the messages in front of her.

Congratulations! Poison Resistance has gained four levels reaching Tin 5.

Hmm . . . wow, that was some really efficient levelling, she thought.

She'd started to feel better due to her passive healing, yet was still sitting on the floor.

"Hey, Glemp, those things that attacked your city . . . is that normal?" she asked.

"Hmm, yes, no. Some young ones saw you leave without violence and also did. Soon they came back with these, yes," Glemp replied.

"Are those the elements of ice you spoke of before? Ice Elementals?"

"Yes, yes, never used to attack but now always, always such violence," Glemp responded, scowling.

I can't think of why they wouldn't attack me when they always attack the goblins, though. It's not like there's much difference between us, except for their mag— Zalia came to a realisation.

"Hey, Glemp, maybe the ice Elementals attack you because of your lava magic."

"Yes, no. Some have thought this, but for many seasons this magic has been ours, and only within many passings of the sun have they attacked, yes," Glemp replied.

"How many . . . passings of the sun have they attacked for?" she asked

"Mmm, yes, maybe fifty?"

So, like, almost two months . . . Do they use months here? Doesn't seem like it, Zalia thought, *maybe it isn't their magic then, hmm.*

"No idea, then. How are you coming with that Silver rank herb I left you. Any discoveries?" she asked instead.

"No, no. Must be very careful, very slow, very precise. Yes, a while it will take me," Glemp said, looking pointedly at where she had poisoned herself.

"I'll concede that point," Zalia grumbled. "Well, what about that creature you wanted me to hunt, think I'm ready yet?"

"No," Glemp said, giving her an almost criminal amount of side-eye.

"So rude," Zalia muttered.

Looking down at her arm, she took out an arrow again.

Probably want to rid myself of this weakness as soon as possible so someone doesn't kill me with my own poison, she thought.

She put the arrow to her arm and cut in again, taking out some more Frozen Heart and chewing it. Once more, as the poison reached her heart and spread across her whole body, she passed out.

Zalia spent the rest of the day slowly bringing up her Poison Resistance until it eventually reached Iron rank:

Congratulations! Poison Resistance has gained
fifteen levels, reaching Tin 20.
Congratulations! Poison Resistance has reached Iron 1.
Poison Resistance - passive
Tin - take reduced damage from poisons and poison based magics.
Iron - gain immunity to poisons of one rank below this passive.
Some incredibly potent poisons may still affect you minorly.
This skill will not rank further until all your classes reach Iron 1.

Damn, that was painful. Definitely worth it, though . . . I think. I guess I'll find out if anyone ever stabs me with my own weapons.

She had only passed out that second time, each additional time handling a bit more and, at the least, managing to remain conscious. She had lived out in the wilds for a good time now and knew to take every advantage she could get.

When Zalia cut herself, the poison only remained for a few moments before fading away again. Glemp had glanced at her a few times as she twitched on the floor in pain, but didn't comment, likely assuming she had some reason for her behaviour. While she definitely had a reason, it might not have been an entirely sane one.

"Hey, Glemp, do you know the direction the other humans live in?" she asked, after testing out her new resistance.

"Yes, yes, if the sun rises in this direction and passes in this direction, then they are this direction, yes," Glemp explained.

"We call those east, west, and south," Zalia said.

Well, at least I know I'm still in the north. That's good news, maybe my home isn't so far away. Hmm.

"Do you know much about other humans?" she asked.

"No, no, only they do not like Those Born of Heat and Stone," Glemp replied, still very focused on whatever they were doing. "You did not come from human lands, yes?"

"Well, yes, I did but I have not been there for . . . many, many seasons," she replied. "I think I'll go there soon, for a few weeks maybe. I've lived in the north for half of my life."

"Many seasons, no, no. You cannot be more than a few, yes, at such a rank?" Glemp asked.

"I only got my magic these past . . . twelve passings of the sun. We call those 'days,' by the way," Zalia responded.

"Yes, no, no, how many . . . days old are you then, Zalia of the snow?" Glemp asked, focused now.

"Well, that's a bit of a rude question," Zalia retorted.

Glemp just stared at her in confusion.

"It's . . . never mind. I am about, ahh, hold on, let me do the maths. Three would be like a thousand, so thirty would be the thousand, plus another two thousand . . . or so. About twelve or thirteen thousand days?" Zalia said. "Or, well, thirty-six years, and there's three hundred and sixty-five days in a year . . . most years."

"No, no, no, no. You are an age half of mine, you should have received your magic many . . . years? Ago, yes. Iron rank you should be, at least," Glemp said, quite thoroughly confused.

"Always have been different," Zalia said with a brilliant smile, "besides, I plan to be much higher than Bronze rank by your . . . Wait, you're seventy?"

"Yes, yes, by your years Those Born of Heat and Stone live for maybe one hundred and fifty? Just about, yes," Glemp said.

Damn, not what I expected, Zalia thought.

"Thank you, Glemp, for your kindness and help. I appreciate your ability to see past our differences," Zalia said, still smiling at the little alchemist.

"Yes, it is not a strong suit of Those Born of Heat and Stone. I appreciate the . . . difference in pace you bring me, Zalia of the snow," Glemp said.

"That's my specialty," Zalia said proudly.

"No, it is?" Glemp asked.

"It is now. Do you have somewhere I can sleep?" Zalia asked.

Glemp rolled their eyes before pointing to the door on the other side of the large workshop. Zalia went in to find a small room padded with various hides, then lay down and promptly passed out again.

CHAPTER NINE

The South

Zalia

Zalia woke up with a yawn and stretched before getting up. She felt surprisingly rested for having slept on a stone floor with very little padding. She definitely needed to find the closest river and wash herself, though, something for later in the day.

Walking out to the other room, she found Glemp still hard at work, staring at a flask as some liquid dripped into it.

"Good morning, what are you doing?" Zalia asked.

"Research, Zalia of the snow, yes," Glemp replied.

"Alright, well, I'll be back in a few hours. I've got a gift for you that I'd like to give before I leave for the human . . . realms for a bit," she said before walking out the door.

Zalia made her way back to her blind and gathered the Ironfur rabbit skins she had collected, ten in all. She also deconstructed the blind, taking her tarp, rope, bag, and sleeping bag. She then headed back to Glemp.

Walking into the house once again, Zalia dropped the hides on a bench.

"These here are yours, aaaand," Zalia said, as she pulled out a few bunches of herbs from her bag, "these are yours too. Maybe now you'll have a whole bunch and you won't need to be so careful with your experiments!"

"Yes, no, yet still I will be," Glemp replied. "I brought this for you, yes."

They held up a deep red root covered in a brighter red, almost bark-like, residue.

"It is, yes, good for fire, heat. Comes only from closest to the lake below, yes," Glemp continued, holding up a few more pieces.

"Oh wow, you really know how to treat a girl. Everybody loves a magic fire root, right?" Zalia said, taking them with a gleam in her eyes. "No promises I won't accidentally set myself on fire though," she added, looking down at Glemp's gift with a grin.

Zalia took the sleeping bag and tarp off her shoulders and folded the pieces neatly into her bag, now that it was emptied of her other herbs. She added in the roots as well, folding them into one of the Ironfur rabbit hides at Glemp's insistence. She still had a healthy supply of berries, Frozen Heart, Bitterbalm and Snow-leaf, all of them in an already prepared state since they took up less space in her pouch that way. She had no doubts that if she spent long enough down south she would have to find something else to swap some of them out for, though.

"Time to go, then. If I don't make it back, assume I died fighting some mythical beast in a heroic battle to save an orphanage or something," Zalia said, shouldering her backpack and picking up her unstrung bow.

"No, no, Glemp does not know what orphanage is and neither will you die, no," Glemp replied.

"What makes you say that?" she asked.

"Yes, because these lands are much more danger than south, yes."

"Well, isn't that just wonderful. Don't worry, I'll find a way to make them so anyways, byeeee," Zalia said as she walked out.

The first thing she did was make her way towards where she knew the closest stream was. She found that the heat of the mountain didn't really bother her much anymore and neither did the cold of snow. It was still cold but not dangerously so, even if she went without her layers and layers of clothes. She quickly washed up before turning to face south and begin her journey.

Zalia didn't really know what to expect from the south. Glemp also didn't know much, and she didn't fully know if she was even in the same world.

Huh, what a funny thought. Of course I'm in the same world, there was just an unexplored mountain of mythical creatures sitting in the snow up here, as well as magic, she thought.

Discounting the theories that she had lost her mind or was suffering some kind of mental issue and was actually passed out in the snow back where the "explosion" happened, she didn't totally rule out the possibility of another world. However unlikely.

Zalia continued travelling for three days. During the nights she dug into the snow and secured her tarp over the top to form a kind of burrow to sleep in. She did as much herbing as she could along the way, managing to gain a few levels.

Congratulations! Flora Identification has reached Tin 8.
Congratulations! Preparation has reached Tin 9.
Congratulations! Harvester has gained two levels reaching Tin 9.

It wasn't a lot, but every bit counted towards getting to Iron rank. She now knew from the Poison Resistance that she would need to get each ability to Tin twenty.

Zalia came over the top of a hill to look out at the landscape below her, and realised the forest was finally starting to thin out—she'd made her way out of the lands laden with snow. Stretching into the distance were rolling plains dotted with trees and bushes, as well as wild animals appearing and disappearing in the distance. A large wildcat was chasing down what she swore was an Ironfur rabbit, though it was hard to tell from this distance.

What caught her eye the most, though, were the two relatively large squads of armed and armoured people. Each was arrayed in a defensive formation, arrows flying over the front lines to hammer into the shields and armour of the other. She saw lines of warriors, moderately armoured with swords and shields, a few plate-armoured knights on horses, and some lightly armoured archers at the back. It looked like only one side had knights, the only cavalry she saw on the battle-field. All in all, it seemed that one side had about a hundred people; the other side had twenty or so more. Another thing that caught her eye about the battle was the magic being thrown about on each side. Some people who she assumed to be mages dressed in cloth were shooting fire, ice, earth, and all sorts of magical attacks at each other across the armies, much like the archers.

While she couldn't see a whole lot of details from that distance, Zalia could see two flags flying above each army. One side had red and yellow flags, and the other had dark green and brown flags. The red and yellow flag side was the one with both the number and cavalry advantage.

Seeing this battle supported the 'different world' theory for Zalia, since she didn't see any way of this sort of thing could happen in her world without it being documented. As the two front lines of the armies came closer over the course of a few minutes, one side suddenly surged forwards with a resounding battle cry, with the other side quickly following. The armoured knights on horses charged around the flanks of their formation and headed for the mages of the other. The two sides collided with a crash of shields and steel that she could hear from her position as the battle began in earnest.

"Of course—I find a peaceful race of cool as hell lava mage goblins, and my own people are warring with each other, as usual," Zalia muttered.

CHAPTER TEN

War

Zalia

At first, it seemed like the battle would end quite quickly. The side that had the number and cavalry advantage quickly took the upper hand, killing or incapacitating the other side's mages and archers in short order. As much magic as the lightly armoured soldiers threw at the knights, they simply didn't seem to notice or be affected by it. At this point of the seemingly decided battle, Zalia heard a resounding crack. She watched as the ground itself seemed to tear open and a large creature made of dirt and stone ripped itself free of the earth.

Zalia hesitated, watching the large, dangerous-looking Elemental start swinging. Her sense of self-preservation was eventually overcome by the urge to help, and she started running down the hill. A fight between two unknown kingdoms or factions was not something she wanted to get involved with, but faced with watching the giant earthen Elemental rip the two armies to pieces, she had to act. She doubted she would be able to kill the thing, let alone harm it, as it was probably a high rank. What she did think she could do was heal those who were injured or dying and provide them an opportunity to get out of there.

Zalia watched as the battle took a complete turn. Faced with an outside threat, the humans stopped slaughtering each other and banded up to face it. The insanity of the situation wasn't lost on her; she didn't have any information about why the battle was taking place, let alone why or how the earth had decided to get up and start a slaughter. The armoured knights immediately began harrying the Elemental, riding around its legs as the slow being swung at them. The monstrosity stood at what she thought to be ten to twelve metres tall, barely seeming bothered by the bombardment the remaining mages and archers were throwing its way. Some of the foot soldiers found a bit of courage and started attacking, but quickly backed off after two were immediately crushed by large, too-long arms.

After a minute and a half of running, during which one knight presumably died after being smashed from their horse and into the distance, Zalia arrived.

? - Gold rank

She immediately used her Protection of the Wilds skill on all the unconscious and wounded soldiers who couldn't walk. A few of the foot soldiers noticed her but didn't attack, thankfully. She also let her Healing Aura affect everyone nearby; it could heal only a small amount but hopefully enough to make a difference. As some of the soldiers that weren't conscious started looking like they weren't going to die anytime soon, she released the Protection of the Wilds from them.

"HEY, HEY!" Zalia screamed at the foot soldiers.

A few of the soldiers looked over and saw what she was trying to do. They came and grabbed the now somewhat stable soldiers and made for the tree line. Soon after, the others who weren't able to contribute to the fight started helping as well. A few actually looked relieved that they had something to do, their commanders too focused on distracting the Elemental to direct them. She watched a few of the mages run out of mana; some were a bit too far over their limit and falling unconscious. The archers started running out of arrows and began moving the unconscious mages away.

Now that she was closer, Zalia did notice that most of the soldiers wearing green and brown were unconscious or dead, the remaining survivors having taken their comrades and retreated back to the east after she yelled at them.

Soon the battlefield was free of the dying, and only the dead remained. All the foot soldiers, archers, and mages had retreated. The ones in red and yellow headed to the west. Zalia grabbed a few arrows from the ground and a roundel dagger from a body before she too retreated, going to the west. She decided that meeting with the army that had a bigger remaining force might be beneficial to her, and hoped they would have a sense of gratitude for her efforts. She checked on the one forcefully demounted knight before she left, finding him dead, as his whole chest plate had been crushed in. The rest of the knights quickly caught on and retreated as well, the Elemental looking a little worse for wear but nowhere near defeat as its cracks and cuts mended slowly.

Zalia followed the stumbling soldiers, those incapable of walking alone who were being supported by others, back to a large war camp. A host of tents in neatly formed lines ran along one side, a few bigger ones along another. The camp itself was surrounded by a slightly raised earthen wall with the ditch the dirt had come from dipping down on the outer side. She followed the wounded soldiers to a group of bigger tents, still allowing her Healing Aura to heal those around her slowly. She went in and got to work, giving those with worse wounds mouthfuls of Frozen Heart. There were a few other healers in the tent, some using spells and others binding wounds with lengths of cloth. She quickly ran out of her small supply of Frozen Heart, deeming the sacrifice definitely worth it considering the horrible wounds and injuries she saw. Her aura was greatly weakened when healing so many people at once but it provided an extended timeframe to bind and heal the worst of the wounds, stabilising those with lesser injuries.

It wasn't long before a woman in full plate came into the tent, walking up to Zalia.

"Thank you stranger, for your help. Who are you, and from where do you hail?" the woman asked.

"I'm Zalia, I come from the north. I wouldn't stand idly by and watch so many be slaughtered, no need to thank me. Who are you people and why are you fighting each other?" she replied, asking a question in kind.

"I am Knight Alara, leader of this war party. Our allegiance is owed to the Kingdom of Endaria and its monarch. The others have splintered from our kingdom, claiming that the king is unworthy and cursed. They seek to dethrone our rightful king. You do not know of the war?" Alara replied, seeming confused at Zalia's lack of knowledge.

Oh boy, I really don't want to get involved with this. Just had to come help the warring humans, Zalia, nice one. "I'd like to talk with you later, once I have finished healing these injured. Where can I find you?" Zalia asked, looking pointedly at the groaning and crying soldiers around them and ignoring the question.

"The biggest tent, over there," Alara responded, pointing.

Zalia looked at the woman, a Bronze rank much like Glemp. She had tan skin, black hair, and green eyes. She stood there, helmet under one arm and the other resting on the pommel of her sword.

"Be with you shortly, then," Zalia replied, getting back to work.

CHAPTER ELEVEN

Cleanup

Zalia

Zalia's next few hours were spent sitting in the tent as the people around her slowly healed from their wounds. Each one who left gave her thanks, some even going so far as to kneel to her, which she very quickly stopped. One of the last few to heal was a man who had lost his leg below the knee. The whole limb grew back over the time she was sitting there. She was amazed by the power her ability provided. As she sat, she looked over the messages she had received during and after the battle.

> **Congratulations! Protection of the Wilds has**
> **gained five levels, reaching Tin 10.**
> **Congratulations! Healing Presence has gained**
> **seven levels, reaching Tin 15.**

She was happy at her progress but sort of ashamed of the power she gained through others' misery. Throughout the process she had to remind herself that the levels were increasing because she was helping. The other healers ran out of mana every so often and had to rest, which really brought into perspective how strong her healing ability was. It didn't necessarily heal a huge amount, but in a situation like this it really came through. The other healers would definitely out-heal her in the short-term, but survival and the long-term were her home court.

Afterwards, Zalia found Knight Alara in what she came to understand was the command tent. Inside was a long table with a map, along with a few different people, some still in plate armour and very obviously other knights, well-dressed officials, and people standing nearby to serve if required. All in all, it looked exactly how she imagined a mediaeval command tent would.

As Zalia entered, Alara gestured and the other people left the tent, some giving nods of recognition, presumably for the help she had given.

Alright then, I guess I've gotten their gratitude, now how can I use it? she wondered, immediately feeling a tinge of shame at the thought of using the soldiers' pain for her own gain once more.

She came and stood next to the map, whereupon looking down, she realised her theory about being in a different world was most likely the truth. The section that the map showed didn't include the north she had come from, only showing a faded area listing it as such. The rest of the map showed some couple hundred kilometres of land to the south before it was cut off, listing the land further south as 'Central Endaria.' She also saw quite a few markers of both the flag of Endaria and the flag of the splinter faction. She assumed each marker was where warriors were known to be, due to scouts and such. Now that she was closer she could see the Endarian flag had a crown with a sword and staff crossed beneath it. The colours were split down the middle, red on the left and yellow on the right. The other flag was the same except with dark green and brown, and the crown was broken in half underneath the sword and staff.

There were a few seconds of silence before Zalia spoke. "What happened to the Elemental?"

"Dissipated once we moved far from where it ripped itself from the ground," Alara replied.

Zalia nodded slowly.

"What are you doing here, Zalia?"

"I was actually on my way down south to find some human civilization."

"You said that you were from the north before, is that true? I don't see how you could have survived up there with your rank," Alara said matter-of-factly.

"It's not so bad once you get used to it, quite nice actually. I only nearly died three times in the past two weeks," Zalia said, giving a small smile.

"Sounds lovely," Alara said sarcastically with a deadpan expression.

"In all honesty, I need some new clothes, a smith, and I'd love to find a magical bow. Know any good bowyers who could make one?" Zalia asked, gesturing to her well-made but quite mundane bow.

"Well, I very highly doubt you're some kind of spy, or you would have left us all for dead. Here, I must insist I pay you for your help, maybe it can buy you some of those new clothes you want. Also, no, I don't know a bowyer," Alara said, handing her twelve shining golden coins.

"How much are these worth? We don't really trade in coins where I'm from," Zalia said.

"Well, it's not enough to get a master crafter to make you an enchanted bow, but it'll do you just fine for some good quality clothes and possibly some light armour if you were looking for it."

That's a good idea. "Well, I won't look down on a gift. Thank you, Alara."

Zalia pocketed the coins before moving to leave the tent. Before walking out, she waved over her shoulder at the knight.

"Good luck with your war, remember to keep mercy in your heart," she said as she left.

Zalia started moving towards the nearest town she had seen on the map, a small place called Alston. It was pretty much directly southwest of where she was, slightly more south then west, and maybe a day more of travel away. Well, a day's worth of travel at her pace, which had significantly increased as her attributes did in kind.

After about an hour and a half of fast walking, her instincts started to feel something. It wasn't her magical abilities triggering in any way; she just caught an odd shadow over her shoulder or an out-of-place sound every now and then. Once she entered a forested area, she decided on a course of action and suddenly burst into a sprint. After about thirty seconds of running through the undergrowth she ducked behind a particularly wide tree and pulled out the long-bladed dagger she had taken from the dead man on the battlefield. A few seconds later, a shadow fluttered past the tree she was hiding behind, and she quickly reached out and grabbed it. The form solidified into a human, a man, as she held her knife to his throat.

"I don't take kindly to being followed," Zalia said in an angry tone. "Go back and tell them you lost me. If I catch you again I'll have to deal with you in a harsher manner." *Probably just tie him to a tree if I have to*, she thought, hoping he wouldn't realise she wouldn't really harm him.

He didn't say anything but she could hear his fast breathing and heartbeat. She let him go and pushed him away in the direction of the camp she assumed he'd come from.

? - Tin rank

Oh hey, there are other Tin rankers, some kind of stealth magic maybe, she thought.

As the man ran away into the trees she started out at a much faster pace towards Alston.

CHAPTER TWELVE

Alston

Zalia

Zalia was still stewing in frustration as night time arrived.

Alara seemed so damn forthright, then sent a spy after me? This is exactly why I moved away from all of humankind in the first place, she thought.

She settled in for the night under the roots of a large tree sitting by itself on a hill. She hadn't slowed down at all that day, hoping to get away from any other people who might be following her, though she doubted she would see them if they were a higher-rank stealth specialist. Either way, it meant she hadn't had time to slow down and inspect any of the new plants she saw around as she travelled. The next day, she would arrive in Alston fairly early if she went straight there, and so decided she could take some time to have a look around first.

Zalia awoke to a herd of strange animals looking down at her. They were much like cows except they grew long thick fur.

I guess some cows in my world do that too, she thought.

Really not wanting to scare the herd, she slowly packed up and started on her way.

She had jumped a few fences on her way to this point so it wasn't entirely surprising that she'd ended up in some farmer's field. As she travelled she found that some of the types of berries that grew up north were still growing here, in a more sprawled out way since more space was available. That was good, because while not needing to eat that much anymore, she still needed food. The plants she harvested were more potent in their use, so berries were enough to sustain her now with how common they were.

Around Alston, the area became more forested as she made her way towards town. It seemed like the town might have originally been there to gather lumber for the kingdom and had grown into a bigger settlement. Since discovering she was in a new world with magic, she'd been looking forward to seeing how most normal people lived and wasn't disappointed. With magic, it seemed that construction and the maintenance of towns was much more advanced in some ways. No longer were they limited to the shapes of materials as they grew or were made. Some pieces of wood on the fascia of the houses looked like they'd grown into place or had flowed and solidified like a river turned home.

As she approached, two moderately armoured people came up to intercept her. She had found a rough dirt road leading towards the town and decided a direct approach to town was probably the best idea.

"Good morning," she called out.

"Morning, miss, welcome to Alston. We must insist that we inspect what you're carrying with yourself there, we've heard word that there are some rebel warriors not too far out of town," one of the guards said as they came to a stop a few metres away.

"Not a problem," she replied.

She handed over her backpack but kept her coins in her coat's inner pocket. The two guards had well-made steel breastplates, spears, and side swords, and a shield slung across each of their backs. The slightly larger of the two was the woman who'd asked to inspect her bag.

"Any weapons?" the other guard asked.

The smaller of the two, the man, seemed a little nervous while the woman remained calm but on guard.

"Indeed, I've got the bow I'm holding in my hands here, a dagger, and a small hand axe I use to cut wood. Will that be a problem?" Zalia asked.

"No," the woman said, looking at the other man. "Where are you coming from?" she followed up.

"North," Zalia replied.

The woman frowned. "Nothing north of here except farmland and we know all the farmers. Where north?" the woman asked, now intently focused on Zalia's face.

"Far north," she replied, "you know, murder rabbits, snow, giant six-legged bears trying to murder you for no reason whatsoever?"

The man started to look a little apprehensive but the woman just laughed.

"Well, alright then, I don't expect trouble from you and if I hear you're getting into fights you'll be kicked out, understood?" the woman asked, still smiling.

"Yes ma'am," Zalia answered, taking back her gear. "Is there an armourer in town?"

"Yeah but a pretty bad one, I'd go to the next town out west. Tell him Eyla sent you and he'll probably help you," the woman, presumably Eyla, said.

"Sounds good to me," Zalia said as she walked past them into Alston.

"You really need to stop acting so nervous if you ever want to find a woman," Eyla said to the other guard as Zalia walked off.

Zalia just snorted and covered her laugh by coughing a few times.

The first thing Zalia found in the town was a big board covered with notices of all sorts. Quite a few were declarations from the king about something or other that she didn't bother reading. What caught her attention were the notices put up by people who needed help. There were small rewards promised for anyone who could do as asked. There was one that caught her eye, a farmer to the northwest needed help with some sort of creature that was slaughtering their herds. The farmer was only offering a couple silver coins but what caught her eye was when the notice mentioned that it had only started happening after they started growing a new type of herb in their small garden. She didn't really care for the money that much, but a new tool she could possibly use would be good. She noted the name of the farm and kept looking around the town.

She quickly found the armourer Eyla had mentioned, but found she agreed with the woman's perspective—nothing was really worth the asking price. What she did find was a seamstress.

Zalia watched in awe as the woman used magic to adjust the entire outfit to her shape.

"Damn, that fits nicely," Zalia said.

She had decided to get a set of hardy travelling clothes and it turned out the woman was also an enchanter. The clothes would self-clean and make minor repairs if needed. They were also designed such that light armour could easily be fit over the top, which was something she'd want later. She also got a mottled green cloak that had similar enchantments, but additionally offered some minor stealth magic. It simply helped her blend in with her surroundings better. She also managed to get the woman to put the repair enchantments on her boots, the runes glowing and hovering over the surface before disappearing. The whole assortment of pieces cost her two and a half gold, but was wholly worth it in her mind. It turned out each gold was a hundred silver, and each silver was a hundred copper, a fairly expected exchange. This brought her total cash to nine gold, fifty silver.

She soon realised she wasn't going to be able to hold on to all of this and asked the woman, "You don't happen to know anyone who would have magical, extra-large bags would you?"

Zalia stood in front of a small door. The seamstress had directed her to this shop, a small place a few streets away. She was currently stuck holding her new clothes since her bag was too small for them. Using one hand to open and push through the door, she had to duck inside. As she entered, the space expanded into a giant room, the size of which wouldn't fit in the building she'd seen from the outside.

The room being an extradimensional space was impressive in itself. More impressive, however, was the fact that the shelves filling the space were lined with an expansive array of enchanted and magical items. All of them seemed to have a common theme in that they were containers of some sort, presumably enchanted with some kind of magic. Behind a counter stood a portly man with an incredible beard.

"Greetings, young lady, how can I be of service today?" the man said, his voice deep and vibrant.

"Good day, I heard you sell some sort of magical bags. I'm looking to be able to carry more than I can right now," Zalia replied, raising her arms filled with clothes to accentuate her point.

"I see, a simple bag, I assume? From the looks of you, nothing flashy, but something that will blend in. I must warn you if you've never used one before, you'll still have to carry the weight of everything in there," the man replied.

"Yes and yes—what do you mean by that last part?" Zalia asked, intrigued.

"I mean, you'll have extra space but the weight of everything will still be there," he answered.

"Makes sense, what do you recommend?" she asked.

The man seemed happy that she wasn't going to argue with him about the whole weight thing, showing her a few items.

? - Silver rank
Congratulations! Aura identification has reached Tin 3.

Silver rank from bag making? This guy must be old to have reached that. Though my Herbalist class doesn't seem to be advancing too much slower than my Hunter one, she thought.

Zalia decided on a bag similar to her own. It was a thin thing, fitting sleekly around her back and holding close to her body. It wouldn't get in the way if she didn't have time to drop it before she fought someone.

"How much?" Zalia asked, preparing herself.

"One gold fifty," the man replied.

It was a little more than she was hoping for but not exorbitantly expensive.

"Alright, I can do that." She handed over the coins and transferred everything to her new bag, putting her snow jacket in there too. She would no longer stand out by being way too overdressed for the weather.

"My name is Zalia, it was nice to meet you, Mr . . .?" Zalia said.

"Taron, and likewise, Lady Zalia," Taron said.

"I'm no lady," Zalia laughed, "just Zalia will do fine."

"Zalia then, good day to you," he replied.

"And a good day to you too, sir," she said, leaving the shop.

Zalia bought a nice pastry roll from a street vendor on her way out of town. It had some kind of meat she thought was probably from one of those cow-like creatures. She felt a little bad for eating it, the animals had been cute.

Zalia left the town on the northwest side, heading in the general direction the notice had said the farm was in. She mentally noted that she should probably get her own map as soon as she could, since it would make life easier. Along her way, Zalia found a new type of herb.

? (Helpful) - Tin rank

Picking as much as she could from the plant, she felt something—her Herbal Magic skill telling her she could perform a ritual with it. She decided to test it out. She pulled some out and used Preparation on it; the plant was dried and turned into a fine dust, after which it gently floated into a small ring around her as some runes formed. The whole thing glowed a light green before it vanished.

Congratulations! Herbal Magic gained two levels, reaching Tin 6.

The whole thing had been almost instinctual; Zalia didn't necessarily understand what was happening, but rather, what it was providing. The ritual would very slightly redirect attacks that came towards her for the next half hour, providing some measure of protection or rather enhancement of dodging. She decided to name the plant Dodge-vine, for its ability and the way it grew up the side of a tree like a vine. She looked back down at some more in her hand.

Dodge-vine (Potent) - Tin rank.

She decided to keep her stash of it in her bag; it didn't activate fast enough to be used in a fight but prior to one would be needed. She thought it probably levelled her Herbal Magic skill quite a bit because it was an entirely new ritual and the first one she had actually performed. Everything else she had done with herbs so far had just been directly applied as a poison or eaten.

Quite happy with her find, Zalia eventually found her way to the farmer's house. She had to ask a few people she saw on her way there for directions, eventually ending up in front of the right door. She had to knock a few times before it opened up before her.

"Hello, I saw your notice on the board in Alston and I've come to help, may I come in?" Zalia asked.

Before her was a very old lady, bent over and wrinkled from age.

"Oh yes, dear, please do. I just baked some fresh bread, would you like some?" the woman asked, turning away and shuffling into the house immediately.

Zalia smiled. "Don't mind if I do," she said.

CHAPTER THIRTEEN

Time for Some Planning

Zalia

The woman led her into a small sitting room with some quite old but nice wooden furniture. She sat down at the low table on a nicely padded chair as the woman shuffled off further into the house. She looked around the room; it was tastefully decorated with nice window furnishings and a small painting hanging on the wall over the mantle of a fireplace. The painting depicted someone she assumed was the old woman and a man in their younger years. Beneath the painting hung a beautifully carved bow that looked extremely well-made to Zalia's eyes.

The lady came back into the room with a younger man.

"My son," the woman said, patting the man on the shoulder. She set down a plate of steaming fresh bread and butter as they both sat opposite Zalia.

? - Iron rank
? - Bronze rank

The older lady was the higher rank, obviously she'd had a longer life to reach it.

"Hey, you're just a Tin ranker? What makes you think you'll be able to deal with our problem when we can't?" the son said to Zalia.

"Now, now, dear, don't be so rude. This woman has been sent here to help," the old lady said.

I was sent *here to help?*

"It's quite alright, I'm Zalia, it's a pleasure to meet you. In answer to your question, I might be a low rank but I've lived in the far north in the snow and been a hunter for the past fifteen years of my life. I'm pretty sure I have an idea of what I'm doing," Zalia said, keeping an even tone.

The man grumbled under his breath a little, but introduced himself all the same.

"I'm Darren, and this my mother, Juniper,"

He had the self-awareness to at least sound a little regretful of his quick words. "It's been a very stressful time with our herd being culled on an almost daily basis by this beast."

"If I can ask a few questions about it, have you seen the creature?" Zalia asked, buttering some bread and eating it as she gave Juniper an appreciative look.

"Nothing too clear, I know it stands on two legs, I caught that. It has fur, attacks with its claws from what I can tell and it's big, real big. My height plus half that, at the least," Darren said.

He looked resigned to the situation and Zalia felt bad for him. His entire livelihood was threatened by whatever the creature was and there wasn't much he could do about it. Based on his appearance, Darren was the son of the man in the painting, who Zalia thought to be Juniper's late husband.

"I've great respect for hunters such as yourself, my pa was one before he settled on this farm," Darren continued, gesturing to the painting and confirming Zalia's thoughts, "but a warning to you. You may be all that you say, but this beast out there is no small thing to play with. It's dangerous, miss, I might say, real dangerous."

"I hear what you're saying Darren, I won't underestimate it. I made that mistake not too long ago and don't plan on repeating the experience," Zalia said. "Here's what I've got for you. I'll track the thing down to wherever it's sleeping, I can do that at the very least. Then, I'll come back here and tell you what I know. If I think I can take it, I'll go back out and do so. Whether I succeed or not, at the very least you'll know where it's coming from and hopefully have a better description and rank," she continued, "how does that sound for now?"

Darren looked at his mother for a moment before turning back to Zalia. "Sounds like a good plan to me, when will you begin?" he asked.

"Darren! Manners," Juniper said before smiling at Zalia and pushing the bread a little closer. Zalia smiled back.

After finally escaping from Juniper, who just really wanted Zalia to eat a little bit more, she made her way down to where Darren said the most recent attack had occurred. She very quickly caught on to a set of tracks leading off into the forested area. Most concerning to her was the fact that her skill and her eyes saw two creatures, not one. She used the Dodge-vine ritual before stringing her bow and moving into the forest.

It wasn't long before Zalia came across a large cave opening set into the side of a hill. The darkness of the cave was deep, and the smell that came from the opening was horrid. Even from fifteen metres or so back, she could smell it. A few things had given her pause before entering the cave. The first problem was that upon arriving she'd noticed her ability was telling her there were quite a few more than two tracks there. It counted upwards of ten separate tracks, meaning there could be even more creatures inside than anticipated. This, plus the fact Zalia didn't know their rank meant she most definitely did not want to go down there. Instead, she had to come up with a plan.

Zalia considered a few things in her planning. Firstly, she absolutely was not going down there, so she needed a way to draw them out. Her idea for that was to use the Flame-root to burn them out. She didn't know if it would work or not, but it seemed like a promising idea. Secondly, she wanted to set up a field of poisoned spikes like she had back in the north. It had worked quite effectively then, and she thought it definitely would here. Next, she would line the clearing with some more of the Flame-root and set it alight when the creatures left the cave, hoping it would deter them from approaching her. She was betting a lot on the creatures being scared of the fire and not completely immune. Then, all she had to do was shoot off her arrows and let her poison do its work. A relatively simple plan that she hoped would work. She quickly made her way back to the farm to tell them what she had found.

Soon, she was resting at the table after giving them the news and watching their expressions of fear and despair.

"I'm going to try," Zalia said.

They looked at her hopefully.

"You've got a plan?" Darren asked.

"*Oh yeah, I've got a plan.*"

CHAPTER FOURTEEN

Now This is Beast Hunting

Zalia

Zalia quickly explained a few of her abilities and her plan to the farmers and thankfully gained their acceptance. She also managed to get out of Darren that the creatures only attacked at night. She hoped that meant the creatures were nocturnal, so attacking them during the day was the best idea. It was around midday now, and Zalia didn't think she could prepare everything she needed within the time she had left that day. The two farmers didn't seem happy that they might experience another attack, but seemed alright waiting once Zalia told them she would be staying around for the night to see if one did attack.

She spent the rest of the day creating little spikes, poisoning them, and storing them in her bag. She would need quite a few to blanket the area she was targeting.

Zalia now waited, relatively hidden in her new enchanted cloak, near a large pen that held some more of the cows she'd seen earlier that morning. She was hiding up in a tree on the side of the fence that faced the direction of the creature's cave. She had to wait a few hours before she saw a duo of the creatures arrive.

Congratulations! Low Light Vision has reached Tin 3.

Zalia saw the creatures were pretty much how Darren had described, standing on two legs, hunched over, and covered in fur. They had human-like hands, but much larger and with wicked claws instead of fingernails.

> **? (Enraged) - Tin rank**
> **? (Enraged) - Iron rank**

Hmm, I think I could probably take the Tin rank one, not sure how I'd go against the Iron rank in a direct battle. Luckily, I'm not planning on it, Zalia thought.

She let the creatures take the animal, not wanting to alert them to the fact they were now being hunted. The 'enraged' affix within their description made Zalia's mind think back to the notice board, where she'd read that the farmers only had issues after planting a new herb. She wondered if the plant was the cause of the creature's enraged status, maybe it was sacred to them or maybe just a simple chemical reaction when they smelled it on the wind. Either way, it gave her another idea for the next day's hunt.

Zalia slept out in the tree, the wide bough providing a relatively safe and stable place to rest. It wasn't the most comfortable, but Zalia had slept in worse and besides, she liked the fresh air and night sky. When morning came, she got to work.

Zalia stood by the cave, looking at her work contentedly. The clear area surrounding the entrance was entirely coated with small poisoned spikes; she'd used a large amount of her stores of poison but it was well worth the effort, she thought. The spikes were all covered now with leaves, only a small path led through, which she had memorised. She had also used all but a small bit of her Flame-root to coat the boundary of the space. After testing a small bit, she did find it would burn on its own for a good thirty seconds before going out. It burnt quite hot too, thankfully, though she expected nothing less from a Bronze rank herb. She had also asked the farmers for some of the new herb and kept it in her bag. It was only Tin rank and might not be the cause of the creatures' enragement, but she would use the advantage if it panned out to be true. She had prepared one last thing. In the centre of the area, in a relatively large space, she had laid out the ritual for the Dodge-vine on the floor. Remembering that Glemp had told her the Bitterbalm was used in cursing rituals, she'd had an idea. While her abilities didn't tell her about anything higher than Tin rank magic, she had coated over the Dodge-vine with Bitterbalm too. The last bit of Flame-root was currently mixed into the gel-like poison coat on the tip of one of her arrows, nocked on her strung bow. She took one deep, calming breath before slowly and quietly entering the cave.

Zalia came out of the small, curved cave tunnel to find a much larger space. She'd thought the smell at the entrance horrendous, but she was definitely long-ing for the mundanity of it now. The smell in this larger cave was almost enough to make her leave immediately. With the small number of Low Light Vision ranks she had, she could see the vague forms of about sixteen of the creatures. A couple were moving around but hadn't noticed her yet, and she wasn't going to give them a chance to. Setting fire to the tip of the arrow with her lighter, she shot it into the largest group of the creatures she could and ran for it. She heard a loud explosion go off as her arrow hit and just as she reached the cave entrance, the shockwave reached her, throwing her forwards.

Zalia opened her eyes a few seconds later, her ears ringing. She had been flung clear of the open pit of spikes and landed painfully on the other side of her ring of Flame-root dust. Thanks to her magic, her hearing quickly healed; then she got up, grabbed her bow from the ground nearby, and got ready. Very soon, the creatures started appearing at the cave entrance. Some of them were much more heavily injured than others, their fur licked by flames, scorched. They stopped at the line of the sun, seeming to not want to come out into the clearing. Shooting one arrow into the leader as she applied her Hunter's Mark, Zalia then quickly hung her slightly scorched bag on a tree nearby and took out a little bit of the new herb the farmers had given her. After a few seconds, the creatures all turned to her. She quickly put the herb back in the bag before igniting the flame ring and drew her bow to shoot once more.

The creatures charged at her as three things happened. She activated the Dodge-root ritual, the carpet of dried leaves began igniting in the presence of the Flame-root's fire, and she began sending out more arrows. She felt the ritual take place and watched as an arrow swerved slightly in the air to strike one of the creatures directly in the eye. The creatures sprinted over her bed of poisoned spikes, quickly limping and slowing down as the Snow-leaf in the poison took effect. One of the creatures seemed less affected than the others. Some of the creatures were already falling over, some were still coming towards her, but this one seemed faster and stronger. Just before it reached her low wall of flames, she activated Nature's Wrath and put her Hunter's Mark on this one specifically. She could now read that it was Bronze rank, but she was a far way off from her first day fighting that bunny. As the creature was set alight by the flaming dried leaves and Flame-root, eaten from the inside by the poison, and scorched by the flaming roots that sprung up from the ground to hold it in place, all of that damage was enhanced by the protection curse ritual and then enhanced again by the Hunter's Mark. Zalia watched it very quickly degrade. She drew one last arrow, the rest of the creatures dead or dying, and activated Kill Shot. She looked the beast in the eyes as she released the string.

CHAPTER FIFTEEN

Going Up in the World

Zalia

As the arrow flew, the creature suddenly jerked to the side with inhuman speed, ripping free of the bonds of Nature's Wrath. The arrow landed with an explosive force, almost severing the creature's arm as it smashed through its shoulder, bone and all. Zalia knew she wouldn't survive in hand-to-hand combat with the beast, even with it being one arm down. Instead, she threw her bow to the side, pulled out her new long-bladed dagger, and ran. She just needed to survive thirty seconds for her Kill Shot ability to return. With Hunter's Mark she could vaguely sense the being, and knew it had started moving after her. She sprinted through the forest, desperately trying to keep ahead, but even poisoned, the creature was much too fast. It caught her, five seconds before the ability came off cooldown, and she used Protection of the Wilds. A shield of thick roots grew over her as the creature slammed into it. She saw it start to rip through the shield, light shining onto her as it tore through. Luckily, there was just enough time. Dropping the magic of the shield just after one last strike by the creature, she burst through the now weak and disintegrating roots, got extra height by pushing off its knee, and slammed her dagger up through its mouth into its brain, using the power and extra damage from her just-off-cooldown Kill Shot to drive it home. The two fell backwards, Zalia pulling the dagger free, jumping off, and rolling back to her feet as they hit the ground.

Zalia looked at the host of messages in front of her. The Flame-root had died down shortly before killing the creature, its thirty second timeframe having run down. She'd quickly gone back and batted down any remaining flames, her Heat Resistance and constant low healing providing enough protection to stop her being seriously hurt. She really didn't want a forest fire on her hands after the fight. She had seventeen kill notifications, seemingly having miscounted by one originally. Most of them were of Tin rank, three of Iron, and the single one of Bronze. Reading through her level gains for her abilities, she saw quite a few level ups.

**Congratulations! Kill Shot has increased by five levels reaching Tin 20.
Congratulations! Kill Shot has reached Iron 1. Kill Shot will
not increase in rank until all classes have reached Iron 1.
Congratulations! Hunter's Mark has increased
by six levels, reaching Tin 19.
Congratulations! Escape has increased by three levels, reaching Tin 8.
Congratulations! Hunter's Sight has increased
by five levels, reaching Tin 14.
Congratulations! Survivalist and associated skills have
increased by three levels, reaching Tin 13.
Congratulations! Hunter class has increased
by three levels, reaching Tin 8.
Congratulations! Flora Identification has
increased by two levels, reaching Tin 10.
Congratulations! Preparation has increased
by four levels, reaching Tin 13.
Congratulations! Stasis has increased by three levels, reaching Tin 9.
Congratulations! Harvester has increased by three levels, reaching Tin 12.
Congratulations! Herbal Magic has increased
by eight levels, reaching Tin 14.
Congratulations! Herbalist Class has increased
by three levels, reaching Tin 9.
Congratulations! Nature's Wrath has increased
by six levels, reaching Tin 11.
Congratulations! Protection of the Wilds has
increased by three levels, reaching Tin 13.
Congratulations! Healing Presence has increased
by four levels, reaching Tin 19.
Congratulations! Druid class has increased by six levels, reaching Tin 11.**

**Kill shot - Iron 1
Tin - Enhance an attack, go for the kill. This ability deals
a tiny amount of damage. The damage of this ability
scales exponentially with targets' remaining health.
Iron - Kill Shot deals increased damage based on how
many separate effects are active on the creature.**

64

LEIF RODER

Well, fuck me. That was a lot of levels, Zalia thought.

She'd felt the surge of power as the battle ended and her attributes increased greatly all in one go, but she hadn't expected that much. It seemed like the kills had given enough experience to level everything at a base of three levels each, plus more for whichever skills were used during the fight. The massive increase in her Herbal Magic skill she gave to the fact she used Iron rank herbs in a ritual, therefore skipping her rank of ritual magic. She had a look at her status page.

Profile - Zalia Taori
Health - Excellent
Mana - Near empty
Stamina - High
Class One - Hunter - Tin 8
Linked Attributes - Strength, Dexterity
Active Skills
Kill Shot - Iron 1
Hunter's mark - Tin 19
Escape - Tin 8
Passive skills
Hunter's Sight - Tin 14
Survivalist - Tin 13
Class Two - Herbalist - Tin 9
Linked Attributes - Vitality, Resilience
Active Skills
Flora Identification - Tin 10
Preparation - Tin 13
Stasis - Tin 9
Passive Skills
Harvester - Tin 12
Herbal Magic - Tin 14
Unity Class - Druid - Tin 11
Linked Attributes - Wisdom, Intellect
Active Skills
Nature's Wrath - Tin 11
Protection of the Wilds - Tin 13
Passive Skills
Healing Presence - Tin 19
General Passives
Heat Resistance - Tin 13
Cold Resistance - Tin 13
Aura Observation - Tin 3

Low Light Vision - Tin 3
Poison Resistance - Iron 1

She didn't know what had caused the initial explosion in that cave but had an inkling it probably had to do with the smell. Very possibly, the accumulated gases in the space had ignited. She had to put down her quick victory to the damage the explosion had very visibly caused the creatures in the first place. Not having known there was a Bronze rank creature in there she couldn't have been sure of her victory. More than anything else, simply having the time to prepare all of her tricks, some now exhausted, had given her this one. Having a supply of higher-ranked herbs definitely helped, their one-time use magic providing a powerful boost to her ability.

Zalia also noted that despite Glemp's insistence, the magic of the herbs seemed to just provide a broad definition, and her intention caused the specific effect, no in-depth testing needed.

In her bags, she now had no more Flame-root, a small amount of Bitterbalm, Snow-leaf, Poisonous Berries, and Dodge-vine. She had slightly more of those of Frozen Heart left as well. All in all, her stocks were looking low after that fight, and she'd need to go back up north at some point to get a bigger stock of the berries and Snow-leaf both. Each of them were integral to her ability to both slow and damage enemies.

Zalia slowly walked back to the farmhouse, quickly finding Darren and Juniper.

"I assume by the blood on you and the fact you're still alive, you managed it?" Darren asked.

"Oh you, always so rude," Juniper said, whacking Darren's arm.

She gestured, and the grime and blood on Zalia quickly dissipated, causing Zalia to feel a little more energetic.

"That's a nice bit of magic," Zalia said, "and yes, come, I'll show you."

Zalia led them back to the combat zone she had created, showing them the Bronze rank creature. She found her bow, and to her dismay, one of the limbs had cracked when she'd thrown it aside. She also took them by the clearing filled with charred and poisoned bodies, warning them not to enter due to the poisoned spikes all throughout the area.

"You did all this?" Darren asked.

"That's right, a little preparation goes a long way. Do you doubt me?" Zalia asked.

"Not anymore, no," Darren said, admiring the carnage before turning to squint at her. "Are you secretly a higher rank?"

"Not that I know of, all three classes are still at Tin," she responded.

"Three?" both Darren and Juniper asked in unison.

"Ahhh, that's not normal?" Zalia asked.

"No," Juniper responded.

"People only have their main class and specialisation class, at least that I've met," Darren added.

Uh-oh, Zalia thought.

Juniper had a thoughtful look on her face, like she was deciding something.

"Well, ah, I've got two main ones and a Unity class," Zalia said, feeling a little worried.

"That explains why you're able to hit much higher above your rank, then. I can't think of any other Tin ranker I've heard of being able to pull off something like this," Darren replied. "Doesn't matter to me, though, I'll take what you've given us, no questions asked."

"I want to give you something extra for the work you've done here, Zalia," Juniper said, looking thoughtfully at her.

Juniper led them back to the house before going into the sitting room and taking down the artfully crafted bow from above the mantle.

"This is the bow that belonged to my late husband. It will see much better use in your hands then either of ours. A relic of a time long past, I'm afraid," Juniper said, handing it over to Zalia.

Hunter's Bow (Heirloom) - Unbonded

Oh, that's new, no rank, Zalia thought.

"Heirloom, unbonded. What does that mean?" Zalia asked, admiring the bow's craftsmanship.

"Well, as a base these types of items will self-repair from most lesser damage. Otherwise, the thing will grow with the user. It's anyone's guess what types of abilities it may form, though some theorise it's usually affected by the user's needs," Juniper said.

"I'm not sure I can take this from you," Zalia said.

"Oh nonsense, I'm giving it to you. Besides, you took care of quite a bit more than the notice described, can't go underpaying you," Juniper responded. "They're not that rare, darling, most households formed by prominent or powerful people have a few lying here and there gathering dust," Juniper continued at Zalia's still unsure expression.

"If you're certain, Juniper. How would I bond it, then?"

"I don't really know, as heirlooms are all different," but you'll figure it out," Juniper responded. "I'm going to make some lunch, will you join us?"

"Sure, if you'll have me," Zalia replied. "Are you ok with this?" Zalia asked the characteristically silent Darren.

"Not like I'll be using it, us farmers are a pragmatic group. If you can go out there and help a bunch more others the way you helped us, sure, why not," he answered.

Zalia wasn't too convinced of his apparent lack of concern, and she decided she wouldn't get too attached just yet in case they changed their minds.

After a pleasant lunch with the duo, they still insisted Zalia take the bow and even still paid her the two silver coins promised. She gathered her things, collecting a few of the poisoned spikes from the clearing that remained undamaged. After a brief but warm farewell, Zalia left in the direction of the next town over, pointed the right way by the farming duo.

CHAPTER SIXTEEN

Little Bit of Travel

Zalia

Zalia restocked on Dodge-vine as she travelled, finding plenty around the place. After the additional two silver she had been given, she now had eight gold, one silver, and ninety-five copper. She hoped it was enough for some actual armour; enemies kept getting in close to her and a little protection would be really nice. It was a couple days' journey to the next town, so Zalia thought about what she could do on the way to train. She hadn't really done much, but with how majorly her strength and dexterity was being affected by the attribute changes, she needed to get used to her body's capabilities. This was especially true if she continued at the rate she was going. She wasn't necessarily inhumanly strong but the draw weight of her bow had gone from comfortable to downright easy—well, that was before she broke it.

Zalia's new bow felt similar in its draw weight but smoother somehow. She couldn't figure out how she was going to bond to it but decided on trying to hunt something. It was called Hunter's Bow after all. As a few days passed, Zalia kept an eye out for the tracks of any creature that would be worthy of such a hunt.

Zalia also thought about how much her Herbal Magic had increased from doing something beyond the ability and involving it. Looking at her Stasis and Escape abilities she couldn't help but feel they were falling behind. She had an idea of how to level the Escape ability but would need someone's help and a lot of rope. As for Stasis, she didn't have any ideas yet but kept it in mind.

Zalia was also pretty sure she had gotten lucky with her hunts so far in that the beasts had been mindless. She felt like hunting something properly sapient would be a lot harder, not that she felt the need to do so. She thought about something Juniper had told her just before she left, about a group of mercenaries in the far west of Endaria who called themselves the Morning's Shade, a group who mostly purposed themselves with helping out humanity against monsters and beasts that threatened the lands. Apparently Juniper's husband had been a part of the group; this was where he had gained his power and prestige as a Hunter. She thought it was probably a good place for her to check out, see if she couldn't learn a thing or two from them.

Congratulations! Hunter's Sight has reached Tin 15.

Her constant track observation paid off, giving her a level, but unfortunately she didn't find anything she felt like hunting that first day. When she camped up for the night she decided on doing some light stretches before she slept, trying to pay attention to how her body moved now.

The next day, Zalia added in some long-stretch runs. She tried to take the most complicated course possible, jumping obstructions, climbing, and so on, all meant to train herself to be as efficient as possible. She spent her time switching between that, scouting for tracks, and gathering herbs.

On the third day, she finally found something she wanted to hunt. She had gained two levels in Flora Identification, bringing it to Tin 12, and one each in Preparation and Harvester, bringing them to Tin 14 and 13, respectively.

The tracks that caught her attention appeared to be from a large, knee-height creature that had what seemed like a hundred legs. From what she could discern it was something similar to a giant centipede, crawling its way through the jungle. The tracks were relatively fresh so she decided to give chase. Shortly after coming across the first tracks, she found a second point of interest in the creature. She found a section of brush that the creature had chewed on. Surrounding the bite marks, the plants were withered and dead as if the life had been sucked out of them. Her Healing Presence couldn't heal the damage to the plants, leading Zalia to believe it was almost certainly of a strong rank.

She followed the tracks to where the creature lay asleep. It was curled up in a circle, resting within a patch of dead, decrepit plant matter. The area was indented into the ground, forming a small out-of-the-weather spot. Looking at the thing from a tree nearby, Zalia could see it had some kind of venom, for sure.

? - Silver rank

Shit, Zalia thought.

She definitely wanted the beast's venom but it would be a dangerous endeavour to get. She started by emptying her small pouch into her bag, the watertight container serving as an alright substitute for a better-sealed glass vial. She could see the venom was dripping from the creature's mouth where it slept, rolling down its carapace to the earth below. The thing slept with its head resting on and across its tail section. When uncurled, she figured it probably was about six or seven metres long.

Zalia quickly performed a Dodge-vine ritual, hoping it wouldn't be necessary, but not willing to give up any advantage she could get. Normally, she wouldn't even consider disturbing the creature. It most definitely wouldn't be killable without another mountain willing to drop a landslide on it, and she wasn't about to risk that. The only reason she considered taking the risk was the fact she was running quite low on her other poison.

She very slowly and carefully approached the small indent in the ground, reaching the side of where it sloped down. Reaching her foot out, she felt at the decomposing, almost mush-like ground, finding it to be slippery but not unwalkable. She chewed her lower lip for a second, trying to make a decision. After a moment, she went to a nearby tree and tied her length of rope around it, then went back to the indent. She used the support of the rope to walk down into the nest of the creature. She gently crouched down next to the large centipede-like beast and put her watertight pouch beneath where the venom was dripping off the creature's carapace. This close, she could see it had six eyes, three on each side, and each of them closed. It had two vice-like mandibles with two smaller, almost arm-like limbs designed to rip at whatever the larger mandibles held still. It was a truly terrifying creature that Zalia had no doubt would be incredibly deadly. She crouched there for almost half a minute before pulling the drawstring on her pouch closed, tying it at her waist before moving to stand. When she looked back at the creature, she saw that its eyes had opened.

CHAPTER SEVENTEEN

Escape

Zalia

Zalia froze for only a moment as the creature shifted slightly and looked directly at her. Deciding her best course of action was to get the hell out of there, she activated Hunter's Mark, Nature's Wrath, and Escape just for good measure, then made a break for it. Old, decomposing plant life took the form of hundreds of small hands, reaching out of the ground and gripping the long-bodied creature as it squirmed in the grasp of Zalia's spell. She dashed up the side of the shallow pit, using her rope to ensure she kept momentum when one of her feet slipped a little. She made it just over the lip as the creature broke out behind her, giving chase with a skittering sound that chilled her to the bone.

Figuring the creature was probably better at getting past obstacles than she was, Zalia decided to take the most direct route through the lightly forested area, sprinting as quickly as she could. The skittering sound chased her for a few minutes as it slowly faded away, getting further and further from her.

Zalia stopped after another two minutes of running. She leaned against a tree, breathing hard, desperately trying to catch her breath as her legs burned from the drawn out sprint.

Oh, good fucking idea, Zalia, go take the spit from a horrific insect creature that wants to eat you, Zalia. Put yourself in a bear's mouth while you're at it, Zalia, she thought, silently reprimanding herself.

> **Congratulations! Survivalist and associated skills have reached Tin 14.**

"Oh, fucking thanks," Zalia muttered sarcastically.

She took out her pouch and inspected the thick venom she had collected.

? (Venom) - Silver rank

She started laughing, a little bit manically. *Oh shit, yeah, this is going to be useful later down the line*, she thought.

Zalia arrived in the next town later that day: Ostoss, as she was informed by the big sign sitting above the gate of the walled settlement. She asked around before being directed to the man Eyla told her to find. There were a few armourers in town, but a passing guard knew Eyla and, subsequently, the man she had directed Zalia to. The guard chuckled lightly when Zalia mentioned Eyla, and told her that the man was a middle-aged fellow named Gurden.

It wasn't long before she found out what exactly had set the guard to laughing at the mention of Eyla. She was standing in front of a low bench, surrounded by armour racks displaying all sorts various pieces. After mentioning Eyla to the man, he set off on a rant.

"Oh, and of course she would send someone to buy from me, like that's going to pay off her debt. 'Oh, don't worry old Gurden, you can just get the money I owe you off this young lady . . .'"

"I'm not a—" Zalia tried to say before being cut off.

"And now look, I'm stuck here with no money and a customer who . . ." His voice faded away as he walked into a backroom, leaving Zalia stunned.

What the fu—

Even her thought was interrupted as the man walked back out.

"—nd now I look like an idiot. Evening, what do you need?" Gurden asked, squinting his eyes at Zalia.

"I," Zalia started carefully, not wanting to be interrupted again, "would like some light armour is all. I can pay, if that helps. For me, not Eyla."

"Hmm, sure, sure should be easy enough. How light?" he asked.

What followed was a lengthy set of questions and answers as Zalia described to him what she wanted. He informed her that he would need a day to make the adjustments but had some pieces that would suit the purpose. He also took some measurements using a piece of blank, flat leather and marking it with a light chalk line. He was no enchanter, so if Zalia wanted some self-repair or cleaning functions like her clothes or cloak, she would need to go find one herself.

She spent some time walking around town, looking for something to do. She tried to find the notice board in this town, but instead found a large group of people amassing in a small square.

"—t's time we took matters into our own hands, anyone who wants to come out with me and take care of this problem once and for all, meet here tomorrow at this time. We'll show them just what they get for plundering our farms and our supplies, slaughtering our friends if they fight back! " a man shouted.

The man was standing atop a crate, shouting across the crowd as they dispersed, his speech now done. Zalia went up to the man.

"What was that about? I only caught the tail end of the speech. New to town, you know?" she asked.

"Oh! Well, there have been a group of bandits extorting our farmers and those who live further out for coin and supplies. Bastards defected from one army or the other and have been giving us no end of trouble since. King won't send anyone out to deal with it and the guard here is too small to do much. Want in?" he asked back.

"Depends, plan on outright killing these people?" she asked.

"We'll bring them in for a fair trial if they surrender but . . . not much of an easy way to go about that if they don't," he responded, shrugging.

"Sounds fair to me, I'll come. Only because I might be able to save some lives, though. I don't much plan on slaughtering a bunch of people," she replied. "Here, this time tomorrow?"

"That's the plan," he said.

"See you then," Zalia said as she walked off.

She felt a bit anxious about this one. She didn't really want to slaughter a whole group of people whose point of view she didn't know yet. To be fair, it wasn't looking good for them, but there could be more to the story. She'd go along and heal who she could, on either side, once the battle was decided. If the townspeople ended up needing help, though, she would do what she could; at least they seemed to be in the right for now.

Zalia made her way to a nice inn she had seen on her way to the square, renting a room for the night and buying herself a good honey mead. She wasn't the biggest fan of alcohol most of the time, but a good, relaxed drink could be nice.

After a relaxing half hour, nighttime came upon the land and Zalia went to sleep in a bed for the first time in a long time.

CHAPTER EIGHTEEN

A Relaxing Mornin'

Zalia

When Zalia woke, she didn't really know what to do with herself. She had the whole morning and a bit of the afternoon to kill, but nothing much to do until then. Deciding she may as well test out one of her theories about how to level her Escape ability, she found a new length of rope that she bought for a few coppers. She asked a passerby to tie her wrists together and using the ability, found it would let her slip free of the bonds. It struck her as a very situational ability, but one that was very powerful in the right circumstances. She just hadn't quite found herself in the right circumstances for it very often. It was both a good and a bad thing, since being in a position where she needed to escape was not a good thing, even with the ability, but she hadn't able to level it so far without. This would allow her to level it slowly, but she didn't feel like finding or paying someone to tie her up constantly. She would probably go back to that enchanter in Alston at some point to see if she could enchant the rope to do it itself.

Walking aimlessly around the town, Zalia stumbled across another Herbalist's shop. She quickly went inside and looked around at the wide array of herbs and spices hanging from strings, arrayed on shelves, in jars, or otherwise. She used her Flora Identification on as many as she could, getting a single level for her troubles that brought it to Tin 13. Most of the herbs and spices looked like they were for cooking or other simple uses, like nice scents. She did see a bunch of Dodge-vine there, recognising the wiry plant. She went up to the wizened old man behind the counter.

"Hey, I have an offer that is a little unconventional," Zalia said.

"Well go on, then, I've not got all day," the man said, absolutely looking like he had all day.

"I have a Herbalist class, and one of my abilities allows me to stop the drying and ageing of a plant or herb that has been harvested. I would like to level it up and wondered if you had any herbs you wanted to keep for a bit longer," Zalia said.

As soon as Zalia mentioned she had a Herbalist class the man's irritable attitude changed. At the mention of her ability, the man even visibly perked up and some of his grouchy body language faded away.

"Well, my, my, I would absolutely be interested in such an ability," the man responded.

"I'm not looking for anything more than just levelling my skill, so don't worry about payment or such," Zalia said. "Shall I get started?"

The man slowly led her to a whole array of different herbs, even bringing her into a smaller room out the back with some rarer Bronze rank herbs. Zalia used Stasis on all the ones the man pointed out.

> **Congratulations! Stasis has gained four levels, reaching Tin 13.**
> **Congratulations! Herbalist class has gained four levels, reaching Tin 13.**

The short hour of work, a lot of it spent waiting for mana to regenerate, quickly gained her a good number of levels, bringing Stasis to level with her other abilities in the Herbalist class, all of them now at the thirteenth or fourteenth level.

Zalia found the man had Bitterbalm and stocked up on it, buying one silver's worth. She also found another herb that interested her while she was there. The man had quite a lot of it, and she did remember seeing it about the place within the city growing up some older walls, but had passed it off as a normal plant. Apparently, the herb was used to provide a physical aspect to any ritual performed. It was only Tin rank, so the effect was not major, but if Zalia picked it herself she knew it would be enhanced. Her instinctual knowledge from Herbal Magic led her to sense that mixed with something like Dodge-vine, this herb could create a dome shield not unlike what Protection of the Wilds did. The feeling she got from it was one of a physical presence, where Dodge-vine gave her a feeling of protectiveness or protection. Zalia wasn't sure about the Bitterbalm, the only time she had used it in a ritual was with the Dodge-vine, and her ability didn't yet give her the instinctual knowledge of Iron rank herbs.

Zalia made her way back to the armourer after having finished up at the herbalists and walking around a bit more. She collected a bunch of the new herb that the Herbalist had called Leaves of Physical Manifestation, but after seeing the name in the little window description, she thought it too much of a mouthful and renamed it to Manifest. She entered Gurden's shop and sat down, still inspecting the herb and moving it around in her hand.

> **Manifest (Potent) - Tin rank**

It had become potent when she collected it off the side of a building, as she had expected it to, due to her Harvester rank. After stocking up on a whole bunch of it, the skill had ranked up.

> **Congratulations! Harvester has reached Tin 14.**

It wasn't long before Gurden walked out and noticed her sitting there.

"Fuck, I didn't notice you in here at all. Here for the armour, I assume?" he asked.

"Mmhmm," Zalia said, getting up and putting away the herb. She gave the man a radiant smile. "Let's see what you've got me, shall we?" she asked.

They were standing in the back room, Zalia now fully equipped with her new armour. She had two leather bracers with small metal plates riveted into the material, covering each of her forearms, the pieces each edged in the same metal. She also had two greaves and cuisses, each with riveted metal plates and similarly edged in metal. Lastly, she had a sleeveless leather cuirass covering her torso, the piece shaped in a way that allowed for good mobility, sacrificing a little defence for it, but it was worth it to Zalia in the end. The cuirass was also edged with the same metal, a few plates riveted into the leather. The metal was a carbon steel, dark in colour with a matte finish. The armour was hardened but still flexible, designed for the highest flexibility to shoot a bow comfortably. It wasn't anything super fancy, no designs or expensive materials used in its make, but she liked it a lot. With her dark, enchanted cloak and bow in hand she looked quite the part of a mediaeval hunter.

"Niiiiice," Zalia said, giving a whistle as she looked at a piece of steel polished to a reflective surface, showing her image.

"It does look quite sturdy, if I do say so myself," Gurden remarked with some pride in his voice.

Zalia handed over the seven gold and fifty silver as agreed, leaving her at fifty silver and ninety copper.

"Now, I've got to go stop some people from murdering each other. Thank you for your work, Gurden, it's quite something," Zalia said.

"You staying around in town long?" Gurden asked.

"Settling isn't how I roll, my friend," Zalia said with a smile. "I'll probably be out and travelling once more when I'm done with this job. I'm heading further out west, going to try to find the Morning's Shade."

"Figured as much—Morning's Shade, hey? You do strike me as the type. Well, good luck in your journey, hunter, I hope my armour saves your life at least once," he replied.

"I'm certain it will, but if it doesn't, at least I'll look good as I die." And then Zalia left, making her way back to the town square where she had been the day before.

She found a relatively large group of people amassed in the square, many wearing different pieces of armour and carrying a variety of weapons. She saw everything from Tin to Bronze rank people, the large majority being Tin. It was possibly the most Tin rank people she had seen since coming to this world. Thinking about those she had seen in the army back north with Alara, they had all been quite high-ranked compared to this lot. If these deserters were actually from an army like what she had seen, they were probably much stronger. She just hoped they didn't have the numbers advantage. If they did this would likely go very, very poorly.

She made her way to the man she had spoken to the day before.

"Quite the turnout. Hey, think this will work?" she asked.

"I sure hope so, it's more than I expected but not as many as I'd hoped for," he answered, looking a little apprehensive.

"I didn't introduce myself yesterday, I'm Zalia. May I ask your name, oh great war party leader?" Zalia asked, letting a little sarcasm into her voice.

"Tristan. Good to meet you, Zalia," he said, giving a small, wry smile.

The man was quite tall, holding a large double-bladed axe and wearing some good sturdy leather armour. It wasn't reinforced with metal like Zalia's but it had definitely seen some battle considering the marks on it. He was also quite well-built, handling the weapon and weight of the armour with ease.

"What do you do with your time for the most part, if I may ask?" Zalia asked.

"Baker," he said.

"Baker," Zalia said, doubtfully, looking him up and down.

"Baker," he confirmed.

"Where is your bakery?" she asked.

"Maybe I'll show you after we're done with this," he said, turning away to the rest of the people.

"Alright! Let's get this thing started then, shall we? I've been told by the guard that the damn deserters are camped up northwards in a small forested area. Some of those guards will be joining us today," he started, nodding towards a few people Zalia guessed were the guards. "We're going to go ask them, real nicely, to come back with us to face trial. If they refuse then we'll just have to convince them, in a much less nice manner."

A couple people gave a few cheers, but there was obvious tension to the situation. These were not fighters or warriors, all of those were off fighting a war. These were bakers and farmers, more used to the tools of life than those of death. She decided then that she would do what she could to keep these people alive; they were obviously a desperate population trying to stop a situation they were clearly not built for.

Tristan began leading the people out of the town, leaving via a gate on the northeast side, the same one she had entered through. Zalia was a little bit concerned for the strength of the human race as a whole so far. Not only was the infighting she saw already equal to what she knew from back home, but these people were very weak, very few higher than Bronze rank. The Silver rank creature she had stolen the venom from could probably smash through this group of people without much harm coming to itself; the Goblins of the mountains up north also wouldn't have an issue with the group and could probably melt them away in mere seconds with their combined ritual lava magic. As they began travelling northwards from the town, Zalia found Tristan once more and told him she would scout ahead. With the slight stealth magic from her cape and her already vast experience living in the wild and hunting, she was most likely their best chance at finding the deserters quickly without being ambushed by some creature.

They travelled for a few hours before it started getting a little dark. Having moved back and forth between scouting and Tristan a few times, she knew they were nearing where they were trying to go. They were taking a short break to rest, hydrate, and eat a small meal. It was at this point that she found some tracks belonging to a human-sized creature heading off into the distance, towards their destination. Zalia didn't remember any other of the villagers doing any scouting, and they sure as hell weren't her tracks. She quickly followed then, vanishing off into the darkness.

A few hundred metres later, Zalia ran into one of the guards, moving away and looking quite suspicious.

"Hey!" Zalia hissed towards the man.

He spun around quickly, half-drawing his sword before seeing her.

"What are you doing out here?" she asked, still whispering.

The man looked around Zalia, and she put her hand onto the hilt of the dagger behind her back, seeing that the man looked ready to spring into action.

"You shouldn't have come after me alone, foolish girl," the man said.

He drew his sword and charged at her. Zalia quickly drew her dagger, readying herself for a fight. The man came swinging, forcing Zalia to backstep a few times to avoid getting hit. On a particularly wild swing, she used the metal plate on her bracer to smash the back of the blade as it whistled past her, pushing the man off balance. She quickly stepped in close to him to get within the reach of his sword. To her surprise, the man immediately dropped the weapon and instead punched her in the head. He made a grab for the dagger, the two of them wrestling for the weapon as Zalia took them to the floor, still struggling. She landed on top, maintaining the upper hand, and pushed the dagger towards his head as they struggled on. With a final effort, the man pushed the dagger to the side, the weapon impaling his shoulder rather than his face. What the man couldn't have known, though, was that Zalia had put a tiny bit of the Silver rank creature's venom on the blade in preparation for the fight to come. She quickly slammed her hands over his mouth as the weapon pierced him, watching in horror as the venom spread through his body, skin and flesh withering slowly while the man writhed on the ground with his screams muffled by her hands. The man was only Tin rank, but the effect of the venom was still startling; it was eating away his body with lethal speed and efficiency. Before long, nothing was left but a withered corpse that looked as if it had been dead more like ten years than ten seconds. She got up and stood above the body for a moment, slightly shocked at the whole encounter. She guessed the man was probably going to warn the deserters and set up an ambush, or maybe they already had one set up and he would have told them that they were coming.

Tristan

Tristan looked around for the new lady in town, not finding her near any of the small fires they had set up. He shook his head.

That woman is more a creature of the wilds than anything else, he thought.

He got up, stretching his back before walking to the edge of the small camp. He wasn't feeling too good about this whole thing. He had been a part of the army that these deserters had come from, he knew they were of quite a high rank. These people around him weren't fighters, he could see that with the experience he had as a warrior. Despite his insistence on being a baker, he really spent most of his life in the army. He heard the sound of metal and leather scraping against the ground to his left and looked that way. To his shock he saw a dark shape in the last remaining light of the day. The cloaked figure was dragging what looked like an emaciated body behind it as it approached him. He put his hand to his axe before finally recognising the figure as Zalia once she got closer. She dumped the body at his feet.

"That one was a traitor," she said.

Traitor? Tristan thought.

He looked down at the body and recognised the clothes and equipment as belonging to Harold, one of the guards who had come with them.

"W-what happened to him?" he asked.

Zalia just looked at him blankly. "He tried to warn the deserters we were coming, I saw his tracks leading from camp. I found him and he tried to kill me," she said, pointing at the body with the sword and sheath she held in her hand. "Now he's dead and I'm not. Figure out the rest."

Zalia

Tristan just stood there staring at her as she finished explaining.

Not my fault the venom was so damn strong, Zalia thought.

Sighing, Zalia turned away from the man, not wanting to see the change in his eyes as he looked at her a little differently than before. She felt bad for the misery the man had gone through before meeting his end, but it was more the method she felt bad about, not the result. He was going to betray his whole town and people, probably just for gold, and would have gotten a lot of good people killed. Despite how she tried to tell herself that she wasn't very affected by having killed the man, her hands had started shaking. She went and sat down at a fire, ignoring the stares of the other villagers as she got a small cup of water to drink. It wasn't long before Tristan came and sat next to her.

"It isn't easy, I do understand," he said.

"I'll be fine, Tristan, I did all I could do in the moment," she replied.

"Still, I understand better than most."

She bumped her shoulder into his. "Just a baker, hey."

"Of course, I'm talking about the trauma of burning a loaf of bread," he said, slowly shaking his head.

She smiled at that, feeling some of the tension and adrenaline from the fight slowly fading away.

"We're going to have to seriously replan our approach now," she said, watching the man as he stared into the depths of the fire, the flamelight flickering over his face.

"That we will," he said, looking over at her, "that we will . . ."

CHAPTER NINETEEN

Confrontation

Zalia

Tristan slowly went from fire to fire, explaining what had happened to everyone and answering their questions. They decided that it was best to sleep here for the night, rugged up as much as possible, not wanting to walk into an ambush in the dark of night. Approaching after sunset would have been an acceptable strategy if the deserters were not yet aware of them, but they didn't know what the guard had told them since the rally in the square the previous day. Once Tristan had explained this to everyone, Zalia stopped getting slightly confused and hostile glances and started receiving appreciative ones instead, mostly. Somehow, that unnerved her even more. She didn't want these people to see her in a better light after killing someone, no matter the circumstances. They put out the fires a short time later and slowly went to sleep—Tristan had also organised a small watch rotation. Zalia would be the last watch for an hour towards the end of the night. Her watch came and went without issue, with morning arriving soon after.

They stood in a small group talking about what they were going to do now.

"I think we should still go find them," a man said.

"I agree, but we need to be real careful about this now, they could know we are coming," Tristan replied.

"We don't even know if what that woman is telling us is the truth, for all we know Harold could have found her sneaking away to rat us out, and she killed him!" the man argued, pointing at Zalia.

There was a moment of silence as a few people looked between her and the man.

"Question me all you want, but even if you were right, in either situation they could know we are coming," Zalia retorted, not bothering to defend herself.

These were townspeople from a quite small town and Zalia was the outsider here. She was more surprised that more of them weren't questioning her story out loud, though she was sure they were internally. Tristan's support was probably what kept her from great suspicion on anyone's part.

"Exactly, so what we should do is send out some people to scout out the forest ahead. We know they are camped in there somewhere, of that I'm sure. Either waiting to ambush us or just enjoying their unearned comforts, I don't know," Tristan said, taking the initiative in the conversation once again.

"I would probably be the best at this, but if any of you are uncomfortable with me doing so, then I'll stay behind with the rest," Zalia said, looking around the group.

"You're damn right, I'm uncomfortable with you going." The man from earlier spoke up.

"Then go scout them out yourself," Zalia replied, maintaining eye contact with him.

"Fine, I will," he replied.

Zalia just rolled her eyes, hoping that his stubbornness wouldn't get him killed.

"Great, anyone else want to volunteer?" Tristan asked.

Only one other person put their hand up.

"I used to go running through the forests as a kid, I reckon I can still remember how to move quietly," a woman said.

"Alright then, we'll move a little closer to the forest edge and you two can go in and have a look," Tristan said, watching for any disagreement.

No one spoke up and they packed up what little they had left laying around. They moved closer to the forest a short way, and the two who had volunteered moved away as quietly as they could manage. The woman was a bit quieter than the man, but both were pretty bad in Zalia's eyes and ears.

I really hope this doesn't go badly, Zalia thought.

About forty minutes later, the woman returned. She was running as quickly as she could while remaining somewhat quiet. She ran up to where Zalia and Tristan were talking in hushed tones.

"We need to hurry, they caught Arthur," she said quickly.

"Shit," Tristan and Zalia said in unison.

They were all already equipped with armour and weapons, ready for the two scouts to come back, but this just complicated the situation further. Zalia strung her bow, still not having used the thing yet but expecting she might need to in the close future.

"We need to be careful," Zalia said.

Tristan nodded. "Aye, but these fuckers are getting on my nerves."

They started pushing through the forest, led by the woman who had scouted it out earlier.

They arrived at the edge of a clearing, trying to keep out of sight. Zalia had pre-poisoned her arrows and dagger, using a tiny bit of the venom on the dagger and her normal mixture on her arrows. She could quickly dip an arrow into the pouch if she needed to but didn't really want to outright kill anyone unless they were close enough to do her harm. She quickly used a Dodge-vine ritual on the townspeople as they grouped up behind a section of thick underbrush.

"This should help protect you a tiny bit," Zalia explained, having received a few odd looks.

She only had twelve arrows, six hers and six scavenged from that first battle-field she had come across. It didn't seem like many, but if she had to fight and landed each shot, the poison and damage this seemingly small number of arrows might inflict on a battle of this scale could be enormous.

They looked into the small clearing. There were tents in the central area with wooden spikes and a ditch along the perimeter. Guards were walking along the perimeter or just sitting in raised chairs designed to look over the spikes. In the middle of the circle of tents, Arthur was tied to a post as someone was lashing him with a whip.

"Those fuckers," Tristan whispered.

Zalia put a restraining hand on his arm, not letting him charge off just yet. She spotted a large tree nearby that offered a good vantage point and gestured, pointing to herself, then upwards.

"If you really need me to shoot someone, point at them. If a battle starts, I'll take things into my own hands," she whispered, moving away in the direction of the tree.

She climbed up and waited, hidden by the leaves as she watched the group of townspeople move out of the clearing edge, approaching the camp.

At least they weren't waiting to ambush us, Zalia thought, watching the guards move about.

There was something off about the way they moved almost robotically. She couldn't put a pin on what felt strange about them, but there was definitely some-thing. She spotted around twelve people, putting them at a disadvantage compared to the townspeople's group of about twenty. They didn't have overwhelming odds like Zalia had wished for but it was definitely better than some alternatives.

She watched Tristan and his group approach the deserters, marking out two archers that would be her first targets if it came to battle. She knew Tristan was Bronze rank, while most of the townspeople were Tin with a few Iron ranks. The soldiers were most likely Iron and Bronze, she doubted there was a single Tin rank amongst them.

One of the guards ran to the man who was whipping Arthur and whispered to him. The man turned to Tristan's group with an eerie smile on his blood-spattered face.

He will be next, Zalia thought.

The man yelled out to the deserters, getting them to group up on the side of the barricade Tristan's group was approaching from. Zalia saw the two archers take position to the side and she nocked an arrow, getting ready to act.

Tristan

Tristan looked at the blood-spattered man he remembered from his time in the army. This had been his commanding officer, once an honourable man.

"Vidar," Tristan said.

"Tristan," the man replied, a dark grin on his face.

The man was Silver rank, something beyond what Tristan had expected to find out here. He had thought the group just some mere deserters, probably Iron and Bronze, but this was something different.

"I hear you're going around, extorting, blackmailing, robbing, and murdering people," Tristan said.

"That I am," Vidar replied calmly.

"You don't deny it?" Tristan asked.

"No point denying the truth, Tristan," he replied.

Tristan saw a brief flash of red behind the man's eyes.

What the hell is that, he thought.

"Come back and face trial, Vidar, you can right some of the wrongs you've done in this place," he pleaded.

Tristan saw the man's face contort as if in pain for a moment before taking a relaxed expression again.

What the fuck, he thought.

"You know that isn't going to happen, Tristan."

Tristan gripped his double-bladed axe, pulling it slightly from its band at his side. "We are only going to ask this once."

"And I'm only going to refuse one time," Vidar said, his grin widening into a visage of mania.

"What happened to you, my friend?" Tristan whispered.

The man whistled and Tristan saw the two archers draw back their arrows. Then, one of the archers dropped as an arrow flew through the side of his head, and the tense field exploded into motion.

Zalia

Zalia quickly released a second arrow, but the second archer ducked back behind a chair using the thick wooden construction as cover. One of the villagers had caught an arrow through the leg and fallen, most likely alive, or so Zalia hoped. The first archer had gone down and not gotten up—definitely wasn't going to survive an arrow through the skull. Applying Hunter's Mark, Zalia carefully aimed and shot a third arrow, creating a light cut across the second archer's arm as a result. If the man was Iron rank, it was all she needed, and she let the poison and Hunter's Mark combination go to work. At her side she had the arming sword she had taken from the guard who had tried to kill her, not planning on using it until she ran out of arrows.

The townspeople and deserters clashed in a mess of flashing swords and shields, axes, and hammers. The deserters were keeping a well-formed line with shield, sword, and spear, using the rough but sturdy defences of their camp to keep from being completely surrounded. Tristan and the person Zalia thought to be the captain of the deserters were engaged in an incredibly fast combat, striking, parrying, and dodging at a speed Zalia could barely keep up with. The villagers were kept at bay due to the spear and shield wall erected by the deserters as Tristan and the captain fought just in front of it. No one seemed to want to interfere in the fight and focused instead on each other.

Zalia let off three more arrows in quick succession, hitting an arm and the chest of two of the spear-wielding back line deserters. The archer who Zalia had shot second was writhing on the ground screaming, contributing no more to the battle. Zalia quickly released another four arrows, leaving two in her quiver, turning the tide of the somewhat stalemate battle in favour of the townspeople. She hopped down from her tree and ran up to the one villager who had taken the arrow and pushed it out through the other side, trying to do minimal damage. Her Healing Presence quickly began healing the wound as she drew her sword and stood over him. The townspeople were quickly disarming and tying up the soldiers who lay screaming due to her poison and killing those who still fought back. She wasn't sure any of them would survive, but if they were of a higher rank it was possible. The one part of the battle she was unsure of was the fight between Tristan and the captain. The captain had started to emit a weird energy, red and decaying. Zalia's aura was countering it with healing for now but there was definitely something wrong. One of the villagers tried to intervene in the fight but was almost decapitated for his efforts. Those two fighters were on an entirely different level than the likes of the townspeople. Zalia took her one remaining arrow and dipped it into the Silver rank venom, nocking it, carefully taking aim, and applying her Hunter's Mark. The two fighters momentarily disengaged as she released the arrow, but to her shock, the captain simply caught it with his hand. It would have been an impressive and singularly incredible moment except for the slight cut he received on his hand for the display. The venom had less of an effect on him than she expected but she realised why when she saw his aura.

? (Corrupted) - Silver rank

Corrupted? she thought.

He soon dropped the arrow and reengaged Tristan, who looked like he was wearing down a lot quicker than the enemy was. Zalia drew her dagger and watched the man closely, hoping for a moment to be able to intervene in relative safety.

The townspeople all stood back, not involving themselves in the dangerous fight but securing the remaining deserters who had not succumbed to the poison. Zalia circled, dagger in hand as Tristan and the captain fought. In a flash, Tristan's weapon was smashed from his hand and a kick to the stomach dropped him to his knees. The captain raised his sword to finish the job but stumbled, gasping.

"Pleeassseee, killl meeeee," he said, coughing and rasping as the red aura subdued for a moment.

Zalia took the moment to act, running up and slamming the dagger into his armpit and his heart. The second she did so, she was backhanded with such force she flew through the air, smashed through a tent—shattering her leg on impact—and rolled to a stop with a thud against a chair. She lay there gasping as she could feel the few broken bones on her body grinding back into place as her healing worked very, very slowly. The pain was immense. She watched through tearful eyes, in denial of her injuries, as the man continued to fight. Tristan had gotten his weapon back and fought on while the captain, dagger still lodged in his heart, smashed against his defences. The captain slowed down once the bleeding and venom took effect. He started looking more and more emaciated as the venom dissolved the water from his body, until eventually Tristan gained the upper hand and struck out, his axe cutting deep into the man's neck. With a second strike, the head came off and silence fell upon the camp.

Zalia used her Protection of the Wilds to heal everyone up quickly, closing gashes and stab wounds, and the surviving deserters, now tied up, also received healing. Four had remained alive, the second archer actually surviving the poison, though still unconscious despite the healing. Tristan and Zalia were now sat numbly next to each other amongst the group of townspeople as they recovered from the extended battle.

"That was one hell of a fight," Zalia said to Tristan.

"A lot of fancy footwork that wouldn't work in a real war," Tristan replied, "and don't think I didn't see that first shot. Took the man out before he even reacted to Vidar's order."

"Vidar? Was that the captain?"

Tristan nodded. "Yep, old captain of mine from back in my army days. Had no idea he was the one leading this group and he was . . . different."

"I noticed something weird with his aura reading. It told me he was corrupted," Zalia said.

"Don't ask me, I have no idea what was going on there," he replied.

"And that red aura coming from him, it was like it was trying to suck the life out of the land around us. Luckily my Healing Presence could counteract it for the most part, but have you ever felt something like it?"

"Ahh, so that was you healing everyone. No, no idea what that was. He never used to have anything like it, but whatever it was, he was obviously not used to it being counteracted like that. His fighting style led me to believe he usually plays it safe, aiming for drawn out battles that are won more by that aura than anything else," Tristan said. "Probably saved my life, since if he went for an aggressive style he probably could have done me in . . . though maybe that was part of him still in there . . ." He trailed off, looking thoughtful and not a little upset.

"Maybe he was still in there, but I don't know that we could have gotten whatever corrupted him out, Tristan. Don't overthink it, you put a friend to rest," Zalia said, trying to console him.

She left to collect all of her arrows once more, finding only one broken. She also read all of the messages she had received during the fight.

Congratulations! Hunter's Mark has reached Tin 20.
Congratulations! Hunter's Mark has reached Iron 1. This skill will not rank up any further until all your classes have reached Iron 1.
Congratulations! Herbal Magic has reached Tin 15.
Congratulations! Protection of the Wilds has gained two levels, reaching Tin 15.
Hunter's Mark - spell - targeted - channel
Tin - Marked by the Hunter, there is no escape. This ability marks a creature you can see. Marked creature takes a small amount of extra damage when damaged by you. You know the general direction of the marked enemy. Marking a second creature removes the first mark.
Iron - You may apply Hunter's Mark to three creatures at once, consecutive marks now remove the earliest applied mark past three.
Mana - very low/s
Cooldown - n/a

Damn, three creatures now. That will only really help in larger battles like these, but I've ended up in quite a few more than I would like, so I won't complain, Zalia thought.

She returned to Tristan, who was still resting, and held out a hand to help him up. "Let's get you back home to the town you saved," she said, giving him a smile.

CHAPTER TWENTY

Back to the Wilds

Zalia

Zalia and the townspeople took everything in the camp they found of use. They took off the simple armours the deserters were wearing, their weapons, food, and supplies that most likely had been taken from nearby townspeople and farmers. One townsperson came up and gave her an extra twenty arrows that they had found on the archers, stating that she had stopped the arrows from being shot at them, so they would give them to her. Her bag was starting to feel quite heavy with the amount of stuff in there. Packed in were her tarp, sleeping bag, metal pan, work knife, lighter, rope, axe, various herbs, old clothes, and now an additional twenty arrows. If she added too much now, the weight would grow cumbersome, slowing her down more than it helped. Obviously this limit would grow as her strength did, but she hadn't reached that point just yet. Arthur, the man who had been caught scouting, was fine after a slightly longer time healing than some of the others. Aside from some lingering mental trauma, that was. Zalia was starting to wonder if her healing had an effect on the mental side of injury as well, though she guessed that not having the scars and injuries of whatever trauma they had received helped on its own.

They stayed for a few more minutes before setting off, prisoners in tow.

"Hey Tristan," Zalia said, walking up next to him.

"What's up?" he asked.

"I have this sword I really don't know how to use. Could you be convinced to show me the basics?" she asked.

"You're not going to become a skilled swordswoman overnight, but I could certainly show you some basics and things to practice. You won't get far without a sparring partner though," he replied.

"I won't be staying around long, my goals are worth more to me than learning how to use a sword," she said, squinting at him. "You won't convince me to stick around for that."

"Worth a try," he said back, laughing.

"To think you thought I'd stick around in one place just for a sparring partner, tsk," she muttered.

"Would you stick around for something more?" Tristan asked.

Zalia winced.

"Ah, I'm sorry, Tristan, I'm not exactly interested in men . . . or anyone for that matter. Not at the moment, anyways. More of the lone wolf type in that regard, I'm sorry," she replied, hoping he wouldn't take it badly.

"Don't need to apologise, Zalia, just thought I'd shoot my shot," he said, not seeming too hurt, to her relief.

"Still up to train me a little?" she asked.

"Of course! I'm not convinced I should let you keep the sword without. More likely to hurt yourself than whoever you're swinging it at, from the way I saw you holding it earlier," he replied, laughing again.

"Ouch, it wasn't that bad was it?" she asked, trying her best hurt look.

He looked at her incredulously before she cracked and laughed with him.

"Not that bad," he muttered.

They made it back to Ostoss without incident, handing off the deserters to the town guard. Zalia hoped there weren't any more corrupt guards, but with the reduced number of deserters, they wouldn't be much of a problem to deal with if they escaped anyways. Before she left town, Tristan showed her some basic footwork and how to hold the sword properly, giving her a few basic strikes to practice, and telling her how to defend against the same basic strikes. It would be a long time before she was anything close to skilled with a sword, but she thought she could hold her own against a similarly inexperienced fighter. Besides, she planned on shooting anyone who wanted to kill her long before they got within reach, not that it always worked out.

She wondered what kind of training the town guards got or if they were just equipped with weapons and told to guard the town. The man she had first killed hadn't seemed particularly skilled as a fighter, especially compared to someone like Tristan or Vidar. Thinking about that man made her hands shake a little again before she calmed herself. This would have made her dismiss her theory about the healing helping with mental trauma, but maybe she would have been far worse off without it. She definitely wasn't going to forget the look on the man's face as his body was sapped of liquid right before her eyes, how she'd muffled his pained screams with her bare hands. No, that experience would haunt her to the end of her days.

It was two days after returning to the town that she left. She was starting to feel restless, claustrophobic, and locked in. Returning to the wilds, she breathed the fresh air in relief, alone once more on the road. She still planned to go west to find the Morning's Shade. She wasn't sure what the entry requirements were for such a group, but she knew she'd find out and get in anyways. A part of her wanted to forget about it and go back north, but she felt that what she could learn from them would be invaluable to her continued living here.

She continued her Mobility training as she went, adding in short rests to practice the basic strikes and defence stances Tristan had taught her. She also began harvesting and using Dodge-vine as she found it, realising she probably should have been doing this all along to train her ritual magic. It also came with the added benefit of having the ritual active constantly, the defensive bonus slight but valuable. She also occasionally poisoned herself, not attempting to use the Silver rank poison, in order to help level her healing skill that was so close to Iron rank. Zalia wondered if other people or creatures had classes linked to all their stats. Her own classes each linked to two stats each, increasing all six of her attributes as she levelled.

Does everyone else with two classes only have an increase to four of their six attributes? What about creatures, it seemed like those bunnies had an increase in resilience and dexterity but was that it? All things the Morning's Shade could teach me, I suppose, though it would certainly explain why I am able to punch above my weight quite a bit, Zalia thought.

The thought of having a distinct advantage over everyone else gave her some comfort for the future. It would mean that at higher levels each attribute would always be equal or greater to others of her rank, but never lower.

About a week passed as Zalia travelled, finding no towns and thoroughly enjoying her journey alone. One day in, a surprise came when she hunted down a small furry creature with two legs that hopped around from tree to tree.

> **Congratulations! You have fought, hunted, and been hunted while wielding 'Hunter's Bow.' The item is now bonded to you.**
> **Hunter's Bow (Heirloom) - Bonded Tin rank.**
> **Tin - Arrows fired from this bow gain a mild seeking effect.**
> **Seeking effect - Arrows will adjust in flight to hit vulnerable spots such as joints in armour or scales, and avoid other natural defences such as bone.**

Testing the effect, she found that her arrows now would almost never hit bone, but hit deep in between ribs or joints. She figured they would have a similar effect when faced with armour as well. She hadn't been aware of the strength of heirloom items, only knowing of the minor self-repair effect until now. It made her truly appreciate Darren and Juniper, the two farmers who had given it to her. It was only minor, but if it levelled to gain Iron and additional rank abilities as she did, it would be another great advantage.

As the week passed, she gained a couple levels in a few skills, as well as a new general passive for her efforts.

Congratulations! Survivalist and associated skills have reached Tin 15.
Congratulations! Flora Identification has
gained two levels, reaching Tin 15.
Congratulations! Preparation has gained two levels, reaching Tin 16.
Congratulations! Stasis has gained two levels, reaching Tin 15.
Congratulations! Harvester has gained three levels, reaching Tin 17.
Congratulations! Herbal Magic has gained three levels, reaching Tin 18.
Congratulations! Herbalist Class has gained two levels, reaching Tin 15.
Congratulations! Healing Presence has reached Tin 20.
Congratulations! Healing Presence has reached Iron 1.
Healing Presence - passive - aura
Tin - Your very presence grants life to all around you. You,
nearby allies, and any flora and fauna you so choose within
your aura are affected by a heal-over-time effect. The heal-
over-time effect heals for low health every second.
Iron - Healing Presence now heals the most grave injuries first,
and you may focus it onto a single target, increasing that target's
healing while reducing the healing other targets receive.
Congratulations! Through your hard work and training,
you have learned the new general passive 'Mobility.'
Mobility - passive
Tin - Your speed is increased. Your stamina is less affected by movement.

The new effect Iron rank gave Healing Presence, plus the fact it was now Iron rank, made the ability a powerful survival tool for Zalia. She found that the fact it was Iron alone made it quite strong and the focused healing part made it sufficient to properly bring her back from an injury that would otherwise be quite dangerous.

The new Mobility general passive came with a noticeable increase to how fast and how far she could run at once before getting tired. It wasn't a game changer, but she would take everything she could get.

She had taken to wearing her armour all the time, taking it off only to sleep. In a town she might not do the same, but out in the wild it was preferable to her. She was sat, about a week after her departure, next to a small campfire she had made. Some very light snow had come down that afternoon, and the light layering made a beautiful scene in the flickering light of the fire. To her, the glittering

of the reflected firelight was calming. It was dark, only the small area around her
lit up, with vague shapes of trees and other plants all around. She was peacefully
eating a small piece of meat she had carved from a kill that still lay roasting gently
on the fire. She was relaxed, listening to the strange clicking sound she found
some creature made for a short time after sunset. The cold didn't bother her at
all anymore, even the heat of the fire was not able to harm her as she passed her
hand through it, carving off a little bit more meat with her bare hands and knife.
She didn't need to eat so much anymore; the closer she got to Iron the less it was
necessary. She felt once she reached Iron in Survivalist she wouldn't need to eat
or drink at all anymore. Not that she couldn't, just that she wouldn't need to. She
found she could still eat as much as a person normally could.

She tensed, suddenly alert and scanning the area as she heard the odd clicking sound stop just off to the right. She flipped up her hood and drew her dagger, standing ready. She started slowly moving away from the fire when a figure
walked out from the shadows, to her eyes apparating out of thin air.

"Relax, relax." A low calming voice came out of the figure, which was holding its empty hands up, palms out.

"Says the person sneaking up on a lone traveller in the wilds," Zalia replied,
only ever taking her eyes off the person to check her surroundings for a few
moments.

"A fair point," the figure said, voice still calm.

"What do you want?" Zalia asked, tense.

"I'd like to sit and have a chat," the person replied.

Zalia stared at them for a few moments before nodding. She crouched down,
still on her toes and ready to move into action should the figure or a hidden
enemy attack. She was a little put off when her Aura Observation couldn't determine what the person's rank was, though she guessed it could be an ability significant to stealth classes.

"Who are you?" she asked.

"I was disinterested and then you noticed me. Now I'm interested. My
name is not important," the figure responded. "Where are you heading to, lone
traveller?"

"Don't see how that's important to you," she responded in kind.

She could see the man's face for the first time, suddenly, as a kind of magic
dropped from his form. His face was bland, nothing memorable or unique about
it except for the singular raised eyebrow.

"Did you just drop your concealment magic to raise your eyebrow at me?"
she asked.

"Expression is very important," the man grumbled.

"The dark and mysterious shadow thing really does not work for you," Zalia
said, relaxing a little.

The man sighed. "It was worth a try, I guess," he said.

"Yeah, definitely not. I'm trying to find my way to the Morning's Shade. Know where I can find them?" she asked.

"Actually, I do. They're based in the fortress city of Endelbyrn. I was just heading there myself, care to join me on the way?" he asked.

Zalia thought for a moment. The man *seemed* trustworthy, but she wasn't about to trust a random lone traveller that stumbled upon her in the wilderness. Though she realised she was also a random lone traveller in the wilderness.

"I don't quite trust you yet, what are you doing out here alone?" she asked.

"I'm a messenger," he said, simply.

Explains all the stealth shit he seems to have going on I guess, some kind of hidden messenger, she thought.

Though she was still unnerved by being unable to detect the man's rank, she slowly nodded. "We might be able to come to an agreement. Some direction would be nice," she finally said.

"Wonderful!" he said cheerfully. He pointed at the small roasting animal she had on the spit. "May I?" he asked.

She looked him straight in the eyes. "No," she said.

Zalia barely slept that night. The man soundly snored away as she kept an eye on him, or tried to, at least. Despite the sound and the fact she knew he was there, she had a very hard time actually seeing or hearing him. She had to focus quite consciously on his form to even see him. It was an odd sensation, as if her eyes slid away from where the man slept.

I wonder how the clicking insects noticed him, she thought, *maybe they have some kind of divination magic.*

She smiled at the ridiculous thought, smiling more when she realised it could actually be possible.

When morning came, the man stood up, brushed himself free of snow and looked to her. "Ready?" he asked.

"Naturally," she responded, having been ready to bolt at any point during the night.

"Quite a paranoid one aren't you," he said, obviously noting her tiredness.

"Alive, paranoid one," Zalia corrected.

"Can't fault that I guess," he replied, before walking off. "Come on! It's about two days' walk, best get to it."

They travelled for two days in near silence, not that Zalia minded. Silence might have felt wrong with a group of people or some others, but it felt comfortable in this situation. The second night she fell asleep, finally, unable to keep herself awake any longer. Thankfully, she woke up still in possession of all her things and un-murdered. It was positively delightful to discover the man wasn't entirely untrustworthy.

The snow had melted away, leaving a glistening and soaked landscape slowly drying in the sun. The land around these parts was quite beautiful, with rolling hills and trees dotting the area. Long, wavy grass grew all across the landscape, forming patterns in the wind.

Zalia didn't practice any more during that time, not wanting to let the man know how incompetent her sword work was. She also left her bow in the bag, except for once a day when she hunted down a small creature to eat. She had consciously been keeping her aura as a focused heal on herself but no longer needed to concentrate on it, the ability coming almost naturally to her after even this short time. Some of her magic still felt unfamiliar but the constant calming, warm presence of her healing had been active the moment she'd gotten it; a constant companion. As they travelled closer and closer to the city she finally spoke.

"So what should I expect from this place?"

"Well, as the name suggests, it's a veritable fortress. The population is quite low for a city of its size, but the average rank is quite high. I expect you'll not find another Tin ranker in there whatsoever. You can expect all the norms of a city, your average people doing all sorts of jobs. The main difference you should expect is the presence of the very organisation you're looking for," he replied, "they're held in very high regard by the people who live there, some even revere them, oddly. Despite my distaste for the reveration of the shades, their reputation is not entirely unfounded. From what I've heard, there are some quite powerful people higher up in the chain of command. There are some theories and rumours, of course, there always are, but the shades I have met are quite polite. Usually."

"Hmm," she murmured.

"That's it!?" the man asked incredulously. "You don't speak for two days, finally ask a question, I give you a thorough description, and your answer is 'hmm'?" He was obviously frustrated.

"Relax, relax," she said, holding up her hands palms out, much like he had when they first met.

She smiled to herself as she walked past, continuing the journey. She could almost feel the disbelief rolling off the man in waves.

Within the hour, it was her turn to be in disbelief. While she had seen a few small towns in this world and had been impressed by the artwork displayed in the construction of the buildings, the fortress city of Endelbyrn was something else entirely. When she crested a ridge, she finally saw it, built at the top of a hill turned cliff edge. The walls were made of a polished stone that reflected the sunlight, and flared outwards with spines as they rose up and around the city, forming an effect that looked like a halo. Within that shining halo of stone stood a large keep, spires pointing to the sky. It was crafted from a dark rock that seemed to absorb the light rather than reflect it. Around the keep, a relatively normal city grew within the bounds of the walls. The whole effect made it seem as if the shadow of a keep sat within a glowing crown of morning light.

"Wow," Zalia said.

The man just smiled.

CHAPTER TWENTY-ONE

Endelbyrn

Zalia

As they got closer to the city, Zalia could see the cliff edge the city sat upon was actually the end of the continent; the sea was below, stretching far into the distance. The two of them walked slowly towards the massive construction, entering the shadow of the huge city as the sun slowly fell behind it.

"I'm thoroughly impressed with the city. Who built it?" Zalia asked.

"I don't fully know," the man responded, scratching his head.

"A shame, I'd love to meet the person who designed it," she said.

"And why is that?" he asked.

"I bet whoever it was could design some really, really good-looking armour," she replied.

The man just snorted in laughter.

Looking at the fortress, she saw that the design was familiar. It reminded her a little bit of how her new bow looked, the designs carved into its surface different yet . . . similar.

They eventually arrived at the city gates, guarded by not two but six guards that Zalia identified as Silver rank. The large gates had the same motif as the city, the dark shade of a keep within a glowing sunlight halo. As they approached the guards, they stepped aside to let them enter without a word, one even going so far as to bow to the duo.

"Who are you?" Zalia asked the man she'd been travelling with, suddenly suspicious again.

"No one important," he replied nonchalantly.

"Says the man with people bowing to him," she replied.

"Fair point," he said, before bowing to her and vanishing into thin air.

"You bastard," she said to the air, knowing he could still hear her.

Some of the guards were looking at her a bit oddly after that display but she ignored them, walking on.

She looked around the inside of the city, a little bit lost. Some of the buildings kept the theme of the city as a whole, but for the most part they were just normal buildings—well, normal for this world. Materials weren't so much nailed and glued together as melded together via magic. She slowly began walking through the streets, taking in the smells of the city, frying street food, dust, and the general odour of a large number of creatures living in close proximity. There weren't some of the usual scents she remembered from cities back in her world, trash and car exhaust, so the experience was slightly better but not by much. She could hear street vendors hawking their wares, people chatting as they shopped or went about their business, the sound of a cart trundling past. The colours of houses and peoples' clothes were vibrant, sometimes clashing and sometimes complimenting each other. All in all it was the chaotic jumble of sensory input that had made her leave civilization in the first place.

You only have to stay as long as you have something to gain, she thought to herself.

She eventually found a small building jammed between two larger ones, a wooden sign gently swaying in the wind above the entrance. It had a mug etched into it, an apparently universal sign for an inn. She quickly went in, needing a break from the constant and overwhelming sounds of a city. She sighed with relief as the sounds faded a bit into the background. She hadn't found a notice board when entering the city but figured it was because they had a giant organisation to deal with any problems they had. Although, there must have been one somewhere for the king to put out declarations, the city was a part of Endaria after all. At least she thought it was. She ordered a random drink from the large board above the bar and went to sit down in a corner at a small round table. There were a couple other people in the small room but not enough to make her feel quite as claustrophobic as the city itself did. She decided she wouldn't immediately go to the Morning's Shade and would instead scout out the city by herself. Moments later, a young woman came and put a mug down at her table. Zalia gave her a smile and a thanks before returning to her thoughts. She was abruptly brought back out of them when she tried the drink, which was slightly alcoholic with a mild sweetness to it. It was excellent in its mildness, not overwhelmingly sweet but just the right amount. Zalia drank a little more, considering her next steps.

I could just go and ask what the entry requirements are, but I have a feeling that isn't the right way to go about it. I'm sure there is something I can do to get their attention, she thought.

She was brought out of her thoughts again as she heard someone whispering very, very loudly.

"Did you hear? The Hidden *himself* was seen bowing to someone entering the city," they said.

Oh good, here we go, she thought.

"He must have been trying to make a point, otherwise he wouldn't have let himself be seen doing it!" their companion replied, whispering equally as loudly.

I'm going to give him so much shit for that name. The Hidden, oooh, scary, she thought, smiling to herself.

After she finished her drink, she went back out, trying to acclimatise herself to the city, its sounds, smells, and sights. She wondered if the man, "the Hidden," was part of the Morning's Shade. It was more than likely, and if he was someone important like those two in the inn seemed to think, she might have already gotten the attention of the organisation. She didn't want to coast into the organisation based on her prior contacts, but she had a feeling that wouldn't happen anyways. Hopefully, it would give them reason to at least consider a Tin ranker, and that she would take.

She decided to wait and try entering the next day. She had found that the organisation was based out of the keep in the city, something she had expected.

A surprise came at night, once the sun set past the horizon: the keep began softly glowing a warm white as the walls of the city faded to darkness, no longer reflecting light.

Darkness in the light and light in the darkness, how poetic, she thought.

She went to sleep that night in a large, wide-boughed tree in a small park within the city, looking up at the warm-lit keep.

The next morning came rudely as a couple of kids ran through the park, screaming as they played. They were kicking around some small circular object, the activity apparently a worlds-spanning sport. She went through her usual morning routine, stretching and going for a run. She started in the park and moved through a section of the city, flying at speed past people casually walking to work or otherwise. She saw a whole array of different people and even someone flying overhead on the wind. She paused for a moment to watch the person in flight, determined to find some ability that provided her with her own flight. Continuing her run, she arrived back in the park to practice her sword work. She still wasn't any good, but with enough work and maybe some sparring partners, she hoped to get somewhere with it. After a half hour practicing the basic forms and strikes Tristan had shown her, she stopped when a new notification appeared, prompting her to read all the notes that had accumulated over the last day.

> **Congratulations! Mobility has reached Tin 2.**
> **Congratulations! You have learnt how to use two different weapon types at a basic level. You have unlocked weapon proficiencies.**
> **Bow - Weapon Proficiency**
> **Tin - Arrows shot from a bow you are using have increased speed and impact based on rank and level of this skill.**
> **Sword - Weapon Proficiency**
> **Tin - You can wield a sword faster and hit harder with it based on the rank and level of this skill.**
> **Based on the proficiency of your skill with the bow, 'Bow - Weapon Proficiency' has reached Iron 1. This will not increase further until all your classes have reached Iron.**
> **Bow - Weapon Proficiency**
> **Tin - Arrows shot from a bow you are using have increased speed based on rank and level of this skill.**
> **Iron - Arrows shot from a bow you are using have increased penetrative power based on the rank and level of this skill.**

Ohhhh shit, that could be really strong, she thought.

She didn't know if shooting a bow in a public park was looked down upon or prohibited, but she was too excited not to try. She pulled out her bow and shot an arrow at a nearby tree. The speed at which the arrow flew had more or less doubled, meaning the impact had quadrupled in turn. She went up and looked at the arrow, now buried a good ten to twelve centimetres into the tree. She tried to pull the arrow out but only succeeded in snapping the shaft, leaving the arrow tip and about a third of the shaft stuck in the tree.

"Well, damn," she muttered.

One arrow down, she was still quite happy and excited for what the skill meant. She could basically use a bow with half as much draw weight and retain an equal amount of power as she had previously. Obviously she wasn't going to do that, but it meant there would be a multiplicative effect on any increase in draw weight she might gain. She was hoping her Heirloom Bow would increase in draw weight by some means once she reached Iron rank in her classes. Or that it did anything at all when she reached Iron rank.

Over the course of her morning she had been preparing herself, trying to feel ready for whatever she was about to get herself into. After the addition of the two skills, one currently much more impactful than the other, she finally felt up to the task. She didn't know if they would make her just sign some paperwork and be done with it, but she had a feeling she would be required to prove herself in some way. She steeled herself and started walking.

She soon found herself standing before the large doors of the keep. It was actually less of a keep and more of a complex of interconnected spires. The ground around the structure was a large, well-landscaped garden with winding paths, water features, and benches. The air was beautifully fresh and the large garden damped out the sounds of the surrounding city. All in all, it made for a refreshing and relaxing atmosphere that Zalia liked very much. She had been dreading staying in the city to learn from the organisation, but upon seeing the surroundings she would be staying in if she were accepted, she could handle it.

Before her sat one of the largest spires, located relatively central to the others. Many covered walkways spanned the distance between it and the floors of the nearby spires. Beside the large doors set into the polished, dark stone of the building stood two guards. Each of them wore a unique set of armour, both variations of a light leather set incorporating metal plates and embellishments. One of them held a short spear, most likely used in close combat rather than as a support in a shield wall, and the other had two sheathed short swords, the blades of which curved very slightly towards the ends. As she walked closer, they gave her a nod.

The spear-wielding guard pushed open the door to let Zalia in. "You're expected," she said.

"I am?"

The woman simply gestured for her to enter. Zalia walked in to see a large circular room, well-appointed with a few comfortable-looking benches and a soft, light grey carpet along the centre of the room. The room's only lighting was a soft glow coming from the very stone the building was made of. At the back was a set of stairs that went up and split to either side, leading to a floor further above. At the very bottom step stood a dark, cloaked figure looking her way.

"I've been expecting you," it said ominously.

"You!" Zalia exclaimed, recognising the figure as the man she had been travelling with.

She heard a chuckle from the door behind her.

"Me!" the man exclaimed back, immediately forgetting to maintain his intimidating, secretive pretence.

"Thought I'd find you here," she said.

"Damn guard at the gate ruined the whole game," he sulked.

"It's what you deserve for trying to be so dark and mysterious all the time and eliciting bowing from people," Zalia explained.

She squinted at the man suspiciously. "You know, I have been here for a single day and people are already whispering about the mysterious new stranger you were seen showing deference to," she said in annoyance.

He laughed. "Oh good, I don't want to be the only one who has to deal with it," he said cheerfully.

"Bastard," she whispered, now approaching the man.

"I assume you're here to 'lead me to my destiny' or some other such mysterious nonsense?" she asked.

"Exactly," he said in complete seriousness, nodding. "Follow along," he added cheerfully and started walking.

"I heard one other thing while I was out and about yesterday," she said, taking on a cheeky tone.

"Oh?" he asked, suspiciously.

"Some person called, 'the Hidden,' *ooOooOohh*," she said, trying to sound as spooky as she could.

"Nooo," he groaned.

"Oh yes," she replied.

"Please, I hate that name so much. Gods damn the sycophants," he moaned.

"Gods?"

He looked at her weirdly.

"I come from somewhere remote," she said in explanation.

"Even the remotest peoples know of the gods, at least the ones people have met."

"Wait, people have actually met them?"

"Yes . . ." he replied, looking at her uncertainly.

"Are you sure they weren't just on a lot of drugs?"

"I didn't intend to sound uncertain about the 'meeting gods' part," he said, looking at her with interest.

"By 'remote,' I meant somewhere really, really remote," she explained further.

"It seems so," he murmured.

During the chat he had led Zalia up a flight of stairs, through a tunnel, up two more flights, through another tunnel, down a flight, through another tunnel, and finally up three more flights to a hallway. At the end of the hallway stood a door.

"Just go through there, some people will interro—I mean, they'll ask you some questions and then tell you where to go from there," he said, a smile on his still hard-to-see face once again.

"Alright, guess I will see you around," she said.

"Yes, you will," he replied, a spark of mystery in his tone again.

She ignored him, walking over to open the door and go in.

"Oh my god," she said in sheer exasperation, and sighed deeply.

Behind a small but wide podium stood three people. On the left was an extremely large woman built like a bodybuilder. She wore a heavier set of armour made entirely of an unknown metal. On the right stood an intelligent-looking man with a hawkish face wearing a light wizard's robe in shades of black and grey. In the middle, and the reason she was so exasperated, stood the mysterious man once again, his form as indiscernible as always.

"You," Zalia said, pointing at him, "are intolerable." Looking to the other two she added, "Zalia, excellent to meet you."

The woman raised an eyebrow, looking at the figure in the centre, while the man on the right looked mildly annoyed at her tone.

"Good to meet you, Zalia, I am Hildebrandt and these two are my colleagues, Matthias and . . . the Hidden," she said, smirking towards the end.

Zalia grinned widely, and the shadowy figure turned to Hildebrandt with a look of betrayal.

"Tell us about yourself," Hildebrandt said.

"I am a hunter from the north, far north where the snow falls. Due to reasons I won't disclose, I only gained my magic as of two or three weeks ago. I'm here to educate myself on what exactly it all entails and perhaps help some people along the way," she said. "I also . . . learnt that receiving three classes is very unusual."

Hildebrandt raised an eyebrow again at the last part; the Hidden only gave a slight smile but Matthias's face was visibly twitching.

"Interesting. If you would like to join us you must know that for your first year here you will be required to do as instructed and work within a group. Is that acceptable?" Hildebrandt asked.

Zalia thought it over for a minute. Working within a group wasn't a deal breaker, though definitely not ideal for her. Having greatly restricted freedom was going to hurt as well if she did choose to join.

"Will I be allowed to leave the organisation at any time I choose?" she asked.

"Yes, but you most likely will not be allowed back in if you do so." Matthias replied.

She thought for a moment more.

"I can accept those terms," she finally answered.

Only a year. It's a steep price to pay for information but I can do a year, she thought.

"Wonderful. Usually, we would test you on three things. One, your ability to deal damage. Two, your ability to perceive things. Three, your ability to hide. However, our colleague here," she said, nodding towards the Hidden, "has already determined you are very perceptive indeed. Tell us, can you track?"

"I was a hunter for many, many years before I even got magic, and with it came an ability to track even better. Yeah, I can track," she replied.

"Acceptable. In that case, we will test you on your ability to strike both single and numerous targets, and your ability to hide from a single or numerous persons. Other abilities will be taken into account, but these three general areas are a part of what makes up our organisation. Finding an enemy, killing an enemy, and hiding from whatever remains," Hildebrandt said.

"I can agree to that, when do we get started?" she asked.

Hildebrandt smiled. "Immediately."

CHAPTER TWENTY-TWO

Initiation

Zalia

The group of four now stood in a small coliseum-like structure that sat further into the grounds of the keep. The round sandy arena was surrounded by a tall, heavily enchanted wall, above which rows of seats rose up in ascending tiers.

"Unlike the other two," Hildebrandt explained, "I have both vitality and resilience attributes linked to one of my classes. This means I'm significantly harder to kill than them. Vitality is a measure of both your health and stamina. Resilience is a measure of your body's ability to ignore damage or remain completely undamaged. It's also thought that a mixture of the two contribute to how fast a person heals. Personally, I believe these two to be the most important stats anyone can have. I know plenty of people who might have lived otherwise if they had them. Unfortunately, which attributes are chosen depend on the mindset of the person and not everyone shares my views, especially when they take their class and specialisation at a young age. Once these are locked in, they can't be changed. Strength and dexterity are relatively simple, being the potency and speed of a body, respectively. Wisdom and intellect are the same, being the potency and speed of a mind, respectively, with wisdom also granting increased mana capacity. Reacting to simple attacks requires only dexterity, but reacting to something more complex in a quick manner requires wisdom—intellect and dexterity working in tandem."

Haven't even joined yet and I'm already learning a lot. "Shouldn't be an issue for me, I've got all six," Zalia said.

She watched Matthias's entire body visibly twitch at that.

What's that guy's issue?

"As you rank you'll become exponentially stronger than the rest of humanity, then. The two unlinked attributes do increase very slightly as you increase rank, but nowhere near to the degree that a linked one does," Hildebrandt said. "Some people get confused about how both wisdom and intellect relate, but the way I've found easiest is to think of wisdom as the *depth* at which you can think and learn, and intellect as the *speed* at which you can think and learn. Now," Hildebrandt continued, "I want you to attack me."

"No holds?" Zalia asked.

"No holds," she replied, giving Zalia a scary smile.

For the first time Zalia was able to see the woman's rank.

Hildebrandt - Gold rank

No holds it is, she thought.

Zalia strung her bow and nocked an arrow after dipping it in the Silver rank poison she had. It might have been reckless, but this was a Gold rank resilience and vitality user. She drew and released in a smooth movement as she exhaled, applying Hunter's Mark in the same moment. The arrow almost teleported the distance between them, swerving in the air a little and slamming into the joint between Hildebrant's shoulder plate and chest plate. It only got about a third of the arrowtip in before it stopped.

Hildebrandt

Actually managed to harm me, Hildebrandt thought, pulling the arrow out and feeling the slight wound close.

Within the wound, she felt a poison striving to destroy her body, but it was also quickly dealt with. It took enough time, however, that she suspected it was at least Bronze rank, maybe Silver.

Now that is impressive.

She hadn't expected Tin rank Zalia to get even close to injuring her, though she suspected the woman probably had a few skills in the Iron rank already. Obviously if she was moving, the arrows would have just bounced off her armour, but she didn't expect the woman to measure up to Gold rank standards.

Zalia

"Very impressive," Hildebrandt said.

Zalia smiled, glad that she hadn't been eliminated after the first test.

"Now, let us test your ability to attack large numbers of targets," she continued.

This was the one she was most concerned about, but hoped Nature's Wrath would help her out here.

Matthias made some gestures, and ten sandy soldiers were formed from the ground before him. They each moved into a stance, surrounding her. She steadily but quickly drew and fired at the soldiers, aiming for the head each time, and took them out in good order. However, it did take much longer than she was sure some others had managed.

"Not so impressive, but still adequate for someone of your rank," Matthias said.

"Make as many as you can within about twenty metres of me," Zalia replied, seething a little.

A huge mass of the soldiers appeared, and Zalia activated Nature's Wrath. Sandstone spikes shot out of the ground, several impaling each soldier as a small fire began to spread across the spikes and soldiers. They all soon lost form, crumbling to blackened sand and ash on the coliseum floor.

"Better?" Zalia asked, looking at Matthias.

"Better," he agreed unwillingly.

The Hidden laughed and Hildebrandt smirked a little, obviously finding enjoyment in Matthias being annoyed.

"I will pass you on both accounts for the damage section of the testing," Hildebrandt said. "Is there any other ability you wished to display before we move on to the hiding section of things?"

Zalia thought for a moment. "Yes, one of my classes is Herbalist and won't be much help in the next part. Essentially it gives me the instinctual ability to harvest and use herbs of my rank, keep them in a form of stasis, and makes them more potent and the like. The most important part of the class, in my mind, is the instinctual ability to enact rituals with herbs of my rank," she explained. "One such is Dodge-vine, as I've named it, which allows me to give some increased defence to anyone I apply it to. As my ranks increase I believe the class will become incredibly strong . . . Oh! And I also have a Passive Healing aura," she added, focusing the healing on each of them in turn so they would feel it more strongly.

"Wonderful, all of that will be taken into account. A healing ability and a good chunk of utility will make you very useful indeed to anyone you work with," Hildebrandt replied.

"Now, for your next test," Matthias said.

What followed was a series of different environments and landscapes, appearing and disappearing as Zalia was tested in each one. The sand rose up and formed each scenario, even going so far as to colour itself the correct colour as Matthias controlled it. She was very quickly found each time, despite her every effort to not be. The man was incredibly perceptive, unbelievably so. She almost wondered if he was cheating and finding her through the sand somehow, but if there was such obvious corruption like that here she probably didn't want to stay anyways.

She desperately looked for anything that could help her as the tests continued, but didn't make any breakthroughs before he called an end to the tests, describing her ability as "lacking but adequate." She actually agreed with the man for once but wanted to figure out how to do better during the next section of the test. It would be the section that would have multiple people searching for her. Her breakthrough came when she was thinking about the nature of her ritual magic. She had already come to the realisation that each component she used in a ritual would provide an essence or type of magic to the ritual. It was the will of the ritualist or more accurately, the runes and forms that they used, that shaped the result. Dodge-vine gave her a feeling of protection, and she had interpreted that as proving some form of physical protection. She wondered, however, if it could also encompass protection from sight or being found.

During one of the last tests, Zalia used Dodge-vine and Manifest in a ritual to embody a physical manifestation of protection from sight. A light layer of shifting material encompassed her. The material changed colour and shape to hide her wherever she chose. She also added the same ritual without Manifest and felt it take effect. It was an ephemeral feeling more akin, she suspected, to what the Hidden did, though the effect was obviously weaker. She felt each would last about an hour, probably longer since they weren't physically defending her in any way.

After this discovery, despite the fact she now had three people searching for her, she actually lasted longer. The longest she managed to hide was a full minute in snowy conditions, her most practiced terrain. The test soon came to an end, and Zalia found herself standing in front of the trio once more.

"What did you change?" Matthias asked, genuinely curious.

"Just discovered some experimental ritual magic, exploring the bounds of my abilities. Something like that," she responded, looking at a new notification.

> **Congratulations! Herbal Magic has reached Tin 19.**

He nodded. "I will also pass you in these tests. While you lack strength in any form, you have an extremely good ability to evaluate a situation and adapt. Strength will come with time and ranks," he said.

Zalia nodded her thanks, taking the insulting compliment in stride.

"What next then?" she asked.

Zalia sat in a small room resembling a dorm. It had a small bed she now sat on, a desk, chair, and a chest at the foot of the bed. It wasn't anything much, and she preferred sleeping in the wilds anyways, but it would do for now. What she liked most about it was that she couldn't hear the city outside whatsoever.

After the tests, the Hidden had given her a tiny little badge in the shape of a flat, shadowy keep in a sun's halo. He had also led her through some kind of ritual that linked her essence to the item. It basically meant someone inspecting it could tell it was hers, and prevented it from being stolen and used by another. He also informed her of a few things. In her first year here she would be required to take one guard duty each day unless on a contract. Guard duties were basically two hours spent guarding an entrance or gate within the keep or city, or patrolling up and down a street. That wasn't an issue for her, some time guarding people was something she could do to help out and might have done anyways. There were a few different opportunities available to her as well. There were trainers for all sorts of things, from advanced magical theory to baking, and there were a few that particularly interested her. She didn't take the archery one—she had been doing that for more than half her life and didn't need any training—but there was a swordsmanship one she would definitely take. There was another about the common herbs of the world, but she had a feeling that relying on her own skills and abilities would teach her how to determine those things on her own. If she learnt the common herbs through study, her progress might be slowed when it came to new ones outside of her knowledge base.

She would be paid a weekly wage for acting as a guard, as well as a percentage of any contracts fulfilled, depending on how many team members she ended up with. She also learnt she could willingly take contracts, but most teams were also given them. She would be assigned to a team the next day and would always have the right to request a change, which she appreciated. They tried their best to assign members based on their skill sets to provide a versatile group ready to deal with most situations. She had been classified by the organisation with a few keywords. Back line, support healer, utility, tracker, and damage dealer. After telling them about the Protection of the Wilds skill they'd given her, the Support-healer tag indicated she was proficient enough with healing to help out in a crucial moment, but not enough to act as a main healer. She agreed with the assessment. Despite the fact everyone had to be able to deal a certain amount of damage and reach a certain skill level for tracking and perceptiveness, the fact that she had a dedicated skill and years of practice meant she would likely be the team's main tracker. That was fine by her, it meant she could spend most of her time in front of and not around the others. Her team would most likely be all Iron ranks, the usual minimum for entry. She had been let in based on her extra class and the firm support of the Hidden. She didn't know why the man was so supportive of her joining, but she'd take the help.

It was about midday and Zalia was bored, so she decided to go find something to do. She kept her bow in her spatial bag, but left her sword sheathed at her side and dagger sheathed behind her back at her tailbone. She wanted to push her Herbal Magic to the next rank, so she went back to the arena and started experimenting.

She used a couple of her normal rituals, finding that they didn't advance her until she decided to experiment with her last bit of Frozen Heart. It was Bronze rank so she hoped it would push her ability over if she managed a ritual with it. She thought about her Protection of the Wilds ability and its similarity to a Dodge-vine and Manifest ritual focused on normal protection. The only difference was in the healing-over-time effect, and she knew Frozen Heart would offer healing-related elements. She made the normal ritual and then overlaid the form carefully with powdered Frozen Heart leaves, using her last bit. Activating the ritual, she found it emulated almost exactly the effects of her ability—on herself only, of course. To her delight, she saw the message pop up that she was looking for:

> **Congratulations! Herbal Magic has reached Tin 20.**
> **Congratulations! Herbal Magic has reached Iron 1.**
> **Herbal Magic - passive - varied**
> **Tin - Minor herbal-based rituals are a keystone of magical herbalists. You gain an instinctual understanding of herbal rituals of your rank or lower. Herbal Magic you use of your rank and lower has slightly increased potency.**
> **Iron - You may emulate the effects of herbs you have used in rituals of a rank lower than this ability.**

Ohhhh, hell yeah! she thought.

Excited by the possibilities of what she had gotten, she also realised she would be able to determine the effects of Iron rank herbs and rituals now. She looked over her herbs of Iron rank, noticing another bit of information popping up in the messages.

> **Snow-leaf (Ice element) - Iron rank**
> **Bitterbalm (Curse element) - Iron rank**

Her old Tin rank herbs also started showing the same information.

> **Dodge-vine (Protection element) - Tin rank**
> **Manifest (Physical element) - Tin rank**

When she thought about the Bitterbalm a bit more, she could feel what was meant by the curse element. It would essentially make the ritual provide a harmful lingering effect based on whatever else she added to it. A combination of Bitterbalm and Snow-leaf would create a damaging, ice-related lingering effect. She was quite excited to explore the effects of the Bitterbalm with some of the other herbs, though she knew what it did with the Dodge-vine. She also realised that she had been going about using it in a very inefficient manner. Previously, she had been overlaying it onto the whole ritual, essentially recreating the entire thing with the Bitterbalm. While that would work, all she really had to do was add a bit of the Bitterbalm as an addendum, rather than an entire ritual. One could say she was very, very excited to test it out. She could also practice with her Tin rank herbs as much as she wanted, now that they could be essentially manifested by her ability and no longer needed to be physically present. She recognised that Herbal Magic was becoming her most versatile skill.

She spent most of the day doing rituals, practicing doing them while at a full sprint, while using her sword, her bow, and during all sorts of activities. The magic would create the correct symbols and shapes so she didn't need to actually place it herself. Now that she could create it at will, she kept using the basic Dodge-vine ritual to have it up constantly. She used it all day and night until it was second nature, something she wouldn't need to think about but could rely on permanently. She kept practicing late into the day, stopping only to run out of the city, catch a small scaled creature with a single eye, eat it, and then run back in to continue her practice.

As she fell asleep that night she checked over her day of practices gains.

> **Congratulations! Mobility has gained three levels, reaching Tin 5.**
> **Congratulations! Sword - Weapon Proficiency has reached Tin 2.**

It wasn't a lot but daily progression was her goal for now, trying to reach a point where survival was easier in a world of powerful creatures.

She awoke feeling alright, not happy with having to sleep inside but dealing with it. In the future she considered going back to the park to sleep, the tree was much more comfortable to her than this room was. She dreaded meeting her group a little bit. It was bad enough that she would have to work with them to get what she wanted, but she knew it would lead to more independence in the future as she gained knowledge and power.

She walked out of her room to find the Hidden waiting for her.

"Good morning, is there something I can actually call you other than 'the Hidden'?" she asked, sighing.

"Yes," he replied.

" . . . And that would be?"

"That would be none of your business," he said, smiling brightly at her.

This day was going to be hell.

She followed the shadow of a man through the confusing path of bridges and stairs until they arrived at a door to a large room.

"Ready to meet your team?" he asked.

"Not really," she said glumly.

"Let's get started then!" he said energetically.

CHAPTER TWENTY-THREE

The Team

Zalia

Zalia entered the room to find a small round table with five seats. Three were currently occupied by people, the fourth and fifth she assumed were for her and the annoying shade she was being haunted by. She sat down, silently inspecting each of the people in turn.

The first person was a tall, gangly woman in a set of robes that looked styled for battle. They seemed designed to allow for a good range of movement, and upon closer inspection, they most likely had some form of padding or armour built in underneath. She had short brown hair, with tight braids and one side closely shaved, lending her a Viking-like look. She had light grey-green eyes but a purple lightning constantly flickered through them.

Sat next to her was a relatively short but sturdy man. He wore full plate armour, with a helm on the table before him. He looked to be well-built but it was hard to see anything beneath the armour. At his side in a loop was a heavy-looking mace, and a tower shield was leaning against his chair. While the tall woman's face held a stern look, the man looked cheery and in quite a good mood. He had short, spiky hair coloured a dirty blonde.

The last person was another woman in light leather armour similar to Zalia's, except it had no metal plating. She had what appeared to be a short-handled, double-bladed staff leaning against the near wall. The weapon was about two-thirds blade and one-third haft. There was also an average-sized heater shield leaning against the wall next to it. The woman seemed almost fragile, but Zalia quickly reevaluated when she saw her move. She would have to remember not to judge someone's strength or resilience based on their looks, the attributes mattered much more. The woman had long black hair, pulled back and bound into a single ponytail with a strip of leather.

The shadow that was following her sat down in the other chair, not commenting or speaking as Zalia sat and inspected each person in silence and they, in turn, inspected her. The man in the middle was the first to break the silence.

"Good morning, I'm Zenis, but my friends just call me Zen," the man said, smiling at her.

Zalia didn't respond for a moment. "Zalia, pleasure," she replied eventually, looking at the rightmost woman.

"I am Lady Leyra Indis, but you may refer to me as My Lady or Lady Indis," she said, holding eye contact.

Zalia just shrugged and looked over at the final woman.

"Ember," she said.

Zalia nodded once to her. "While I can figure out some basics from what armour you're all wearing and what weapons you wield, I'd like to know what your roles are."

"Tank, damage, buffs, front liner, with the strength, intellect, resilience, and vitality attributes," Zen said, pointing to himself. "She's healer, damage, utility, front liner with the dexterity, intellect, wisdom, resilience attributes. And she is damage dealer, utility, and back liner with the same attributes," Zen said, pointing to Ember and Lady Indis in turn. "How about you?"

"Damage, support healing, utility in the form of rituals, poisons, herbs, tracking, and mobility. Attributes are all of them," she replied.

"All of them?" asked Lady Indis doubtfully.

"What are your classes?" Zalia asked, ignoring her questioning tone.

"I'm a Mage with lightning specialisation," Lady Indis replied.

"Tank with leader specialisation," Zen said.

"Healer, combatant specialisation," Ember said quietly.

"And you?" Lady Indis asked with furrowed eyebrows.

"Hunter and Herbalist with Druid Unity class," Zalia replied.

"What the hell is a Unity class?" Ember asked.

Zalia just shrugged. "Dunno, but it means I have all six attributes unlocked. If I could tell you how to get it I would, but it started out this way for me," she said.

She gave them a brief rundown of her abilities and what they all did, each of the others giving theirs in return. It seemed like Indis's abilities from her Mage class were focused around mana regeneration and magic empowerment, while her lightning specialisation was focused on ways for her to direct and form that power. Zen's Tank class was focused around being able to take more damage and draw attention to himself, while his leader specialisation was focused around buffing allies and providing them opportunities. Ember's Healer class was just that, a very healing-oriented main class that would make them pretty hard to kill unless done so outright. Her Combatant class focused on being able to get in close and deal some damage; some of the effects actually allowed her to heal allies more efficiently.

All in all, it would be a pretty rounded team if they could learn to work together. Each of them had the Resilience attribute, meaning they would be quite hard to kill in general. Indis was probably the easiest to kill due to Zalia and Zen both having vitality abilities, and Ember had an ability in the Combatant class that increased her resilience even more.

"I suggest we go on a contract as soon as possible," Lady Indis said.

Zalia thought for a moment, inspecting the woman further. Getting out of the city for a time would be good. She nodded, looking to the two others who quickly agreed.

The Hidden finally spoke, trying his best at being dark and mysterious again. "Excellent, we had a contract prepared in case." He dropped a stack of hardy-looking papers on the table. "Reported sightings of a pack of Garroi near Bur, a small town to the north," he explained.

The other three had gone silent, seeming concerned.

"Anyone care to explain what those are?" Zalia asked.

"Garroi are a relatively small Iron rank creature by birth. They are quite weak," the Hidden explained, "but have extremely sharp, bladed protrusions made of bone running down their arms. The fact that they are pack creatures makes them quite dangerous. The real issue, and probably the reason your team-mates are so silent right now, is that if they begin a frenzy they will become exponentially larger and stronger. A small town would be the perfect place for them to become strong enough to become a threat. A frenzy needs blood and, well, people have plenty of that."

"I see the issue. When do we go?" Zalia asked.

"You've got to be kidding," Zen said, "we can't fight a pack of Garroi, can we?"

"I don't see why not, they're only Iron rank," Zalia said.

"You're not even Iron rank!" he exclaimed.

Zalia shrugged. "So?"

"You may go when you're ready, just be quick about it," the Hidden replied.

Zalia thought she might be ok working with these people on occasion. It wasn't preferable, but to learn from others, she had to actually be in an environment with others. It was quite the conundrum. Ember was quiet and thoughtful—which was a good sign in Zalia's books. Lady Indis was uptight but didn't talk much either. Zen, however, already spoke too much for her liking.

Zen-is bad for my Zen, she thought, smiling at her own joke.

"I'll meet you guys later at the entrance, maybe in a couple hours? We can leave for the town today if you all want," Zalia said, standing up.

The others agreed, Zen quite reluctantly, and Zalia walked out.

Zen

Zen watched the woman walk out of the room, closely followed by the Hidden. He turned to Indis and asked, "So, what do you two think? She seems quite . . . abrupt."

"I like her," Ember said.

"She is a little short-mannered," Indis said. "Only Tin rank too, but if they let her in as a special case below the minimum requirements, she must be strong. Three classes, all attributes linked. Hmm, yes, she will be a good ally if she doesn't die in the early ranks."

Zen rolled his eyes. "Of course you're thinking about alliances," he muttered.

"Of course I am! I am the future of my house, young man, and making powerful alliances is quite important, thank you very much," Indis retorted.

"Young man! We're the same age."

"Not that you act like it."

"Can you both please shut up?" Ember muttered.

Zalia

Zalia walked through the confusing labyrinth of stairs and bridges between spires thinking, *We're a good team, with complementary powers. Besides, working in a team is safer and there's plenty to learn from them. They're not completely annoying and don't seem incompetent either, at least. There will be plenty of things to do in my free time, solo hunts and the sort.*

She continued in the same vein of thought as she walked, trying to convince herself she wasn't going to hate having to work with other people for an entire year.

She got lost a few times in her walk to find the exit, but eventually found a door set into the base of one of the spires, and was able to leave the complex of structures. She walked through the gardens, trying to settle her mind. But even the gardens were beginning to annoy her, the curated plant life not giving her the same feel as the wilds beyond the city. She would be glad to be back out amongst the trees and rolling hills of the nearby lands.

Zalia made her way down to the park she had slept in the first night in the city and began going through her morning routine: sword work before a run, before going back to sword work once more, and performing her Dodge-vine ritual with magic throughout it all. She only had an hour and a half to train but went back a little early, wanting to find somewhere to wash herself off. Her clothes were self-cleaning, thanks to the enchantress back in Alston, but she still had to bathe. Her armour was kept free of sweat by her clothes, though they needed to be cleaned of dust and dirt sometimes. She was going to get a self-cleaning enchantment on the armour when she was back from this contract. She didn't know how much it paid but hoped it was enough to fund a couple small things.

She soon made her way back to the spires, having gained one more level in each Mobility and Sword Proficiency. Her Aura Observation also went up one level to four as she scanned over a strange duck-like creature floating in the park's pond. After arriving at the spires she had about fifteen minutes left before their scheduled departure. There had been a section of one of the spires that the Hidden had told her was a washroom on the way past. It wouldn't be an equal substitute for a nice, cool dip in a half-frozen river but it would get the job done, at least. After a few accidental detours, she found the place and went in. The hallway led off into another much shorter hallway with six doors leading off it. She tried one of the doors and found a small room inside with enchantments on the walls. Unlike the enchantments on her clothes and bag, these were visible, which led her to believe they were more powerful. She wasn't entirely sure that was how it worked but it was her best guess. She wasn't an enchanter, after all. She stepped in and closed the door, flicking a small lock on the inside. Immediately, the runes glowed brighter and she could feel the sweat dissipate off her body. She could also see the dirt and dust disappear from her armour, along with the blood stains on her bracers. She had tried to scrub them off but hadn't had much luck. She pulled items out of her bag and found them nicely cleaned as well.

She returned to the main spire entrance and found her newly acquired team waiting for her. She was a few minutes late, the ridiculous layout of the spires mainly at fault.

"Ready?" she asked as she entered the space.

"Waiting on you," Lady Indis said coldly.

Zalia ignored the remark, containing her annoyance at having to be around people. Glemp had at least been direct, logical, with a good sense of humour. Glemp was also not human. That helped.

Deciding on a course of action, Zalia thought just walking out the door would be best. The others followed as she left.

"Anyone know the town and the best way to get there?" Zalia asked.

"Been there a few times," Ember replied.

Zalia gestured for her to lead and they began their journey.

Zalia immediately felt better after they left the city, her annoyance fading away to a background chatter similar to the sound of her teammates bantering behind her. Ember had also joined Zalia at the front and was leading them all down a road that was more of an indentation in the dirt than anything else. Zen and Indis seemed quite familiar and had a habit of going back and forth slightly insulting each other, in a friendly way. It seemed to annoy Ember just as much as it did Zalia, but she found it hard to maintain that annoyance while traveling through the rolling hills and fresh air of the wider world.

They were most of the way to the town of Bur by the time night fell, and they began setting up camp. The others pulled out supplies and began eating their own relatively large meals made of travel supplies and rations. The meals consisted of mostly dried fruits and meat, as well as nuts and other similar items. Zalia chuckled quietly at the sight and walked off.

She came back ten minutes later with another one of the small, scaled creatures she had caught the other day, quickly and efficiently field dressing, skinning, and cooking the creature. She used some basic herbs and a little bit of salt she had acquired in the city to season the animal as it cooked, then ate it right off the fire, unbothered by the heat. The others looked enviously at her fresh food as the smell drifted over to them. She decided it was probably best they learn how to hunt and cook themselves, or she would teach them if they asked.

> **Congratulations! Survivalist and associated skills have reached Tin 16.**

Zalia smiled. The skill seemed to passively level as she continued to live. It made perfect sense to her.

After eating, the others set up tents they seemed to have been carrying in spatial bags of their own, while Zalia just climbed up into a tree and lay with her cloak wrapped around her. It was as comfortable to her as a fluffy warm bed was to Lady Indis, most likely. She fell asleep in the boughs of the tree.

Morning came, and Zalia awoke as the sun rose. She had to wait for a good half hour before Ember awoke and another half hour again before the other two got up. Each of them had to eat a meal and pack up their belongings as Zalia waited. She refrained from making a snide comment about the wait, as Indis had done. During the wait, she instead did her morning routine, practicing sword work, running, and practicing once more. Ember actually joined her for the second session of sword work, giving her a few pointers that raised her Sword Proficiency another level. Soon, they were back on the road and near to arriving in Bur.

After another two and a half hours' walk they made it to Bur. Saying it was a small town was an understatement. There were seven buildings in total; the place was more of an outpost than a town. The people there recognised Ember as the group entered the small but active community.

"Oh, healer, thank the gods you've come back, and at a good time," a woman said, rushing over.

"Poor Onyl has taken sick, could you spare a moment to care for him? We really don't want it spreading," the woman asked, a pleading look on her face.

"Of course," Ember said warmly, following the woman.

"She'll be a moment, shall we find whoever sent out the warning that the Garroi have been sighted?" Zen asked.

"Yep," Zalia replied.

They knocked on one house's door, and the elderly man inside directed them to a house across the way, saying it was the home of the man who'd seen them. They went to the directed place and knocked once more. A limber-looking man in rough but thick clothes opened the door.

"Oh good, you must be here to help," the man said, looking over their armour. "Come, come." He walked out of the house and closed the door behind him.

As he led the group down the path a little, Ember caught up with them, having finished what she'd been doing. Leaving the town limits, they travelled through a section of thicker forest to where the woods began thinning out into grassy plains. At the edge of the forested area, Zalia found some tracks of relatively small humanoid beasts.

"Saw them just here, I did. See those tracks? Bunch of ghastly beasts, I tell you. Horrid business. I'm just a forester, not some adventurer or warrior. Will you be taking care of the problem?" the man rambled.

"Don't worry, sir, we certainly will be," Zen replied.

Lady Indis looked over to where Zalia was crouched down, running her fingers over the tracks. "Find anything?"

"Yes," Zalia said, smiling. "The hunt begins again."

CHAPTER TWENTY-FOUR

Garroi Pack

Zalia

Zalia tracked the creatures for about two minutes before noticing something strange about the tracks. There were about thirteen of the creatures, but that wasn't what was strange. What was strange was that a few times she'd seen tracks that looked more human than Garroi.

"Hey, do you know of any people living out here?" Zalia asked the man who led them to the tracks.

"No, I'm the only one who comes out here often," he replied.

"I only ask because it seems like the pack that left these tracks were tracking something else. A human." She looked up at the rest of the group before adding, "These tracks are relatively fresh too."

"So?" Lady Indis asked.

"Well, here's my thinking, this man here is the only one to come out here, the beasts are tracking someone, and relatively recently. I don't know how good they are at tracking, but if they're any good . . ." Zalia trailed off as the others finally seemed to get it.

"The town," Ember whispered.

"The town," Zalia agreed.

The group began making their way as quickly as they could back to Bur.

They arrived just as a resounding scream echoed through the forest.

"Oh no," Zen said.

Zalia took off her bag, pulling her bow out and quickly stringing it. She began running towards Bur; she was faster than the rest of the group due to her increased Mobility, especially in a forest.

"Zalia, locate any Garroi stragglers within the village. Zen, get their attention. Ember, you know what to do," Lady Indis instructed.

They arrived in the small town to a horrific scene. The pack of Garroi had found Bur. To the right, a group of eight beasts were surrounding a house, trying to break through the walls and door. Further into town, Zalia saw five more, each of them trying to find a way into different homes. As the group entered, Zalia began shooting at the Garroi. The one furthest into town had managed to break through a window, and was entering a house. She cast a Dodge-vine ritual on all her allies, then saw a lone villager backing away from the pack of Garroi.

Zen let out a resounding cry, and a strange feeling vibrated through the air. The sensation was extremely strange, though the effect was immediately visible. The Garroi that were still in the street immediately turned and charged in their direction. Zalia had taken down two with her arrows, landing headshots on both creatures with the arrowtips punching most of the way through their skulls. The third and fourth creatures tearing across Bur had also received an arrow each, one in the leg and one in the shoulder. She slung her bow across her back and drew her sword, sprinting down the street to the house one Garroi had broken into.

Meanwhile, Indis was charging some kind of lightning energy within her hands and all over her body, standing a good distance away from Zen or Ember. The lightning arced between her body and the ground, spitting up chunks of dirt where it made contact. Ember was standing close to Zen, ready to back him up when the Garroi got close. Zalia didn't let that happen, though. As she got closer to the large pack charging in their direction, she activated Nature's Wrath, binding the whole group in place as thorny vines dripping with some kind of poison sprouted from the ground, wrapping around the beasts. She sprinted around the group towards the two Garroi furthest away, drawing her sword.

Zalia drew her dagger from behind her back and threw it as she neared the first creature. It didn't hit blade first but achieved its goal—the creature flinched back a little. She used the creature's hesitation to get in close and swing at its head. The strike connected, cutting most of the way through before coming to a stop. The creature had swung at the same moment as her, unfortunately, but its claws had deflected off a metal plate on her leg armour, leaving deep scratches. She let go of the sword as the body dropped, unslinging her bow once more when she saw the second creature approaching. It was greatly slowed both by the poison and the arrow in its leg, so Zalia carefully aimed, used Kill Shot, and released. This arrow flew straight through the creature's head and slammed into the wall of a house ten metres behind it.

She slung her bow again and took hold of her sword—after planting her feet against the dead Garroi, she gained enough leverage to free her weapon. She sprinted once more for the breached home. As she reached it, the world lit up and she heard a thunderous crack and loud explosion behind her. She ignored it, hoping her Iron rank teammates could easily deal with the bound creatures. She vaulted through the window, also ignoring the quickly healing cuts she received for her haste, and found a scene of chaos before her. The room once was a cozy living room with a fireplace; now it was a complete mess. A bloodied metal fire poker lay on the floor by two figures violently wrestling. One of them, a human, was on his back, fending off the smaller creature using a light wooden chair. The creature was above the man, snarling, as the villager desperately tried to defend himself. Unhesitant, Zalia ran up, applied Hunter's Mark, and slammed the sword through the creature. Or tried to at least. It jerked around at the last moment, hearing her approach, and darted away with a deep cut across its side.

She could see its right arm was a mess, presumably where the blood on the fire poker came from. She didn't have enough poison to cover her sword, so she couldn't play the waiting game with this one and would have to act while she had the advantage. She stepped forwards, executing a basic strike, but the creature dodged and stepped away. Zalia could see the Garroi was beginning to frenzy, gradually increasing in size and muscle mass. She didn't know how to deal with it, but continued attacking. Each of her simple attacks were dodged, and she didn't have another dagger to use as a distraction. An opportunity came when the brave townsman arrived, wielding the fire poker once more. He charged in, swinging the improvised weapon with as much power as he could muster. The creature, now much larger and significantly stronger, easily blocked the blow and delivered a powerful blow in return, its bladed arms ripping into the man. Zalia took the opportunity the man gave her. She activated Kill Shot and stepped her back foot forwards, extending her two-handed grip towards the creature, blade point first, executing a simple thrust. The creature was fast, but not fast enough. It only managed to bring its arm up to catch the blade through the hand while the sword continued forward, pinning its own arm to its chest. Zalia let go of the sword as it stumbled backwards, unable to maintain her grip without being pulled over. She watched the creature slowly pull the blade from its chest, but didn't give it an opportunity to retaliate: she unslung her bow in the close quarters and put an arrow right between the creature's eyes.

Zalia quickly focused her healing on the man, stabilising him before she opened the locked door to look outside. She watched from a distance as Zen and Ember finished off the last two of the creatures. Zen deflected a swing from one and used the momentum of the deflection to hurl his mace around, crushing the creature's head. Ember moved with more fluid motions, severing a hand before impaling the creature, then pulling the blade out to immediately behead it. Near to them, where she had initially immobilised the pack of creatures, lay a steaming and charcoaled pile of Garroi bodies, the obvious result of Indis's lightning magic funnelled into one giant lightning blast to obliterate them. The woman had actually gone unconscious from the mana usage. Zalia shook her head at the risky tactic but stayed where she was, focusing the healing on the man. She went and retrieved her sword as her heart calmed after the fight. It had ended as less of a hunt and more of a battle, but as far as she knew they had saved the people in the town from any serious injuries, with two healers being present, after all. After killing the final Garroi, Ember came to check up on Zalia. Zen remained to guard Indis.

"You're well?" Ember asked.

"Fine. This guy could use some extra healing, though," Zalia replied.

Ember walked over and touched the man, a burst of healing entering his body and quickly sealing up the remaining wounds across his torso and arm. Ember's healing was significantly stronger than Zalia's. This was due to the fact that her healing was buffed by not only passive but active abilities that used mana. It made her stronger but also required resources, and as such, could run out. Zalia much preferred the slower but seemingly infinite healing her aura gave her. She hadn't yet run out of mana like Indis just had, but she'd come close. Usually, using both her long cooldown abilities from the Druid class nearly depleted her mana. The fact that her wisdom attribute increased as her Druid abilities did was a large contributor to that, increasing her mana as it levelled. Zalia watched the healing as she checked her messages.

> **Congratulations! Escape has increased by three levels, reaching Tin 11.**
> **Congratulations! Hunter's Sight has increased**
> **by three levels, reaching Tin 18.**
> **Congratulations! Survivalist and associated skills have**
> **increased by three levels, reaching Tin 19.**
> **Congratulations! Hunter class has increased**
> **by three levels, reaching Tin 11.**
> **Congratulations! Flora Identification has increased**
> **by three levels, reaching Tin 18.**
> **Congratulations! Preparation has increased**
> **by three levels, reaching Tin 19.**
> **Congratulations! Stasis has increased by three levels, reaching Tin 18.**
> **Congratulations! Harvester has increased by three levels, reaching Tin 20.**
> **Congratulations! Harvester has reached Iron 1.**
> **Harvester will not progress further until all classes have reached Iron.**
> **Harvester - passive - skill enhancement**
> **Tin - The Herbalist harvests herbs and other flora, with which**
> **they do what they will. You gain an instinctual understanding**
> **of how to harvest flora of your rank and lower. When harvesting**
> **flora of your rank or lower, it has increased potency.**
> **Iron - You are able to sense nearby herbs and flora**

> **of a type you have already harvested before.**
> **Congratulations! Herbalist class has increased**
> **by three levels, reaching Tin 18.**
> **Congratulations! Nature's Wrath has increased**
> **by five levels, reaching Tin 16.**
> **Congratulations! Protection of the Wilds has reached Tin 16.**
> **Congratulations! Druid class has increased by five levels, reaching Tin 16.**
> **Congratulations! Mobility has reached Tin 7.**
> **Congratulations! Sword - Weapon Proficiency has reached Tin 5.**

As always, fighting seems to increase skills by a lot more than anything else, Zalia thought, inspecting her new Iron rank Harvester ability.

She could already sense quite a bit of Dodge-vine around the place, but that wasn't really required anymore. The part that would be important was the herbs of the rank of her ability that she couldn't just reproduce with Herbal Magic. She could also now gather more potent herbs of the Iron ones she had. They wouldn't have any added effects, but they would be stronger than before. Zalia and Ember made their way over to Zen once they were done, healing the man in the small house. He had fallen unconscious after the strike but would be fine now, besides the destroyed house. It seemed like the people of Bur were tough, though, so she wasn't particularly worried for them.

"How is she doing?" Zalia asked Zen.

"Alright, I think, just a little mana burn," Zen said.

"Used up all her mana?" Zalia asked.

"No, just channelled way too much without releasing it," he replied.

Indis had an ability that let her over-cast a spell by channelling more mana into it than it required. It was what she had been doing before Zalia ran off, channelling one of her lightning strike abilities. Apparently holding too much mana within your body was just as detrimental as running out of it.

Zalia began focusing her healing on Indis, hoping it would help with her recovery. Ember narrowed her eyes at Indis as Zalia did so too. Ember's other healer class abilities allowed her to understand the injuries and state of a creature's body.

"The low but constant healing is actually helping quite a bit, whereas mine would cause more damage," Ember said.

Zalia just grunted in response. *I wonder if healing energy is some form of mana . . .* She walked around, picking up her dagger and arrows and inspecting the corpses. She couldn't help but marvel at the destructive force Indis had wielded as she looked at the smoking pile of ash and charcoal—all that remained of the Garroi that Indis struck.

Zalia pondered the situation she was in. On one hand, she probably couldn't have handled these creatures by herself, but on the other, she most definitely could have if she was prepared enough. She would have arrived in the town earlier if she didn't have to wait for the others, and as such, probably could have caught the creatures before they arrived. Alternately, though, she wouldn't have known the way to the town and so might not have even arrived in time at all. She did have to admit there were a couple advantages to having a team, but still preferred going it alone.

Indis eventually woke up, and they began making their way out of Bur and back to Endelbyrn. The people of the town thanked them with some small pieces of food and a couple coins, but it wasn't much to speak of. Zalia also wasn't really here for money or food and so didn't take any. The man she'd saved was particularly thankful, telling her his house was open to her any time she visited and to ask for anything she needed. Zalia waved him off, saying it was something anyone would do. That wasn't necessarily true, but she didn't want the thanks. After another day and a half's journey they arrived back in Endelbyrn. Zalia gained another level in both her Sword Proficiency and Mobility skills during her morning routine. She was quite close to reaching the Iron rank and was excited to see what her other abilities had in store for her once she ranked up.

Arriving back in the keep of the Morning's Shade, Zalia found the cleaning rooms once more and washed away the blood of battle and dirt of travel. This simple and quick method of washing was extremely practical, and Zalia loved it for that very reason. They were not required to take a guard shift that day since they were back from a contract. During the year she would train under supervision, Zalia wouldn't have to pay for any of the facilities or trainers, but she would also not make any of the money from the contracts taken and completed. They would be given a weekly stipend of a single gold coin, which was more than enough for her. She could always make a little more selling Tin rank herbs to herbalists within the city if she had to, since she didn't really need them anymore. Having the day to herself, she bid farewell to the others and went to find the sword training instructor. They were available during certain time slots during the day, this one holding sessions within the same colosseum arena that she had been tested in. She found the instructor there, already training a group of three people. She was quickly integrated into the session, taking up one of the other students as a sparring partner and beginning her training.

It was two hours before she stopped, having been pushed to the edge of her stamina as she was hit over and over, failing to dodge, parry, or block whatever strike was coming her way. Luckily her healing was enough to take care of any bruises or even cracked bones as they fought—the teacher let them go a bit harder due to her Healing Presence. She left the arena sore despite the healing, and gained another two levels in her Sword Proficiency, bringing it to eight.

Despite the relatively small number of levels gained, she felt like she had definitely learnt quite a lot about her weaknesses and failures as a sword wielder. If she kept attending the classes, she felt she would get quite good, quite quickly. She went out of the city after another pass through the cleaning rooms and began walking around, picking herbs and scouting tracks. She stayed long enough to gain another level in each of her active Herbalist skills.

> **Congratulations! Flora Identification has reached Tin 19.**
> **Congratulations! Preparation has reached Tin 20.**
> **Congratulations! Preparation has reached Iron 1.**
> **Preparation will not progress further until all classes have reached Iron.**
> **Preparation - spell - targeted**
> **Tin - The careful preparation of herbs, poisonous or healing, can enhance their effects. You may magically dry, cut, or otherwise prepare various foods, herbs, and other similar items that are plant-based.**
> **Iron - Preparation can now be used to magically harvest plants. All bonuses from harvesting manually are still applied. You may also dry, cut or otherwise prepare foods that are not plant-based.**
> **Congratulations! Stasis has reached Tin 19.**
> **Congratulations! Herbalist class has reached Tin 19.**

It looked like her Herbalist class would be the first to reach Iron, something she was happy about. The utility the class provided her was incredible, even more improved now that she could harvest plants and herbs just by walking near them and thinking about it. She could also prepare foods without a pan, knife, or other utensil, which would be very cool even if that was all she could do. Zalia smiled as she walked through a small forested area, magically picking, preparing, putting into stasis, and then storing herbs as she walked. Being able to sense and harvest them without sight or movement was truly amazing; the casual magic was no longer foreign or scary to her but normal and convenient.

CHAPTER TWENTY-FIVE

A Few Fun Bits

Zalia

Zalia spent the next three weeks mostly training, going on small hunts by herself, or standing guard. She didn't go on any more contracts during that time as her team wasn't given any and didn't take any. The first few days, she got her last abilities in the Herbalist class to Iron, ranking the class itself up.

Congratulations! Flora Identification has reached Tin 20.
Congratulations! Flora Identification has reached Iron 1.
Flora Identification will not increase in level
until all classes have reached Iron.
Flora Identification - spell - targeted
Tin - Poison, cure, or food, you'll know. You may identify whether
targeted flora is poisonous, helpful, nutritious, or all of the above.
Iron - You may now identify what elements different flora contain.
Congratulations! Stasis has reached Tin 20.
Congratulations! Stasis has reached Iron 1.
Stasis - spell - targeted
Tin - Can put a small amount of herbs into stasis.
Iron - Herbs in stasis may now be put into a spatial storage.
Congratulations! Herbalist class has reached Tin 20.
Congratulations! Herbalist class has reached Iron 1.
For reaching the next rank, linked attributes of the
Herbalist class have increased significantly. Increase
all other classes to Iron to progress further.

The new Flora Identification ability allowed her to determine what elements were in herbs, which was quite useful. She'd gotten the sense of what they contained already from her Herbal Magic passive, but now she could see it defined in the small text box that came with Aura Observation. She checked out all her stored herbs with the new effect.

> **Snow-leaf - Iron - Use in a ritual to add an element of Ice.**
> **Bitterbalm - Iron - Use in a ritual to add an element of Curse.**
> **Dodge-vine - Tin - Use in a ritual to add an element of Protection.**
> **Manifest - Tin - Use in a ritual to add an**
> **element of Physical Manifestation.**

She had no Frozen Heart or Flame-root left but wanted to see what kind of element they would contain. The next level of her Stasis ability allowed her to put herbs into their own little spatial storage that was kept . . . somewhere.

She couldn't identify where the herbs went but could feel they were there and how much she had of each. There was room enough to store quite a lot of the Iron rank herbs, she only kept Tin ones in the short-term to sell in the city. She found that herbs she was using Preparation on she could store, otherwise, she needing to be touching them. It was the same for summoning them; she could bring them back into her hand or as part of using Preparation. This meant she could harvest, cut up, and store herbs magically without touching them, putting them into a timeless space to be used at a later time. The synergy of the abilities was quite satisfying to use.

It was quite something to feel the increase to her vitality and resilience attributes that accompanied the rank up from Tin to Iron for her Herbalist class. She could physically feel the significant increase in health and toughness. It was almost as if the density of her body changed, as if she were now harder to cut into and required more damage to destroy.

Across the three weeks, she spent a lot of time in the forests near the city and managed to net about sixty silver daily from selling herbs, retaining a good stock of the Iron ones. This meant by the end of the three weeks she had amassed twelve gold and sixty silver, along with the extra three gold from the Morning's Shade. This brought her to a total of sixteen gold, ten silver, and ninety copper, including the fifty silver and ninety copper she still had from before. She also continued her Mobility and sword training across the weeks, gaining six levels in Mobility and five in Sword Proficiency, raising them to fourteen and thirteen respectively. The speed at which her Sword Proficiency progressed had slowed quite significantly after her initial learning curve but almost stopped completely once she got more comfortable. She was now pretty good with basic sword work, still nothing compared to someone like Tristan, but she was on a good track to getting there. She wanted to change up what weapon she used, though, the short sword didn't feel quite right. Another type of sword would fit her better; she just hadn't figured out what she wanted. She had her mind on something lighter, something she could use in a more graceful way than the thicker short sword she used now.

Over the weeks, Survivalist and Hunter's Sight also ranked up to Iron, only requiring one and two levels respectively.

> **Congratulations! Hunter's Sight has gained two levels, reaching Tin 20.**
> **Congratulations! Hunter's Sight has reached Iron 1.**
> **Hunter's Sight will not gain further levels**
> **until all classes have reached Iron.**
> **Hunter's Sight - passive - body enhancement**
> **Tin - The Hunter tracks their prey. You can track creatures easier.**
> **When tracking, you learn very basic information such as number**
> **of legs, number of creatures, and general size of creatures.**
> **Iron - You now learn how long ago a creature left tracks and may**
> **apply a Hunter's Mark if tracking it for more than an hour.**
> **Congratulations! Survivalist and associated skills have reached Tin 20.**
> **Congratulations! Survivalist and associated skills have reached Iron 1.**
> **Survivalist will not gain further levels until all classes have reached Iron.**
> **Survivalist - passive - body enhancement**
> **Tin - The body of a Hunter shall not fail easily. Gain the Heat**
> **Resistance and Cold Resistance passive skills. They level alongside**
> **this ability. You are able to survive with less nutrition.**
> **Iron - Gain the Stealth and Trapper passive skills. These**
> **also level alongside this ability. You require less sleep.**
> **Heat Resistance - passive**
> **Tin - You take reduced damage from high**
> **temperatures and heat related magics.**
> **Iron - You may manipulate fire and heat to a minor degree.**
> **Cold Resistance - passive**
> **Tin - You take reduced damage from low**
> **temperatures and cold-related magics.**
> **Iron - You may manipulate ice and snow to a minor degree.**
> **Stealth - passive**
> **Tin - Normal vision and sight-based skills and**
> **abilities have a harder time seeing you.**
> **Iron - Other senses are also inhibited and you**
> **blend with your surroundings.**
> **Trapper - passive**

> **Tin - Your traps are magically hidden from sight.**
> **Iron - Your traps are magically enhanced.**

Hunter's Sight gaining an ability that specifically affected how she could use another confirmed one of her theories about the skills and the further effects she was gaining. It seemed like the new abilities were forming themselves based on her preferences for using her existing skills. Preparation interacting with Stasis the way it did had formed the theory for her, but this confirmed it.

The effects Survivalist gave her were a complete game changer. It not only gave her two extra passives in the form of the Stealth and Trapper passives but also brought her Heat and Cold Resistance to Iron with it. The minor manipulation skill wasn't super useful, but she thought it might level with the skills to become better. They were very fun to use, however, and she often found herself playing with the fire of her campfire, forming it into shapes and making it flow around her body.

The Stealth passive allowed her to sneak up on creatures a lot easier, and she could immediately see how changes to her form and colouring matched to her surroundings, making her much harder to see. The Trapper passive was very interesting, and she tested it with some of her spikes. When she placed the small spikes, they were magically hidden within piles of leaves or roots, whatever fitted where she placed it. When a creature stepped on the spike, it extended as if it shot up from the ground, impaling the foot of the unwary victim.

The last part of the skill was the reduced sleep, which she also immediately noticed, as she woke up earlier than she usually would have the next morning. If she didn't have to sleep while the skill progressed further she would have a lot more time on her hands. At this point, she only needed to eat a small meal once every two days due to the Tin rank effect.

She also gained a single level each in Low Light Vision and Escape, and two levels in Aura Observation, Nature's Wrath, and Protection of the Wilds. This brought her Druid class to Tin eighteen and her Hunter class to Tin twelve.

The final thing she did during the three weeks was get her armour enchanted with the simple self-repair and self-cleaning functions. It was done by an enchanter she found in the town for a gold coin.

At the end of the three weeks she was found by her group at the entrance to the keep as she returned to complete her guard duty for the day.

"Zalia," Ember greeted.

"Ember," she replied.

"Hey, Zalia! How are you? How have things been?" Zen said, moving in to give her a hug.

"Good," she replied, taking a step away from the bear hug.

"Zalia, back to civilization once again I see," Lady Indis said.

"Unfortunately—is there a reason you are ambushing me with social niceties?"

"We've been given a contract," Ember said.

"Ah, let's go see what it is then," Zalia replied.

They made their way to the same room they had met in. It was just a standard meeting room for any team that wanted to use it, Zalia had found out. During the three weeks she'd been out and about, she hadn't really seen any of the others from her team apart from the occasional meeting in the halls or about the keep. She spent most of the time sleeping out in the wild, only coming back for her daily guard duty.

When they entered, the Hidden was sitting in a chair, casually leaning back and looking relaxed. Zalia gave him a nod as she entered, getting one in return.

"Alright, what have you got for us?" she asked as she sat down, ignoring any pleasantries. Indis gave her a look for the apparent breach of conduct, but she didn't care.

"We've had reports coming in from all over the lands about Elementals raising trouble. That, in addition to the war happening across the eastern borders of Endaria, has caused quite a stress across the martial forces of the kingdom. While we aren't an extension of the kingdom's military, we are a big martial force all the same. As such, the kingdom has decided to pay us to take care of some of the Elemental nuisances around the lands, and the Morning's Shade has accepted. We do this to protect the people of the lands rather than to assist the kingdom's plots and will be doing some investigating of our own. Elementals acting in this way are usually responding to something, and we plan to find out what. Obviously none of this can leave this room," the Hidden explained.

There was some silence in the room before Zalia spoke up. "Where are you sending us?"

"You and two other Iron rank groups will be going into a large abandoned mine a few days south of here. They had some issues a couple of months back; different Elementals were attacking the miners and it has been abandoned since. It was a part of the deal with the kingdom that we are allowed to choose where we send people, and this was one of the first noticed awakenings of Elementals that we know of. It's been getting worse these past weeks, and it's time something was done about it," he replied.

"I did hear of this mine being abandoned, it was a great blow to House Darial," Lady Indis said.

Zalia zoned out for a minute as Indis went on to explain the economic difficulties the house had after the mine's abandonment and what the resulting impacts to the economy were.

"When do we leave?" Zalia eventually asked, interrupting Indis.

"You and the other teams are to meet up in the marshalling yard on the east side of the keep grounds," the Hidden replied, smiling at her impatience.

"Excellent, if that's all, I'd like to report for my guard duty so I can leave the city again," Zalia said.

Indis just rolled her eyes but Ember actually gave her a smile; Zen just seemed to be deep in thought.

"Actually, it isn't. May I have a word with you in private?" the Hidden asked.

"Sure," she said.

Indis seemed to get the message and prodded Zen, leading him and Ember out of the room.

"I wanted to talk to you about that bow," the Hidden said once the others had left.

"What about it?" Zalia asked, a little worried.

"I knew its owner."

"You knew Juniper?" she asked, a little surprised.

"Yes, I did. We were close, once," he replied, smiling a little sadly. "I was once the familiar of the man who first wielded it, Zayes."

"Wait, what? You're a familiar? What does that even mean?" Zalia asked, now quite confused.

"Yes, I am, in fact, not human. I am a shade, once non-sentient but brought to sentience when Zayes formed a bond with me. I found you because I sensed that bow and the essence of my old friend upon it. I believe Juniper gave it to you for that very reason, she must have known there was something special about you."

Zalia was silent for a moment, thinking about what the shade had told her.

"Who was he, this Zayes?" she asked.

"The founder of this organisation. The name, the Morning's Shade is in reference to how I met the man. His death was, in part, my fault. I will not go over the details, but I believe the bow is in good hands now and would leave it with you—not that it's my right to take it, but it's how I feel, all the same. There isn't anything special about the bow other than its status as an heirloom item, but it does mean a great deal to me and some of the older members of our group."

The explanation the shade had given her did connect a few dots for Zalia, explaining some oddities she had noticed in Juniper's actions and how easily she had been let into the order.

"Why tell me all this?" Zalia asked the shade.

"Because I believe you are a good person, despite your dislike of dealing with others. I thought you should know the history of the weapon you use," he said, simply.

"Thank you, I do appreciate that. You aren't all that intolerable," Zalia said, smiling.

"I am the most tolerable, I will have you know," the shade responded, adopting an exaggerated aghast expression.

"Of course. Am I allowed to know your name now, oh mysterious shade?"

"Nope."

"Ugh, I take it back, you're completely intolerable."

"How dare you!" he replied in mock anger.

Zalia chuckled quietly. "I'll see you around, Shade." Then she stood up, grabbing her bag.

"See you around, Zalia," he replied.

The shade had a slightly sad expression on his face as she left the room and made her way to the guard shift she'd taken for the day.

CHAPTER TWENTY-SIX

Travel Buddies

Zalia

Indis found Zalia as she finished up her guard shift.

"We're to meet tomorrow morning, be ready," Lady Indis said.

"Yes ma'am," Zalia said sarcastically, giving a salute.

"What is that gesture you did?" Indis asked, frowning.

"Gesture of respect," Zalia replied.

"Didn't feel that way," Indis muttered.

Zalia walked away, smiling. She gave her profile an inspection, checking what she needed to rank up.

Profile - Zalia Taori
Health - Excellent
Mana - Full
Stamina - Full
Class One - Hunter - Tin 12
Linked Attributes - Strength, Dexterity
Active Skills
Kill Shot - Iron 1
Hunter's Mark - Iron 1
Escape - Tin 12
Passive Skills
Hunter's Sight - Iron 1
Survivalist - Iron 1
Class Two - Herbalist - Iron 1

Linked Attributes - Vitality, Resilience
Active Skills
Flora Identification - Iron 1
Preparation - Iron 1
Stasis - Iron 1
Passive skills
Harvester - Iron 1
Herbal Magic - Iron 1
Unity Class - Druid - Tin 18
Linked Attributes - Wisdom, Intellect
Active Skills
Nature's Wrath - Tin 18
Protection of the Wilds - Tin 18
Passive Skills
Healing Presence - Iron 1
General Passives
Heat Resistance - Iron 1
Cold Resistance - Iron 1
Aura Observation - Tin 6
Low Light Vision - Tin 4
Poison Resistance - Iron 1
Mobility - Tin 14
Stealth - Iron 1
Trapper - Iron 1
Weapon Proficiencies
Bow - Iron 1
Sword - Tin 13

Both Druid actives would rank up relatively soon, and then she was just waiting on Escape to rank eight levels still. Hopefully, due to it being the only skill that could gain levels at this point, it would go by much faster. She felt she had gotten past the Tin rank quite quickly, and though she wasn't done yet, she soon would be. Now that she thought about it, though, most creatures would have reached that rank in the early years of their life and probably only took longer due to being young and inexperienced.

Zalia walked slowly through the streets, thinking about the time she had spent in this place so far. Remembering Alara and the army back up north, she realised she had forgotten to do something.

Shortly afterwards, Zalia walked out of a small store crammed between two others, holding a map of the lands. It seemed to have most of the towns, but obviously not all of them since Bur wasn't on it. It showed the Kingdom of Endaria up to its borders and then past it in some parts. It didn't show any of the north, but it did show that on the southern edge of the border there was a desert stretching an unknown distance further south. The western edge of the kingdom came up against the edge of the continent, except for further south near the desert where it started widening out, going further out east once more. She put away the map, feeling suddenly claustrophobic in the city once more. She put her bag back on as she burst into a sprint, making her way towards the city's exit.

The activity was much harder now that she had the Stealth passive, some lower rank people didn't see her until she was much closer, so she had to avoid everyone much more carefully.

She sat against a tree in the small forested patch near the city, breathing deeply as she inspected the carvings on her bow. They didn't seem meaningful but knowing where the bow came from and who had owned it did help her feel as if she understood the weapon, like a friend who had shared an important memory from their past.

> **Congratulations! You have learnt about the past of 'Hunter's Bow.' Your bond has deepened and you may now summon and store the item within its own space.**

Zalia could immediately feel the change, sensing the weapon in her mind. She tried it out a few times, storing and summoning the weapon from and into her hands. It was like it had become a new limb she could control, only one that appeared and disappeared. She smiled as she looked at the bow: through it she could hunt and eat, and through her it could fulfil its purpose. It was a good, practical, two-way relationship that left nothing else wanted or expected.

Zalia started practicing summoning the bow in the midst of close combat in case her sword was taken from her. It probably wouldn't work and she'd end up getting stabbed, but it could be a good emergency plan to have in the right situation. She couldn't really practice properly without a sparring partner but was content trying some things out first by herself.

Zalia spent the rest of the day performing her various routines: practicing sword work, Mobility, and newly added attempts to walk as quietly as possible. She properly thought about what she was doing and where she was trying to get to in life. She had spent such a long time fighting for survival out in the cold north of her world, but even there she could most likely survive easily now. She considered what her class descriptions had been when she had gotten them. The Druid class said she was meant to be some protector of the balance between life and death. In some regards, she did think it important that the world's ecosystem maintain balance between all creatures upon it, but what did that mean in a world where some were born so much stronger than others?

Do I even want to be some protector of nature? she asked herself.

She wasn't sure.

She had survived the journey here, trying to learn about this world and what the magic she now had entailed. It had been her goal since leaving the north to find such an opportunity, and now she was achieving that. What came after, she did not know. As she went to sleep that night she thought about where she wanted to end up once she was done learning.

Zalia woke up the next morning still undecided as to where she wanted to take her future. For now, however, she could push the thoughts into the back of her mind as she had a short-term goal to work on. She and her group were meant to explore some sort of abandoned mine that was very possibly overrun by some sort of Elementals. She suspected they would be earth or metal Elementals but didn't really know what parameters they worked under, if any. She had seen an earth Elemental once before, the day she first learnt of the war currently going on. She made her way into the city of Endelbyrn as she considered the task before them, and headed towards the marshalling yard that the shade told her to go to the day before. None of her abilities were particularly strong against an Elemental; she wasn't even sure if her poison would work or not. Hopefully ritual magic could provide some utility to a fight, but she didn't hold out hope it would be super useful. Fortunately or unfortunately—her opinion switching from moment to moment—she had a team. Zen would be quite useful with the large mace he wielded.

And Indis might just turn them into earthing Elementals with her lightning, Zalia thought. She chuckled at her own joke, constantly amused by her terrible humour. She was decidedly unimpressed with the world when she realised no one here would get the joke.

Zalia arrived at the marshalling yard early and began practicing her sword work. Soon after, another team arrived, speaking amongst each other in low tones.

"They're sending a fuckin' Tin ranker with us," a man whispered.

"What a joke," the man's companion replied.

Ignoring the not-so-subtle conversation, she continued her practice.

It wasn't long until the others arrived, the last of the lot being a Silver rank woman. All together there were twelve people: Zalia's group of four, a group of five that included the two not-so-quiet whisperers, a duo of male and female twins, and the one Silver ranker. The twins were Bronze rank and the other group of five were all Iron rank.

"Morning everyone, name's Larel," the Silver ranker introduced herself. "I'll be in charge of making sure not too many of you die on this contract since the hunted's number and strength are unknown. Any questions?"

"Why is the Tin ranker on this contract?" the man from earlier asked.

"What's your name, shade?" Larel asked.

"Eston," he replied.

"Well, Eston, she is here because the people in charge of organising the contract decided she should be here. One of the said people who organised the contract would be the Hidden himself. Any more questions?"

Eston shut his mouth after that, speaking no more on the matter. Larel ran her eyes over the rest of the group, lingering on Zalia for a moment before speaking once more.

"Let's get moving," she said.

They began moving out of the city, Larel at the front, followed by the twins, followed by the group of five, and finally followed by Zalia's group.

"So what have you been doing all these weeks?" Zen asked Zalia, in a good mood as always.

"Living," Zalia replied, still unhappy being within the city walls.

" . . . Great! Any interesting hunts recently?"

"Not particularly."

"You're such a bore Zalia," Lady Indis said.

"Thank you," Zalia replied dryly.

The woman just rolled her eyes.

"How about you Ember, what have you been up to?" Zen asked.

"Living," Ember replied, grinning.

"I'm surrounded by introverts with dryer-than-desert humour," Zen muttered.

"Sorry, Zen, I'm just not fond of being around so many people," Zalia said.

"But we're alright aren't we?" Zen asked.

Zalia stared at him for a few seconds. "You're people."

"Yeah, but we're the super interesting and fun-to-be-around kind of people," Zen said back.

Zalia didn't say anything, not agreeing but not disagreeing either.

"I'll take the silence as acceptance of my duly stated fact," Zen said happily.

Zalia stared at him deadpan for a few moments. "Sure!" she said in an overly excited yet quite sarcastic tone.

"Why, thank you, Zalia," Zen said, missing the sarcasm entirely.

Zalia let him have his moment, not having a reason to shatter his illusion. Ember just laughed quietly while Lady Indis muttered, "Commoners," as she shook her head.

"Are you actually from a noble house?" Zalia asked Indis, genuinely curious.

"You don't know of House Indis?" Lady Indis asked.

"Do I need to remind you that I've been living in the snowy north for the past . . . let me see . . . most of my life?" Zalia asked.

"I still find it hard to believe with your rank, I apologise. I did forget you're uncultured. Yes, House Indis was previously quite an influential name in the Kingdom of Endaria but took a bit of a plummet in the past few years. I intend to bring honour and influence back to my house to restore what my parents managed to destroy."

"And you will do this by walking about doing contracts and insulting us 'commoners'?" Zalia asked.

"Of course not, this is just a stepping stone in my plan."

"Wonderful, I get to be a stepping stone for Her Ladyship, Leyra Indis," Zalia said dryly.

"Of course, it is good you know your place. And it is Her Great Ladyship Indis to you; the use of my name is above you," Indis replied.

Zalia just shook her head, trying to pretend there wasn't a kernel of belief in Indis's words. She might be stuck-up, but she had some potential to be a good person, or so Zalia thought.

"What about you, Ember, what are you here for?" Zen asked.

Ember looked at the man for a short time as they walked. "To help the people who can't help themselves," she said simply.

Zalia swore she saw a little emotion behind the words, there was some history between them, maybe. Ember quickly hid it, however, so Zalia didn't push, and Zen didn't seem to notice.

"How long will this journey be?" Ember quickly asked, changing the subject.

"The Hidden said a few days, but from how slow some of these people are I'd expect about three," Zalia answered, looking pointedly at the group of five in front of them.

"I don't know about the rest of you, but I really don't feel like going three days without a proper meal. What do you say, Zalia, up to teach me?" Ember asked.

Zalia squinted at the woman. It was the most she'd ever heard her talk, and right after Zen had asked her that question.

"Oh come on, Zalia, surely you can show us a trick or two!" Zen said, jumping in and supporting Ember's suggestion.

"It would be nice if you could hunt some food for us, Zalia, really," Indis said.

Zalia considered it for a moment. Ember and Zen would at least like to learn a thing or two, which wasn't so bad. It would mean they were less reliant on Zalia, and she liked that. What finally convinced her was the pleading look that Ember had hidden in her expression, as if she really wanted to talk about anything else at that moment.

"Fine, fine, I'll teach you. But you have to listen very carefully to what I say. I'm not fond of speaking once, let alone twice," Zalia said, giving in.

Looking at her two new students, Zalia had a feeling one of them would pick it up a lot better than the other.

* * *

It was much later in the day and the group had camped for a quick break. Some people brought out travel rations while others, such as Zalia, Zen, and Ember, had gone off to hunt. Zalia began showing them the ropes of hunting properly. They were each at least at a certain level of perceptiveness, which was necessary in order to meet the Morning's Shade entry requirements. Both Zen and Ember had the intellect attribute, so they picked up what Zalia told them relatively fast, thank the stars. Ember also had the wisdom attribute, and she seemed to understand what she was taught on a deeper level than Zen did. Zalia did have a huge advantage, with her Hunter's Sight ability pretty much doing the tracking for her, but she'd also done this for years before she had any magic at all and still knew what she was doing.

"You see where these tracks split just a little? It seems two creatures were passing through here, following in each other's steps for the most part," Zalia explained, gently pointing to where some small creatures with furry tails had passed through. "Their tails hide the tracks quite well, but this section here has two footsteps next to each other, that's what shows us it's more than one creature. It could be the same one moving through twice, but each track seems the same age to me. Don't worry about identifying the ageing of tracks just yet, that's much more difficult to do and requires a lot of experience. My ability confirms for me that two small, four-legged creatures did indeed move through here, about five minutes ago. If we follow quickly enough we can catch them soon," Zalia continued, explaining all the little details she saw as they walked along.

The other two seemed extremely attentive. She wasn't sure if it was because they were actually quite interested in what she was showing them or if they were just surprised at how much she was talking now.

Zalia tracked the creatures, describing what she saw until her knowledge and ability told her that they were quite close. She stopped making noise and motioned for Ember and Zen to move quietly as she continued following the tracks. She summoned her bow into her hand, getting a look from them as she did so. Zen wasn't wearing his plate armour at Zalia's request, knowing the man most likely wouldn't have been able to sneak properly in it.

Finally, they came upon two small creatures bouncing around in a clearing, playing some sort of game. Zalia stopped and nocked an arrow, then drew the bow as she aimed carefully. Zen stepped on a stick just as she released the string, causing the creatures to panic and flee. Zalia, however, no longer relied just on luck but now could depend on her abilities and magic. Her arrow flew at an incredible speed, cleanly passing through both creatures' heads as the arrow curved in the air before it struck a tree. The two creatures fell dead to the ground, and Zen whistled in appreciation.

"Don't make noise when I'm about to take a shot at my prey, or you'll be my next hunt," Zalia said grumpily.

"You still got them though!" Zen said in his own defence.

"Only because of magic. Not so long ago, I wouldn't have hit either because of you," she retorted.

"It was quite an impressive shot, I must say," Ember said.

"Thank you, it is kind of what I do. Obviously, neither of you have ranged weapons, but we can get you both some small hunting bows when we're back in Endelbyrn. You could also learn trapping but it usually takes too long on trips like these, it's more of a home version of hunting," Zalia said, walking up to the kills. "Now, field dressing is very important after making a kill, listen closely."

CHAPTER TWENTY-SEVEN

A Little Bit of Hunting

Zalia

They were sitting at the camp once more as Zalia used Preparation to skin and clean the rest of the two animals. The skill could now work on animals as well, an influence from her Hunter class, or so she thought. What would have usually taken her a good amount of time was finished in an instant as the two creatures were perfectly prepared using her Iron rank Heat Resistance passive to efficiently help the fire along. She found she could also use the ability to spread heat through a kill evenly, cooking it to perfection even while on an uneven cooking surface such as the spit she was using now.

"That's probably the most I'll ever hear you talk," Zen said as they watched the creatures roast.

"I think it's important to only speak when there is something worth saying," Zalia replied.

Ember nodded to Zalia's statement, seemingly agreeing.

"And why is that, mysterious hunter?" Zen asked.

Zalia just shrugged.

"I do wish you would follow her advice sometimes, Zen," Indis said.

"What's that supposed to mean?" he asked

"It's supposed to mean if you're going to keep talking so much, you should probably find something worth saying," Indis replied.

"Ow," Zen said.

"How old are you, Zen?" Zalia asked.

"Twenty-two—what does that have to do with anything?"

"Ahhh, that makes sense. Don't worry, you'll learn some wisdom when you grow up," Zalia said.

"When I grow up? We're probably the same age," Zen retorted.

Zalia gave him an odd look. "Not even close."

"Well, how old are you, then?" Zen asked.

"Zen! Have some manners, don't you know it's rude to ask a lady her age?" Indis scolded.

"Oh, I'm a lady now, am I? Thought I was just a commoner," Zalia said sarcastically.

"See!" Zen exclaimed.

"Still not answering you, Zen," Zalia added.

"Oh," he said.

The food was ready, and Zalia reached into the fire to grab a piece of the meat that was cut away as she used Preparation. She ate it appreciatively, gesturing to the others that they could feel free to eat.

"It's a little strange how casually you reach into the fire like that," Zen said.

All three woman stared towards him as he said that.

"Heaps of people can do that, fire magic is a thing," Ember said.

"Yeah, but fire magic is a thing she doesn't have," Zen said, gesturing to Zalia.

Zalia smiled at him before continuing to eat. She hadn't told anyone about her Survivalist skill, keeping her Cold and Heat Resistances in line with one another, which significantly increased the respective resistances' levelling speeds.

"So?" Lady Indis said.

"No, he does actually have a point," Ember said.

"I do?" Zen said.

"He does?" Indis said at the same time.

"Yeah, how high is your Heat Resistance, Zalia?" Ember asked.

"Mmm, why should I tell you?" Zalia asked back.

Ember just shrugged.

"Fair enough. Iron," Zalia answered.

"How did you manage that? One, you lived in the snow most of your life, and two, you don't even have all your classes in Iron," Indis asked, looking suspiciously at her.

"No, I didn't torture myself, if that's what you're thinking, though it's definitely an option with healing. It's a trade secret," Zalia responded.

"A trade secret of what, Hunters? Herbalists? Bloody Druids?" Zen asked.

"Yes," Zalia replied.

She was being difficult for no reason other than she didn't want the trio getting used to getting answers. They might talk at her more if they did.

"Anyways, I think we're getting ready to leave, so pack up," Zalia said as she stood and collected her things, killing the fire with her minor fire manipulation.

The rest of the groups had already begun packing up, and they were all on the road again shortly after.

* * *

For the next two and a half days as they travelled, Zalia taught both Ember and Zen how to track. On the last day she barely even needed to show them; the only way they could learn now was from experience. Until they finished learning the basics, at least. On that last day Indis even joined in. Zalia spent most of her time showing the woman how to track as the two others from their group went ahead. She even went as far as lending Ember her bow for a short time, showing her how to properly use it. Lady Indis seemed to pick up tracking much slower than the other two, obviously not used to that kind of work. Zalia idly wondered if the woman had gotten into the organisation based on influence in addition to her skill, not just based on her abilities. From time to time, Zalia caught the Silver rank leader of their contract giving her approving looks as she taught her teammates. The other group of Iron rankers seemed to be spending their idle time playing around, joking with each other. Not to say that her group didn't do that, but they were also productive during the trip. Zalia even gained a new passive:

Congratulations! You have unlocked the general passive 'Teaching.'
Teaching - passive
Tin - You gain a better understanding of what methods of teaching will work with certain people, scaling with the level and rank of this ability.

Not a passive I hope to be using much, Zalia thought. But immediately after, she reconsidered.

She actually didn't mind teaching her group, for the most part, they were attentive and quick learners. She would never be the type of person to sit in a classroom and teach a whole room of students, but teaching practical skills in a small group like this, she didn't mind at all.

On the last day of the trip, they were due to arrive at the mine within the next few hours, and had settled for one last break. Zalia's group went off as they usually did to hunt, the four of them walking to a thick-canopied section of forest nearby.

There, they found the tracks of a small group of gazelle-like creatures that travelled through the thick undergrowth with surprising nimbleness. They followed the tracks until they found something. Zalia knelt next to the body of the creature, its blood still fresh. It was slender with graceful limbs and a body covered in a short, sleek coat of fur. It ranged in colour, from shades of golden brown to deep chestnut, with elegant patterns and shimmering highlights that most likely helped it blend in with the dappled sunlight of the surroundings. In stark comparison, the bright red blood coming from deep gashes in its body stood out amongst the greens of the forest.

Zalia summoned her bow, nocking an arrow. "I don't think we're alone," she whispered to the others.

The rest of the group immediately tensed, drawing weapons. They stood in silence, observing the forest around them as Zalia performed a Dodge-vine ritual for the whole group and prepared another trick she had been working on. With Zen's help she had carved a bunch of small wooden caltrops, dipping a tiny bit of each spine into poison. She had very little left, but it would be worth using since she didn't know how long it would remain potent. She threw a bunch of the caltrops around them; the small spikes dug into the ground and were covered by leaves as her Trapper passive got to work. She also prepared a Dodge-vine major and Manifest minor ritual, ready to activate it at a moment's notice. It formed a small ring around them, with bits of herbs and leaves floating in the air. Another ring of intricate runes began to form from the finer pieces of plant matter and manifested closer to the ground.

"That ability is really cool, Zalia," Zen whispered.

"Shut up and keep an eye out," she hissed back at him.

She began to relax, hoping whatever had killed the mottled gazelle-like creature had left when they arrived. She tensed back up as a slight crack of wood came from above. She immediately activated the ritual, and a shield of roots, vines, and leaves formed around the group moments before a creature crashed into it from above. The shield immediately broke, but it was enough time for Zalia and Indis to get out of the way as Zen and Ember stood in front of them. The creature that smashed through the quickly dissipating shield was an animal with the graceful elegance of a great cat, with a sleek muscular body and an agile build. Its coat was adorned with vibrant foliage, including leaves, flowers, and vines that shifted and changed colours to match the surrounding forest. It had six legs rather than four, much like that first bear creature Zalia encountered. She could barely see the cat creature, even as it hit the ground, hissing at them.

? - Bronze rank

Might be doable, she thought. She quickly put her Hunter's Mark on it; it was difficult to follow the creature's movements, and it would be extremely helpful to know its general location.

Zen immediately got to work, engaging the creature with his giant tower shield. He smashed the shield into its face as Ember circled around its side with a smaller heater shield and double-sided blade at the ready. It nimbly dodged her quick thrust—it was extremely fast for a creature of its size. Zalia took a shot as it came into clear view after leaping away from Ember and Zen's attacks. Even with the tracking aspect of her arrows, the creature was only grazed by the shot, enough to be poisoned, though. Indis began charging electricity, and the creature, seeing it, turned and jumped nimbly through the small clearing, running up a tree into the canopy once more. Zalia tracked where it was moving with her mark, the others following where she pointed her bow. The ability allowed her to vaguely see its shape as it jumped from the canopy towards Indis. Zalia activated her Protection of the Wilds around the woman as she shot an arrow at the creature midair. It turned an ethereal colour momentarily, the arrow passing straight through it before the creature hit the shield. Indis was still charging her lightning attack within. It scratched off the shield, tearing parts of it away as Zen smashed it in the side with his mace. The creature stumbled sideways, stepping onto one of Zalia's caltrops, which promptly expanded, stabbing up through its paw. Ember quickly took advantage of its temporary immobility, slashing across its side. Indis came around the creature's other side right when it turned to snarl at Ember and punched the thing straight in the head, releasing a blast of electricity that shocked through its body. The creature went stiff, shaking as it fell to the ground. The strike signalled the end of the battle, and Ember stabbed her sword through the relatively still creature's chest, into its heart.

> **Congratulations! Escape has gained two levels, reaching Tin 14.**
> **Congratulations! Hunter class has gained two levels, reaching Tin 14.**
> **Congratulations! Nature's Wrath has reached Tin 19.**
> **Congratulations! Protection of the Wilds has**
> **gained two levels, reaching Tin 20.**
> **Congratulations! Protection of the Wilds has reached Iron 1.**
> **Congratulations! Druid class has reached Tin 19.**
> **Protection of the Wilds - spell - area - counter execute**
> **Tin - You call upon the Protection of the Wilds. You and nearby allies are protected by a biome-specific shield and are subjected to a moderate heal-over-time effect. The heal-over-time heals exponentially more based on how low the target's health is and remains until the shield is broken.**
> **Iron - Protection of the Wilds now has a more ethereal and moving visage. You and allies within a shield created by this ability may still see and move as normal. Additionally, you may enhance this ability with a single effect replicable by the Iron rank ability of Herbal Magic.**

Oh daaaamn, Zalia thought.

Moving and seeing through the shield would greatly increase its use. The added Herbal Magic section didn't add much use yet, but if she found some good Iron rank effects she could add, it might be nice.

"Damn that creature is sneaky, I can still barely even see it," Zen said.

"Sneaky, but not that strong," Indis said, a light bit of smoke still rising from her body.

"You are kind of scary sometimes, Lady Indis," Zalia said.

"Oh, that's so sweet of you," Indis said, smiling brightly.

"Think this thing will taste good?" Ember asked, eyeing the creature.

"Mmm, not with my poison in its veins . . . maybe I can do something about that now, though," Zalia said.

Now back at the temporary camp, they were getting glances from the other group as Zalia prepared the creature. Her ability was able to drain the poison from the dead body, along with skinning, field dressing, and nicely cutting it into sections. They did this all on top of her now filthy tarp.

"Want the pelt?" Zalia asked Ember.

"Nah, it's definitely more your style," Ember said.

Zalia shrugged, taking the thing to a nearby stream to wash before putting it into her bag. It would make an excellent adornment to assist with her Stealth, that is, if its magic could still be shaped to work as it had in life. She idly wondered if Endelbyrn had any magic leather workers, and decided it probably did.

When she returned, she found the expedition leader talking to her group.

"That is a good catch," Larel was saying, gesturing to the once agile creature that was now a pile of meat.

"Wasn't so hard with a larger group. Besides, it probably would have killed one of us outright if Zalia hadn't been there," Zen said.

"And it probably would have killed me if I were alone," Zalia responded as she walked up.

"No, it wouldn't have," Ember said.

Zalia didn't comment. She might have been fine, it was true, but it would have surely been a much more difficult fight. The last time she fought a Bronze rank creature it had required a hell of a lot of preparation. Granted, she had been considerably lower rank then, but the difference might not have been enough.

"The fact you can say probably instead of definitely in regards to a Bronze rank creature killing a Tin rank one is impressive in itself," Larel said.

The woman seemed to approve of Zalia and how she had acted during the contract so far. Someone at as high of a rank as Silver considering her abilities impressive surely meant she was on the right track.

"Thank you," Zalia replied.

"No thanks needed. Be quick about your kill, we leave soon," Larel said before walking away.

They quickly cooked and ate; Zalia only had a tiny bit as she had already eaten the evening before. There was definitely something about eating a higher-rank creature that added to its taste, maybe something about how much magic its body held.

Before long they were off once more, not far out from the mine.

They arrived about four hours later, Zalia's Protection of the Wilds still on cooldown from the fight earlier. Before them stood a relatively small mountain, really more of a large hill. Set into the side of it was a mine that looked more natural than a man-made structure. It seemed like the stone itself had flowed into the shape of the mine's entrance; probably a result of magical mining methods.

"Alright, everyone, listen up, entering the mine I'll be taking lead, followed by the twins, the group of five there, and you four last," Larel said pointing to each group in turn. If we encounter any creatures of Silver rank you must not get involved in the fight—retreat until I have defeated it. If we encounter a Gold rank creature, I'll distract it while you all escape, and then I'll be escaping as well. Any questions?"

"They're putting the weakest ones at the back." The man from the group of five earlier snickered quietly, Eston was his name.

They're putting the ones who can actually watch for danger at the back, Zalia thought.

"What was that, Eston? I didn't quite catch it," Larel asked.

"Just wondering what to expect in there," Eston called back.

"I'm not entirely sure, you know as much as I do. We'll just have to watch our backs," Larel said coldly.

"How do you actually kill an Elemental?" Zalia asked.

"You have to dissipate or break off enough of its form. It varies depending on what type it is, and some are better at recovering than others. Usually the more solid the material, the tougher they are, but the slower they recover," Larel explained.

That answered Zalia's question so she stayed silent, thinking it over.

"Alright if there aren't any other questions, let's get moving," Larel finished.

They began moving into the mine in the order specified by Larel, everyone carefully keeping an eye in front of and behind themselves. Zalia used her Heat Resistance Iron rank ability to keep a flame hovering above her hand.

They travelled slowly through a winding tunnel as they descended into the ground. The tunnel was relatively large, big enough for two to travel comfortably next to each other. The ceiling was also quite high for Zalia, though Indis was just a bit too tall and had to stoop a little. They travelled for a short time, Zalia's Low Light Vision levelling once to Tin five.

The tunnel widened as they entered a large space that Zalia could only see a few metres into. What she could see as they grouped up at the entrance was a wooden walkway with stairs leading down—she could barely see the ground below, but did notice a bunch of small creatures crawling along the floor. They looked to be made of different stones and metals.

"Shall we get started?" Larel asked.

CHAPTER TWENTY-EIGHT

We All Know What Happens When You Dig Too Deep

Zalia

Zalia slowly and quietly drew her sword, surmising that her bow would probably not do very much against earthen Elementals.

She watched as Larel vaulted over the rail off the walkway, falling to the ground below. The woman vanished into the darkness below without making any sound as she came into contact with the floor. The entire room was lit up for a moment—Indis released an arc of lightning towards the centre of the room. In the brief flash of light, Zalia saw the silhouettes of hulking Elementals roaming amongst hordes of smaller Elementals made of all types of materials, from rusting iron to various stones. They were all rough-hewn creatures made of jagged edges and shapes. She saw a smaller Elemental explode as their Silver rank leader punched straight through it, and she saw the two Bronze rank twins vaulting over the handrail as well. The other group began making their way to the ground in a more conventional manner via the stairs. The room was quickly and more substantially lit up once one of the other groups' damage dealers began throwing fire through the space.

Zalia knew she wouldn't be much help in this fight and stayed back, using her healing to keep everyone refreshed while her team followed the others down the stairs. She would play the healer in this fight as Ember took a more frontline role to keep Zen from being surrounded.

The other team reached the bottom of the stairs and got to work. Their second damage-dealing back liner was some sort of gravity or telekinesis-focused mage, busy crushing smaller Elementals in swaths while their fire mage aimed at some of the larger creatures, melting through their rocky bodies. They had two front liners, Eston and another man who used two large, heavy gauntlet weapons to smash through Elementals—less impressive than Larel but still quite a sight. Eston focused more on defending the two mages and their last member, a healer.

Zalia's team reached the fight soon after, and Indis began letting off blasts of lightning. The magic homed in on the larger metallic Elementals and failed to do any real damage but the member of their team that really shined in this fight was Zen. He laid waste to the creatures with his large mace and buffed strength attribute, using his taunting abilities to gather the smaller creatures into large groups he could essentially blow up with a few hits. Zalia used rituals to increase her allies' defences and then began using Dodge-vine and Manifest rituals to create small walls that funnelled some of the smaller Elementals to add to Zen's grouping efforts.

The room was lit up by molten rock and patches of fire that flickered as lightning arced through the air, and Zalia could see further into the room as Larel started using her actual abilities against a large composite Elemental made of metals and stones. She only kept a watch on the fight out of the corner of her eye, but she could see Larel was some sort of fist-fighting ice mage. An icy mantle that seemed quite flexible had formed over her body and she was expertly dodging the slow but weighty strikes of the Elemental, and periodically slammed her fist into the creature. A large icy spear grew from the ground, impaling the side of the creature and holding it still as Larel laid waste to its body, smaller Elementals exploding just from the force of the strikes. Zalia finally saw the twins as they appeared on the back of the creature using some sort of joint ability to summon shadowy tendrils that snaked across its surface and began digging into the stone, slowly pushing it apart and cracking it.

Zalia had to properly focus back on her fight, ignoring the incredible display of magic as Zen took a hit to the side. She focused on healing the man as the fight continued on.

The fight finally ended with Larel kicking one last small Elemental, which exploded into dust and tiny stones as it was hurled across the room. Zalia had needed to use Nature's Wrath far into the fight when it had looked like the other team was going to be overwhelmed. The ability had held down everything long enough; numerous stone tendrils impaled creatures and held them still for enough time that the other team could recover. While using the ability, she noticed one more interesting thing when two small Tin rank stone creatures had ripped themselves from the ground and gone to work on the other Elementals. Now that the fight was done, she checked her messages, finding exactly what she had expected.

> **Congratulations! Escape has gained four levels, reaching Tin 16.**
> **Congratulations! Hunter class has gained four levels, reaching Tin 16.**

> **Congratulations! Nature's Wrath has reached Tin 20.**
> **Congratulations! Nature's Wrath has reached Iron 1.**
> **Nature's Wrath will not gain further levels**
> **until all classes have reached Iron.**
> **Nature's Wrath - spell - area**
> **Tin - You invoke the wrath of nature. Nearby enemies are bound**
> **by vines, sinking sand, or other area-related hazards. Enemies**
> **are also subjected to a damage-over-time effect relevant to the**
> **biome that lasts until the restraint has ended. The damage-**
> **over-time effect deals moderate damage per second.**
> **Iron - When used, Nature's Wrath now summons two short-lived**
> **allies of nature. The allies are one rank lower than this ability. The**
> **allies are of a type based on the surrounding environment.**
> **Congratulations! Druid class has reached Tin 20.**
> **Congratulations! Druid class has reached Iron 1.**
> **For reaching the next rank, linked attributes of the**
> **Druid class have increased significantly. Increase all**
> **other classes to Iron to progress further.**

Her Nature's Wrath ability had levelled during the fight from experience gained by killing the Elementals, and the added effect had come into play as she used it. As her Druid class levelled to Iron rank, she could definitely feel the effects. It was less of a physical feeling like the Herbalist class had been, but more of a mental sensation. Her wisdom and intellect attributes had gained a large chunk of power, and she felt as if she had been half asleep her whole life. Her mind raced, being able to see and understand things now so much easier and quicker. It would have taken a while to get used to this overwhelmingly improved ability to perceive and think, if not for the fact that her mind was now much more capable of dealing with its own improvement.

Zalia looked around the room, the floor strewn with broken rock and ore, larger bodies lying still where Larel and the twins had taken care of the higher-rank creatures. They hadn't encountered anything above Silver and so had remained in the space, with the two Iron rank teams keeping far away from where the higher-rank teammates fought.

"What's next?" Zen asked.

"We find out what's through that door," Larel said, pointing to what appeared to be a solid stone wall.

"What door?" three members from the other group asked simultaneously.

"This one," Larel replied as she walked forwards and punched the wall.

The wall reacted by promptly exploding inwards.

They filed through the small hole in the wall, one by one. Inside was the scene of a massacre, dried blood coated the walls and floor, and within the centre of the room sat a small, undulating rip in the fabric of space. Surrounding the anomaly was a ritual in old, dried blood.

"What the hell," Zalia muttered.

This sentiment was shared by the others. A low rumble went through the room, stone shaking for a second as they slowly moved further inside, examining everything.

"Just a tremor," Eston said, sounding a little unsure.

"Any idea what that is?" Zalia asked, pointing to the strange rippling portal in the middle of the room.

She swore she could see through it into some kind of space beyond, but the sight was too blurry to make out any details.

"Yes, some, though I need to confirm with the higher ups before I say any-thing," Larel said.

The room trembled again, dust falling in clouds from the ceiling.

"We should get out of here soon," Zalia said.

"A little bit longer," Larel replied.

She was about to argue the point when a message popped up in front of her.

? - Gold rank

She turned to Larel, about to relay what she had just seen, but the woman's eyes were already wide open.

"GET OUT!" Larel yelled.

Everybody immediately jumped to action, running out of the room from their separate locations. They sprinted through the battle-torn cavern, getting to the stairs and quickly ascending. The same message was everywhere Zalia looked, telling her something Gold rank was there.

Oh no, Zalia thought.

They sped up the stairs and began sprinting through the tunnel towards the entrance, the Silver and Bronze ranks getting ahead of the others. She made it out of the tunnel mouth, turning after a few more metres of running before seeing the final person make it out of the tunnel just as the mouth of the mine snapped shut. Two circles much higher up on the rock face opened, molten cores glowing within as Zalia recognised it for what it was: a face.

She turned and ran, the rest of their teammates doing the same. Zalia heard a thunderous crack as an enormous, rough arm ripped itself from the ground, slamming down and flattening the fire mage from the other group. She kept running, as fast as she could, moving ahead of the pack due to her high Mobility passive. She saw Larel stop and turn to face the monster as the ground beneath them shook. Another crack and thunderous boom sounded as a second arm ripped itself from the ground and slammed down. Getting far enough away, Zalia turned around in time to see a huge, hunched humanoid figure rip itself from the hillside, sending chunks of dirt, stone, and dust flying through the air. Standing before the monstrosity was Larel, silhouetted against the light shining from the molten cores of the creature's eyes. Time seemed to stand still for a moment as Zalia's heart beat in time with the boulders crashing into the ground. The creature opened its mouth—once the mine entrance—letting out a deep grinding sound. Within the pit, she could see a deeper red glow. Larel was the only one with a chance of fighting the creature, as she was significantly faster than the comparatively sluggish Elemental. If they let this thing loose, it could level cities and towns, destroy infrastructure, and possibly even push the kingdom over the edge towards destruction, as it was already teetering on the brink due to the war.

As she watched, shadowy tendrils began sprouting from the ground and wrapping around the creature's thick, trunk-like legs and arms. It was standing on all fours as a gorilla would. Larel dashed forwards; though she said they would run from a Gold rank creature, this one was slow enough to be defeatable. That was Zalia's thinking, at least.

As the Silver ranker sprinted forward, the creature raised its arm to crush her. As it swung down, an icy spike grew from the ground, intercepting the fist as the creature impaled itself on the spike. It provided a moment for Larel to get to its legs and begin punching, small shockwaves exploding outwards from every strike. It looked like she was focusing down one leg as the shadowy tendrils and icy spike kept it still. The icicle snapped as the creature pulled sideways and tried to stomp Larel into the ground. She dodged around, avoiding the stomps and getting in more strikes whenever she could. Dark clouds formed above the creature and black rain started falling down, sizzling as it landed on the creature's back. Considering their rank, the joint magic of the two Bronze ranks was working to great effect.

None of the abilities had a range large enough to affect the two groups of Iron ranks watching from afar, but to them, the raw magic on display was nearly tangible. They watched as a large-bladed chunk of ice formed and slammed into the creature's face, splitting it a bit. The creature let out another grinding sound at that and opened its mouth once more, a blinding bright light coming from within. A wave of molten stone flowed out over where Larel stood, and for a second Zalia thought she might have been caught in it. As the stream of stone stopped, Zalia could see a section that had cooled and solidified around a dome of ice. Larel exploded out of the structure, charging once more at the creature and going to work on its legs.

A change in pace finally came when the creature tried to stomp Larel once more and its leg finally snapped, leaving it unbalanced. Larel's strikes seemed to get stronger and stronger as she fought, possibly using a ramping skill that made each consecutive strike stronger. At the start, each of her strikes had been visible, but now every one looked like a veritable explosion. As the creature toppled sideways, Larel formed ice into a large spike that its head impaled itself on. She proceeded to grow ice around its body, trying to hold it down. The shadowy tendrils also gripped the creature, slowly pushing their way in and holding firm. The Elemental struggled and pushed, resounding cracks echoing through the area as ice cracked, but held. Larel went to work on its neck, smashing through at great speed. The creature managed to break free, standing unbalanced, but as it pulled away its head came free, leaving the stone impaled on the ice spike. The creature seemed unfazed but now stumbled blindly as if it couldn't see. It wildly swung its arms and legs around, desperately trying to smash the little bug pummelling its body, molten rock now freely flowing from its severed neck.

The fight drew to an end as Larel cut more off the same leg, managing to take the whole limb off as it fell this time. The next leg soon followed, and the arms not long after, signalling the creature's final moments. Zalia and her group stood watching from afar in awe as the other group mourned the loss of their friend.

> **Congratulations! Escape has gained three levels, reaching Tin 19.**
> **Congratulations! Hunter class has gained three levels, reaching Tin 19.**

She watched as Larel came up to them, the twins appearing at her side. She noticed something a little different.

> **Larel - Gold rank**

"Congratulations," Zalia said sombrely.

"It came with a price I'd rather not have paid," Larel replied. "I was close and would have gotten there sooner or later."

Larel walked up to the now group of four.

"I'm sorry for your loss," she said gently.

All she got were teary-eyed nods and weak smiles.

The whole party slowly made their way back to Endelbyrn over the course of the next few days, taking the trip easy. It was like the entire group had been muffled, all emotions overshadowed by the death of their team member. They'd tried to find the body, but there had been too much rubble and once-molten stone strewn about.

Zalia continued training and helping the others to learn hunting as they went back. She checked her messages from the six-ish days of training as they arrived at the city gates.

> **Congratulations! Mobility has gained five levels, reaching Tin 19.**
> **Congratulations! Sword - Weapon Proficiency**
> **has gained four levels, reaching Tin 17.**
> **Congratulations! Teaching has gained two levels, reaching Tin 3.**

Making steady progress across the board, Zalia reentered Endelbyrn with a slightly better understanding of the dangers of this line of work and what they could take from you.

CHAPTER TWENTY-NINE

Back Home

Zalia

After returning to the keep and giving Hildebrandt a brief recounting of her point of view during the mine contract, Zalia was now back in the small forested area near the large city. Her Escape ability was now at Tin nineteen, and she wanted to get it to Iron so she could finally begin levelling up her other skills again. First, though, she needed some time to decompress from the contract and think about things. As such, she spent the next three days building herself a medium-sized log cabin from nearby trees, immersing herself in her thoughts as her body was engaged in the therapeutic task. She only ever went back to the city to perform her guard duties, leaving immediately once they were done. The first time she'd ever built a cabin it had taken her almost a week straight of constant work, but she was now significantly stronger and more experienced.

As the three days came to an end, Zalia laid her sleeping bag down in the finished structure, now ready to move forwards into Iron rank without it. She was more comfortable now sleeping within the boughs of trees than in a cozy cabin anyways; leaving the sleeping bag behind was almost a statement about her leaving behind the mundane life she had led, devoid of magic and powers. She had come to the conclusion that what she was doing now probably wasn't any less dangerous than her old life had been, just that the scale of power was significantly more drastic.

Zalia had gained one more gold coin during the course of the last week, given to her by the Morning's Shade. She made her way into the city, entering for the first time since the Elemental contract for a reason other than guard duty. She checked her messages from the last three days, reconnecting with her new reality.

> **Congratulations! Mobility has reached Tin 20.**
> **Congratulations! Mobility has reached Iron 1.**
> **Mobility will not gain additional levels until all classes have reached Iron.**
> **Mobility - passive**
> **Tin - Your speed is increased. Your stamina is less affected by movement.**
> **Iron - You may step on air one time before**
> **stepping on a solid surface once more.**
> **Congratulations! Sword - Weapon Proficiency has reached Tin 18.**

She read over the Mobility upgrade once more, smiling, then grimacing when she realised she had managed to get it to Iron before Escape. She had definitely been neglecting the skill more than she should have.

Zalia went into the keep and found Ember sitting in a small dining hall, eating a light meal.

"Hey," Zalia said.

"Hey," Ember replied, looking up at her.

"I need you to tie me up a bunch," Zalia told her.

"What for?" Ember asked.

"Training," Zalia said as if it explained everything.

Ember just shrugged. "Alright."

Soon, they were standing in the training grounds, Ember tying up Zalia for a third time. As she used Escape, the ropes unknotted and fell to the ground—and the ability finally levelled up.

> **Congratulations! Escape has reached Tin 20.**
> **Congratulations! Escape has reached Iron 1.**
> **As the last skill to reach Iron, 'Escape' has evolved**
> **into 'Fight or Flight,' gaining an extra ability.**
> **Active 3 - Fight or Flight - spell - cleanse - body enhancement**
> **Tin - choose one:**
> **When used, your perception increases greatly for five seconds.**
> **Remove all slowing and restraining effects, and prevent further**
> **slowing and restraining effects for the next five seconds.**
> **Iron – Option one now grants the ability to sense if**
> **you're going to be hit by an attack and where the attack**
> **is coming from within the duration of the ability.**
> **Option two now grants you increased speed and**
> **dexterity within the duration of the ability.**
> **Mana - medium**
> **Cooldown - 1 minute**

She ignored the other messages for a moment, rereading the skill. She tried out the new section first, increasing her perception. The ability seemed to slow time but actually allowed her to perceive things significantly faster, which achieved a similar effect, except she couldn't move any faster than normal. She also tested her new Mobility upgrade, jumping off the air a few times. Then, she paired it with the second option of Fight or Flight and found she could pull off some pretty acrobatic manoeuvres with the increased dexterity and speed. The increased dexterity and strength from her Hunter class advancing also contributed to the extremely increased stat. After running around like a very well-trained headless chicken for a few minutes, she finished reading the rest of the messages.

> **Congratulations! Hunter class has reached Tin 20.**
> **Congratulations! Hunter class has reached Iron 1.**
> **For reaching the next rank, linked attributes of the Hunter class**
> **have increased significantly. Ascend to Iron to advance further.**
> **Congratulations! All of your classes have reached**
> **Iron. Would you like to ascend to Iron?**

Zalia thought about it for only a moment before accepting; she had already made her decision.

> **Congratulations! You have ascended to Iron rank.**
> **Bow - Weapon Proficiency has advanced to**
> **Iron 9 to better match your skill.**

She opened her profile.

> **Profile - Zalia Taori**
> **Health - Excellent**
> **Mana - Full**
> **Stamina - Full**
> **Class One - Hunter - Iron 1**
> **Linked Attributes - Strength, Dexterity**
> **Active Skills**
> **Kill Shot - Iron 1**
> **Hunter's Mark - Iron 1**
> **Fight or Flight - Iron 1**
> **Passive Skills**
> **Hunter's Sight - Iron 1**
> **Survivalist - Iron 1**
> **Class Two - Herbalist - Iron 1**

Linked Attributes - Vitality, Resilience
Active Skills
Flora Identification - Iron 1
Preparation - Iron 1
Stasis - Iron 1
Passive Skills
Harvester - Iron 1
Herbal Magic - Iron 1
Unity Class - Druid - Iron 1
Linked Attributes - Wisdom, Intellect
Active Skills
Nature's Wrath - Iron 1
Protection of the Wilds - Iron 1
Passive Skills
Healing Presence - Iron 1
General Passives
Heat Resistance - Iron 1
Cold Resistance - Iron 1
Aura Observation - Tin 6
Low Light Vision - Tin 5
Poison Resistance - Iron 1
Mobility - Iron 1
Stealth - Iron 1
Trapper - Iron 1
Teaching - Tin 3
Weapon Proficiencies
Bow - Iron 9
Sword - Tin 18

Zalia looked at her now all-Iron rank class abilities with pride, glancing over to Ember with a wide grin.

"Congratulations," Ember said.

"Thank you. Let's duel," Zalia replied.

"Certainly." Ember quickly moved away to get a set of training swords.

Zalia's next goal was achieved after her short bout with Ember, and then attending the sword training session for that day.

Congratulations! Sword - Weapon Proficiency
has gained two levels, reaching Tin 20.
Congratulations! Sword - Weapon Proficiency has reached Iron 1.

> **Sword - Weapon Proficiency**
> **Tin - You can wield a sword faster and hit harder with**
> **it based on the rank and level of this skill.**
> **Iron - The durability of a sword wielded by you is**
> **increased based on the rank and level of this skill.**

Zalia found the increased durability noticeable; she was able to strike stone quite a few times before tiny dents in the bladed section of the sword appeared. But they were small enough to be easily fixed with some quick sharpening, a skill she learned from the sword training lessons.

Zalia wanted to go back north and see Glemp again to learn whether they had made any discovery about the Silver rank herb she had given them. She also wanted to stock back up on the vital berries and Snow-leaf that made up the potent poison she often used. She was running dangerously low and would have run out if it had been usable on the Elementals. Unfortunately, unless she was on a contract, she wouldn't be exempt from her daily guard duty until she had completed the first year of her time within the Morning's Shade. She thought about it for a moment before going to find the Hidden.

She found the shade a half hour later after having to ask directions to his office space multiple times, still utterly confused by the layout of the many spires. She knocked before entering, finding him in deep focus reading a book.

"Shade," Zalia said in greeting as she entered.

"Human," the Hidden said in answer.

Zalia frowned. "I have a name."

"So do I."

"The big difference being that you know mine."

The shade just shrugged, still reading.

Zalia rolled her eyes. "I'm here to ask if you have any contracts in the north."

"Go on then."

"Go on then, what?"

"Ask."

"Have you got any contracts in the north?" Zalia asked, letting out a deep, frustrated sigh.

"Of course! Why didn't you just ask?" the shade replied. "There are all the open contracts, of course, various people wanting any and all information about the land, plants, creatures, and other such things. No one really wants to go up there due to all the snow, pain, and death waiting for them."

"I'm looking to go on an extended trip there, could I take some of those contracts?"

"Well, as I said, they're open so anyone can work them, although you specifically cannot, but your team could. You would have to convince them of it, though," he replied.

She considered for a moment, thinking over how she might accomplish that. "You can't just assign it to us?"

"I could, but I'm not going to," he said.

"And why is that?" she asked.

"Because, one, it would be giving you preference over the rest of your own and the other teams. And, two, I would not send someone north who did not want to go," he replied.

They were both good points.

"Fine, if I can convince them to go, will you allow it?"

"Yes, a longer term contract could do you all good as a team. You are from the north, if my memory serves, so a worse place could be chosen for such an activity. Yes, I will allow it," the shade replied, finally putting down the book to look at Zalia.

"Thank you. And what are you reading, if I may ask?"

The shade looked at her for a few moments before answering. "Have you heard of Cormaine?" he asked.

Zalia looked at him blankly.

"Of course you haven't. Cormaine is known only peripherally throughout the lands, some think it is where those of evil go when they die, some think it is simply another realm. There are many theories but most agree that it is a horrid place that none wish to ever enter. I'm reading up on it and everything that is known or theorised about the place."

"Cormaine, interesting. Does it have something to do with the Elementals?"

"That is yet to be seen. That is all I will speak on it however. Go, convince your friends," the shade said, raising his hand when Zalia was about to ask another question.

"I will try, thank you, milord," Zalia said sarcastically, giving an exaggerated bow.

The shade scoffed at Zalia's performance, going back to his book as she left the room.

I really need to stop being so sarcastic with this man . . . shade, Zalia thought. Something about the way he spoke and acted just made her feel like being overly sarcastic.

But after a moment, her thoughts moved on to how she would convince the others to come north with her. She felt like Ember might be easy to convince, Indis would be the hardest, and Zen would be a wild card. She could never really guess how the man would react, other than it was sure to be in a loud manner.

She found Ember first and with her help, quickly found the other two, and the four of them now sat under a tree in the gardens surrounding the spired keep.

"Sorry, repeat that, I must have misheard you," Zen said, an expression of disbelief on his face.

"I said, I want to take a contract to go north," Zalia repeated.

"For what reason?" Lady Indis asked.

"A few, I wish to see a . . . friend, and gather a resource I'm running low on, but mainly I want to explore more of the north now that I'm a higher rank. Having you all along would be . . .helpful," she said, adding the last part with some hesitation.

She hated to admit that the four of them together would have a better chance at survival but it simply was the truth.

"Alright, I'm in," Indis said.

What? Zalia thought.

"By Enar, I'm not!" Zen said.

"Enar?" Zalia asked.

"Oh shut it for once, Zen. I would like to explore the north, even just for a change of pace in the environment," Ember said.

"You too?" Zen groaned, looking at Ember.

"Yes, me too," Ember said, "and you're coming too."

"Oh really, and why is that?" Zen asked.

"Because I said so," Ember replied.

Ember gave Zen a hard stare, holding contact until the man eventually backed down.

"Fine," Zen grumbled.

She hadn't expected it to be that easy. The fact that Ember had pushed Zen that much to get him to agree was almost as shocking as Lady Indis agreeing from the get go.

"Thank you all, I'll let Hidey know," she said gratefully.

"Hidey?" Zen and Indis asked simultaneously, while Ember just smiled.

"Yeah, idiot shade won't tell me his name so I'm choosing one for him," Zalia said.

Zen put his face in his hands, groaning, while Indis just laughed lightly.

"How did you even come up with 'Hidey'?" Zen asked, his voice muffled by his hands.

"The Hidden, Hidey, it comes pretty naturally, I think—and one of my classes is Druid, I know all about natural," Zalia said as she promptly backed out of the room.

Her preparation was well placed as Zen's hand instinctively went to his mace. Zalia softly ran out of the room, laughing.

Zalia found Hidey once more and was given a list of different contracts that people had put out for objectives related to the northern lands. Some wanted different herbs and plants from the north while others wanted hides or different body parts of creatures, all apparently having some kind of known use. She took copies of them all, not necessarily to try and complete each and every one of them but just to keep in mind what people were looking for that they might come across. She thanked the shade before putting away the pages, leaving to do her guard duty for the day.

After her guard duty, Zalia once again found her group, and they organised when and where they would meet to depart on their journey. It had only been three days since they'd returned from their previous contract, so they wanted to give it a short time before they went traipsing off into the wilderness once more. Zalia was more than happy to do so, much more at home in the wilderness than the others, but Ember and Zen had family in the city they wanted to spend a day with before they left again. As such, they agreed to meet the day after next at the marshalling yard. Zalia figured she should find something to spend her time on and had an idea.

Back in Bur, when she had killed the Garroi, she had thrown her long-bladed dagger—more of a stabbing weapon than a throwing knife—at an enemy to distract them. So, she went off and bought three throwing knives, much more suited to the task than her other weapon. She did have her bow, but the knives would be much quicker to use. She also bought a sheath for them that fit along the outside of her right leg, with a few adjustments. It came to a total of one gold and five silver, not too expensive but still significant, or so she thought. She thought about buying some potions but still had the one Glemp had given her, having had no need for it yet. The only person she might have used it on was that fire mage, and they had died so quickly it wouldn't have helped. She decided to put off buying anything and thought to have a look at what Glemp had cooked up whenever she saw them again.

The next day she spent preparing herself, stocking up on travel supplies like food just in case she would need them, however doubtful she was of that happening. She also spent some time in training, testing out the limits of her newfound power. She found that unlike before, where she felt like her brain was moving faster than her body could keep up with, the two were now on par due to them both being Iron rank. She felt young again; though her body was not deteriorating by any means, she was still reaching her mid-years. Now though, with constant healing flowing through her and the increased strength, dexterity, and other attributes, she felt better than she had in a while.

The day finally came and she met Ember, Zen, and Lady Indis within the marshalling yard, ready as always to head back out into the wilderness.

CHAPTER THIRTY

Travel and Old Friends

Zalia

Zalia and her team were travelling along the path she now knew would lead back to the small walled town of Ostoss. It had taken her about a week and two days to travel from that town to Endelbyrn, but she suspected it might take slightly longer than that to travel back the other way. Above all else, Indis and Zen were just . . . slow. They wouldn't be called slow by a normal person's standards but by the standards of the Morning's Shade they definitely were. They had only been travelling for two days, with seven to nine days of travel still ahead of them. She had started integrating the air step upgrade from the Mobility rank up into her sparring, trying to get it to fit into different strikes and positioning manoeuvres. She hadn't yet had much luck but knew with time and practice she would make it work and hopefully, make it do much more than just work.

Zalia sighed, slowing her walking speed down once more as Zen and Indis fell behind again.

"Do either of you have the Mobility passive?" Zalia asked.

"The what?" Zen asked.

"No," Lady Indis replied.

"That explains it," Zalia muttered.

"Explains what?" Zen asked.

"Why we are so slow, Zen," Indis said.

"You two should both join my training every morning," Zalia suggested.

"What for?" Zen asked.

"So I don't have to consciously slow myself down when I'm travelling with you," Zalia replied.

Zen paused for a moment. "Alright, fair, how bad could it be?"

The next morning, Zalia woke everyone up as the sun rose. This elicited complaints from Zen and Indis, which was expected, but she also received some from Ember, who had not agreed to do the training.

"You're slow too," Zalia said to the stormy-faced, grumbling woman.

They all stood now, with the small camp still set up around them. The other three tended to use tents and bedrolls rather than sleeping in trees like Zalia.

"Who are you calling slow?" Ember growled.

"You," Zalia replied.

"Bullshit," Ember said.

"Keep up then," Zalia replied, before taking off into the forest.

The other three quickly followed but not one of them could match Zalia's speed. She eventually slowed down, Ember catching up as Zalia fell to Zen and Indis's relatively slow paces.

They ran for a time, before Zalia led them in a loop back around to camp once more. Their route took most of a half hour, and she returned with all three of her teammates gasping for air as she gently came to a rest from the light stroll. They had been moving at what they would consider a sprint, while for her, it was barely a run, more of a jog.

"Seem a little out of breath, Ember," Zalia said.

Ember didn't respond, simply touching her thumb to the centre section of her middle finger and angling her palm out towards Zalia.

"What does that mean?" Zalia asked.

"It means . . . shut up . . . or I'll . . . hit you," Ember wheezed between breaths.

Zalia smiled. Getting words out of Ember was hard at the best of times, getting visibly strong emotions was all the more of a task. She was proud of her accomplishment, even if it was just annoyance or anger the woman displayed.

Zalia waited for the others to recover while she practiced her sword work. It wasn't long before they all were breathing normally, with their Iron rank bodies working on a different level than normal peoples'. At least, what she used to consider normal.

During the run she managed to acquire two levels in her Teaching skill and one in Mobility. As she raised a few abilities above Iron one, it occurred to her that she could begin raising her other abilities once more. Poison training was now on the list of activities she could introduce to her daily routine. She grimaced at the thought but knew it was probably wise to do, getting the resistance to Bronze quickly might provide a useful tool. She also knew it would take a while to manage with her current poison, and she most definitely was not going to use the Silver rank poison as it would probably kill her. She was ok with having to wait some time to get to Bronze, though, and would have to unless she found a poison with a strength between the two.

The next week and a day were spent in a very similar fashion. Zalia woke up the rest of the team, much to their annoyance, they trained Mobility, close quarters combat, tracking, and additionally, archery. It turned out that the others had actually bought bows after Zalia's training in tracking and wanted to learn how to shoot as well. So, she showed them all the tips and tricks it had taken her a long time to figure out. They benefited greatly from her expertise, learning very quickly over the week due to their increased mental attributes. Zen learned more slowly than the others, though, due to him not having them linked. The bows they had were only smaller hunting bows, more for small game and probably much less effective in a fight than Zalia's bow would be. She doubted the small bows would even be able to penetrate through some thicker leather armours. They were quite good for small game, however and she showed them how to use the weapons, each finding some success during small hunts they undertook during the short journey.

Towards the end of the last day, Zalia finally saw the walled town of Ostoss on the horizon and decided that they could probably make it before nightfall. They arrived just as the sun set below the horizon, walking through the small checkpoint with no issue, as Zalia recognised the guard. She simply gave a nod to the man, recognising him as one of the guards who had come with her and Tristan to stop the deserters. The image of the man she had killed flashed through her mind as she remembered the events that had taken place in this town not so long ago—his body wracked with pain as she muffled his screams, and his body rotting around him as he died an excruciating death. She shuddered.

"We're going to go find a place a friend of mine owns," Zalia said.

"You have friends?" Zen asked.

"Of course I have friends, not everyone talks as much as you," Zalia retorted.

Indis actually slapped Zen upside the head, shocking him and Zalia.

"Lead on," Lady Indis said.

Zalia found the small bakery that Tristan ran and went inside, finding the man closing up shop.

"Tristan!" she called out.

"Zalia! Welcome back to town, it's good to see you," Tristan said as he turned, a grin spreading across his face. "And you have some friends as well, I'm surprised," he added with only a hint of sarcasm in his voice.

"Why do people keep saying that?" Zalia muttered.

"Lady Indis, a pleasure," Indis said to Tristan.

"I'm Zen, this is Ember," Zen added, poking Ember and getting a glare from her.

"Pleasure's mine. Tristan's the name, as Zalia so thoughtfully yelled earlier," Tristan replied, actually bowing to Indis.

"Why are you bowing?" Zalia asked.

"That's a lady of a great house behind you there," Tristan pointed out.

"So?" Zalia asked.

"Sooo, you bow to ladies of great houses," he replied.

"Finally someone with some common courtesy and respect," Indis said haughtily.

"Must not be as common as you think," Ember muttered.

They spoke a bit longer, mostly idle conversation, before—at Zalia's request—they were directed to a nearby inn that had the best rooms in town, according to Tristan. They organised to meet the next day, Zalia more than eager to test herself against Tristan now that she had made so much progress with her sword fighting. He was still a Bronze rank with a good bit of actual battle experience from the army so she didn't expect to beat him in even a single bout, but she thought she might be able to hold her own for a little bit, at least.

The next morning Zalia, her team, and Tristan all stood outside the walls as Tristan smashed Zalia's blade from her hand once more, ending the fight.

"Damn it, you're just so fast," Zalia said.

"And significantly more experienced, trained, higher rank. Not to mention handsome," Tristan added.

Indis let out a half snort, half laugh.

"Your face being aesthetically pleasing by the subjective standards of society has nothing to do with how good you are at hitting people with an axe," Zalia retorted.

Everyone looked at Zalia weirdly.

"What language was that?" Indis asked.

"What do you mean what language?" Zalia asked.

"It sounded like gibberish," Zen said.

"Only because you don't know what any of those words mean," Zalia said.

"I didn't either," Indis said.

"Whatever, I'm here to spar, not talk. The rest of you should spar with Tristan as well," Zalia said, ending the conversation

Later, they all sat together in the inn, Tristan as well, having a light beer each. Zalia was the exception, just drinking water, as she didn't see the point in drinking alcohol that could no longer affect her and was more expensive.

"How did you two meet, anyways?" Zen asked.

"You wanna tell the story or shall I?" Zalia asked Tristan.

"No, no, I'll do it," Tristan said.

He launched into a dramatised version of what had happened, the deserters, the villagers gathering and going after them, the betrayal by the guard, and then the final battle in which he overplayed Zalia's part while severely underplaying his own. He finished up with the final battle between himself and the deserter captain, explaining how without Zalia's intervention he would have died that day to the man.

Zalia carefully watched his face the whole time he spoke, knowing the topic was a touchy one for him, but he seemed alright and in good company so she wasn't too worried. As he finished, Zalia remembered a detail about the fight he hadn't included.

"The man had a tag after his name that I could see with Aura Observation. It said 'corrupted,' have any of you heard of anything like that?" Zalia asked.

Ember and Indis shook their heads, but Zen looked thoughtful.

"Zen?" Zalia asked.

"I have heard of such things before, actually, yes. I heard of someone who tried to contact a dead family member after their passing and ended up being corrupted. The man had to be put down as he went insane, lost his mind," he answered.

"Strange," Zalia replied. "Tristan, did you ever know the man to try and raise the dead, or whether he talked to any dead family members?"

"No, never, but . . . well I didn't know the man well in recent years, I suppose. He could well have done those things after I left the army. It would explain why he ended up deserting if he got caught up in stuff like that," Tristan said, looking thoughtful.

I wonder if it has something to do with Cormaine. Hidey did say that the place is known to some as where those who did evil in life go when they die, Zalia thought.

As she had the thought, a realisation came to her. The strange portal or rip in space that they had seen within the mine might have been one that went to Cormaine. Maybe it even had something specific to do with Tristan's old captain.

"Tristan, did your captain ever have any reason to go to the old mine? The one that is now abandoned?" Zalia asked.

"I don't recall him ever going there, why?"

"Just a thought about something we found on a contract there not so long ago, might be unrelated."

"You're thinking about the weird anomaly we found in the mine?" Ember asked.

Zalia nodded.

"I don't think it is related, though it might be. It's probably what caused all the Elementals to gather there, though," Ember said.

Zalia perked up. "What makes you say that?"

"Elementals tend to gather wherever there is an imbalance in the strength between nature and . . . other forces. They're like nature's own defence, or so I've been told," Ember explained.

"Who told you that?" Zen asked.

"None of your business," Ember told him.

"Well, that would certainly explain how such a high-rank Elemental appeared there, but do you have any idea what the weird anomaly was?" Zalia asked Ember, interrupting Zen.

"Not really, though Larel said she might know, and I would guess the leadership of the Morning's Shade will tell us at some point," Ember replied.

"So that's where you found all these nice people," Tristan said.

"Yep, I was accepted into the Shade," Zalia said mysteriously.

"Spooky, congratulations are in order then. Most likely the lowest rank person to ever be brought into the group, from what I hear," Tristan said, raising his mug.

"That she is," Indis said.

"And while we are at it, congratulations on Iron rank!" Tristan added.

"Doesn't feel like that much of an achievement. Only took me what . . . four weeks?" Zalia said, trying to recall how long she had been here.

"That itself is quite an achievement, not many make it to ancient without getting any magic," Zen said.

Zalia narrowed her eyes at the man, hand going towards her dagger. "Who are you calling ancient, youngling?" she growled.

"Youngling! I'm almost in my midtwenties!" Zen retorted.

"Yet you still act like you're twelve," Zalia pointed out.

The rest of the table laughed and they chatted away through the rest of the morning until about half past midday.

They left the city that day, Zalia bidding a fond farewell to Tristan, as the man was unwilling to come along with them. According to him, his fighting days were over long ago, but Zalia didn't begrudge him the decision. They made their way, led by Zalia, in the direction she remembered Juniper and Darren's house to be. She was looking forward to seeing the two farmers again and wanted to thank them for the weapon they had given her. Already it had helped her in many ways, from being a good weapon for hunting to allowing her to defend her friends, to helping her with entry to the Morning's Shade. She also wanted to ask them about Juniper's late husband, Zayes. He had been the one to help Hidey gain sentience and form the whole organisation that she was now a part of. She was unsure if any of her team knew about it, but she wasn't really one for keeping secrets just for the sake of secrecy.

She knew it would be three days travel, likely four with her team, to the farmhouse. They set off travelling once more, soon to see another set of her new friends in this world.

They continued on as they had been before entering Ostoss, a routine of training and travelling, hunting for themselves, and repeating it all again the next day. Before long they arrived at the small farmhouse Zalia remembered so well. The small house was surrounded by a lovely garden tended to by Juniper and

Darren. She remembered the herb that she had gotten some of to help enrage the beasts she had killed here. It hadn't turned out to be anything special, mostly just good for cooking, other than having a powerful enraging effect on that one particular creature. She decided it might be good to get some while she was here and put it into Stasis, just in case. She checked her messages from the past almost two weeks of training.

> **Congratulations! Kill shot has reached Iron 2.**
> **Congratulations! Hunter's Mark has reached Iron 2.**
> **Congratulations! Fight or Flight has gained two levels, reaching Iron 3.**
> **Congratulations! Hunter's Sight has reached Iron 2.**
> **Congratulations! Survivalist and associated skills**
> **have gained two levels, reaching Iron 3.**
> **Congratulations! Hunter class has reached Iron 2.**
> **Congratulations! Stasis has reached Iron 2.**
> **Congratulations! Herbal Magic has reached Iron 2.**
> **Congratulations! Healing Presence has reached Iron 2.**
> **Congratulations! Aura Observation has**
> **gained three levels, reaching Tin 9.**
> **Congratulations! Low Light Vision has gained**
> **three levels, reaching Tin 8.**
> **Congratulations! Mobility has gained two levels, reaching Iron 4.**
> **Congratulations! Teaching has gained six levels, reaching Tin 11.**
> **Congratulations! Bow - Weapon Proficiency has reached Iron 10.**
> **Congratulations! Sword - Weapon Proficiency has reached Iron 2.**

It was good, solid progress across the board. She couldn't help but notice that now she was Iron rank herself, her Tin rank abilities were levelling significantly quicker. Some sort of catch-up experience went to them from everything she did, maybe.

She saw Juniper kneeling down in a patch of the garden and rushed over in her direction, yelling and waving. "Juniper! Juniper!" she called out.

The woman stood, shading her eyes as she looked in their direction. "Zalia, dear, how are you?"

"I'm quite well, thank you. Is Darren around?" Zalia asked.

She watched as Juniper's face darkened a little, before taking its usual look as the woman noticed Zalia's companions. Zalia made introductions before giving the woman a questioning look, wondering what the earlier expression had been.

"You had better come inside my dear, I've news you should hear," Juniper said.

CHAPTER THIRTY-ONE

Back North

Zalia

Zalia, her team and Juniper all sat around the low table, now holding a few plates of various treats and cups of tea. Juniper had refused to allow them to help, quickly and efficiently moving through her kitchen and setting everything down within minutes.

"What did you want to tell us?" Zalia asked finally as the woman settled.

Juniper slumped, the energy leaving her body. "They conscripted my poor boy—" Juniper got that much out before a sob wracked her body and she began crying.

Zalia didn't know how to react, but she didn't need to as Ember moved across to the woman and put her arms around her. For her part, Juniper seemed to recover quite quickly, possibly due to some magic Ember had used. Zalia did know that healing magic had a calming effect on the mind and began focusing her aura on the woman too.

"The kingdom conscripted him?" Zalia asked.

"Y-yes, apparently the king has decided to begin forced conscription to swell their numbers and put down the rebellion in force," Juniper answered, wiping her eyes.

"Damn," Zalia whispered. *That would explain why there seemed to be fewer people in town in Ostoss. I wonder if they'll recruit from Endelbyrn too.* "How long ago?"

"Only three days past, recruiters that had come up from the south. They took Halden from down the road too."

"I'm sorry. I'm sure Darren will be fine, he is strong and young," Zalia said, trying her best to be comforting.

But she wasn't sure of that, to be honest. It seemed like most of the people fighting in the one battle she'd seen all had classes related to combat. Darren most likely had some kind of workman class with a farming specialisation. She just hoped the army was smart enough to keep the newly conscripted people as backup rather than using them as some form of fodder.

"Shit," Zen said.

It seemed like it was weighing on everyone's minds. Indis didn't seem too well off either, the news probably meant something to her too. Zalia was aware that both Zen and Indis knew people that might have been conscripted, even she knew people—Darren and possibly others from towns further away. It was likely that people like Tristan would be conscripted too. The thought sickened her, Tristan had done enough fighting in his life and was just trying to live peacefully as a baker, but the fact that he was relatively young, in shape, and experienced meant he would be one of the first they took when they got to Ostoss. Others, such as Gurden the blacksmith in Ostoss, Taron the enchanter in Alston, or Eyla the guard, also in Alston, could be taken as well. Those were the few people Zalia knew after only a couple weeks in the kingdom. Each of the others would know hundreds of people that could be conscripted, and although Ember hid her emotions well and hadn't ever talked about any family or friends, she must've certainly had some.

They spoke for some time, mostly avoiding bringing up Darren or the army as the topic settled in the back of everyone's minds. Zalia pulled aside Juniper later into the day to talk to her one-to-one.

"I wanted to thank you for what you did for me," Zalia told her.

"And what did I do for you?" Juniper asked.

"You gave me Zayes's bow, your husband's heirloom, because you knew that our shade friend would recognise it and help me," Zalia said.

This elicited a real smile from Juniper, one she didn't have to put on. "Oh, it's good that he did, I do miss the overdramatic shade. What does he go by these days?"

"The Hidden, but I just call him Hidey."

This got Juniper to let out a chuckle. "Oh my, the Hidden. He certainly hasn't changed much."

"Do you know his actual name?"

"Oh yes, I most certainly do," Juniper said, some joy brought back to her posture.

"What is it?" Zalia asked eagerly.

"That is not for me to tell, my dear."

"Oh what the—Not you, too. It can't possibly be this big of a secret," Zalia said, exasperated.

"Of course it isn't, but I would not want to ruin my dear friend's . . . *games*," Juniper replied, almost innocently, the smirk ruining her attempt.

Zalia narrowed her eyes at the woman. "That wouldn't be becoming of you to do, not at all," she said, clipping each word.

The woman gave Zalia a wide smile before dropping it again, thoughts of Darren clearly resurfacing.

"I'm truly sorry, I would help if I could," Zalia said.

"I know you would, I just hope this whole thing comes to a close soon. Such terrible business war is," Juniper said sombrely.

Zalia nodded in agreement. "That it is."

They had spent the rest of the day at the farm, sleeping the night there as much as for a good night's rest in a building as to keep Juniper company. It wasn't right to leave an old woman, even a Bronze rank one, alone and take her son from her. With Juniper's permission, Zalia took some more of the herb she called 'Enrage' from the garden. She couldn't use it for anything, but if she found any creatures similar to the ones she'd hunted down previously, it could come in handy. The next morning they left early, heading straight north. As much as Zalia wanted to check in on Eyla and the rest of Alston, it was a tiny bit south of the farm and they were trying to get into the north. It was bad enough that she had detoured so much eastwards rather than just going straight north from Endelbyrn, but seeing Glemp again was part of the purpose of venturing there, at least for her.

As they travelled, Zalia explained everything she knew about the north and what type of creatures they would find there. She told her team about the Ironfur rabbits, six-legged bears, the ice-magic-wielding wolf creature she had encountered, and then went on to explain who Glemp was and where they were heading. It was about four days' travel by her reckoning, and the others had plenty of questions about the various topics she brought up, all of which she answered.

About halfway through the second day, they entered the snow once more. Zalia avoided the area where she knew the war camp of Alara to be, assuming it was still there. As soon as they entered the snow, Zalia began harvesting Snowleaf and her special poison berries, some worry leaving her as she had a good stock of the vital plants once more. She also found plenty of Bronze rank Frozen Heart, explaining to the others what it did, where to find it, and how to use it. It would be a good tool for anyone to keep on them, in Zalia's opinion. She wanted to get more Flame-root as well, the fiery magic it provided being an excellent tool to keep in her arsenal.

Before long, she had the others hunting their very own Ironfur rabbits as well. This was an exceptionally easier task for the three, as this was a target that did not flee but one that threw itself at them with violent abandon. While most of the rabbits sat at Iron or Bronze, Zalia did know that they could be found in Silver rank as well. On their way to the mountain they didn't encounter any of the six-legged bears, though tracks were seen. Zalia had a theory that the creatures usually dwelled further north, where the team would soon be travelling after visiting Glemp. During the journey she also started adding the Poison Resistance training to her daily routine; however, she was unable to convince the others to do the same.

On the fourth day, they finally arrived at the mountain that had been visible for a long time. She went to the place she knew the doors to be and knocked as hard as she could. They waited for a few moments.

"Are you sure you found the right indistinguishable mountain face?" Zen asked.

"Shut up, Zen," Zalia and Ember said simultaneously.

A rumble sounded through the rock face as a split appeared and the doors ground open, swinging inside the mountain. Two short creatures stood looking at the group of four. Then, their eyes began glowing the deep red Zalia remembered oh so well.

"Wait! Wait! I'm a friend of Glemp, Glemp," Zalia said quickly.

One of the Born of Heat and Stone stopped, jabbing the other with its hand to get it to stop too. A conversation in their language then followed, quick and short, filled with clicks and guttural sounds. Their language was quite hard to even get a sense of. The first creature, the one that had understood what Zalia was saying a little, slapped the other in the back of the head before gesturing for the group to enter. That was apparently a universal sign for calling someone an idiot.

The teammates entered the large cave tunnel, holding onto each other's hands since they couldn't see in the darkness—darkness that Zalia was fine with herself. She led them by the hand down the tunnel until they could see again by the warm light filtering into the space from the large opening up ahead. As the room heated from the lava Zalia knew was up ahead, the others began taking off some of the thick layers they'd put on for the journey. She entered the large spiralling town of the small peoples that had first welcomed Zalia in this world. Haphazard homes were built up the twisting and often dangerous stairs, and tunnels were built into the sides of the large cylindrical space. Still remembering the way, Zalia led her group on the twisting path that would take them to Glemp's home.

She entered the residence and found the small creature hunched over one of their workbenches, working on some meticulous alchemical study, no doubt. She knocked on the wall with a dull sound, Glemp loudly speaking in their language before Zalia spoke.

"Hey Glemp, I'm back," she said.

The small creature turned to her, large eyes widening even further as they took in Zalia. "Wait, just wait, yes, yes. Important discoveries, yes," Glemp said, before turning right back to their work.

Zalia rolled her eyes, turning back to the others as they entered.

"What was that language you were speaking?" Indis asked.

"What language?" Zalia asked back.

"What do you mean what language? The one you just used. Couldn't understand it," Indis said, walking into the room past Zalia.

What? She turned around, still looking at Indis. "I only spoke the same way I do with you."

"Yeah, definitely not, only a couple words were the same," Indis said back.

Zalia looked over at Ember, who just shrugged.

"Couldn't understand it either," Ember said.

What the hell? Zalia thought.

"It sounds exactly the same to me," Zalia said in confusion. She then heard a small hissing before a tiny pop sound came from where Glemp was.

"No! No, no, no, damn it, fire and stone, no," Glemp yelled.

"What are you doing?" she asked Glemp.

"You are speaking that language again," Indis pointed out.

"No, very specific amounts, yes. Very precise," Glemp said looking at Zalia.

"You can't understand that?" Zalia asked Indis.

Indis shook her head and Glemp looked at her in confusion.

Some kind of translation power? "Oh," she said.

She spent the next ten minutes trying to introduce Glemp and her team, having to work as a go-between for the two groups. If she had been given some kind of translation power when she came to this world, it would explain some things. It wouldn't have made any sense if the people here were speaking English. It didn't work on Glemp's primary language, however, which led her to believe maybe it only worked on languages that were similar enough to her own in structure. It would explain why back in Ostoss, the group had been confused when Zalia tried speaking in a complex manner.

After she made introductions, she explained to Glemp that they were here for various reasons, but mainly to hunt different beasts and find various plants. The creature's eyes shined at her mention of hunting and she remembered when she had first been here there was something Glemp had wanted her to hunt for then, but had never deemed her worthy. She asked Glemp, but they still seemed uncertain, so Zalia let it drop for now, hoping to maybe prove her group's skill in the coming days.

After they had all finished talking, the three went to find somewhere to sleep; Zalia pointed them to the backroom of Glemp's workshop.

"Glemp, have you found out anything yet about that Silver rank herb I gave you back then?" Zalia asked.

"Yes, yes, some. Elements of ice, time. Purpose? No," Glemp said.

"Elements of ice and time, hey, interesting," Zalia said, musing over Glemp's words.

It didn't seem they had found a purpose yet but knowing the elements, Zalia might be able to use it preemptively in some ritual. If she found more, that was.

"Thanks, I appreciate knowing that much at least. We might hunt some things over the next coming days or weeks, would you be interested in getting some pieces of creatures? Oh! And did you find that large six-legged bear I told you about when I left?" Zalia asked in rapid-fire.

"Yes, yes, yes. Would want many things, yes. B . . . e . . . a . . . r was good find, yes. Very good pelt," Glemp said, struggling to pronounce 'bear.'

Now that she thought about the possibility of having a translation power, she could almost feel it, hear it. It was a strange sensation to pay attention to, being able to speak a language that by all rights she shouldn't be able to. She had never learnt another language before either, which added to the strangeness for her.

"Excellent, I'll let you know when we catch anything impressive then," Zalia said

She went to sleep right there on the floor, looking at the few messages she had from the days of travelling up to the north.

> **Congratulations! Teaching has gained three levels, reaching Tin 14.**
> **Congratulations! Survivalist and associated skills have reached Iron 4.**
> **Congratulations! Flora Identification has reached Iron 2.**
> **Congratulations! Preparation has reached Iron 2.**
> **Congratulations! Harvester has gained two levels, reaching Iron 3.**
> **Congratulations! Herbalist class has reached Iron 2.**
> **Congratulations! Poison Resistance has reached Iron 2.**

The next morning, Zalia once more had to wake the others up as they slept in relative, but importantly, warm comfort. They were all prone to sleeping way too much, in Zalia's opinion, which might just be due to the fact she was bored after waiting for too long. It was most likely the fault of the reduced sleep section of her Survivalist ability, an unforeseen downside to the upgrade that made working alone rather than in a group an even better prospect.

They went through their morning routine, Glemp apparently still hard at work on their alchemy project. She wasn't sure Glemp actually needed sleep but, who knew. After their morning routine, Zalia took them all out of the mountain and back into the snow. She took a deep breath, appreciating the cool, fresh northern air. The air in the mountain wasn't necessarily toxic but it was definitely stifling, with an ashy tinge to it. She led the group to the north, breaking into a run as her team tried to keep up. Before long, she slowed back down again before stopping. She looked to the others.

"Who wants to have a go at tracking today?" she asked.

"I've got it," Indis said.

Zalia was surprised, since the woman usually had to be persuaded to take part. Though, it would be exciting for anyone to explore a new land that no human had ever explored, as far as they knew, at least.

Zalia spent the next few hours slowly moving further north, explaining to them all, mainly Indis, how tracking changed when you were in snowier lands. In some ways it became easier, in others harder, but in general it was just some different signs you had to look for compared to the usual ones from forested terrain. After a few more hours they found what she had been looking for, some tracks of one of the six-legged bear creatures, smaller than usual. It was most likely a young adult of the species and Zalia hoped that meant it would be a Bronze rank one, not Silver. They tracked the beast for a half hour before finding it, the four of them crouched in the snow at a distance as they watched the creature foraging for berries from a bush.

"Wait here," Zalia said.

She was definitely the most stealthy of the group and snuck just close enough to see that it indeed was a Bronze rank creature. She then made her way back carefully to the group.

"Let's hunt," she whispered excitedly.

CHAPTER THIRTY-TWO

Relaxing Vacation in the North

Zalia

Zalia and her team spent the next two weeks hunting in the north and exploring the lands further into the wilds, away from the mountain home where Glemp lived. They constructed a small camp area with a short spike wall emplaced by Zalia, the construction magically enhanced and hidden by her passive. The other three had set up tents that the whole group worked together to hide properly in the snow of the stark white landscape. As the weeks passed, the north grew colder but as it did, so too did the others gain more levels in Cold Resistance. The first bear creature they had hunted, a species they had named Seybears, had been a rough fight; the others were unused to the creature's immense strength. They had quickly adapted however, the faster group members having an easier time than others. They'd hunted a few during the weeks, each hunt going better than the last. Zalia had shown them how to properly prepare the hides of the beasts to be used, and the others all now used the thick warm hides as blankets. Zalia herself wasn't much bothered by the cold, wearing her usual outfit of rough travelling clothes, armour, and enchanted cloak. Both her cloak and passive stealth ability had environment-blending effects on her appearance so she moved through the snow and undergrowth as more of a mottled effect than a perceivable creature.

Zalia had also experimented a little with her Herbalism. When she looked at Snow-leaf it now displayed extra information.

> **Snow-leaf - Iron - Use in a ritual to add an element of Ice.**

This was an addition that was added when her Flora Identification ability had reached Iron rank. Playing around with some rituals, she found she could create a ritual of Manifest, Snow-leaf, and Bitterbalm to create a creeping ice that slowed and even harmed a target depending on its Cold Resistance. A simple Manifest and Snow-leaf ritual would manifest a chunk of ice, the shape of which she could play around with to a small degree, making a wall, ball, and various other things. She felt that there were two different types of herbs she had discovered when it came to her rituals so far. The first was a shape-type herb that helped guide how the affected ritual appeared in the world. Examples of this type would be Manifest or Bitterbalm, which allowed her to create rituals as curses or physical manifestations. The second type of herbs had elemental aspects that dictated ritual effects, examples being Dodge-vine and Snow-leaf, each of which applied effects based around protection and ice, respectively. This distinction gave her an easier time figuring out how to use some of the higher-rank herbs in rituals. One such higher-rank herb was Frozen Heart. She had figured out how to use it in a ritual that applied a healing-over-time effect by replacing Dodge-vine in the protection ritual she had grown so accustomed to using. She was sure there was a much more efficient way of using the herb then in a ritual designed for a Tin rank herb, but for now it was another healing capability she had.

Zen had gotten significantly better at learning tracking and hunting, strangely being much better at the task in the snow than in the woods. Maybe it just had something to do with how different the two activities were or maybe something had just clicked in his head and he had finally figured it out. Either way, he was quite good enough now to go about hunting without Zalia and actually have a good chance to catch something. This brought some stress off Zalia as she didn't have to really teach any of the others tracking anymore, only giving tips and tricks here and there as they asked for them. Zalia had a bit more time each day then to practice stealth and trapping, exploring how her Trapper passive could enhance different traps she set that traditionally wouldn't be of much use in the moment. She used sinew from the animals she killed to create a few different lengths of string, which could be used as bowstring though this wasn't what she wanted it for. Instead, she attempted to use it as a trap.

Running it between two trees, she found it blended in extremely well, seeming almost as thin as a spiderweb, nearly invisible to the eye. When she made Zen run through it, the string tied itself around his legs, holding him down until he could undo the complex knot that the string formed. He could also have just cut it, but Zalia wanted the length of string back so asked him not to. She also made sure to keep a bunch of her caltrops in her bag, knowing them to be useful, though wary of when to use them, since she did have allies around. She also traded with Glemp for some small metal spikes she could easily slam into a tree as she ran past. Similar to the caltrops, the spike would extend from the tree in an instant like a spear, impaling whatever had triggered it. Finally, she had begun training with her throwing knives, gaining a new proficiency along the way.

Ember had gotten quite good at using the bow and was the furthest along in her bow weapon proficiency, though Zalia was not surprised by that. Indis had actually taken quite an interest in what Zalia had to teach, catching up quickly to the other two in tracking and archery. Despite the first appearances of snobbishness and privilege that the woman gave off, Lady Indis was actually quite a hard worker and a good listener when it came down to it. Zalia probably shouldn't have expected anything else from a woman who was desperately fighting to keep her whole house from failing.

Zalia gained quite a few levels in a range of abilities over the two weeks.

> **Congratulations! Kill Shot has gained three levels, reaching Iron 5.**
> **Congratulations! Hunter's Mark has gained four levels, reaching Iron 6.**
> **Congratulations! Fight or Flight has gained four levels, reaching Iron 7.**
> **Congratulations! Hunter's Sight has gained three levels, reaching Iron 5.**
> **Congratulations! Survivalist and associated skills have gained five levels, reaching Iron 9.**
> **Congratulations! Hunter class has gained three levels, reaching Iron 5.**
> **Congratulations! Flora Identification has reached Iron 3.**
> **Congratulations! Preparation has gained three levels, reaching Iron 5.**
> **Congratulations! Stasis has gained two levels, reaching Iron 4.**
> **Congratulations! Harvester has gained three levels, reaching Iron 6.**
> **Congratulations! Herbal Magic has gained five levels, reaching Iron 7.**
> **Congratulations! Herbalist class has reached Iron 3.**
> **Congratulations! Nature's Wrath has gained two levels, reaching Iron 3.**
> **Congratulations! Protection of the Wilds has gained two levels, reaching Iron 3.**
> **Congratulations! Healing Presence has gained four levels, reaching Iron 6.**
> **Congratulations! Druid class has gained two levels, reaching Iron 3.**
> **Congratulations! Aura Observation has gained two levels, reaching Tin 11.**
> **Congratulations! Low Light Vision has gained two levels, reaching Tin 10.**
> **Congratulations! Poison Resistance has gained three levels, reaching Iron 5.**
> **Congratulations! Mobility has gained six levels, reaching Iron 10.**
> **Congratulations! Teaching has gained six levels, reaching Tin 20.**
> **Congratulations! Teaching has reached Iron 1.**
> **Teaching - passive**

> **Tin - You gain a better understanding of what methods of teaching will work with certain people, scaling with the level and rank of this ability.**
> **Iron - When teaching someone, they have an easier time grasping concepts that you explain, scaling with the level and rank of this ability. You are also able to convey simple concepts even when there is a language barrier.**
> **Congratulations! Bow - Weapon Proficiency has gained three levels, reaching Iron 13.**
> **Congratulations! Sword - Weapon Proficiency has gained two levels, reaching Iron 4.**
> **Congratulations! You have gained a new Weapon Proficiency in 'Throwing Knives.'**
> **Throwing Knives - Weapon Proficiency - Tin - Knives thrown by you have increased speed based on rank and level of this skill. They will also better spin in the air to hit with the part of the weapon you want.**
> **Congratulations! Throwing Knives - Weapon Proficiency has gained six levels, reaching Tin 7.**

A part of Zalia's success in teaching Zen came from the upgraded Teaching passive, or so she thought. She was also getting quite far ahead in her Bow Proficiency, which she put down to her previous life experience. Additionally, she had begun to trust the 'Tracking Arrows' ability provided by her bow, and was now able to make shots that would have been otherwise impossible or improbable without.

The final discovery during the two weeks was one made by Glemp as he finally managed to make something from the Silver rank herb she had gotten for him. It was a potion he described as a haste potion. It would essentially allow the user to be faster for a short period of time, after which they would be slowed for a small time. It was very simple, but the way it worked was by time magic, which is what gave it its Silver rank. It seemed like something that Zalia wanted and so she was going to try to find more of the herb and convince Glemp to make her one. After talking about his discovery for some time, Zalia pestered him once more.

"It has been two weeks now, Glemp, are you sure we aren't ready to fight whatever that beast is that you want hunted?"

The small creature that was her friend eyed her. "No, yes. Maybe you are ready, yes. Up high, yes, in the mountains, a creature of flight. Bronze is its rank, yes, but near to Silver it must be. Very strong, very strong, yes, very," Glemp said, relenting finally.

"How would we get there?" Zalia asked.

"Glemp will lead you, yes."

"Why does it interest you? Why do you want us to hunt it?"

"Very good for alchemy, yes, much of its body. Various uses, many uses, yes. Ah, and it guards the slopes, the slopes that hold a plant more useful, yes," Glemp said, a gleam in their eyes.

"A plant? A herb? On the slopes of the mountain?" Zalia asked, eager now.

"Mmhmm, yes, yes," Glemp replied.

"Oh, I'm in and I'm sure my team will be too. Speaking of herbs, would I be able to get some more Flame-root?"

"If you can reach the root, you can have the root, yes. By the pools it grows."

If I can reach it, I can have it. Seems fair.

Her team was still outside, engaging in a hunt of their own. She thought it might be a good idea that they hunt some Ironfur rabbits by themselves to solidify their tracking skills.

Zalia left Glemp's workshop, making her way down the twisting paths, stairs, and tunnels of the mountain home of Those Born of Heat and Stone. She had to descend for quite some time, eventually reaching a tunnel that looked out onto the bubbling pits of magma near the bottom. The space was much wider here and had many paths crossing around and between the pits; the whole area was littered with the charcoal-like roots that Zalia knew to be Flame-root. Her Heat Resistance was being put fully to the test now and she was only able to stand the heat by the use of the second tier Heat and Cold Resistances, keeping herself and the air near her as cool as possible. She ran quickly into the room, using Preparation mixed with Stasis to harvest and store as much Flame-root as she could before she left the room once more, sweating profusely. She had to repeat the action twice more before she collected enough to last her a while. She went back to Glemp once she was done, thanking them and leaving to find her team once more.

Before long, she found their tracks and began following the path they had taken, tracking her team as they had tracked another creature not long before. She found her team, sneaking up on them as they sat hidden near the den of an Ironfur rabbit.

"What are we looking at?" she asked, whispering in Zen's ear.

"AH! F— *Zalia,*" Zen yelled, then hissed.

She watched Ember and Indis jump too; neither of them noticed her approach. She smiled, satisfied with her advancement in stealth.

"Hi," she whispered innocently back.

"Don't sneak up on us like that, especially when we're hunting," Zen hissed at her.

"Pay more attention to your surroundings," Zalia shot back quietly.

She saw Ember roll her eyes out of the corner of her vision.

"You guys do remember you don't have to stake out the entrances of these bunnies' dens, right? They're bloodthirsty little creatures," Zalia said.

"We know," Indis said.

"Then why are we just crouching here?" Zalia asked.

"You'll see," Lady Indis replied.

Indis said nothing more so Zalia just waited—being short of patience was not one of her failings, fortunately. She watched as one of the Seybears came sniffing into the clearing before the small Ironfur rabbit den, and suddenly a burst of eight rabbits came out of the den they were watching, along with two more entrances nearby. The Seybear was overwhelmed in short order, brutally pummelled by the Ironfur rabbits before being ripped apart and dragged into the dens, along with two rabbits that had been killed in the fight. Within a few minutes, the ground upon which the slaughter had taken place was once more covered by the light snowfall.

"Oh," Zalia whispered.

"I think this is the first den of young ones we've found," Ember whispered appreciatively. "It looks like they work together while they are younger before moving into their own dens later in life. Must be how they get to the rank they do."

"It is quite a smart tactic, and one I don't think we should mess with," Indis said quietly.

"Agreed," Zalia whispered back.

They moved slowly and silently away from the clearing, though it seemed they would have to go between the den entrances to fall prey to the tactic.

"Well, ignoring that horrific sight, I have some good news!" Zalia said to the others once they were much further away.

"News?" Zen asked excitedly.

"Glemp wants to lead us to the creature they want hunted. Looks like we might finally have something new to hunt!" Zalia said happily.

"That could be interesting," Ember said.

"Might be something we can bring back to Endelbyrn too," Indis added.

"Yaaaaay," Zen said unconvincingly.

Zalia knew the man missed his home and family, but he would have to get used to this kind of thing if he wanted to work for the Morning's Shade, so she didn't feel too bad. She explained quickly to the others what Glemp had told her as they went back to the mountain city to find Glemp. Those Born of Heat and Stone led them upwards for a long while, winding through tunnels and paths up into the mountain so far that the air even cooled down a bit. After a time, they exited onto the slopes, far, far above the forests below. She could see for hundreds of kilometres in every direction, the horizon lit up by the falling sun as the land below glittered, billions of snowflakes reflecting the day's last light.

"Oh wow, it's quite a view you guys have up here," Zalia said to Glemp as the others murmured their appreciation of the view as well.

"Yes, yes, but dangerous, very. Good luck, Zalia of the snow, in your hunt, yes," Glemp said, retreating back into the cave.

Zalia could already faintly see some of the creatures up in the sky, large winged beasts leaving a trail of soft snow in the air as they flew. They wouldn't be able to hunt one of those but if they went higher to find a nest, they might have some luck. The other alternative was to react when one of the creatures decided to hunt them.

They trekked for some time through the snowy mountainside, climbing higher to find one of the nests before Zalia spotted one of the creatures making a spiralling descent towards their location. She stopped the others with a waved hand, crouching down and watching the creature as she summoned her bow to her hand. Luckily, the creature was not going for them but some other creature nearby and they watched as it soon dove out of the sky. They quickly followed, tracking where the creature was landing with their eyes before it hit, and a cacophony of sound followed. They ran up and lay down, looking over the small ridge to see the battlefield beyond.

The first thing Zalia saw was the bird creature with large, feathered wings that shimmered with a blend of silvery-white and pale blue hues, resembling the colours of frosty clouds, its body sleek with similar colouring. The wings left the same frosty trail as when they were flying high up above, the now fading misty path it had taken still visible in the air. The creature had several razor-sharp talons that were dug into the second thing Zalia noticed. It held a large, streamlined feline creature with thick fur in patterns of grey and white. It had piercing silver eyes and slender, almost translucent shards protruding from its shoulders, back, and tail. Extending from the feline creature's large paws were sharp icy claws that it was using to strike back at the bird. Unfortunately for the feline creature, the bird had ambushed it and the fight was soon over.

The fortune of the bird wasn't much better as Zalia's team ambushed it in turn and the fight quickly began again. It started with Zalia firing off three silent arrows in quick succession, all three hitting the creature in the wing and crippling its flight. As it tried to leap back into the air, and failed, Zen ran down the short ridge towards it with shield and mace raised. Just behind him was Ember, keeping pace with a double-bladed sword and shield drawn. Next to Zalia, Indis started sparking as she channelled lightning through her body, while Zalia focused her healing on the woman to provide an extra boost as she channelled. Zalia managed to fire off one more poisoned shot; Hunter's Mark was already locked on and a Dodge-vine ritual completed on all her allies before Zen reached the creature. The large man finished the job of crippling the creature's wing as he smashed the thrice-pierced limb with a sickening crunching sound.

This was a Bronze rank creature, however, and it wasn't going to go down that easy. It let out a piercing howl that loosed a cone of frosty breath from its mouth, blowing over Zen and Ember as they held up their shields. They managed to block the breath but were both encased in a frosty prison. Zalia sprinted down the hilly ridge to the two front liners while Indis kept the creature busy by blasting it with a charged lightning bolt that slammed down from the sky above. In the brief pause Zalia had, she reached her allies and performed a Dodge-vine ritual, overlaid with Flame-root. The magic pressed into her two allies, melting ice and warming their bodies as she channelled Nature's Wrath. Her two summoned Elemental allies occupied the bird creature as Indis began channelling one of her now Bronze rank abilities, forming a storm above the creature. Zalia was slowly backing up, firing off more shots as Zen and Ember broke free of the remaining ice and went back on the offensive.

Multiple bolts of lightning now struck down from the storm above every few seconds, blasting against the creature with a sizzling sound and creating rancid smoke that filled the air, the smell a mix of ozone and burnt feathers. Zen drew the creature's attention; Zalia prepared a Manifest and Dodge-vine ritual around him from afar using his taunting shout. Just as the creature turned to Zen and struck, Ember slashed out, taking off one of its legs. While the creature's beak strike now managed to smash through Zalia's finished ritual, Zen absorbed the rest of the force with his shield, and deflected the strike. Zalia's two icy air Elementals struck at the sides of the creatures, but were blown away as the creature desperately flapped both its wings with pained cries, trying to escape the grasp of her spell. Zen and Ember weathered the strong wind by going to one knee and angling their shields against the gusts; Zalia was now far enough away to manage. The fight came to a loud resolution as the final and strongest lightning bolt came from the storm above, directly hitting the bird with a loud blast. Zalia put down her bow and let out a breath, puffing from the short but intense fight.

"Solid work everyone, any injuries?" Ember asked.

Zalia checked herself over, finding the light lacerations on her face from shrapnel quickly healing.

"All good," she called out, along with Zen and Indis.

They grouped up around the large sizzling bird, the creature mostly intact except for its head, which had been half destroyed by the last strike. Zalia began tying some rope to the creature but handed off the job to Zen when she heard a mewling sound. She walked over to the body of the large feline creature that the bird had killed and looked around, finding a very small version of the larger creature. A kitten.

"Aw, hey, little buddy," Zalia said soothingly, reaching out to pick up the small creature.

It hissed at her hand and Zalia hesitated but, making up her mind, reached out and picked it up, hugging it close to her chest. The little cat scratched at her armour but eventually calmed, pushing into the warmth of her body. She walked back over to the others, showing them.

"Look, guys, I found a friend," Zalia told them, smiling brightly.

"Oh gods no, of course you would," Zen said, pressing his hands to his face when he saw what Zalia was holding.

"Really, Zalia, you can't keep that," Indis said.

"Watch me," Zalia said, still smiling.

CHAPTER THIRTY-THREE

Little Boreal

Zalia

After the fight, they had trekked back to the cave entrance with Zen and Ember hauling the body of the creature between them. Zalia had used her abilities to harvest a good amount of a new plant she found on the way back. She assumed it was the herb that Glemp had told her about, and it being an Iron rank herb, she was able to identify it.

> **? - Iron rank - Use in a ritual to add an element of Air.**

She called the new herb 'Zephyr' and its description promptly changed to match her new name for it. They were now all gathered in Glemp's workshop, sitting around a table and watching as Zalia played with their new companion, dangling a length of string as a toy. What Zalia thought of as a small kitten was probably more along the size of a normal house cat. The reason she still thought of it as a kitten was because of its comically large paws, ones she knew it would grow into based on the size of the creature that had been its parent. She watched as the small kitten began wiggling, preparing to pounce. As it did, a light glow could be seen deep within the icy shards growing from its shoulders, back, and tail. The kitten leapt, landing on the piece of string and released a small blast of icy magic that froze the piece of string solid.

"That is some strong magic," Zalia said, praising the small kitten.

"You're really planning to keep the little murderer?" Zen asked.

"You're just upset it doesn't like you," Ember said, watching as Zalia flicked the string around the kitten, who now was laying on its back, paws flailing.

"I don't see why not," Zalia said.

"Maybe because it is going to grow into a giant creature built to hunt and kill," Indis said matter-of-factly.

"I still don't see the issue," Zalia replied.

"You won't be able to just keep that thing as a pet in any city I know of," Zen added.

Zalia only graced that point with a more pointed look.

"Yeah, yeah, I forgot you're basically as wild as this thing," Zen grumbled.

"I'll train it," Zalia said.

"You'll train it," Indis said disbelievingly.

"I will," Zalia said.

"And how will you accomplish that? Do tell," Indis said, still unconvinced.

"Mystic arts, generational knowledge, magic, skill, and most importantly, food," Zalia told her.

Ember snorted a laugh and Indis just shook her head, smiling despite herself.

"Oh, you can't be considering this, Lady Indis," Zen said, seeing the woman's smile.

"I don't think we can stop her, little Zen," she said, giving in.

"Little Zen!" he exclaimed in outrage.

"And look how cute it is!" Indis pointed at the furry kitten that was batting at the air as Zalia played with it.

"Its cuteness does speak for itself," Zalia said.

"Whatever, not like I have a say in this anyways," Zen said, finally giving in as well.

"That's the spirit!" Zalia said cheerfully.

The little creature was already Iron rank, most likely born that way. Zalia felt that if she did manage to train and raise the kitten, it could become a powerful ally.

"What should I name it?" she asked the group.

"I wouldn't even know where to begin," Ember said.

"What about 'Frosty'?" Zen said.

"Absolutely not," Zalia told him.

"You should think of a name if you're going to be training it, Zalia, not one of us," Indis said.

"Yeah, alright, I'll think about it. Do you all want to explore further up the mountain, or go further north next?" Zalia asked the group.

"I think we could have a search further up the mountain," Indis said.

"Sounds fine to me," Zalia said.

The first bird creature they killed was gifted to Glemp at the mountainside cave entrance. The goblin had shown them the path to the mountain now, so they could always go get another for themselves if they really wanted. Zalia really wanted to see what was higher on the mountain, somewhere even the people who lived here avoided due to the danger.

"Let's go then," she said as she stood up, grabbing the kitten.

The next week was spent exploring and climbing up the mountainside, getting further up each day before returning—they didn't quite feel safe enough to stay the night there.

During the week, Zalia added another activity to her routine. She began trying to teach the kitten various different commands using fresh catches as motivation. Her Teaching passive seemed to actually help in this regard, the kitten was picking things up quite quickly. After Ember had called the kitten her "Boreal buddy," Zalia had taken to the name, using it for her new friend. Boreal was an energetic little thing, bouncing around and barely sleeping a wink except for in the evenings, when it passed out for a few hours each day. Zalia discovered that Boreal did indeed have some impressive natural magics that it could use, the first being its ice magic. It could control the cold and snow to a small degree much like how Zalia could with her Iron rank Cold Resistance, maybe even from the same source as her. It also left small icy footprints wherever it walked, the reason for which Zalia didn't understand until she saw it walking outdoors. The natural effect made its tracks almost vanish into the ice and snow underfoot. Boreal also seemed to have some natural stealth magic similar to Zalia's, and was able to blend in with the surroundings scarily well. Zalia did wonder if its currently limited control over the ability was what caused the large bird creature to attack it and its parent, since it could appear almost invisible when it was active, even to Zalia. Zalia's study of the kitten allowed her team to properly react when they were first ambushed by one of the creatures, knowing of the icy magic it wielded and coming out on top in the fight.

Zalia experimented with the new herb she had found, finding many uses, from providing a wind-blocking barrier to masking her scent, to creating mild wind effects. Mixing the Zephyr in with any Flame-root ritual helped amplify the effects, fanning the flames.

Everyone eventually got along with little Boreal; Zen was the only one to get scratched by the kitten while Zalia was there. He wasn't very good with animals, Zalia surmised. Even Glemp didn't seem to mind having the murder kitten around, though they might not have even noticed with how focused they were on experimenting with the various bits and pieces of bird they cut out.

All of Zalia's and her team's skills got good use while they were exploring the mountainside, and Zalia had a feeling that Ember was getting closer to Bronze rank, with Zen and Indis not far behind. Zalia was trying to keep up, but it was bound to be harder since she'd reached Iron much later than the trio had. She checked her messages from the week over which they had hunted and caught quite a few of the bird and feline creatures.

Congratulations! Kill Shot has gained two levels, reaching Iron 7.
Congratulations! Hunter's Mark has gained two levels, reaching Iron 8.
Congratulations! Fight or Flight has gained two levels, reaching Iron 9.
Congratulations! Hunter's Sight has gained three levels, reaching Iron 8.
**Congratulations! Survivalist and associated skills
have gained three levels, reaching Iron 12.**
Congratulations! Hunter class has gained two levels, reaching Iron 7.
**Congratulations! Flora Identification has
gained three levels, reaching Iron 6.**
Congratulations! Preparation has gained three levels, reaching Iron 8.
Congratulations! Stasis has gained two levels, reaching Iron 6.
Congratulations! Harvester has gained three levels, reaching Iron 9.
Congratulations! Herbal Magic has gained three levels, reaching Iron 10.
Congratulations! Herbalist class has gained three levels, reaching Iron 6.
Congratulations! Nature's Wrath has gained two levels, reaching Iron 5.
**Congratulations! Protection of the Wilds has
gained three levels, reaching Iron 6.**
**Congratulations! Healing Presence has gained
three levels, reaching Iron 9.**
Congratulations! Druid class has gained two levels, reaching Iron 5.
**Congratulations! Aura Observation has gained
three levels, reaching Tin 14.**
**Congratulations! Low Light Vision has gained
five levels, reaching Tin 15.**
**Congratulations! Poison Resistance has
gained two levels, reaching Iron 7.**
Congratulations! Mobility has gained three levels, reaching Iron 13.
Congratulations! Teaching has gained four levels, reaching Iron 5.
**Congratulations! Bow - Weapon Proficiency has
gained four levels, reaching Iron 14.**
**Congratulations! Sword - Weapon Proficiency
has gained three levels, reaching Iron 5.**
**Congratulations! Throwing Knives - Weapon Proficiency
has gained four levels, reaching Tin 11.**

It was, all in all, some good progress, but definitely not enough to keep her caught up with the rest of the group. The constant hunting day in and day out was definitely an excellent way to quickly level all of her skills, though, especially with the variety of prey she was hunting.

During each hunt, she brought little Boreal with her. The kitten managed to hide during the fights while Zalia kept an eye on the small creature, but it was obviously wise enough not to interfere with such larger creatures fighting. Zalia also barely needed to sleep at this point, with Survivalist at Iron twelve now. She spent most of the time that the others were asleep interacting with the tiny, clawed menace.

Towards the end of the week, Zalia and her team made a discovery. Much further up the mountain they found a small cave within which was a familiar sight. It looked like a ritual, eerily familiar to the one that the expedition contract had found in the mines much further south. They walked in, looking around the blood-soaked ritual on the ground. Luckily, there was no rip in space like they had found in the other one.

"Oh what the hell," Zalia muttered.

"Yeah," Zen said.

It was extremely similar to the previous one they had found, though the time they had spent investigating it had been minor due to the Gold rank Elemental complications. This time around, the cave entrance was right there, but they still remained vigilant. Luckily, no tremors or extremely powerful Elementals appeared out of nowhere. Indis got out a small notebook and started sketching sigils and runes, drawing out the ritual.

"What do we do?" Zalia asked.

"We're going to have to go report this to the Morning's Shade," Ember said.

"It appears so," Indis agreed.

"Damn, I was really enjoying myself up here. We'll go immediately, then?" Zalia asked.

The two of them nodded.

"Finally, back to the warmth of civilisation," Zen said.

"Unfortunately," Zalia added.

They finished up investigating the ritual site before beginning the journey back down the mountain. Zalia collected as much of the herb from the mountain as she could; she was able to hold much more weight in her bag now that her body could support it. The spatial pocket from her Stasis ability was already stuffed with various herbs.

Upon reaching the cave entrance, Zalia informed Glemp of what they had found and how it might have something to do with the Elemental attacks that their people had been dealing with. This finally drew Glemp's attention away from their experiments, and the news caused the Born of Heat and Stone to move down the interior of the mountain to find their king, something Zalia was just now learning that they had. Zalia and her team, however, didn't wait for Glemp to come back, making their way out of the mountain and beginning the long journey back to Endelbyrn.

They travelled for three days before finally leaving the snow and as they travelled past the point Zalia had first encountered other humans, she remembered something from that time. During the battle that had taken place, a large earth Elemental had risen and fought both armies. Zalia had intervened, saving many lives but wondered what had caused that one to rise up. She realised it might mean there was another ritual that had happened nearby.

"Guys, guys, we should explore to the west a little," Zalia said, halting in her tracks.

"Why?" Indis asked.

"I saw a Gold rank Elemental here once," Zalia said.

"You did? Similar to the one we saw in the mine?" Zen asked.

"Quite similar, now that I think about it. It was in the middle of a fight between two armies but one side was losing, bad," Zalia explained. "Maybe they caused the Elemental to appear on purpose? I'm not certain of it, but it's a possibility, right?"

"Might be worth a look," Ember said.

The other two nodded slowly and Zalia led them to the west, where she remembered the rebel faction soldiers fleeing after the battle. She eventually found the remnants of a war camp. It looked like it had been torn down quite some time ago, though still recently enough for debris and dug-up earth to be visible. They searched through the soil and ashes for a little bit, finding nothing of interest before Zalia pulled out her map, looking for the nearest town.

"Every place I've seen those Gold rank Elementals, I've also seen one of the rituals. There must be one nearby somewhere," Zalia said, pointing to a location on her map. "There is a town just a half hours walk away, we might find something there."

"It's a long shot, Zalia, but if you really think there is something to be found then we can go," Indis said.

"It's not very far out of our way, why not?" Zen said in agreement as well.

Ember simply gave a nod and they were on their way once more. Little Boreal was making the journey half-wrapped around Zalia's neck and shoulders like a furry scarf. They made their way to the town quickly at a near run, though haste wouldn't necessarily help them. They arrived just as the sun was setting, walking around town for a short time before deciding to head to the nearest tavern. They couldn't see anything extremely obvious like an army or ritual site, and so decided to talk to some of the local people and see if they couldn't find something out.

Zek

Zek's life hadn't been going so well since he had decided to join the rebellion. They had recruited him, citing their need for spies and the importance of what they were doing for the kingdom. He had foolishly believed them, being a young man with some ideals about the world that he now knew to be naivety. They had assigned him to this tiny out-of-the-way town in the north end of the kingdom ever since; the only interesting thing to have happened was the big fight between the armies that had occurred and the follow-up chase he'd gone on. His commanding officer told him to follow that woman, find out who she was, and if the information he got was important enough, he would be promoted out of this shithole town. Well, she had caught him and sent him packing, now he was going to be in this place for the rest of his life. At least she hadn't killed him.

He was sitting in the tavern having a drink by himself and listening to the many conversations happening around the room, a normal activity to occupy his nights. He saw the doors swing open and a group of four entered, making for the closest empty table. Normally he wouldn't care about the newcomers, but the woman he saw with them made him freeze. It was the same cold-eyed, sharp-faced woman with the grey-and-white hair that he'd been sent after that first time. The only large difference he saw now was the equipment, rank, and most noticeably, the wild cat she appeared to have slung around her neck. He stared for a moment before quickly turning away, putting his head down.

Oh shit, oh shit, I gotta get out of here, Zek thought to himself.

He sat for a few more minutes, trying his best not to bring any attention to himself and listening to the group of four as best he could from where he sat. Before long, he stood and stretched, walking casually towards the door. The woman had been Tin rank when she'd caught him, and he was still Tin rank himself. She was now Iron rank and he definitely did not want to be anywhere near her; he had no idea if the woman would recognise him or not. He'd just reached the door, heart beating quickly, and was reaching for the handle when he heard footsteps behind him.

"You!" the woman said loudly, grabbing his shoulder and spinning him around.

"You," Zek said, scared.

Zalia

"You," the spy said in a scared tone.

"It's probably best you come sit down and we have a little chat," Zalia said, pushing the man, gently, to her table where Ember, Indis, and Zen all still sat.

"Zalia, who is this?" Indis asked between gritted teeth, obviously annoyed at Zalia's lack of tact in grabbing the man.

"This is an army spy and someone I once caught following me. I believe he owes me a favour," Zalia said brightly.

"Oh, of course," Zen said, the sentence muffled by his hands as they covered his face.

CHAPTER THIRTY-FOUR

A Nice Tavern Chat

Zalia

The tension at the table was palpable. Zalia's team was on edge, tense like a spring ready to shoot into action; Zen slightly less so, as his face was in his hands. This was most likely a result of the three-odd weeks spent in a frozen landscape filled with dangerous creatures. The spy, Zek, was an observant man and was currently surrounded by a group of people above his rank, ready for battle. The tension in the man was so high it was nearly visible, his muscles sometimes straining as if to escape bonds that were not there. Despite all this, Zalia was relaxed and casually leaning over in her chair. There was a long pause in the conversation as the man inspected them all, slowly relaxing as he realised he was not about to be assaulted. Zalia's team also relaxed as they realised the man wasn't about to make a huge scene, considering she had essentially abducted him from his day-to-day business.

"Sooo, what did you want?" the man asked, finally breaking the silence.

"You're in the army right?" Zalia asked.

"Not . . . specifically, no. I work *for* an army, but I'm not in one," the man replied.

"Right, exactly what I meant," Zalia replied to the man, before turning to Indis, "We could ask him about what we're looking for."

Zen finally took his face from his hands and looked like he was about to object before Indis spoke up.

"We could, but do you trust him whatsoever?" Indis asked.

"No, not really," Zalia admitted.

"Would he even know about what we're looking for?" Indis asked.

"I don't know, he might. I'm pretty sure he is a spy or something so knowing things is in the business," Zalia replied.

"Know what?" the man asked.

"That adds to the argument in not asking him about anything though," Ember added in.

"Well, sure, but if we don't, we could be walking around looking for a while, or just give up and not find anything at all. We could save time this way," Zalia argued.

"That is true," Indis said, looking thoughtful.

"We're not actually going to ask this army spy about this, are we?" Zen asked.

"Why not, he's technically on our side, is he not?" Zalia asked.

"You guys are rebels too?" the man whispered.

A hush fell over the table as they all stared at him.

"Oh, well maybe we aren't," Zalia said.

The man paled as he realised he had given himself away.

"We aren't on any side, Zalia, we're mercenaries hired to hunt monsters," Indis admonished her.

"Alright, well, I guess that means we aren't technically not on his side then, just neutral," Zalia said, a little questioningly.

"Kind of," Indis said.

"We've been hired by the kingdom he is fighting against, though," Zen said.

It was Indis's turn to put her face in her hands as Ember slapped Zen in the back of the head and Zalia groaned.

"Why, why would you say that in front of him?" Zalia asked.

"Whoops," Zen said sheepishly, rubbing the back of his head.

"I can pretend I never heard that," the spy volunteered, still looking a little pale.

"Stop being so scared, we aren't going to hurt you," Zalia said.

"Screw it, just ask him, then we can go home," Ember said.

"Oh go on, tell him our every little secret since Zen is going to anyways," Indis said, giving up.

"Excellent! Hey, spy man, know anything about any crazy blood rituals going on around here?" Zalia asked quietly.

"Crazy blood rituals?" the man asked suspiciously.

"Yeah, like, some kind of blood ritual with portals? Maybe portals that . . . might be affecting the Elementals somehow. Oh, and they might be corrupting people, turning them into blood-frenzied crazies," Zalia explained further.

"You're saying the king has performed a ritual here too!?" the man asked quietly but intensely.

"The king? What, no, not that I know of," Zalia said, confused.

"Oh good, worried me a little there," the man said, calming down.

"Why would you assume the king did it?" Zalia asked.

"That's the whole reason we're fighting this war, to stop the usurper king from dooming us all with the blood rituals he performs," he explained.

"Don't be crazy, it's not the king performing those rituals. Right?" Zalia said, asking the others for confirmation.

"We don't know who is," Indis said, looking a little disturbed.

Zalia calmed little Boreal, who had started waking from her nap, patting her on the head. She had determined the little feline was female, though she was an exotic animal, she was similar enough to most cat-like creatures that Zalia felt she had got it right. She took Boreal off her neck and put the feline on the table. Boreal yawned and stretched before looking around to inspect her loud, nap-hostile surroundings.

"Well, that doesn't matter at the moment. If you're unaware of any rituals being performed here we can pack up and move on," Zalia said.

"Unless the rebels are the ones who did it and the man is lying to us," Ember said.

Zalia sighed. "Yeah," she said grudgingly, "unless that."

"I'm not lying, I swear it," the man said quickly, looking disturbed as Boreal came and sat in front of him on the table, inspecting him with too-intelligent eyes.

"Yeah, but you're a spy with nefarious plans, we can't trust your words or your morals," Zalia said dramatically.

"I don't feel like you're taking this very seriously, Zalia," Zen said, also looking a little disturbed by Boreal.

"No," Zalia admitted, "I'm not very good at this kind of thing."

"You're really not," Zen said.

"Don't you start talking, spiller of secrets," Zalia retorted.

"Hey, I—" Zen started.

"How can we know you aren't lying?" Indis asked the spy, interrupting Zen and getting the conversation back on track.

Zen crossed his arms, simmering. Zalia stuck her tongue out at him before retrieving a little piece of meat from her bag, trying to get Boreal's attention.

"There's not much I can really say to convince you, other than . . . the thing you're talking about is exactly why an entire rebellion is fighting against the king's rule right now," the man said.

"That's pretty convincing," Ember pointed out.

Boreal crouched and started wiggling, getting ready to pounce as she noticed Zalia flicking a piece of meat around on the table.

"What do we . . . do then?" Indis said, glaring at Zalia as Boreal pounced across the table, landing with a puff of ice magic.

"I vote we go back to the Morning's Shade with what we know and let them deal with it," Zalia said, patting Boreal.

"Would be less of a headache than doing it ourselves," Ember agreed.

"We also don't know what has happened since we left, some of the other expeditions may have found something," Zen said.

"That is a good point," Indis agreed, sounding surprised.

"Alright, seems that is decided. What about this guy here?" Ember asked, pointing at the spy.

"He hasn't hurt anyone, we should just let him go," Zalia said.

"We should take him back with us. He might know something," Indis rebutted.

"Might. Or he might know nothing and we would be kidnapping a man for no reason whatsoever," Zalia argued, holding her ground.

"I vote we leave him too," Ember said.

Indis looked to Zen.

"I'm not getting involved," he said, holding his hands up in mock surrender.

"Alright, we let him go then," Indis said, sighing in annoyance.

"Settled, off you go, then," Zalia said to the man.

The spy hesitated for a moment. "If you ever find out the truth and want to fight back against the king, come and find me. I'm Zek," Zek said, before getting up and leaving the table.

"He seems pretty convinced," Zalia said once the man had left.

"He might well be right about the king being the cause of this," Indis said.

"That doesn't make any sense, though. Why would the king perform all those rituals, anger the Elementals, and then hire the entire Morning's Shade to deal with them and look into why it's happening," Zalia argued.

"So he can better hold off the rebellion as we deal with the Elementals instead of his army, plant information pointing to the rebellion as the cause, and then get our help with putting down the rebellion," Indis suggested.

Zalia paused for a moment. "Damn politics," she muttered, "you would know better than me and I guess that is possible. Have you ever met the king?"

"Once, when I was much younger. He didn't strike me as an evil man then but the minds of the young can easily be deceived," Indis said.

"Hmm," Zalia said, now entirely focused on Boreal as the feline jumped around, trying to catch her sleeve.

"Hey, Zen, want to get some drinks for us all?" Zalia asked.

"Not particularly," Zen said.

"Thanks!" Zalia said, handing him two silver coins.

Zen grumbled but stood, moving off to the bar.

"He's a good kid," Zalia said once he had moved away.

"Sure is," Ember agreed.

"What do we do if it's the king who's performing the rituals?" Zalia asked.

"What is the purpose of the Morning's Shade?" Indis asked back.

"I'm not actually entirely sure, but it seems to be to protect the people from whatever threatens them and get paid for doing it," Zalia said, thinking it over.

"That's pretty accurate to how it ends up but the purpose of the organisation is to protect the people no matter what. Payment is required so the people who do it can afford to live," Indis corrected.

"So, what is your point?" Zalia asked.

"My point, Zalia, is if it is the king who is performing these rituals that seem to involve a sacrifice, if it is the king who is disturbing the Elementals that are harming countless people across the lands, if it is the king who is lying to his people for some purpose beyond what is happening, then I don't see a way we do our job without having to take that man out from where he stands," Indis said, steel in her tone.

"Fair enough," Zalia replied, after a moment's pause.

Zalia considered Indis's words as she watched Boreal curl up in her lap and try to fall asleep once more. She would probably do what had to be done to stop the rituals from happening and Elementals from awakening. The Elementals themselves were a danger to most people's day-to-day lives, but they was also a danger to Those Born of Heat and Stone in the mountains and definitely a danger to those in Zalia's line of work. That was reason enough for her to do what she could to help stop the king if it came to it. They still didn't know what the rituals were meant to achieve but it couldn't be anything good.

Zen came back with a round of drinks and they spent the night chatting idly before sleeping in a few rented rooms. Tomorrow, they would worry about what was to come.

The next morning they woke up early and left, no training and no wasting of time, as they needed to get back to Endelbyrn as quickly as possible. They had acquired a few key alchemical ingredients that Glemp had pointed out to them from kills they'd made up north, along with all the various herbs that Zalia had collected. Zalia had tried to draw out a map of the surrounding area but even with her increased dexterity and mental stats, failed miserably at the task. Ember had stopped her on the second day and had taken over, drawing up a passable map of the area. That, plus the new information they were bringing back about the ritual high up in the mountain should have been enough for the Morning's Shade to consider their time up north well spent.

They travelled light and quick, sleeping less, only hunting when absolutely necessary, and not taking time out of the day for training, towns, or any other distraction along the way. It took them two days less than the expected week and five days to finally reach the city of Endelbyrn. When they arrived at the keep that hosted the Morning's Shade, they found activity had kicked up while they were gone. Many more groups and people than they were used to seeing around the grounds were going on about their own separate business, many hurried. There was also a much larger percentage of higher-ranked individuals, though many couldn't be specifically distinguished due to some aura-masking abilities they must've had.

"What is happening here?" Zalia asked in wonder.

"Seems something has happened," Indis said.

"Or is happening," Ember added.

They quickly went up through the confusing stairs and walkways of the keep to find one of the leaders they were used to communicating with. They found the Hidden in his office.

"Hidey! How are you?" Zalia asked as she entered.

Zen groaned at Zalia's use of her nickname for the shade.

"Wonderful, on such a sunny day," Hidey said, smiling.

"You like the sun? But you're a shade," Zalia said in mock confusion.

"We have news," Indis said, interrupting Zalia's stream of inane babble.

"I'd love to hear it," Hidey said, watching the feline creature on Zalia's shoulders. It was half hidden by its magic, and currently playing with strands of Zalia's hair, batting at some and chewing on others.

Indis went on to describe their findings in the north, the mountain, and the ritual, as well as giving a shortened version of their conversation with the spy they found in the tavern. She did leave out the information Zen had given away, and the slightly unprofessional manner in which they had conducted themselves. She also mentioned the peoples Born of Heat and Stone but didn't expand on the relationship, their strength or numbers, simply noting their existence.

"That is some news, indeed," Hidey said, raising a hand to his face as if in deep thought.

"What has happened since we left?" Zalia asked.

"Oh! Of course you would not know," Hidey said distractedly as Boreal jumped to the floor and began inspecting the room. "What is that creature?" he asked, instead of elaborating.

"That's Boreal, my new companion," Zalia said simply.

"Right, right. Well, essentially, you are not the first group to come back with news of more ritual sites found. Many more have been discovered by groups that have been sent out to deal with issues related to Elementals within the lands across the kingdom. Many of these rituals have taken place within infrastructure key to the continued efficiency of the army, as if done to purposely awaken Elementals as an act of sabotage. It is also noted that none have been found outside of the kingdom's borders," he added.

Indis turned to Zalia, raising an eyebrow as if to say, "See, I told you."

"And who do you think is doing it?" Zalia asked.

"The obvious perpetrator would be the rebellion, as for the most part, none of the rituals have taken place in locations that would endanger civilians of the kingdom. The mine that you were sent to was a large producer of iron that House Darial sold to the kingdom and was used to properly arm the kingdom's armies, for instance. I, however, don't think it is them," Hidey replied.

"As I said, the rebellion seems to blame the king for the rituals," Indis said.

"Yes, though I can't see it being the king either. Purposely sabotaging his own army's infrastructure just to get us involved with the war when he could just fight the war outright instead as he suggested? No, I think there is something larger at play," Hidey said.

"Well who else could be responsible?" Zen asked.

"Honestly, I do—" Hidey started before he was interrupted by Boreal climbing up a bookshelf at the back of the room and pulling a section of books off as she fell. The books clattered to the floor with the feline as Zalia rushed over to clean up the mess.

"Sorry," Zalia said, a little sheepish.

"No need to worry. As I was saying, I really don't know who else could be responsible. It seems way too convoluted of a plot for the king to be using to gain our support in the war when they were initially stronger to begin with. It would be over faster with our support, to be sure, but the cleanup afterwards wouldn't be worth it. The rebellion using the very rituals they accuse the king of using to destabilise the kingdom's army doesn't seem likely either, though maybe a smaller faction amongst them is responsible," Hidey continued.

"We need to know more then. Do we know the purpose of the rituals yet?" Zalia asked.

"Ah, yes, I do believe we have ascertained their purpose. They are meant to either open a portal of some kind to Cormaine or . . . possibly summon something through. However, they are either sabotaging it on purpose, or simply have not yet discovered the correct method of application. Each ritual has only had the result of either causing an Elemental awakening or driving the practitioner mad. That is as much as we know," Hidey explained.

"Well . . . what next?" Ember asked.

"In that, your timing is excellent. Come with me," Hidey said, standing from his chair.

CHAPTER THIRTY-FIVE

A Few Little Mysteries

Zalia

Zalia scooped up Boreal as they left the room.

"Where are we going?" she asked.

"We believe that whoever is performing the rituals is not choosing the locations idly. The additional location you reported to us may prove vital in deciphering what exactly is going on," Hidey explained.

"Do you think they are performing some sort of wider scale ritual, based on the placement of all these smaller ones?" Indis asked.

"Possibly, we shall see," Hidey replied.

They walked for a short time through the keep before arriving in a large room with not a small number of people walking around. Centred in the room was a large map of the kingdom with small red pins placed in several locations near to Endelbyrn, the old mine being one of them. The ritual sites found so far were in two small arcs, one smaller than the other, with a few in between the two ranging about as far out as the mine. Hidey added a small pin on the mountain where their team had found the ritual, and it fit into the pattern, though it was much further out than any other discovered site. The broader arc of pins would connect the mine to the mountain of Those Born of Heat and Stone, and if it continued, it'd make a large circle with the kingdom's capital at the centre. The second arc would fit within the larger one, with the kingdom's capital also at its centre if a full circle were drawn through it. Not all of the pins were located within the two arcs' paths, some were dotted in between and within the two outlined circles. The majority of what they had discovered was relatively close to Endelbyrn, with Zalia's team's pin being the furthest out.

"So, it has something to do with the capital?" Zalia asked.

"What makes you say that?" Zen asked.

"If you continue the pattern, it forms two circles both centred around the capital," Zalia pointed out.

"Yes, that was my thinking as well," Hidey said.

"Is a ritual on that scale even possible?" Zalia asked.

"I'm not sure . . . I've never seen something like it. Whoever is doing it seems to think it is possible, however, and that's reason enough to try to stop it," Hidey replied, looking deep in thought.

"So what do we do?" Zen asked.

"Until we know more, we stop it," Hidey said simply.

"How do we do that?" Ember asked, frowning.

"Well, we destroy the ritual sites as a start, though I do not know if it will stop what is coming or not," Hidey explained, looking just a little worried.

"I guess it's a start," Ember said, still frowning.

Boreal

Boreal watched the other two-legged ones from her perch on the warm one's shoulders. They were making sounds at each other, some form of communication, she had discovered. She'd started to understand some of the sounds the two-legged ones made but was entirely uninterested in the current goings on. She decided to take things into her own paws, hopping off the warm one's shoulders and walking innocently around, inspecting the room as the warm one watched her. Once the warm one was making sounds at the others and distracted, Boreal began sneaking from the room. The familiar feeling of her power activating flowed through her as she left the room, inspecting each direction before choosing to go left.

Boreal travelled for a few minutes in the winding stone corridors of the strange spiky mountain, examining each doorway as she passed and looking for something fun to do. A flash of feathers and talons passed through her mind as she remembered the last time she'd gone wandering. Her fur began settling as the memory faded once more; this time it would go differently. The warm one was a good leader and a strong hunter, there was much she could learn from such a hunter who was always well fed, but the warm one also tended to spend time in the most boring situations and that didn't interest Boreal. No, she was more interested in what secrets she could find in the winding tunnels of this spiky mountain.

Eventually, Boreal happened upon a room that smelled quite interesting indeed. Within, she found some more of the two-legged ones standing throughout a large room, doing some sort of ritual with their food. Boreal had not seen fire until the warm one had found her but she now knew that the two-legged ones often performed a ritual of fire before eating their kill. It seemed strange and inefficient to Boreal, but she was young, so maybe the two-legged ones knew something she did not. She snuck up a stack of small boxes onto the long bench the two-legged ones were performing their ritual at. They did not look like they would be able to run very fast, and so she struck. Boreal grabbed a large chunk of meat with her teeth and sprinted from the room as yells and clattering noises erupted, the two-legged ones throwing some hard objects and sounds at her as she fled.

Boreal quickly made her way back to where she had left the warm one, holding her prize as she padded through the winding halls.

Zalia

A few minutes of conversation passed as they came up with theories and ideas as to what was happening in the lands, but each was quickly shut down. It was quite obvious that they would need to find out more before they could come to any conclusion. Zalia had begun zoning out of the conversation, her mind idly floating away as she couldn't focus on the theories and ideas any more. It was at this point she realised she didn't know where Boreal was. She quickly looked through the room and found the small feline finishing off some kind of meat.

What? she thought.

She walked over to Boreal, Ember glancing her way before focusing back on the conversation.

"What have you been up to?" Zalia asked Boreal before picking up the small feline and receiving a mew of protest in response.

She walked back to the table holding Boreal in her arms as it seemed the others finally came to the same conclusion she had.

"So what do you want us to do?" Zalia asked Hidey directly.

"Want us destroying some ritual sites?" Zen asked.

"Mmm, no. I believe the ritual sites are too dangerous for you to visit without the help of a Gold ranker, considering each manifestation of Elementals around a site has been of that rank. At that point, we may as well just send the Gold ranker and you would only get in the way," Hidey said, looking thoughtful as ever.

"Where do you want us then?" Indis asked.

"I thought you might actually go back and contact that spy you spoke to. I would be interested to know what the rebellion knows about the rituals, if anything," Hidey replied.

"We could do that . . . I guess," Indis said, looking a little worried.

"Concerns?" Hidey asked.

"Well . . . isn't that kind of a risky thing to do? I mean, there is a war going on and we're working for the people who are at war with the rebellion," Indis said quickly.

"Indeed, but just because the kingdom is paying us to look into the Elementals does not mean we work for them. We work with them, and if they are the ones responsible then they will be ones facing the consequences. Yes, for now, go and contact the spy once more and see if you can't set up a meeting with someone higher up. Be discreet about it, but also be careful. You have full discretion to call the whole thing off if you ever think that you are at risk of serious harm. Understood?" Hidey said, finished.

"Understood," Indis said, still looking a little unconvinced.

They began to leave the room when Hidey called out, "Zalia, a moment."

"Yeah?" Zalia asked once the others had left.

"Be careful with that little one you have adopted, keep it safe," Hidey said, looking at tiny Boreal.

"I will, don't worry," she replied, smiling.

"Juniper contacted me about Darren, said you knew what had happened to him," Hidey said.

"I know what has happened, yes," Zalia said, looking unhappy.

"I have a small amount of sway with a few key people in the army and have organised for him to be kept on inner territory patrols for a while. Hopefully, that will keep him out of danger for some time, enough time for this damned war to be over. Let Juniper know on your way back, would you?" Hidey asked, a mixture of emotions very visible on his face and in his posture.

"I will," Zalia said.

"Thank you, now be quick, there is much to be about," Hidey said, waving at Zalia in an imperious and dismissive way.

She rolled her eyes. "Oh, just had a thought. Could you perhaps have a look into someone called Vidar? He was a captain in the army that one of my friends knew. We found out he was corrupted. Something might come up," she asked.

"I can, I'll let you know if I find anything," Hidey said.

"Thanks," she said.

Zalia left the room, finding the rest of her team waiting for her in the hallway.

"Everything good?" Ember asked.

"All good," Zalia replied.

"What now?" Zen asked.

"We go to that town again and find the spy, though I need to drop by Juniper's farm on the way," Zalia said.

"Can we have a day or two to see our families?" Zen asked, almost pleading.

"Don't see why not," Zalia said, looking to Indis.

"It would be nice, though I have only a cousin in this city," Indis said.

"Alright, we'll wait a day or two, then. See you all around," Zalia said, walking off as she scratched Boreal's head.

She heard quick footsteps behind her before Ember caught up.

"Mind if I come along with you?" Ember asked.

"Sure," Zalia replied.

She inspected the woman closely for any emotion, but it was like reading a book that had been glued shut. She had thought that maybe Ember had family in the city, but the fact that she wanted to spend the day or two with her, rather than family, meant they were either estranged or not around.

They walked for some time in silence before Zalia spoke up. "Why did you join the Morning's Shade? I kind of understand why Lady Indis and Zen are here but I can't figure you out."

Ember inspected her for a long moment as they walked before replying. "Someone has to step up first and help others."

"Is that the only reason?" Zalia said, trying to pry further.

Ember paused for another moment. "I . . . I had a tough life growing up, and there were many times that my life could have turned around if someone had just stepped up and helped," she said, unsteadily at first.

Zalia stayed silent, waiting.

"And then someone did, and my life did turn around, so now . . . Well, someone has to step up first and help others," Ember said, finishing off with a shrug.

"It makes sense to me," Zalia said, finally.

"And you? I can't figure out what your deal is either," Ember said.

"I don't know, to be honest. I came here to learn about magic but I seem to be fine figuring it out on my own with a little help here and there. Then I got swept up into whatever this politics and ritual nonsense is, and I don't really have anything else in this world so . . . I'm just going along, for now. It seems like I could do some good for a whole lot of people by helping with this," Zalia replied, feeling oddly comfortable talking with Ember.

Zalia sighed before continuing. "That isn't the main reason I'm here, but it's as good as any to finish whatever this is that I'm already involved with. Sometimes I think about just going back to the wilderness, but I'm not sure I could live with myself if I walked away and something terrible happened that I could have stopped. As much as I hate dealing with all of it, I feel I'll hate what happens if I ignore it more. Then, once this is all done and dealt with, and my year of service is done, I'm going to use as many Morning's Shade resources as I can to go explore the wild places of the world," Zalia finished, smiling at the thought of wandering the world, just her and Boreal.

"Sounds nice," Ember said.

"Doesn't it?" Zalia agreed.

They walked for some more time in silence before ending up in the park that Zalia had once spent a few nights sleeping in. They trained for a time before Zalia called a halt.

"So, what do you usually do when we aren't on a contract?" Ember asked.

Zalia shrugged. "Hunt, train, and train some more. I don't really have any other hobbies; have something in mind?" Zalia asked.

"Yeah, I actually do," Ember said, before taking off at a jog.

They ran through the city, soon arriving at the entrance gate and passing into the small plains beyond. Ember picked up the pace and Zalia matched her speed, the two of them began sprinting across the land.

They ran for a time before Ember slowed down, puffing. They then walked for some time before taking off at a run once more, alternating the pattern until arriving at a small farmstead near Endelbyrn. Zalia watched as Ember walked up to the door and knocked, the door opening as the people inside greeted Ember with open arms and wide smiles. The farmer couple took Ember around the side of the house, with Zalia following, to a small pen holding some of the animals she recognised as the cow-like creatures. They led Ember to one that had trouble walking and Ember healed the creature. The couple tried to give Ember a few coins, but she refused and walked back over to Zalia, gesturing to the road once more.

"Shall we?" Ember asked.

Zalia nodded and they took off down the road once more, running ever onwards.

They stopped off at two more farms, a small town, and a way stop at a cross-roads. Each time they stopped, Ember was greeted as if she were a close friend or family member and then led to an animal or person. Not all of them had injuries, but those that did didn't hesitate when they saw Ember. Zalia was a little bit in awe as the woman refused any coin or token of gratitude, simply healing whoever or whatever needed it and moving on once more.

"Is this what you do with your spare time?" Zalia asked.

"Sometimes," Ember replied.

"I'd ask why but I think I know what you'll say," Zalia said with a chuckle.

Ember smiled. "I thought I would show you what I meant. These people can't afford a healer, they aren't rich or powerful. Many reach a high level through the hunting of monsters and beasts, but these are simple farmers and merchants, they level much slower than we do and will take a long time to reach Bronze rank, if even that. I can spend a single day of my time and heal animals that might have struggled for months, or people that would have been out of work for weeks due to injury, and all it costs me is a little time," Ember explained.

"I understand why you do it," Zalia said.

"I'm glad," Ember said, smiling.

They continued for some more time, stopping off at a few other places as they ran in a loop back to Endelbyrn. When they arrived Zalia was actually quite exhausted, Ember looking similarly so. Zalia had tried to get Boreal to run beside them, but the poor feline had only lasted a short time before becoming exhausted and passing out, needing to be carried. It was getting dark as they stood before the city gates.

"I usually make a few days' trip out of it, walking the roads slowly, but I thought I would make it into some Mobility training as well. To keep you from dying of boredom, of course," Ember said, looking amused.

"Ha ha, funny. In all seriousness though, I appreciate you showing this to me. I think I understand you just a little bit better now," Zalia said.

"Of course, you did strike me as someone who would understand why I am doing it," Ember replied.

"I do, yes. Now if you don't mind, I'm going to go to the forest and pass out in a tree or something," Zalia said.

"Naturally," Ember said, laughing.

They went their separate ways as Ember reentered the city and Zalia went back to her small log cabin home in the forest nearby. She fell asleep curled up around Boreal, thinking about the day's events. The increasingly mysterious rituals and Elementals all around the kingdom, disrupting people's lives and sometimes even ending them. It was at odds with the thought of Ember running through the lands, healing and helping for one simple reason: if she didn't do it, who would?

The thought that maybe there were other people out there like Ember helped Zalia relax as she drifted off.

CHAPTER THIRTY-SIX

Ever More Twisted

Zalia

Zalia only needed to sleep for a short time, just a few hours, before she woke up feeling refreshed. Her Survivalist skill had really cut down on the amount of hours she needed to sleep each day, and she was sure it wouldn't be long until she could go days without. At this point she rarely needed to eat anymore, though she still could eat as much as normal if she so wished.

Boreal audibly protested as Zalia got up and began her usual morning routine, practicing sword work, then throwing dagger practice followed by archery practice—a new addition now that her other skills were catching up—and finally, finishing with a long run through the woods. Returning from her run, she practiced each of her weapon proficiencies once more before she was ready for the day. She poked and prodded Boreal until the small feline woke up and started moving around. She noticed that Boreal wasn't looking so small anymore, having grown a good amount since Zalia had found her. She wasn't anywhere near what Zalia thought fully grown was but was still definitely looking more like a larger predator than a house cat with too-large paws. She tried training Boreal a little, but the feline wasn't interested in the cured meat Zalia was using as motivation. Zalia sighed before searching the immediate area for some smaller tracks, hoping to find something that Boreal could hunt. She quickly found the tracks she knew to be from the small reptilian creature she had often hunted in the woods and got Boreal's attention before pointing to the tracks. The feline looked confusedly at Zalia for a moment before seeming to understand and leaning down to sniff where she had pointed.

Hunting seemed more like a natural instinct to Boreal than something that needed to be learnt, but still Zalia had to stop her and point her in the right direction. Zalia was a little surprised that Boreal had caught on to what she was trying to do so quickly, but knew from the past few weeks that the feline was actually significantly more intelligent than she'd expected. Eventually, Boreal found the creature they were looking for and stealthily moved towards it. It appeared that she was much more motivated by a hunt and a fresh kill than she was by cured meat that had been sitting in Zalia's backpack for a few days. Boreal crept up before pouncing on the reptilian creature, a wave of icy magic spreading through it before Boreal struggled with the half-frozen creature for a bit. The struggle came to an end when Boreal latched onto its neck, securing the kill. With the level of her Low Light Vision passive, Zalia barely had any trouble seeing by the light of the stars anymore, and it definitely seemed to her that Boreal had a natural ability to see in the darkness as well.

Boreal walked up to Zalia and dropped the fresh kill at her feet, surprising Zalia once more with her intelligence. She considered trying to train Boreal some more with the fresh kill but felt a little weird about teaching such an intelligent creature like it was a dog. She felt that if she treated Boreal more like a companion than a pet, she would get further towards mutual understanding. As such, Zalia simply used Preparation on the creature, slicing it into nicely sized sections for Boreal. Her companion hastily ate up the fresh kill, Zalia standing nearby lost in thought as she waited.

The sun was close to coming up at this point, and Zalia decided to make her way into the city. She arrived at the gates and noticed a group of five well-armed people leaving the city. As she got closer she recognised one of them as Larel, the Silver-turned-Gold rank who had led the expedition to the mine. She assumed the other people in the group were most likely Gold rank as well, though her ability didn't inform her of any ranks besides Larel's. She gave the woman a nod as they passed each other, with Larel nodding back, before Zalia scooped up Boreal and entered the city proper, making her way towards the keep. It seemed like Hidey was acting quite quickly in sending out a group of higher-rank people to take care of the existing ritual sites. Although now that she thought about it, those people were most likely fully fledged members of the Morning's Shade and had decided along with the others how, when, and who would be going to complete this particular objective. She walked around in the city for a while before deciding to go and take up guard duty if she could, just to get it out of the way for the day. It felt like she had so much more time within a day when she only needed to sleep for a few hours, and realistically thinking, she did.

Zalia was quite sure that Zen would at least want to stay for this day too, and so decided that it was best she find Ember once more, after guard duty. So when guard duty was completed, with Boreal having been wrapped around her neck like a scarf for half of it, she heading off to find Ember. She wasn't quite sure where Ember stayed, but the sun was now up and morning had definitively begun. Ember was the one to usually wake up the earliest, except for Zalia of course, so she felt she had a good chance of finding the woman walking around somewhere. It took a half hour but Zalia eventually found Ember eating in one of the food halls within the spires.

"Morning," Zalia said in greeting.

"Sure is," Ember replied as Zalia sat down across from her.

"Want to go on a town tour again soon? I think we should find the others tonight and leave tomorrow morning, so that leaves most of the day," Zalia asked.

"Sounds good to me," Ember replied.

Zalia sat in silence for a while, petting Boreal as Ember finished off her breakfast.

"Let's go," Ember said, standing and moving to leave the room.

Zalia followed and the three of them left the city once more. The majority of the day passed the same as it had on the previous day, with Ember, Boreal, and Zalia running through the lands, healing people as they went. Zalia actually joined in with her own healing abilities this time, the two of them taking turns as they travelled. It was an oddly cathartic experience, a very simple activity, passing through various places as they healed any in need simply because they were in need. After a time, they found themselves back at Endelbyrn again and returned to the keep. It was getting late in the day, so they started sparring near the gate to the spires, keeping an eye out for Indis and Zen. The two days of running through the wilds and towns nearby Endelbyrn had actually gotten Zalia two levels in Mobility and three in Healing Presence.

They sparred for a little while before Indis showed up. They pulled her aside once they noticed her, then waited for Zen, the man arriving through the gate about forty-five minutes later. They organised to meet there the next morning and then each went off about their own business. Zalia once more found herself with nothing to do but train, so train she did.

The next morning they met as organised and all moved off into the wilderness, making their way in the direction of Juniper's farm. During the travel to the farm they fell into their now familiar patterns as they hunted, trained, and travelled, often talking into the night over a campfire easily tended by Zalia's skills. Before long, they were travelling along the road past Juniper's farm, Zalia telling the others to continue on while she quickly ran up a side path to talk to Juniper. She had asked the others if it was okay that she talk to Juniper alone this time. She found the woman quietly gardening in the small patch near the house, a sad expression on her face. She quickly walked up and greeted the old woman with a light hug before delivering the news that Hidey had asked her to deliver about Darren. The news seemed to bring some weight off the woman's shoulders, and the sad expression faded just a little.

"Hey, before I go, I've been wondering—why is it that our mutual friend and shade keeps his real name hidden?" Zalia asked, once the news had been delivered.

"It is not something many know, though it isn't necessarily a secret. But a shade can be controlled if the wrong person knows their true name. As far as I know, only Zayes ever knew his true name, it partly being the reason he was able to bring sentience to our dear friend," Juniper explained.

Zalia frowned, a theory and concern shaping in her mind. "What happened to Zayes, Juniper?"

"I . . . I don't know. He had this home built for us, he wanted to retire and never really wanted to live with great prosperity and fame. This was meant to be our retreat from the wider world, and for a time it was. One day he told me he needed to finish off one last piece of business before he was done with the Morning's Shade for good and . . . and he never came back. I asked everyone I could about what they knew but nobody seemed to know what had happened to him. I've lived without closure ever since, though Darren has brought me much joy," Juniper said, the sad expression returning in full to her face.

"I'm sorry for what you've been through, and I hope the news I've brought can bring you some comfort. Hopefully the war will soon end, as it seems the king is trying to bring about peace, and you can have your son back," Zalia said, trying her best to console the older woman.

"It does bring me a measure of comfort, dear, and I do appreciate your help. Now go, I see you are in a rush, so don't let an old lady hold you up any longer," Juniper said, giving Zalia a light but weak smile.

She returned the smile before turning and running back down the path to catch up to her team.

It wasn't long before Zalia caught back up with the others as they trod down the path.

"Is all well?" Indis asked.

"Maybe. I need to think a bit longer about it," Zalia said.

"Alright," Indis replied, inspecting Zalia a bit before turning back to the road.

Zalia thought about what Juniper had told her. The manner in which Hidey had always hidden his real name had struck her as odd, but now she realised there was a deeper motive behind it. It also meant that it was possible someone was able to control Hidey's actions, and that scared her a little. The shade had always seemed trustworthy to her but if someone else was able to control him, then she was not sure he could be fully trusted. Juniper seemed sure that the only person to ever know Hidey's true name had been Zayes, but she also didn't know what had happened to her husband in the final days of his life, or if he even was dead and gone. She considered telling the others right then and there but decided against it, wanting to let the full meaning of what she had just learnt sink in before she acted.

* * *

They travelled for a few more days and Zalia became more and more sure that she should tell the others what she had learnt. Just before they reached the little town that they had last met the spy in, she spoke up.

"Hey, guys?" Zalia said, still a little unsure.

"Yeah?" Ember said questioningly.

She explained what she had learnt and knew about the whole situation involving Hidey, his name and what it could mean. The others listened intently and as she finished, Indis let out a deep sigh.

"Oh damn, that complicates things. Best case scenario?" Indis asked.

"Best case, Hidey doesn't tell anyone about this weakness because he doesn't want people searching for his true name, and he also doesn't want people distrusting him like we are doing right now," Zalia said.

"Worst case?" Indis asked.

"Worst case, he is being controlled by somebody, might have something to do with all these rituals, and could be under the control of whoever is orchestrating the entire thing," Zalia said worriedly.

"Alright," Indis said.

"What do we do?" Zen asked, voice filled with concern.

"What do we do?" Zalia echoed questioningly, looking at the others.

"I don't know," Ember said.

Indis took a deep breath. "Simple, we prepare for the worst and hope for the best. I believe we should still learn what we can from the rebels but we should treat anything we have learnt from Hidey—the Hidden, as possibly untruthful or misleading," Indis said.

"Simple," Zen muttered.

"Alright, we can do that. Sure as hell makes this even more complicated," Zalia said.

"What is hell?" Zen asked.

"It's kind of like . . . just don't worry about it," Zalia briefly tried to explain, but gave up.

"Bloody people," she added in a mutter.

They walked in silence to the town, each of them deep in their own thoughts and worries, considering what to do. Zalia wasn't really sure what it meant or if she was just totally overreacting, but the others seemed to be in agreement. Had what the shade told her about Cormaine and the purpose of the rituals even been the truth? Questions floated around her mind as she went over each and every conversation she'd ever had with the shade, picking at everything he had said. The conversations she remembered at least.

They arrived at the town, still in silence before realising that they hadn't even talked about what to do once they did arrive.

"Should we just go to the tavern?" Zalia asked.

"Seems like a good place to start," Indis said.

They went to the tavern they had been at last time and entered, taking a seat near one of the walls. Looking around the room, Zalia couldn't see the man, but they decided to wait for some time anyways. It was midday, after all, and the man must have other responsibilities other than sitting in a tavern listening to the locals.

They waited for a few hours before the man finally entered. He immediately saw them and rather than being concerned, actually walked over to them all on his own. He seemed to be significantly more confident and less scared then the last time they met him.

"Well, what a wonderful day!" he said enthusiastically.

Zalia gave him an odd look.

"We have been sent to . . . learn a little bit from you and your people," Indis said, ignoring social niceties, something Zalia found to be very unlike her.

The spy gave a short nod, looking around the table.

"I'm not entirely sure I can trust you lot, especially after you mentioned you were working for the kingdom last time," he finally said.

"It's hard to argue with that," Zalia said, giving a glare to Zen who was looking a little sheepish.

"But, and this information comes free, we do happen to be struggling a little in the war and the help of the Morning's Shade would definitely turn the tides. Take that as a token of our goodwill," the man said.

"Though you could be lying about that in an effort to plant the idea that the rebellion is weaker than it actually is," Indis pointed out.

The man just smiled. Zalia was quite confused with how he was acting; it was as if he was a completely different man than who he'd been the last time they were here.

"And I suppose we need to provide a token of our goodwill?" Indis continued after the spy didn't speak.

"I'm glad you asked," he said, smiling brightly.

"You have something in mind?" Zalia asked.

"Indeed I do, a little problem that I could really use your help with," he said.

"Go on," Zalia said, narrowing her eyes a little. *This is getting more and more suspicious by the second.*

CHAPTER THIRTY-SEVEN

Puzzle Pieces

Zalia

Zalia and her team followed the spy as he walked, heading towards the eastern edge of town. Zalia glanced over at the others, hoping they had also noticed the strange behaviour of the man, and Indis caught her gaze, giving a small nod. Zalia gestured towards the west with her hand, a silent question to ask whether they should leave or not. Indis shook her head, indicating that she thought they weren't in danger just yet. Zalia looked back towards the man walking in front of them.

"So where exactly are we going?" Zalia asked.

"To meet one of my colleagues," the man answered.

They didn't speak any further as they walked, eventually arriving at a small house on the outskirts of the town. The man knocked once, then paused, then knocked twice more. They heard footsteps, then the sound of a deadbolt unlatching, and the door swung open. Standing before them was a large humanoid covered in thick fur wearing simple clothes and equipped with a large boar spear. They stood at around seven feet tall, and ducked their head to see through the doorway as they looked at each member of the group in turn, stepping out of the doorway once their gaze fell on the man leading them. Zalia stared at the creature, wondering what or who they were. They didn't seem like a beast, more like an intelligent creature, another race maybe? The only other race she had seen had been the Born of Heat and Stone, and she was definitely excited to meet another. By the 'extensive' research she had conducted with a grand total of one other race, they seemed to be much more welcoming than humans generally were.

As the large person stepped aside, the man leading them began to lead them all inside. Zalia hesitated, looking to Indis's guidance, following when the woman gave a small nod of approval. She trusted the other woman's insight when it came to people much more than she trusted her own. They followed the man into the small house and immediately went up a flight of stairs into a small but comfortable room, the furry person staying behind. The room was well-appointed with nice-looking chairs and other decorations that were soft on the eyes. The room lit up when the man waved at the walls, the flameless lights similar to the ones in the keep at Endelbyrn coming to life. The man sat down with a sigh, and then something that Zalia considered incredibly strange happened. The man's face shifted and warped, turning into the face of a different man. Indis sat down nearby, completely ignoring the fact that the man's face had changed, though both Zen and Ember had expressions similar to how Zalia's must have looked at that moment.

"Sorry about all that," the man said.

"Not at all, such care for secrecy is commendable," Indis said diplomatically.

"Always good to be wary of watching eyes," the man said knowingly, tipping his head towards Indis.

"Someone want to clue me in to what is happening?" Zalia asked.

"As you have probably gathered by now, I am not the person who you met with last you were in town. They sent someone a little more . . . capable to deal with you should you return, which, thankfully, you did. We have been hoping for contact with your organisation ever since the help you are rendering to the kingdom began affecting the outcome of the war," the man explained.

"Right, and the task you need us to do?" she asked.

"A fabrication, in case there was anyone listening. I have a few plans for fabricating a falling out once you leave this building as well, to ensure any peeping eyes will not believe us to be working together," the man added.

"You seem pretty confident that it will be a fabrication at all," Ember said, finally taking a seat as well.

Both Zalia and Zen followed suit and sat down as well.

"Indeed I am, time is short so I will cut to the chase and give you the full explanation of my side of things," the man replied.

"I and the people I work with hope that you are here to gather more information about the rituals, am I right?" he asked.

"Yes," Indis said.

"Excellent. Many of the people in the rebellion have worked with, hired, or previously been a part of the Morning's Shade, and many know of the good reputation of your organisation. As such, even though you are working with the kingdom at the moment, we hope that the proof we can provide of the king's involvement in the creation of the rituals can sway you to our side," the man told them.

"You can provide actual proof of this? How?" Zen asked.

"Simple, not a small number of our cause are defectors from the army. Very simply put, many of those men were once loyal subjects to the royal family, and many come from long lines of army soldiers. The ones that defected are the ones that know the king is not who everyone thinks he is; the creature that now holds the throne usurped the real king and is ruling in his stead. They were asked by the usurper to commit atrocious acts in his name, and many took a dislike to the orders and they started to speak out about it. Those who spoke most loudly against the orders were quickly . . . silenced, one way or the other. Many were corrupted somehow, their bodies taken from them and moved by some other entity. Others still were sent on missions to out-of-the-way locations and were never heard from again. The remaining few loyal to the real king realised what was happening and defected, starting the rebellion. It is thanks to them that it is even possible at all, many have keen military minds, the only reason we have held out this long," the man responded.

Zalia thought about the lengthy explanation and a few pieces fell into place for her. The deserter captain she had helped take down some time back with Tristan might have not been a deserter at all. Tristan had said that the man used to be a loyal and well-liked captain in the army, his desertion had made no sense to her friend but fit neatly into what the spy before her said. The captain had been camped out near where the outer line of the giant ritual circle would have travelled and could very likely have had something to do with them as well. The missing farmers and travellers that the deserters had taken very well might have been fuel for the rituals in the first place. The thought sent a chill down Zalia's spine. Due to this knowledge, some of what the man before her now said rang true to her ears. It didn't mean the whole story was true, but if it was then Zalia was sure she couldn't fully trust Hidey. The shade had so strongly argued against the king having anything to do with the rituals. The thoughts nauseated her, if her friend was truly being controlled by the king then she would do whatever she could to free him. Zalia decided to trust this rebel just a little for now.

"Would it be possible for us to meet these people you are talking about, the army defectors?" Zalia asked.

"Yes, though it would take some time to organise," the man replied.

"I think I might believe you," Zalia said.

Her team looked to her with a little confusion.

"Do you know Captain Vidar?" Zalia asked the rebel.

A look of recognition passed over the man's face. "Ah, I believe I do. One of the first to become corrupted, if my memory serves," he said.

That confirmed it a little for Zalia, the fact that the man seemed to know about Vidar at all. He could have been faking it and guessed, of course, but she didn't think so. Zalia explained to her team who Vidar had been, how he had been corrupted, where Zalia had found him, and what she had put together about his possible involvement with the rituals. After her explanation, they seemed to understand her quick acceptance of the rebel's story a little more. Still, she would not act without further proof, but these puzzle pieces fitting together was enough for her to hear them out.

I wonder why Hidey sent us out here if he's being controlled. If he is, maybe some of him still remains in there, fighting to stop what is happening, Zalia thought.

"I think we are willing to go a little further and hear out what more proof you have," Indis said, looking to the others for agreement, which she got.

"Excellent. I do hope we can come to an agreement with the Morning's Shade to turn the tides of this war," the man said.

Zalia didn't mention that it was most likely both a bad idea and an impossibility with what she knew, but wanted to learn more before she let the man down.

"So what now, then?" Zalia asked.

"Now, we fabricate a heated exit and meet ten minutes' walk out west of the city," the rebel said excitedly. It seemed like the man really liked theatrics.

"What's the plan?" she asked.

"So, to begin with . . ." he started explaining.

Zalia and her team rushed out the front door of the house, slamming it as they exited. The rebel, who had finally introduced himself as Eztari, quickly followed out the door after them.

"How dare you ask us to commit such an atrocity!" Indis said in mock but believable anger.

"Please, I did not mean it in such a way!" Eztari said pleadingly.

"Bah, there is no other way to mean it. Begone with you!" Indis said before storming off.

"You are a disgusting man," Zalia said in a more controlled but still angry voice.

Eztari disguised as Zek looked down in shame.

"Forgive me, please," he begged.

"May you find Cormaine when you perish," Ember said before the rest of them walked off after Indis.

They walked for some time before finally letting go of their seriousness, and Zen was the first to laugh a little.

"That was ridiculous but fun, as unnecessary as it probably was," Zen said.

"It was certainly a strange plan," Zalia agreed.

"If it makes him feel comfortable, it's not so much to deal with," Indis said.

"Do you all realise what this might mean for Hidey?" Zalia asked, looking sombre.

"Yes . . . I do. It's unfortunate if true but the knowledge of his predicament could provide us with an advantage," Indis said.

"I suppose it could. I want Eztari to be wrong, or lying, though, just because I don't want this to be true about Hidey," Zalia said.

"I know, Zalia, but you must not let your emotions cloud logical thinking here. If Eztari really does provide compelling evidence, we must heed it. It doesn't mean that Hidey is necessarily being controlled either, maybe he is just simply wrong about the whole situation," Indis said, trying to comfort Zalia.

Zalia didn't know what to think anymore, but she had a feeling the whole situation had something to do with Juniper's husband's disappearance. Zayes had disappeared on some final quest for the Morning's Shade and ever since, Juniper hadn't seen Hidey even once. It compelled Zalia to believe it might be true, especially since maybe whoever was theoretically controlling Hidey didn't know if Juniper knew his true name or not and was keeping him away from her. She felt sick to her stomach thinking about it, but the more she did the more she was convinced it was true.

They walked in silence for some time, each of them lost within their own thoughts as they considered the ramifications of everything they had learnt in the past few days. Should what Zalia thought turn out to be true, then at this point they couldn't trust anyone within the Morning's Shade, outside of their own team. The thought of having to navigate both their own organisation and the rebel faction, while retaining any important information that could cause harm in the wrong hands made Zalia's head spin. Luckily, they had Indis, who was the child of a once powerful political house within the kingdom. If anyone knew how to go about doing what they needed to do, it was her. Zalia picked up Boreal, hugging the fluffy feline for comfort as they walked.

They met up with Eztari a short time later as they found him leaning against a tree in a small field.

"So, where to?" Zen asked.

"Now, we travel for a while south towards one of our war camps where I can start to get some meetings organised. You're all sure you want to go through with this?" he asked.

Each of them nodded their assent as he turned his gaze to them in turn.

"Well alright, let's get going," he said, moving south as they began their journey.

CHAPTER THIRTY-EIGHT

The General

Zalia

They travelled south, then southeast for four days, arriving at a large war camp surrounded by a tall log wall. Unlike the war camp Zalia had seen when meeting Alara and her small band, this was more of a permanent camp and there were many, many more soldiers here. The camp looked to hold a few thousand soldiers, most likely an encampment right on the battle line of the war. Zalia knew, of course, that a war had been raging while she and her team had been off hunting and exploring Elementals, rituals, and the north, but being here and seeing how large the army was gave her a little bit of a shock. For some reason she had thought that there were smaller battles and skirmishes and that was about it, but the truth was the scale of the war was much greater than she had previously thought. From what she knew, Endaria stretched much further south and there were most likely a few more war camps just like this one along the southern stretch of the battlefront.

The war camp itself had a tall, spiked log wall as she had previously noted, along with towers at regular intervals, each with the silhouette of a person atop. The wall had a large two-door gate on the side, facing west towards central Endaria.

"Soo, what now?" Zalia asked, a little nervous.

"We go in," Eztari said.

He looked back at the four of them.

"It's not too late to turn around and go back, if that is what you want," he said.

Zalia and her team all looked at each other, but no one made any objections so Indis turned back to Eztari, giving the man a nod. Saying nothing, but looking pleased, he left the shade of the small patch of trees and led the way towards the war camp. Once they were closer, a guard noticed them and stood, looking like they were about to sound an alarm. The guard stopped when Eztari held up a small object in his hand, gave a short but sharp whistle, and made a strange gesture with his other hand.

The guard turned about and shouted down towards the doors, "Open the gate!"

With a groan of wood, one side of the large gate began swinging open. They reached it just as the gate stopped, the door open only far enough for them to enter before swinging back closed behind them once more. Whatever happened, they were committed now; Zalia didn't think that escaping the camp would be anything close to easy if it came to that, but she still made sure to keep an eye out for possible escape routes. Towers, the gate, anything she could think of. They followed Eztari as the five of them passed by rows and rows of neat and well-ordered tents. No soldier sat idle as each man and woman went about their tasks, whether it was sharpening weapons, polishing armour, eating, training, or other mundane but important tasks.

"The operation of this army speaks a great many words as to the proficiency of its generals," Indis said diplomatically.

Eztari nodded. "Indeed, the false king made a grave error in alienating these men to his cause."

"You truly believe the king is at fault for all of this, don't you?" Indis asked.

"I do, and you will soon believe it too, or so I hope," Eztari said.

Indis seemed to inspect the man for a long moment, though she must have detected only honesty, for she didn't respond.

They walked for some time through the camp, past soldiers and various aides going about their duties. They even saw a group of soldiers patrolling in full armour, weapons held at the ready. As they got closer to the centre of the camp, tents got bigger, and even more permanently constructed buildings started appearing. They closed in on a large building that wasn't really decorated in any way; it looked mundane and no different than any of the other nearby buildings. It was the bunker of a building, a large stone construction that looked like it had been grown from the very ground around it. As they approached, Eztari motioned for them to stop and walked up to the two guards at the door. He whispered something quietly and moved into the building. The two guards eyed Zalia and her group warily, very obviously sizing them up and preparing themselves in case a fight should occur. Zalia noticed the others were doing the same and realised she was too, though she didn't like their chances if it came to a fight, considering the Silver rank of both the guards and the entire army around them. In this situation, diplomacy was key.

A few tense moments later, Eztari came back out of the building, looking between the guards and her group, shaking his head.

"Come, time to meet some of our generals," Eztari said.

He led the way into the building with Zalia's group following, though she noticed the two guards had a tight grip on their weapons. They entered into a well-lit room with a large table in the centre and a few chairs set around it. Around the edges of the room stood several attendants holding various items, from pitchers to sheafs of paper or rolled-up maps. One of them even had a large, complex-looking object made of various metals and precious stones. The man holding the object looked like he was tapping a flat stone plate while watching another similar plate as various swirling patterns appeared on it. She watched the man for a moment, and to her surprise the best comparison she could make was that it resembled typing. It seemed the man was typing on the flat stone plate and interpreting the images on the other, some form of long-range communication, maybe. Zalia thought back to the last time she had used a keyboard, a long time ago when she still lived with her parents. She hadn't spoken to either of them in many years; she didn't really have any form of internet in her log cabin in the snowy north and now existed within some other planet or realm.

She looked around the rest of the room, noting the four sharply dressed military people around the central table, the surface of which was covered in a large unfurled map, stones holding down the four corners. The four people were looking at Zalia and her group as they entered, different expressions on each of their faces. There were two men and two women, each of them dressed in similar uniforms. The uniforms each had metal plates sewn onto the shoulders, three of them holding two plates on each shoulder while the fourth person, a woman, had three plates. Zalia guessed that was some form of rank, which would make the woman the general or leader of this camp whilst the others were most likely advisors or lower-ranked military squad commanders, or something similar. One of the three that only had two plates had plates of a different colour, distinguishing them in some way that Zalia didn't yet understand.

Neither Zalia's group nor the four at the table spoke for a short time until Eztari finally spoke up.

"General, advisor, and commanders, these are the emissaries from the Morning's Shade I mentioned earlier. Emissaries, this is the general of this camp, her advisor, and commanders," Eztari said.

"An honour," Zalia said, giving her best nod of respect. It probably wasn't very good. She didn't know if saluting was even a thing here.

"Likewise, may I ask your names?" the advisor asked.

Zalia hesitated for a moment, glancing at Indis before replying.

"I am Zalia, this is Ember, Zen, and Lady Indis," Zalia said, motioning to each of her companions. "And may I ask your names?"

Zalia was hating this. She was not the best with people and she had expected

Indis to take the lead but the woman was just inspecting the equally silent general who was inspecting her in turn. Stupid politics.

"Of course. I am Advisor Ryn, this is General Faian, and Commanders Gurz and Lynette," the advisor said.

The woman he introduced as Commander Lynette was the only one at the table who held an openly hostile expression. Both the general and advisor held neutral expressions, while the other commander had an air of general disapproval about him.

"We may as well cut to the point. We would like proof of your claims that the king is behind the rituals and is causing the Elemental attacks. Eztari has already explained the claims to us, most of it, but we would like direct testimony and if possible, irrefutable proof," Zalia said, deciding to cut away with the bullshit and get to it.

"Why should we tell you anything, your organisation has caused us trouble enough already," Commander Lynette said.

Zalia frowned. "What trouble have we caused you?"

Both Zen and Ember seemed content to let Zalia talk for now, not wanting to get involved almost much as Zalia herself didn't want to be.

"You have freed up the kingdom's armies by dealing with the Elementals in their stead. This means they now have overwhelming numbers against us, despite their general disorder and lack of skilled generals," Commander Lynette said, a little anger in her voice.

"Enough," General Faian said.

Despite the general's command, Zalia still replied, "You would prefer we ignore the Elementals and let them rampage through the lands uncontested, harming people and destroying towns as they see fit?" Zalia asked, feeling herself get a little angry.

The commander had the sense of mind to look a little ashamed at the suggestion and Indis finally spoke.

"I have heard of you, General Faian. You were once a general within the kingdom's armies, if I recall correctly," she said, moving past the argument with tact.

"I was and still am. I serve the people of Endaria first, always," Faian said.

"The fact you are here and not serving under the king's armies already does bring some truth into Eztari's stories but I would like to hear your story anyways," Indis said.

"Very well. As you have said, I was once a general under the king, loyal as any. The previous king was a good man who deserved the loyalty those that served under him gave, he was well-respected. When he died, his son took his place and all was well for a time, though many grieved the loss of the old king. I myself was among the new king's advisors when it came to military matters in the beginning. I can still recall the day that something . . . changed in him. I don't know exactly what happened and at the time, I thought it to just be the foul mood of a son who had finally realised he had lost his father. I thought the truth of the situation had finally sunk into the boy and that was the cause of his strange behaviour, but I couldn't have been more wrong," Faian said, pausing for a moment looking deep in thought.

"One day, not so long after the death of the king, I received an order from the new king, an order for me to send out one of my more trusted companies far north of here and with the orders came a sealed and stamped letter from the king himself. I never learnt the contents of that letter, as I still trusted the king at the time and sent along the men with the sealed letter, under orders to only open it when they arrived at their destination. The men I sent were good men, loyal as any to the new king. I guess it is because of their loyalty that they followed through with whatever it was the king wanted them to do, though I believe it was one of the first rituals to have taken place. I didn't know it then, however, all I knew was that the company came back but they were . . . different. Not all of them returned either, some lost, though the survivors would not say how or why. The ones that did return were crazed in their actions, wild and impossible to control. The king eventually called for us to send the men to him to be taken care of and we did so, still believing in his good intentions. Unfortunately, this was only the first of such happenings and soon me and some of the other generals and commanders realised what was happening. We foolishly approached the king and confronted him about the horrors that were happening to our soldiers but we were waved away," she continued, some very deeply hidden emotion beginning to show on her face. "Soon after, the first of us disappeared and was never seen again. Soon after, another of the generals suddenly stopped communicating with us and was found to be crazed, much like the others. It was then that those of us who remained made plans to flee and begin this rebellion. We were the only ones who yet knew what was happening to the soldiers and the king himself, though many of the army knew as well. Many came with us, and many were lost in our flight. We weren't yet a big enough number to contend with the remaining army at that time and had decided to regroup far to the east of the kingdom and make plans there. Many of us did make it, though not all. Now, we fight. We fight the king's crazed soldiers and we try our best to protect the people of this kingdom from the threat they do not yet realise. Not all of the king's armies are corrupted and crazed such as those that we fight, some he has kept normal to keep up pretence to his people but more and more have realised the truth and come to our side. Not so long ago the tide had actually turned in the war. We were winning for a time and had started taking ground, getting closer to the capital, and this is where your organisation comes in. We think the king is using you as a desperate move to take back momentum in the war, and so far it is working. It will not work for long because his armies do not fight with order, discipline, and planning but through madness and thirst for battle. It is the only reason I believe we have held out as long as we have. Soon, as more realise the truth, we will take back momentum once more and push forwards, but I fear it will be too late," the general finished explaining.

She paused for a moment.

"I fear we will be too late, I fear that the reason he has gone to the measure of getting your organisation involved is the simple fact that he needs but a little more time. Just a little bit more time to put into motion whatever nefarious plan he has, whatever it is the rituals are meant to accomplish. We destroy the ones we find, but I fear it is simply not enough," she finally finished, looking intensely at Zalia and her group.

Zalia found it hard not to believe the woman. The story was so compelling, spoken with such conviction and detail that she had a hard time believing it was anything but truth. She looked to her friends and saw that they too seemed to believe in what the woman told them; Indis herself seemed the most convinced, though maybe it had something to do with the fact that she had previously known of the general.

"I must admit, I find your retelling of the story to be quite compelling," Indis said.

Although a compelling leader is one requirement for such a strong rebellion, Zalia thought idly.

"Because it is truth, Lady Indis," the general said.

"How long do you think we have?" Zalia asked.

"I don't know for sure, but time is running short," the general replied.

Suddenly, Zalia remembered something. She gently patted Boreal as the feline woke up from her nap on Zalia's shoulders.

"The battle in the north, near the town where Eztari met us. What was that whole fight about? The people there didn't seem crazed to me, but like normal soldiers," Zalia said.

"The battle that took place some two months ago? How do you know of it, were you there?" General Faian asked.

"I was, in fact I saved quite a few of your people that day," Zalia said.

"So you are the one that the few who returned here spoke of. You have quite strong abilities for an Iron ranker," Faian said with a thoughtful expression.

Soon though, her expression turned to a frown.

"That battle. Bah! A waste of good men, it was. I told those who were camped there not to engage, they were meant to be a simple vanguard against an attack from the north, to stop any army from crossing freely past our lines, but the idiots got too confident. Our recent successes in battle, and the war in general at the time, bolstered their courage and they took it upon themselves to go and push our lines forwards. A foolish decision that cost many lives, more so if you had not been there. I thank you for the work you did that day," Faian explained.

"Saving lives is an action that needs no thanks," Zalia said, looking to Ember who nodded appreciatively.

The general nodded, obviously in agreement with the sentiment.

"We must retire for a time and talk amongst ourselves about what we have learnt, if it is acceptable to you," Indis said.

"Of course, Eztari will show you to a private tent in which you can talk," Faian said, gesturing to the man.

"Thank you, we will get back to you shortly with our decision and we can plan where to go from there," Indis said.

The general nodded and they began moving out of the room. As they were about to step out the door, a loud horn sounded through the camp, quickly followed by a second and third blast.

"What have you done! Who have you led here?" the general asked in anger.

"This is not us," Indis said firmly.

The general looked to Indis for a long moment before standing and rushing out the door.

"To arms! To arms!" General Faian yelled over the clamour of the camp.

CHAPTER THIRTY-NINE

Battle Crazed

Zalia

The sounds of battle clamoured through the camp and reached Zalia's ears as she left the building in a hurry. Faian, her advisor, and the two commanders all rushed past Zalia and her team towards the sounds of battle as other groups of soldiers in various states of armament rushed past in different directions, some towards the battle and others towards racks of weapons or armour. Zalia and her team started moving towards the sound of battle as well, wanting to see what was happening, though she thought they should stay hidden if possible.

"An attack by the king's army?" Zalia asked.

"Seems the most likely scenario," Indis said.

"Should we get involved?" Ember asked.

The woman obviously didn't like standing around when she could be off helping to heal others. Zalia felt uneasy as well, as they hadn't decided on either side yet, despite the compelling nature of Faian's story.

"No, not in this one. We defend and heal only, from either side," Indis said.

Zalia nodded in agreement and gently patted the restless Boreal. They moved through the rows of buildings and tents towards the sounds of battle, a fire now visible as it raged in one corner of the camp. They finally got close enough to see what was happening and got their first proper piece of proof that supported the general's story. There was a hole in the defensive wall that looked like someone had set off an explosion. It was suddenly obvious to Zalia that such defences were much less useful when faced with the power of a high-rank soldier. Rushing through the gap were soldiers in armour, most of it looking like it was in need of a lot of care. Some pieces of armour were rusted, some dented, and many had scratches and other marks. What struck Zalia the most as she observed the soldiers, and what gave some solid proof to Faian's story were the soldiers' eyes. Within their gaze was a crazed madness that Zalia could only describe as other-worldly. It was almost as if there was a corrupt fire burning deep within them, distorting their perception and driving them into a rage. They didn't fight as a well-organised unit of an army, but rather rushed in, attacking whoever first caught their eye. There were no tactics to the attack, it was more like an assault by mindless animals.

Zalia turned to Indis and saw that the woman had noticed all the small details that she had.

"Could be a ploy by the rebels to support their story," Indis pointed out.

Zalia sighed, she was quite sick of humans and their politicking. She wished to be back in the wilds once more where everything was as it seemed; the hunting of an animal turned into a ruthless fight for survival. It was a harsh way of life, but it was at least honest and forthright.

"I suppose you are right. Do we fight now? I'm still not quite convinced," Zalia asked.

"No, not yet," Indis said.

They watched from a distance with unease, Zalia trying to focus her healing at a distance on anyone who went down but did not die. The soldiers of the rebel army were quickly organizing, but the initial attack of the supposed king's men had punched quite far into the camp; the fire now raged further in as soldiers fought and died in the heat. Zalia watched with unease, unsure about their decision to not join this fight. Some of the crazed soldiers ran straight through patches of burning fire and attacked the quickly forming blocks of rebel soldiers even as their clothes caught ablaze, not caring about the fire that consumed their bodies as they fought. Smoke and ash filled the air, clogging their throats and eyes while the relentless onslaught continued.

Zalia and her team had to retreat further back when one of the crazed soldiers saw them and sprinted their direction. Despite their attempts to push the man back and retreat, they ended up having to kill him, Zen using his large mace to smash the man's head in. The man had been Iron rank as well but simply attacked with thoughtless rage, no skill or tactic behind the sword work. The tide of the battle finally turned when the two commanders arrived with fresh and properly armoured and armed soldiers, forming a shield wall and pushing back the attackers. Before long, the battle was over and General Faian approached them on the edges of the battle zone.

"Apologies for the outburst earlier, I did not mean to lay blame for the assault at your feet," Faian said.

"It was unfortunate timing, no apology needed," Indis said, diplomatic as ever.

"Oh it's not the first time they have attacked and I know it will not be the last," Faian said.

Hearing the words, Zalia did notice that there were signs of battle if one looked closely enough. A patch of ash that could have been an extinguished campfire but could also be a burnt down tent, a section or two of wall that looked newer than the rest. She also noticed that Ember was looking apprehensively towards where the battle had been. She caught the woman's eye and nodded. Ember ran off towards the battle, checking bodies and injured, helping where she could.

"She is our healer," Zalia said, at Faian's questioning expression.

The general seemed to accept that explanation and spoke once more. "You see now why we rebel. The false king would have us all made into those mindless beasts," Faian said, a hint of well contained venom in her voice.

"I do," Indis said with a nod.

"You keep calling him a false king. Do you think it is no longer the man you knew?" Zalia asked.

"I . . . I don't really know. I simply cannot piece together the man I knew, raised by the king I served, with the man who would order something such as this," Faian said, gesturing to the battlefield.

Zalia actually felt a little bad for the woman. She had obviously been loyal to the previous king and the people of her kingdom but was now forced to fight them and even kill some of them. Those that she killed very well might have been loyal and disciplined soldiers, but were now turned into these mindless brutes.

"We still need to talk amongst ourselves about what we will do," Indis said.

"Of course, Eztari will take you. I must help clean up here before anything else, anyways," Faian said, turning away as she watched the scene before her.

Eztari came forwards, appearing as if from nowhere. "If you'll kindly follow me," he said.

"One minute," Zalia said.

She went over to the battlefield where Ember was still healing the injured.

"Come, we need to talk. They will take over," Zalia said, gesturing to an arriving group of healers.

Ember nodded and they returned to the group, looking to Eztari. He led them to one of the stone buildings, letting them in and telling them, "If you need anything you need only ask."

They entered the building and sat on the chairs around the small central table. The room was very similar to the one the general had occupied, most likely they switched which buildings they held meetings in just as a safety measure.

"So?" Ember asked.

"I think we should trust them," Zalia said.

"You are too quick with your trust once again, Zalia," Indis said.

Zalia frowned but internally acknowledged the truth in the woman's words. "What do you think we should do moving forwards, then?" she asked.

"I think we should see if we can arrange talking with another of the generals in the army. As far as I know, they don't have any particular leaders, just a bunch of military people revolting against the kingdom. We will hear the story from at least one other and see if any cracks in the narrative crop up. If not, then we can begin to trust their story," Indis said.

"And what do we do if we decide to trust them? Do we go back to Endelbyrn and inform Hidey? I'm feeling quite lost on how to move forward here," Zalia said.

"Me too, I feel way out of my depth," Zen said, speaking for the first time in quite a while.

"We decide together," Indis said.

"I don't see the path forwards," Zen replied.

"We all came to join the Morning's Shade for one reason or the other, but I think the one thing that does bring us all together is that we all strive to help others in one way or another. I search for a way, any way, to bring my family from the brink of ruin. You, Zalia, despite how much you say you detest people, have a caring heart and I know you would sacrifice for others if it came to it. Ember, don't think I haven't noticed how often you go travelling from the city, how the people of Bur treated you like one of them. I know you go and heal the people of Endaria for no other reason than the good of your heart. Zen, despite how often you say stupid things I know there is good in your heart too. This is how we figure out the path forwards," Indis monologued.

"I think I see what you're saying," Zalia said.

"I don't," Zen grumbled.

"It's simple. If we end up accepting that the king really is responsible for the rituals, the Elementals, the crazed and mindless soldiers, then we do whatever we can to stop him. We do this for the good of the people, and that is that. We simply have to make a decision and stick to it. I don't think we should go back to Endelbyrn, if time is as short as Faian seems to think. No, a woman as intelligent as her must have some plan to act soon, and we should help with that, assuming we agree with their story in the end," Indis explained.

"Alright, sounds like a plan then," Zalia said.

She was a little relieved that it had been so easily sorted for the near future at least. She had been feeling a bit lost in all the complexity of the situation and was glad for Indis's expertise and mind in figuring out their next move.

"I think I can agree to that," Ember said.

"Well, alright, let's go inform Faian shall we?" Indis said.

They left the room and found Eztari nearby, the man making no comment and leading them back towards where the general was without preamble. They told the general of their decision and the woman agreed to allow them to meet another of the army's generals, though they would have to organise for them to travel, or for the general to travel here. Indis wanted to speak to Faian a bit more about specifics; Zalia trusted her to deal with it and moved away, taking Boreal down off her shoulders. The feline was getting quite large and was probably going to be too big to rest on her shoulders like that anymore. She walked through the camp with Boreal at her side, trying to listen to the soldiers' conversations as she passed. She wanted to get a sense of the general mood of the camp; were these people confident in their cause? Were they unsure of their actions being for the greater good? Were these good people, ones worth working with to help provide a better future for the lands around? She wasn't quite sure yet, Indis's comment about her being too trusting had thrown her off once more.

As she walked, she did think about the easy trust she often gave people. For some reason, she believed people when they showed her who they were on the surface. She trusted that who they were at face value was real and genuine and not some form of trick to gain her trust. It might be a flaw she had but it was also not something she wanted to lose, the faith that humanity could be better, despite how many frustrations she had with people in general.

She poured over the story Faian had told them, considering each word, but she just couldn't believe any of it was some form of lie or trick to gain their cooperation. The woman truly did strike Zalia as genuine. It was probably good Indis was here, her read on people was not always the best.

As she listened to the soldiers' conversations and looked at their general mood and posture, she came to the conclusion that they most likely did believe in the cause they were fighting for. Mostly she felt there was some sadness or anger at the recent attack, a sense of hopelessness in the situation they were in, but there was also an undercurrent of resolve to everything they did, evident in their posture and dedication to each task they performed. She might have been imagining all of that, as she thought she wasn't the best at reading people's thoughts and emotions but she decided to trust herself anyways.

She started making her way back to where Indis was, having made the decision that she wanted to help the people here achieve their goals, and that she did believe the king had some large role in everything and needed to be stopped. Maybe she wasn't the person for the job, but she would do what she could to help the people of Endaria.

CHAPTER FORTY

The Scarred

Zalia

Zalia returned just as Indis finished her conversation, Boreal following closely in her footsteps and giving a wide berth to any moving soldiers.

"All sorted?" she asked.

"The details have been decided, yes," Indis replied, looking over at her.

"Wonderful, what's the plan?" Zalia asked.

Indis shrugged. "We have the rest of the day to ourselves before they can get in contact with the closest other general to organise a meetup. Faian did mention, however, that there is actually a soldier here who is a survivor of one of the rituals. The man apparently saw it firsthand."

"Oh, we definitely need to go talk to that man," Ember said.

"Agreed," Zalia said.

She looked around and saw Eztari was still hanging around, keeping an eye on them.

"Hey!" she called out.

The man walked over. "Yes?"

"We would like to talk with the man who has seen one of the rituals firsthand," Zalia said.

"I know of the man and see no issue with that, come along," he replied.

They followed Eztari for a time as he led them through the camp until they arrived at a stone building that looked a little different from the others. Entering, they discovered the reason for that, as they saw that it was some sort of hospital. The men in the building didn't look injured however, many of them were staring mindlessly at the walls or rocking back and forth as they sat.

"Oh no . . ." Ember whispered, trailing off.

Zalia mirrored the sentiment, looking around the room at the mind-scarred people. An unfortunate reality of war; some people suffered such grievous wounds or experienced so much horror that their minds simply broke. It seemed that despite the wonder of magical healing, some parts of war here were the same as Zalia's own world.

"It is a heart-wrenching sight, isn't it?" Eztari said, looking around the room with sadness in his eyes. "We do as much as we can for them, try to keep them comfortable. A constant source of healing can relax their minds, take away some of the pain for a while but it very rarely sticks. Some have recovered this way but for many we can only hope."

He led them past rows of beds, many occupied by people in various states of distress. Some few seemed to notice their passing, though none spoke to them. Amongst the scarred soldiers, many healers walked from bed to bed, giving healing or comforting words. They were led to the back of the building where a man sat on a bed in the corner, facing the walls. He was rocking back and forth while idly scratching at the wall with one hand, the quiet scraping sound accompanied by a low whisper as he spoke.

"Fire and death and fire, the lands below where they stir in their torment. Terrible, oh so terrible are the lands below. They speak in whispers and murmurs, murmurs and whispers, always in pain, so much pain. In those lands of fire and death and fire, the lands below where they stir in their torment . . ." the man whispered as he scratched the wall, repeating the phrases over and over.

Ember looked more and more disturbed as she watched the man, before turning around and leaving. Zen looked at Zalia and Indis before following after.

"I assume he has been like this ever since you found him?" Zalia asked.

"He has, nothing we have done has been able to break him from repeating the same thing, over and over," Eztari said.

He must have seen into Cormaine and seen much more than we could through the small distortion at the mine. Is the place really so terrible as to break a man so soundly? Zalia thought.

"Where did you find him?" Indis asked.

"He was found at one of the rituals further east. We have been destroying them as we go but this one we found early on, soon after the ritual itself was completed. The men had all turned mad and we had to kill them, but this man just sat there on the floor, covered in the blood of the sacrificed, scratching at the floor and repeating those words, over and over," Eztari said, shuddering as he recalled the memory.

"You were there?" Zalia asked.

"I was . . . it is something I never wish to see again. Seeing one of the rituals after it has been cleaned up and abandoned is one thing, but when it is fresh . . .

the blood, the pieces of bodies ripped apart . . . it is no wonder this man is so broken," Eztari replied.

He had a haunted look in his eyes and Zalia thought maybe Eztari hadn't come out of the experience fully alright either.

"Why do they do it?" Indis asked.

"Do what?" Eztari asked back.

"Why do they follow through with these rituals if they are just normal soldiers before they take place? No sane person would do such a thing," Indis said.

"We don't really know," Eztari admitted.

"There is still something we don't understand about these rituals," Indis said.

"Corrupted," Zalia muttered, having thought of something.

"Corrupted?" Indis asked.

"When Tristan and I fought that captain, my Aura Observation passive titled the man as corrupted," Zalia said.

"So?" Eztari asked.

"And yet the crazed soldiers who attacked this place didn't have that," Indis said, coming to the same realisation Zalia had.

"Exactly. There was also . . . some kind of aura that the man had. I didn't mention it before because I didn't think it was really important, but he had some kind of aura that was affecting everyone around him. My Healing Aura managed to counter the effects for the most part, though," Zalia explained further.

"You think that has something to do with why the soldiers are going through with these rituals?" Indis asked.

"I don't know, but possibly? I wouldn't rule it out," Zalia replied.

"I think I know what you're talking about, we have seen a few of those types. They're much harder to kill than the normal crazy soldiers," Eztari supplied.

"Another mystery to solve," Indis said.

Eztari said something in reply but Zalia had stopped listening.

I wonder . . . she thought.

She focused Healing Presence on the man scratching at the wall and for a moment he stopped, falling silent as his hand dropped.

"Oh gods, oh gods, please, no," the man said. He turned to them with a crazed look in his eyes, but he did seem to see them, at least.

"You have to stop them, you must stop them!" he screamed at them.

Eztari looked at the man with wide eyes, speechless. A few of the healers in the room ran in to see what the commotion was, but the man had gone back to his whispers, scratching at the wall once more.

"What was that?" Indis asked.

"I just tried to focus my Healing Aura on him for a moment . . ." Zalia said.

"Please, you must leave while we tend to him," a nearby healer said, motioning for them to leave.

"I . . ." Zalia started.

"Come on," Indis said, interrupting her and gently pushing her towards the exit.

Eztari followed them, still looking a bit stunned by the whole thing. They finally exited the building to find Zen gently hugging Ember as she cried softly.

"I've never heard him say anything else," Eztari said, looking at Zalia.

"I don't know what I did," Zalia said helplessly.

"Maybe your type of healing is different?" Eztari said questioningly.

"My classes are different, maybe that has something to do with it," Zalia said, unsure.

"How so?" Eztari asked.

"I have . . ." she started saying.

"She has gained them in a strange manner is all," Indis said, giving Zalia a warning look.

"Yes, that," Zalia agreed, failing completely at lying.

She could tell Eztari didn't believe the obvious lie Indis had told, but he didn't push further. He did look at her with vague suspicion, though, and she just looked back awkwardly until he turned away. She picked up Boreal, who was used to being carried and made no complaint, and walked over to Ember. Ember turned to Zalia as she approached and pushed Boreal into the woman's arms. Ember hugged the very fluffy and very warm feline closely. Boreal stared into Zalia's eyes from under Ember's embrace.

"*Why?*"

Zalia heard the voice project into her mind and almost jumped with surprise. She looked closer at Boreal. "*Because she needs comfort and you are very fluffy,*" Zalia thought back.

She watched Boreal but no more words were forthcoming.

What the hell? she thought to herself.

She had no idea if the thought had come from Boreal or something else, but it had definitely not been her own. It looked like Boreal had accepted her fate so maybe Zalia's thoughts had been heard. She shook herself out of her confusion.

"Are you alright?" Zalia asked Ember.

"I will be alright. I'm sorry, the sight just struck a little close to home," Ember said, putting Boreal down on the ground and trying to regain her composure.

Zalia didn't prod further, she knew that the woman would open up about what that meant if she felt like it; pushing would only cause more harm.

"Maybe we can go talk to some of the soldiers and hear their stories," Indis suggested.

"That's a good idea," Zalia said.

"Sounds fine to me," Zen said in agreement.

They spent the last hours of the day walking through the camp, asking soldiers why they were fighting, what their stories were, and what they thought about their leaders and the entire war in general. There were a wide array of responses but the main ones that came up were stories of soldiers with friends who were turned by one of the rituals; or squad leaders or commanders deserting and taking their squads with them, as well as other horror stories of heinous orders being given to the squads. Every soldier seemed to have at least one friend or ally who had been turned mad by the ritual, and each of them spoke with strong conviction for the cause they'd chosen to follow.

While the stories were varied, the messages were all the same. Each of them believed the king to be some form of usurper or corrupt creature, and they wanted the man gone. They seemed to all truly believe that it would be best for the Kingdom of Endaria and its peoples.

The sun was close to setting when Eztari found them again, informing them that a nearby general would be able to join them in this camp within three days. He would be coming with his own contingent of soldiers to reinforce their position and was happy to explain his story to the group. As the sun set, they were given their own large tent to sleep in and they settled in, talking about everything they had learnt.

"I had an idea while we were talking to the soldiers earlier," Indis said.

"Oh?" Zen said questioningly.

"Alright, basically I figured if we want to help the rebellion, and if we assume we are right about Hidey, we can feed false information to him to help make a mission more likely to succeed. If we are short on time like General Faian thinks, an assassination attempt is something we should consider," Indis explained.

Assassination? Zalia thought, a little disturbed.

As much as she disliked the idea, it was probably the track they were going down if they did help the rebellion. They wouldn't be the ones doing it, but even helping make it happen didn't quite sit right with her. She would have to think a lot about her feelings in that regard.

"It is a viable option," she replied.

"We'll have to work with the rebellion and figure out the details but it could be promising," Ember said.

Ember was still a little red-eyed but had managed to get her emotions under control for the moment. Zalia was now sure Boreal had not only heard her but understood her words because the ever growing feline was now curled up next to Ember, purring gently.

"I'm a little unsure, I'll have to think about it," Zalia said.

"Of course, we haven't decided on our path just yet. It is only an option I thought worth bringing up," Indis said.

Zalia nodded, looking at Zen and trying to decipher his expression. He seemed . . . lost.

"You alright, Zen?" she asked.

"Hmm?" he said, breaking out of his thoughts.

"Yes, I just . . . I just feel so out of my own depth here, in this situation," he said.

Zalia definitely understood what he meant. Not only were they a bunch of Iron ranks, but the situation was growing ever more complicated, and she was personally getting more and more concerned that she might get things wrong and doom many, many people to a horrid fate. Depending on what the large ritual was actually meant to accomplish, supporting the wrong side could possibly spell the end of the Kingdom of Endaria and its people entirely. It was a scary thought.

"Yeah, I get that," Zalia said, knowing it probably wasn't comforting to him.

"Can we just . . . can we rest and talk about it tomorrow?" Ember asked.

"Of course, some sleep might be best for us all," Indis replied.

Zalia looked at the woman and realised that despite how she appeared to be in control, the Lady might be feeling just as lost and worried as the rest of them were.

The others all settled in to sleep for the night and Zalia tried to as well. For once, her ability that allowed her to sleep less wasn't as much of a blessing. As the others fell asleep, Zalia was left restless and awake, stuck with her thoughts deep into the night before she too finally fell into slumber.

Morning came, and Zalia awoke to the weight of Boreal sitting on her chest, gently poking her in the face with her paw.

"What th . . ." she mumbled.

It felt like the feline was getting payback for all the mornings that their positions had been reversed, and Zalia had woken Boreal up instead.

"*Hunt.*"

"*What?*" Zalia thought, confused.

And then she realised Boreal had spoken into her mind again.

"You want to hunt something?" Zalia murmured, still bleary eyed from sleep.

No thoughts popped into her mind, but Boreal jumped off her and walked over to the entrance so Zalia took that as a yes.

She got up and quickly got ready to go for a short hunt. As always, her bow was stored in its space so she didn't need to worry about packing it, and she left her bag behind, so all she really needed to do was strap her armour on before leaving the tent. All her allies were still asleep and despite having gone to sleep so late, she had awoken quite early in the morning, thanks to her ability. She went to the gate and quickly explained to the guard what she wanted to do. The man ran off to talk to a superior and came back soon after, allowing her to leave and promising she would be allowed entry once she returned.

She followed Boreal as the feline led her into a thicker section of forest. She watched as Boreal quickly picked up the tracks of a larger beast and began to track it into the woods. Impressed, she followed along but was unsurprised at how much better Boreal was at tracking already. She did forget sometimes, but Boreal would grow to be a large and very dangerous predator and had the natural instincts of one.

They moved quickly through the forest as Boreal tracked, with Zalia only having to guide the feline once. Zalia constantly kept an eye out for any new herbs but was not lucky enough to see anything of note before they found the creature they were hunting. Zalia looked from Boreal to the creature they had found and raised an eyebrow at the feline, hoping she had learnt how to decipher facial expressions along with her newfound ability to speak into Zalia's mind. Boreal now weighed somewhere around twelve to fifteen kilos by Zalia's reckoning and the creature they'd hunted down was a large moose-like animal with two large, sharp horns growing from its head. The moose creature probably weighed somewhere around seven to eight hundred kilos.

"I think you chose some prey way out of your weight class," Zalia whispered to Boreal.

Boreal just looked up at Zalia with wide, round eyes, looking innocent and oh-so-cute.

"You little extortionist," she whispered. She couldn't believe she was about to hunt down a giant creature just so Boreal could eat it.

Boreal gave one small, quiet mew and Zalia gave a heavy sigh before summoning her bow.

She got a little closer and saw that despite the size of the creature, it was only Iron rank, much like herself. That was good, though she knew not to underestimate the thing.

Zalia drew her bow as Boreal stalked off into the woods to her right. She let off a shot, a second quickly following, and two dull thuds sounded as both arrows impacted the head of the creature. One of the arrows deflected off its thick skull, but the other managed to penetrate through its lower jaw. The creature let out a strangled but still extremely loud cry of protest before spotting Zalia and charging. It crashed through the undergrowth as Zalia let off another arrow, another dull thud sounding when it pierced the creature's chest, driving in deep. She activated Kill Shot as she let off one more arrow, this one managing to embed itself so far into the creature's chest that even the feathers vanished within its flesh. Her poison had started its work and the creature had begun to slow down, but it was still charging quite fast towards her and she was forced to stow her bow once more. Just before the creature reached her, she saw a flash of mottled grey fur as Boreal exploded from a patch of thick undergrowth and latched onto the creature's neck. Zalia dodged towards the right as Boreal's attack caused the creature to stumble a little to her left.

The moose creature was now doomed to die and was alive only because of adrenaline, and yet it still fought on. It crashed around trying to shake Boreal free but wasn't able to, and Zalia summoned her bow once more, now free to shoot as the creature's attention was elsewhere. With a good side view and a closer shot, her last arrow fired off from the bow and struck deep into the creature's eye, the tip of the arrow piercing through the other side of its head. The moose creature finally stopped struggling and fell to the ground, twitching as it took its final breath.

CHAPTER FORTY-ONE

Beast Bond

Zalia

Congratulations! You have formed a Beast Bond with Boreal. Your passive ability 'Survivalist' now expands to affect Boreal. Boreal's passive ability 'Feline Eyes' now expands to affect you. You and Boreal are now able to slightly sense each other's location in reference to each other, as well as gain a vague sense of each other's emotions.

What? Zalia thought.

The first thing she noticed as she rushed over to the dead creature was how much her eyesight had improved. She could see considerably better in the dark of the early morning and everything seemed sharper, more in focus. She found Boreal and saw the feline had somehow pulled herself up onto the side of the creature's neck that hadn't hit the ground. Thankfully, she seemed unharmed.

"That was a little dangerous," Zalia chided.

Boreal looked up at her but didn't reply, instead looking back down at the moose. Zalia rolled her eyes but used Preparation to field dress the animal before preparing a small bit of meat from it for Boreal. The feline didn't eat the piece of meat, instead still looking at Zalia expectantly.

"You're growing soft," Zalia said, realising Boreal wanted her to cook it.

She reluctantly obliged, using heat manipulation from her Heat Resistance passive to start a small fire and cook the meat. Boreal finally ate the meat once it was done cooking, and Zalia used her ability to cool it down so it wouldn't harm Boreal.

"There's a reason I never did want children," Zalia thought, eyeing Boreal.

At least Boreal would quickly grow up to a size where she could hunt for herself. The not-so-little feline was steadily growing bigger by the day. She could vaguely sense Boreal in the back of her mind now, almost as if another mind was gently poking at her consciousness. The sensation was weird; the feeling of Boreal's location was similar to her Hunter's Mark, something she was familiar with now, but feeling the emotions of her feline friend along with sharing one of her passives was another change to get used to.

Zalia took a look at the rest of the moose creature and considered what to do with it. She didn't really want to waste the meat, even though hauling back such a heavy creature would be a bit of a task. With her increased strength she could probably manage dragging the corpse; carrying it was off the table. She was kind of wishing she had brought her tarp now but she hadn't been expecting to make such a large kill.

"We can't just let this all go to waste," Zalia said, gesturing to the beast as she looked at Boreal.

The feline had finished eating and now looked back at Zalia.

"And you're not going to be of any help," Zalia grumbled.

She thought about the limitations of her Preparation skill and turned to a nearby patch of a vine-type plant growing up the side of a tree. It allowed her to magically dry, cut, or otherwise prepare various foods, herbs, and other similar plant-based items. She figured that the vine was plant-based so there was no reason it wouldn't work, right?

Zalia went over to the vine and activated Preparation. Focusing her thoughts on what she wanted it to do, the skill was able to cut off a few lengths of vine and dry them. The prepared vines dropped to the ground with the light sound of rustling undergrowth. She picked up the few lengths and intertwined them, then wrapped the whole thing around the body of the moose creature with a great amount of effort. She tied it to itself with a slipknot and then stepped back to look at her makeshift rope. She took up the loose end and gave an experimental tug, managing to pull the creature some distance with a lot of effort.

"Oh man, this is gonna suck," Zalia mumbled.

While it had only taken her about twenty minutes to get out as far as she had while tracking the creature, dragging it back took her three times that long. She struggled and strained, pulling the big creature through the undergrowth back towards the camp. It was a lot of effort for little reward but the simple and achievable task gave her mind something to focus on besides the convoluted problems she had been dealing with lately. Eventually, she arrived at the gates. She was coated with sweat and would have been covered in dirt had it not been for her clothes' and armour's self-cleaning enchantments, but accomplishing her self-given task gave her a sense of accomplishment. The gate opened, the guards on duty recognised her and were aware of what she had been up to, and she entered the camp once more. She slowly dragged the creature through the camp, getting not a small amount of odd glances from the soldiers she walked past; as it was still early morning, many were just waking up. She arrived back at the tent that her companions were still sleeping in and finally dropped her burden with a grunt and a long sigh of relief.

She began building a small fire with some wood she found in a nearby stockpile, while she also used Preparation to magically begin cutting up the moose creature into a stock of well-butchered meat on top of her tarp. She very carefully began cooking choice sections of meat and seasoned them with various herbs she had, and some salt and various spices she managed to convince a nearby soldier to get for her. The man left happy after she gave him a nice chunk of well-cooked and seasoned meat as payment and told him to spread the word in case anyone else was hungry.

Ember awoke first, leaving the tent and sitting down next to Zalia.

"Good morning, sleepy," Zalia said cheerfully, handing the woman a nice piece of skewered meat from her campfire.

"It's so unfair how cheery you are in the mornings," Ember grumbled, accepting the food despite her annoyance.

Zalia didn't comment, happily focusing on her task. She really did enjoy the simple things in life, cooking, walking the wilds, and fighting powerful creatures to the death in a violent bid for survival.

Before long, a few more soldiers began arriving and accepting food from her small campfire with thanks given. Each of them arrived with a small token of cooking herbs, spices, salt, or pepper. At first she found the small tokens funny, guessing that the first soldier had spread the word about the meat and told them to bring her spices or herbs as payment. After the first ten or so soldiers, however, she was getting a little concerned. She need not have worried, though. Indis and Zen soon woke up, also accepting her cooking, and after a few more soldiers came by her fire, she ran out. She had started giving them larger amounts to take back to their friends, hoping to get rid of it before she ended up with too many small pouches of herbs and spices. The soldiers probably had some army chefs around, but they most likely had not yet begun serving and the food they served would probably not be as good as the fresh meat.

"So, what's the plan for today?" Zalia asked.

"There isn't one, the general won't arrive for three days' time. Have something in mind?" Indis asked back.

"Not really, I'm always up for a good hunt, though," Zalia replied.

Ember looked at the last piece of food she was still eating. "Did you not just hunt?" she asked.

"Yes, so?" Zalia said, a little confused.

Boreal made a small chirping sound as if in agreement. Ember looked down at Boreal somewhat confusedly as the feline stared at her.

"Zalia?" Ember said.

"Yeah?" Zalia asked.

"Why is Boreal staring at me like that?" Ember asked.

"Because Boreal is in agreement with me and wanted to let you know," Zalia replied.

"What does that mean?" Ember asked.

"I don't know, Boreal seems to be starting to understand words and has even started speaking into my mind sometimes," Zalia said.

"She's started doing what?" Zen asked.

"Is that not normal?" Zalia asked, stopping cleaning up for a moment.

"Not particularly, no," Zen said.

"Have you ever seen others of Boreal's species, though? It could be normal," Zalia reasoned.

"I . . . guess," Zen said, frowning.

"Could be a useful ability in the future," Indis said thoughtfully.

Zalia rolled her eyes.

"Always thinking about how you can twist things to your advantage," Zalia replied, tsking a few times.

Indis just shrugged.

"It is what I must do," Indis said a little morosely.

They were all silent for a moment after that, remembering the situation they were all in.

"I formed something called a Beast Bond with Boreal," Zalia said.

Ember whistled. "Damn, Zalia, that's lucky. Though, I guess not too unexpected with both your classes and the fact you somehow managed to befriend a murderous predatory kitten," she said, a little awe in her voice.

"Is it rare?" Zalia asked.

"Mmm, not super rare. I have heard of Beast Bonds before, it's not something so rare as the Familiar Bond Zayes had with Hidey, for instance," Ember said.

The mention of Hidey brought the mood back down again immediately.

"Maybe it would be good for all of us to go on a hunt," Zalia suggested.

"Why is that?" Ember asked.

"To take our minds off things for a little while. It's better than sitting around thinking about our situation when nothing can be done about it at the moment, right?" Zalia asked in reply.

"I suppose so, three days isn't a long time to find something that can challenge us around here, though," Ember said.

"We could ask Faian or Eztari if there is anything worth going after nearby, they might know of something," Indis suggested.

"That's a good idea," Zen said.

"Of course it is, it's my idea," Indis replied, trying to put some of her old poshness into her tone.

Zalia hadn't realised how long it had been since Indis had played the part of spoiled noble and also realised she had missed the playful, if not annoying, side of the woman.

"Naturally, My Lady," Zen said in a formal tone, giving a mock bow.

"It is good you recognise your betters, peasant," Lady Indis said, raising her chin and looking down her nose at Zen.

"Cut it out, you two," Zalia said.

They both laughed and Zalia found herself joining in. Being able to joke around and have a laugh was refreshing and something they all needed.

"Shall we go and talk to Eztari or Faian, then?" Ember asked once they had settled once more.

"Yeah, sure, just let me finish cleaning up," Zalia said, standing once more and going about cleaning off her tarp with some water from a large barrel on a cart nearby.

Boreal followed behind her as she dragged the tarp, pouncing on the trailing edge and momentarily sticking it to the ground with some icy magic. Zalia had to yank it to break off the ice and gave the feline a glare. Naturally, Boreal pretended nothing had happened and carried on innocently, cleaning herself.

"You're a pest," Zalia told Boreal.

Boreal looked up and she swore she could see a humorous twinkle in the feline's eyes.

She is becoming more and more intelligent by the day, Zalia thought.

She finished cleaning up and returned to her friends.

"Ready to get going?" she asked.

"Yeah, let's go find ourselves something to do!" Zen exclaimed.

CHAPTER FORTY-TWO

Spirits or Scoundrel

Zalia

They went about trying to find Faian, but seemingly out of nowhere, Eztari appeared. The man suggested they instead find the camp's huntmaster, the man in charge of organising hunts and foraging in the local area. It was a joint effort between the huntmaster and the quartermaster to ensure all the soldiers and camp workers were well-fed.

"I've heard he actually has been having a little bit of a problem recently that you might be able to help him with," Eztari said as they walked.

"Oh?" Zalia said, interested.

A chance to build some more goodwill with the soldiers and army around them was an opportunity she would take. Couldn't hurt, right?

"Yeah, some thief has been stealing food and no one can track or find the damn criminal. You lot are supposed to be excellent hunters, maybe you can," Eztari explained.

"It's worth a look," Zalia said.

Neither Zen or Ember said anything, and she assumed Indis agreed with her thoughts. The woman would have spoken up otherwise.

They ended up on the other side of camp where something akin to an entire kitchen was set up. It was a mostly outdoors affair, with various large kilns, fires, benches and other cooking stations set up under a large waterproofed cover. Under the cover a few chefs organised and ordered around a whole host of soldiers, the men and women running back and forth, preparing various ingredients in anticipation of their soon to wake comrades. In the centre of the whirlwind stood two people, a man and a woman, who were writing and talking over several books and sheets of paper.

"Just in there," Eztari said, pointing to the man and woman Zalia had spotted. She looked dubiously at the quickly moving storm of people rushing around.

"Should we wait until they're free?" Ember asked, looking similarly dubious.

"Oh I think you may end up waiting a very long time if you do that. No, just go and talk to them now," Eztari said.

"You're not going to introduce us?" Indis askes, obviously detecting something in the man's words and tone.

"Good luck!" he said before fading into the camp once more.

"Sooo, who wants to go in there?" Zalia asked.

All of them turned to Indis, who just sighed.

"Only because all three of you are terrible at talking to people," she muttered.

They watched as Indis walked into the people blender that the camp kitchen currently was. She was pushed around and had to struggle and shove through the mess towards the centre. After a minute or so, and half a bowl of soup spilt on her arm, Indis finally made it. They watched as she quickly spoke to the two organisers and pointed back towards them before saying something more. Both of the people listened, and once Indis was done talking, they spoke again briefly before nodding. The man put down the paper he was holding and made his way towards Zalia, Zen, and Ember. Unlike Indis, the man barely struggled to move through the crowd as people noticed him and moved out of his way as fast as possible. Indis quickly followed in his footsteps, using the path he created to make her way out as well. The man who approached looked well into his fifties with greying hair and weathered skin. He was somewhat short and wore simple work clothes, but despite the toughened and weathered appearance, had a kindly expression on his face.

"Greetins, I heard you lot wanted to volunteer ya help," he said.

Much like his appearance, the man's voice was rough but kind.

"We heard you have been having a theft problem?" Zalia said inquisitively.

"Aye, some rascals have been having a heyday with our supplies. Makes feeding this lot a real pain in my ass," he said, pointing a thumb over his shoulder.

"We can imagine. Would you mind showing us where you keep your supplies?" Indis asked.

"Aye, I can do that. We've had plenty of our men lookin' around to see what they can see but nothin' so far. Might be you lot can find something we can't, being in the profession and whatnot," he said.

He turned on the spot and began leading them towards an area on the other side of the kitchen.

"Started about the time we set up this damned camp, some of the lads reckon it's forest spirits stealin' our supplies but I've seen cheeky sods pull all kinds of tricks claimin' spirits before, I ain't tricked by it," he explained as they walked.

"How do you know it isn't spirits?" Zalia asked.

"Spirits don't want no food, lassie, they have no need for it. If they wanted us gone from their forests there're much easier ways they could go about it," he replied.

"Fair enough," Zalia said.

They then arrived at a large storehouse that was sat on the other side of the kitchen area than where they'd first arrived. It was somewhat near the wall of the camp, so Zalia could definitely see how it could be possible that something from the forest was making its way into the camp to take food.

"Any ideas what could be taking the supplies?" she asked.

"Not one. Whatever it is only takes fresh meat from our hunts, and only at night. We've tried postin' guards but they either don't see nothin' or end up claimin' spirits in the morn. Bloody sods probably fell asleep at the post," he said, still maintaining a cheery expression despite the scathing words. The two guards standing by the door looked down at their boots.

"We'll see what we can find," Indis promised.

"I've no doubt about it." He then unlocked the door, leaving them to it. "Lock up behind ya," he called out as he walked off.

"That was the huntmaster, in case you didn't catch on," Indis told them.

"Yeah, thought as much," Ember said.

"Should we have a look around?" Zalia asked.

"Yeah, split up and see if we can find anything," Zen agreed.

"*Hunt*," Zalia thought towards Boreal.

"*Hunt!*" an enthusiastic reply came into her mind.

Boreal began walking around the building and Zalia went in another direction, focusing on her Hunter's Sight passive. It would passively work without her conscious thought, but when it came to very subtle tracks, it definitely worked better when she focused. She first walked around the outside of the building, carefully examining the ground as the rest of her team went inside. She did a full circle of the building, finding plenty of tracks, just none that seemed suspicious. The biggest issue was the fact that it was a busy area, especially in the morning as breakfast was prepared for the waking camp. This meant that there were tracks from many soldiers and cooks around the area. Even with her newly improved sight from Boreal's shared passive, she was still not able to find anything. She went inside just as Boreal trotted up to her, looking a little annoyed.

"Find anything?" she asked the others.

Indis and Ember shook their heads.

"An apple," Zen said, chewing.

She sighed at him.

Zalia and Boreal joined the hunt inside, inspecting each corner and print they could find. She was about to give up on this path and suggest they wait until night to see if they could catch something when Boreal meowed. She turned to look at her and found Boreal looking up towards the ceiling. Zalia looked up and saw that in one of the corners, a piece of meat appeared to be stuck halfway inside the thatched roof.

"What the," Zalia murmured. "Hey, guys, come look at this."

The others came over and looked at it as well.

"They're slipping through the roof somehow?" Zen asked.

"Looks that way, though it looks like it's almost . . . a part of the roof," Zalia replied. She frowned. "Hey, come outside and give me a boost," she told Zen.

They went outside and with Zen's help and her single air step, she managed to jump up onto the roof of the building. What she found was both surprising and what she expected. The piece of meat was half sticking out of the roof on top as well. She tried to move it but it was like it had become a part of the thatching. She nimbly jumped back down to the others.

"Yep, sticks out of the top. It's almost like it got half phased through the roof before getting stuck again," she explained.

"Hmm," Indis said.

"I have heard of some creatures with the ability to move through solid objects, like spirits," Ember said.

"I was thinking just the same thing," Indis added.

Zalia looked up to the ceiling and then to the nearest wall. It was about fifteen metres, a jump she would have previously thought impossible, but with her newfound strength and abilities, she could probably do it herself at this point. She walked towards the closest part of the wall, carefully inspecting the ground as she went. She found nothing and moved back towards the others who were looking at her oddly.

"Sorry, I thought I would check for tracks. I'm thinking they might be jumping from the wall to the roof, then phasing through somehow," she explained.

"It's possible, might be tracks on the other side of the wall. We could check it out if you want," Indis said. It seemed she was coming to trust Zalia's intuition.

"From those towers, wouldn't the camp watch have seen anyone jumping over the wall?" Zen protested.

But Zalia was already moving; she ran towards the wall and jumped as high as she could, using her air step to reach the top with her arms, and hauled herself up. She grinned down at the others. "Be right back!" And then she nimbly jumped over the other side.

"Zalia!" Indis protested.

She landed lightly in a crouch on the grass, now on the other side of the wall. She looked around carefully, focusing on the ground and the marks on it. Going slightly further out, she finally found something. It was the footprints of a four-legged creature with giant paws, except the imprints were much less deep then she would expect them to be. She frowned at the tracks, inspecting them. The ones closer to the fence were slightly deeper, indicating the creature had jumped at that point. She wasn't surprised the camp's men hadn't been able to see the tracks, she barely could with her years of experience and abilities focused on this exact task. She turned around and with a run-up, leapt forwards to grasp the top of the wall and haul herself over again. She jumped back down, landing gently to see Indis glaring at her.

"Oh yeah, some kind of animal is jumping the wall, alright," Zalia said.

Indis gave her a pointed look.

"Hey!" she protested.

"Good find," Ember said, trying not to laugh.

Boreal meowed at Zalia indignantly, annoyed at having been left out of the trip over the wall.

"Don't worry little one, we'll be going out there in a minute anyways," she soothed.

"I don't think Boreal can understand you, Zalia," Zen said.

"I'm pretty sure Boreal is more intelligent than you, Zen," Zalia retorted.

"Anyways, let's go around the other side of the wall since the rest of us can't jump it," Indis interrupted.

"Sure, see you there," Zalia replied.

"Oh no you don't," Indis said, but it was too late.

Zalia had scooped up Boreal and put her on her shoulders, quickly running away to jump over the wall once more.

She began closely inspecting each track again and tried to determine why a creature with such large paws would leave such shallow indents in its tracks. Eventually, Indis, Zen, and Ember came up from around the side of the wall.

"See the tracks, here and here," Zalia said, pointing them out.

Indis was giving her some pretty poisonous stink eye but they all looked at the tracks she pointed out anyways.

"Bloody hell, Zalia, I can barely see those even when you point them out," Ember said appreciatively.

"Let's track them, shall we?" Zalia asked.

"Sure, how many of them are there do you think?" Zen asked.

"Not sure, it's quite hard to tell. It looks like one most of the time, but some-times . . . maybe two," Zalia replied.

It was quite hard to see, but she thought the creatures might actually be intelligent enough to walk in each other's tracks, giving the appearance of only one creature. Added to the fact that they left such light imprints, it meant there could be one, two, or three and she wouldn't be able to tell. What her ability did still manage to tell her, however, was that the creatures had come not so long ago, maybe just four or five hours ago.

The tracking took a long time. Thankfully, they had left in the morning and had a lot of daylight left, but still, even with Zalia's skill it was difficult. She kept having to backtrack, sometimes having to search the nearby area as the tracks simply vanished. Each time, however, they managed to find the tracks once more. Finally, after an hour, she was able to apply her Hunter's Mark to the creature. This helped greatly, as she could determine its general direction, which meant she could find the next sets of tracks much more easily than before. Zen, Ember, and Indis were of basically no help in tracking, but she'd expected nothing less considering the difficulty even she had. Boreal surprised her, though, managing a couple times to find the next set of tracks before her. They had to stop once for Zen to eat again—Apparently as Zalia had to eat less and less each day, the large front line warrior had needed to eat more and more.. But finally, after four and a half hours of tracking, they stumbled onto something.

Zalia knew they had found what they were looking for as the sky above them began to darken by some magic. She gestured for her team to be quiet and stay where they were as she slowly and carefully moved up and over the small ridge ahead. She began crawling until she could see over the other side.

Over the ridge sat a small pool that glittered like it was reflecting the stars. The sky above had gone dark and though the sun could still be seen, its light had been reduced to that of the moons. There was a clearing around the pool, the space occupied by stones of various sizes, upon which the creatures she had been tracking lay. They were large, wolf-like creatures—some were sleeping on the stones, and some were walking around. Each of them was translucent, as if not quite real, and their thick fur coats sparkled with stars, much like the pool they surrounded. The entire clearing was surrounded by the large ridge that Zalia now peeked over, with thick trees that had grown into an almost wall-like defence for the area. She had a feeling that without her Hunter's Mark ability, she would not have been able to find this place. As she looked closer, a stone deep within the pool was reflecting light like it was mirrored, and emitting a soft light in the darkness of the water. Her initial guess of there being just one or two of the creatures was obviously very wrong; a dozen or more of them were visible in the clearing, with more possibly gone or hidden. She very slowly and quietly moved back away to her team.

As she arrived to regroup, she signalled that they should move away and so they did. Only once the sky was normal again did she dare speak.

"We have a little bit of a problem. I don't think we can deal with this alone," she told them.

Seeing Indis's frown, she explained what she had discovered: the pool, the sky, and the many wolf-like creatures.

"Did you manage to see what rank any of them were?" Indis asked.

Zalia shook her head. "Didn't want to get close enough to see, too dangerous," she replied.

"We should definitely get some help then, it's not worth the risk," Ember said.

Zen and Indis also agreed, and so they made their way back towards the war camp. As they moved quickly through the forest, Zalia's thoughts were stuck on the ethereal beauty of the creatures she had seen.

It would be a shame to kill them, she thought.

And in thinking that, she realised she really didn't want to. There was something about the creatures that made her unwilling to disturb them, some instinct that they were on her side, in a way. She pondered those thoughts, trying to come to a decision.

CHAPTER FORTY-THREE

New Eyes and Deeper Thoughts

Zalia

Before they arrived back in camp, Zalia called a stop for a few minutes, wanting to talk to the others.

"I don't think we should tell them about the ethereal creatures just yet," she told them.

Indis frowned.

"Why not?" Zen asked.

"It's just a feeling I have," Zalia said, trying to figure out why she felt that way.

"A feeling?" Indis asked.

"I don't know . . . I feel like we shouldn't disturb the creatures," Zalia tried to explain.

"Any reason in particular? We could gain a lot of goodwill for telling the huntmaster about them, whereas we gain nothing if we don't tell him," Indis tried to reason.

"It's not always about what you can and cannot gain from a situation, Indis," Zalia said, feeling somewhat defensive of the creatures.

"Alright, alright," Indis said, putting her hands up in surrender, "we won't tell them just yet. But Zalia, you have got to give us a reason."

"This is quite unlike you, Zalia, usually you would be excited for such a hunt," Ember pointed out.

At the mention of the word "hunt," Boreal meowed at Zalia. But she just scratched the bloodthirsty predator behind the ears.

"I know and I will, just give me a bit to think it over," she told them.

There was a moment of silence.

"You've been really quiet recently, Zen," Zalia said, trying to change the subject.

Indis nodded and Ember scrunched up her eyebrows as if she'd also just realised that.

"I've been thinking," he said simply.

"About?" Ember asked.

"About stuff, I don't really want to talk about it yet," he answered, leaving it at that.

There was another moment of silence, and Zalia began to look over the messages she'd left sitting in the back of her mind, the list popping into her vision at her thought. She had taken to ignoring messages for longer periods of time as her progress slowed down after reaching mid-Iron rank in a few abilities. She thought her advancement had slowed because a few things had reached a more natural level for her age, though she couldn't prove that, it was just another instinctive feeling.

> **Congratulations! Hunter's Sight has reached Iron 9.**
> **Congratulations! Flora Identification has reached Iron 7.**
> **Congratulations! Aura Observation has**
> **gained two levels, reaching Tin 16.**
> **Congratulations! Low Light Vision has gained**
> **two levels, reaching Tin 17.**
> **Congratulations! Teaching has reached Iron 6.**
> **Congratulations! Sword - Weapon Proficiency has reached Iron 6.**

It wasn't much progress, though she hadn't really done much recently other than travel and talk. Hunter's Sight had gained an extra level from the hours of tracking, and her other abilities had levelled through various small bits of training and observation she was always doing. Looking at her profile, she did notice another section had been added to the bottom.

> **Profile - Zalia Taori**
> **Health - Excellent**
> **Mana - Full**
> **Stamina - Full**
> **Class One - Hunter - Iron 7**
> **Linked Attributes - Strength, Dexterity**
> **Active Skills**
> **Kill Shot - Iron 7**
> **Hunter's Mark - Iron 8**
> **Fight or Flight - Iron 9**
> **Passive Skills**
> **Hunter's Sight - Iron 9**

Survivalist - Iron 12
Class Two - Herbalist - Iron 6
Linked Attributes - Vitality, Resilience
Active Skills
Flora Identification - Iron 7
Preparation - Iron 8
Stasis - Iron 6
Passive Skills
Harvester - Iron 9
Herbal Magic - Iron 10
Unity Class - Druid - Iron 5
Linked Attributes - Wisdom, Intellect
Active Skills
Nature's Wrath - Iron 5
Protection of the Wilds - Iron 6
Passive Skills
Healing Presence - Iron 12
General Passives
Heat Resistance - Iron 12
Cold Resistance - Iron 12
Aura Observation - Tin 16
Low Light Vision - Tin 17
Poison Resistance - Iron 7
Mobility - Iron 15
Stealth - Iron 12
Trapper - Iron 12
Teaching - Iron 6
Weapon Proficiencies
Bow - Iron 14
Sword - Iron 6
Throwing Knives - Tin 11
Beast Bond - Boreal - Minor
Shared Passives
Feline Eyes - Iron

She focused on the last ability and was rewarded with an ability description.

Feline Eyes - passive - body enhancement
Tin - The sharpness of your vision is dramatically increased.
Iron - When activated, you may see heat in
addition to your normal vision.

Oh? Zalia thought.

She should've had a look at all this earlier, but now was as good a time as any.

"We should get moving again," Indis said, the silence having stretched on as Zalia read through her profile.

They got up and began moving, and Zalia thought about the shared passive, how it could activate the heat vision. The change was instant and extremely noticeable, Zalia was able to see the heat emitted by everything around her. Her three teammates were the obvious sources nearby, emitting quite a lot of heat into the area, but she could also see a multitude of small critters amongst the leaves and undergrowth. She could even faintly see where her teammates had walked simply by the heat difference they left behind in the air, minor thought it was. It might have been something she wouldn't have previously been able to see or notice, but with her dramatically increased vision and mental attributes, she could distinguish it faintly.

She looked around the world with literal new eyes, taking in every single piece of information provided by this new type of vision. She squinted at Boreal, who didn't leave behind any type of heat trail or emit anything at all. Zalia knew for a fact that Boreal was one warm kitten, and yet she was unable to see Boreal at all with the new vision; the feline blended in perfectly with the surroundings. Only by also using her normal vision was she able to see Boreal. Due to some kind of innate magic, maybe?

"*So this is how you see the world,*" Zalia thought towards Boreal. She forgot that she could share mental messages with the feline and only remembered when Boreal looked up at her and mewed.

Zalia began playing around with her Heat Resistance passive Iron rank ability, trying to mask herself, using the new vision as a guide to her success. The Iron rank allowed her to manipulate heat to a small degree, and she did have some success in lowering how much of the heat escaped her body. It would be a long time until she managed to match what Boreal was doing to any degree, but if she worked at it, it could be a possible advantage in future.

She immediately felt guilty about berating Indis for seeking any advantage she could, because in a way, she did the exact same thing. While Zalia sought any advantage in survival, Indis sought any social advantage, anything that could allow House Indis to survive. Whilst the two were somewhat different, it was a similar mental attitude, just in two different situations. She would apologise later; with the strong front she put up, Zalia did sometimes forget that the woman had her own struggles. Indis was also much younger than her, in her midtwenties, another thing she forgot about because of how mature the woman acted most of the time.

Having read over her profile for the first time in a while, and having thoughts about the ethereal creatures on her mind, she made a connection between two things. Her Druid class description had said,

> **"You are a protector of nature and the natural cycle of life and death. Through your instincts and knowledge you understand both the flora and fauna of the wild places of the world. You use this ability to preserve the balance as you see fit."**

Maybe the instincts she had to protect the ethereal beings was some unwritten ability granted by her Druid class. In fact, she had been growing steadily less joyful about the prospect of hunting at all as her classes had grown stronger. At least, hunting without purpose. Now, the definition she put behind the word "hunt" was different. Now, she was hunting down the perpetrator of the current imbalance in nature, and in that cause she still felt resolute. She hadn't really considered it before and had never asked anyone, but it might be possible that her classes were affecting her mind and how she thought. They could affect her body, abilities, and all other aspects of her senses. Why not how she thought and acted?

She didn't feel like her other two classes were affecting how she thought, necessarily. They definitely affected how she could respond in any given situation, but the Druid class was her Unity class, the class that was meant to tie the other two together. At least, that's what she thought it meant. She had never really learnt what it all meant; despite originally going to the kingdom to learn about it all, no one else had three classes like she did. Nobody else she met had a Unity class, so as far as she knew, she would have to figure that out herself. Honestly, other than the basics, the only thing she had really learnt so far about her magic was that it was much different than everyone else's.

"Hey, Indis," Zalia called.

The other three were walking slightly ahead of her and Boreal, her pace had slowed as she was deep in thought. Indis fell back to keep pace with Zalia.

"Yes?" Indis asked.

"I'm sorry for getting on your case about finding every advantage you can in any given situation. I sometimes forget what you're dealing with, you always keep up such a strong and confident face," Zalia said quietly.

Indis sighed, a crack appearing in her ever-stoic expression. "I appreciate the apology, Zalia. You are right, though, that I should not always look for the most advantageous outcome. Sometimes, it is simply best to do what is right," she said, a faraway look in her eyes.

"Do you know if our classes affect our mind, thoughts, and actions?" Zalia asked.

Indis's eyes refocused and her expression became neutral once more. It was strange to see behind the mask the woman always had up and Zalia wasn't quite sure what to say, so she'd chosen what was safest and changed the subject. Indis would talk when she was ready, maybe.

"Some research has been done into the topic, though it is hard to come to any actual conclusion about it. Many think so, though it might simply be that the manner in which we can respond to any given situation is determined by our abilities, which may slowly change our mind and temperament to fit the situation," Indis replied.

"I think that my Druid class, called a Unity class in my profile, might have something to do with my instincts about the ethereal creatures. When I gained it, the class description talked about using my instincts and knowledge to preserve the balance of life and death in nature. I just . . . there is something about them that feels pure and natural despite their otherworldly appearance. And I think we should leave them be," Zalia explained.

Indis gave her an appraising look. "Maybe. I have learnt it is often a good idea to trust your instincts, so I will go with you on this one. What do you want to tell the people in camp?" Indis asked.

"Tell them we may be onto something but need another few days to look into it. Maybe I can communicate with the creatures somehow?" Zalia said questioningly.

"Not impossible, though highly dangerous," Indis said.

"Maybe I can catch one when it's out taking food again; it would be significantly less dangerous than walking into the whole pack of them," Zalia suggested.

"That is a much better idea. With us there to support you, and the camp nearby, we could at least get some help," Indis said, looking a little less apprehensive at the better idea.

"Alright, that's decided, then. Thank you, Lady Indis, for your help," Zalia said warmly.

It was the first time that Zalia had ever called her "Lady Indis" without some level of sarcasm or flippancy in her tone. She swore she saw another small crack in the woman's mask before she schooled herself into a neutral expression.

"Of course, Zalia of the Wilds," Indis replied.

It took them significantly less time to get back to the camp than it did for them to track the creatures all the way back to their glade. The largest part of the major time difference was the amount of backtracking and examining tracks that Zalia had needed to do on the way there. The time it took to travel back was almost a quarter of what it took to get there in the first place. Now that she wasn't so focused on tracking anymore, Zalia had time to appreciate the surrounding nature with her new type of vision. She'd never really considered just how alive the forest was, with hundreds of various critters and creatures going about their own business. Did insects also have a rank? Were there little tiny Gold rank ants waging incredible battles with each other down in their own small worlds in the woods?

She closely observed everything with her newly gained vision and heat vision, appreciating nature so much that the time flew by and before she knew it, they had arrived back at camp. They entered through the gate, the four of them known to the guards by now as people to be let in, and made their way towards the far right end of the camp. They arrived to find it much the same as when they had left; the kitchen area was a nightmare of movement as the soldiers prepared lunch for their comrades.

"I've got it this time," Zalia said as she noticed Indis looking with dread at the storm of movement.

As she approached, she tried something to keep the soldiers from her path. She simultaneously pushed her healing into the ones nearby whilst also cooling the air in her path to freezing temperatures. The strange contradiction of freezing air and warm healing pulsing through their bodies made the soldiers stop and look around, moving out the way as Zalia forged towards the centre where the huntmaster stood.

She made it through quickly and without much hassle, only having to shove past a duo of people who were quite focused on their tasks.

"Huntmaster," Zalia said by way of greeting.

"Cat tamer," the huntmaster said, looking at Boreal, who stood by Zalia's legs.

"We may have found something but will need an extra day or two to investigate," Zalia told him.

The man just nodded, going back to jotting down a few numbers like he was doing some math.

Zalia shrugged and turned away, guessing the man didn't really expect much to come from their investigation and probably thought they were making an excuse for more time.

"So?" Zen asked.

"He didn't seem to care, so we have ourselves some more time," Zalia said.

"Alright then, what's the plan?" Ember asked.

"The plan, is we make a plan," Indis said.

"Thrilling," Zen said in a bored tone.

CHAPTER FORTY-FOUR

Druid Things

Zalia

Always with the planning," Zen complained.

"Oh shut it, you," Zalia told him.

They were sitting in their tent, Ember with the small booklet she had rescued from Zalia's grasp the first time she tried to draw a map of the north. They had decided if they were going to do some more planning, they may as well write it all out, right?

"Ok, so here's what we've got so far," Ember started.

"Working for the Morning's Shade, we are trying to find the truth about the rituals by gaining what information we can from the rebellion. In coming here, we've realised that not only can we not fully trust our own organisation's leader but the rebellion might be truthfully founded after all. Now, we are trying to get as much information out of the generals as we can, and potentially assist them in any way we can through our connections in an effort to take down the king," Ember finished, reading off the page.

"Right, now add at the bottom, 'Gaining trust by helping with an issue in the camp, but that has now turned into another complicated issue because of Zalia's Druidic life-and-death balancing powers'," Indis said.

Boreal meowed.

"And add that at the end," Zalia said.

Ember dutifully wrote "meow" on the page. She turned the book to show them and everything was written in bulleted, summarised points.

"Right, so what now?" Zen asked.

"We catch out one of the creatures alone and Zalia somehow communicates with it?" Indis said questioningly.

Ember jotted down the idea.

"Could work. We catch one out as it tries to enter camp, it might be a higher rank, but if it was, I can't see why it would be sneaking into the camp for food the way it does," Zalia added a little distractedly.

She was still working on manipulating the heat around her to make herself invisible to the Heat Sight. In a way, the process felt similar to a type of training she had done previously. When she had first gained the ability to perform the Dodge-vine ritual, she had begun casting it constantly to make it a never-fading power around her. She now cast the ritual subconsciously all the time on herself, her allies and even a couple of times accidentally on passerby. The heat trick was similar, except performing it was much more complicated and would probably take much, much longer to do subconsciously.

"What are you doing?" Indis asked.

"Huh? Oh sorry, what was that?" Zalia asked.

She had completely missed what the woman had said as she focused on working her magic.

"I said, do you have any ideas about how to communicate with it once we do catch it out?" Indis repeated.

"Um, not really, no. I was just kind of hoping I'd be able to, or something would come up. I want to ask if they'll stop stealing, and maybe we could solve our problem that way," Zalia said.

"Hoping isn't really a good plan," Indis pointed out.

"Yes . . ." Zalia said.

"And yet you think it will work?" Indis asked.

Zalia sighed. "No, I don't know. All I know is I want to somehow resolve this in a peaceful manner. How do you normally communicate with an ethereal wolf creature?" Zalia asked back.

Back in Zalia's world, that might have seemed like an insane question. Here, her teammates just looked thoughtful.

"No clue, never seen them before and still haven't," Ember said.

"Boreal understands you a bit," Indis said hopefully.

"Took weeks for that to happen and I have no idea if that is because of our bond or her own intelligence," Zalia said.

"Damn," Indis muttered.

"Yeah," Zalia agreed.

There were a few moments of silence as they all considered what to do.

"Maybe . . ." Zalia started, having an idea.

"Go on," Ember urged.

"Well, they're coming here for food, right? Or at least that's what they're taking. Why don't we just hunt something and give it to them as a sort of peace offering?" Zalia suggested.

"That could work," Ember said.

"We don't have any idea how they'll react, though. These could be aggressive beasts for all we know," Indis said, sighing.

"We have to try," Zalia insisted.

"Because of your weird instincts, I know," Indis grumbled.

"What if they attack us when we try?" Zen asked.

"We defend ourselves, of course," Indis replied.

"Seems like we have a plan down, then," Zalia said.

"Finally, I'm hungry," Zen said.

"Hungry? Again?" Indis asked incredulously.

"Yeah, so?" Zen asked defensively.

"You're ridiculous, come on," Indis replied as she stood up and walked out of the tent.

Zen stood up and followed her.

"Get me something small as well!" Ember called after them.

Both Zalia and Ember sat in silence, the only sound being Boreal's purr as Zalia petted her. Ember read through the notes again before dropping her arm to the ground.

"Did you always live in the north?" Ember asked.

Zalia didn't respond for a moment, trying to decide how to answer the question.

"No, not always," Zalia replied.

"I've been thinking about what to do once this is all over, where to go. I'm not sure I'll stay with the Morning's Shade after all we've learnt. Why did you move to the north originally?" Ember asked.

That was a hard question.

"Where I come from, the human race was well on the way to destroying the natural world. Forests and ecosystems were destroyed, the very air around us was turning to poison, and the land was turning into endless cities filled with millions of people. The north was one of the only places that hadn't quite been tamed by our people yet, and so I moved there. I moved to get away from everything, from the daily news of horrific accidents or disasters. Different nations were consistently at war, killing each other in a constant bid to claim what others had. I couldn't deal with it," Zalia explained.

"It sounds horrible," Ember said sombrely.

"It was. When I came here, I thought maybe people here were different, maybe there wasn't so much death and disaster everywhere, and so I came back to human civilization. Not that different so far," Zalia continued, gesturing to the tent walls and the army surrounding them.

"You'll go back once this is over?" Ember asked.

"Oh yeah. I plan to go much further north than I was before. As far as I know, no one has bothered to explore further, so I may as well see what's up there," Zalia replied.

"Sounds exciting," Ember said.

She didn't make it explicit, but the meaning was clear. If Zalia wanted, Ember would come with her.

"I can't wait. Back where I'm from I had no power whatsoever, no magic, no increased strength, and so I left. I left because I felt there was nothing I could do to change the course of the world. Here, I might not be as strong as some, but I have the power to actually have an impact on what happens next. Maybe, just maybe, I can help prevent a disaster. I would have left already otherwise," Zalia said.

Ember nodded slowly, seeming to understand. At that moment, Indis and Zen pushed back into the tent, the former holding a platter of food and the latter almost stepping on her heels.

After the other three had finished eating, the five of them left the camp for the forested area beyond the walls. Neither Boreal or Zalia had eaten, and neither would need to for the next two days or so after the hunt they'd gone on that morning. One of the reasons Zalia didn't mind being in the human lands so much was because they had, as of yet, failed to tame the wilds. Despite the cities and towns around, much of the land was still covered in forests filled with hundreds of animals.

"You guys go ahead, I want to spend some time looking around," Zalia said to the others.

"You sure?" Ember asked.

"Quite sure, I'll be able to find you, no worries," Zalia said.

"Are you saying we aren't stealthy?" Indis asked.

Zalia just looked pointedly at Zen.

"Fair point," Indis conceded.

"Hey!" Zen said in protest.

"Oh shush, you'll scare away everything within a kilometre," Ember complained.

They moved off, continuing in that vein as they went. Zalia smiled as they left, amused at their bantering. Despite her early misgivings about working with anyone at all, they weren't so bad, for humans. She began walking around, using her Flora Identification on all manner of plants around her—from trees, to bushes, to ground covers. She didn't find anything new that her Herbalism magic indicated would be useful, but had come to enjoy the simple process. She did find some Bitterbalm and Dodge-vine around, both of them very common in the forested areas of the north, though not so far north as the snow. She pulled out some Zephyr, the plant she had discovered on the high-up slopes of the mountain that Glemp called home. She hadn't yet really played around with what she could accomplish with the herb, having been too distracted by the current situation.

Once she held it, she could immediately feel how it could be used, in a general sense. It could add the element of air to any ritual she performed, and on its own, had a wide variety of uses. She was excited for a moment but after thinking about it, she was given the information that it wouldn't allow her to fly. Slightly disappointed but still hopeful, her ability informed her that it could be used to fall slowly if needed. Thinking of her bow, she was also informed that it could be used to enhance the flight of an arrow, giving it an increased range and reducing the impact of wind. It had a variety of other uses as well, though one she was most interested in was mixing it with Dodge-vine, which would create a barrier of wind that would be quite effective on small projectiles. Using a combination of the barrier and the enhancement on her own arrows would mean she could shoot from relative safety while her own projectiles were unaffected by the barrier. In addition to the standard Dodge-vine ritual, she would be quite protected from any small projectiles of her own rank.

She played around for a while, using the slow-fall ritual on Boreal. When she did, she realised it didn't just have a slow-fall effect. Boreal bounced around, jumping from tree to tree as she was lightened by the magic, each of her jumps going much higher than usual. Zalia decided to try it herself and found she could jump almost twice as high as she previously could. It wasn't quite as good as flying but for now it would do.

Zalia and Boreal jumped through the boughs of the trees, her Hunter's Sight easily able to track where her team had walked, even at a distance. Being able to semi-fly through the treetops was exhilarating; though she miscalculated a few times early on, her increased dexterity and mental attributes allowed her to move quite speedily. She quickly caught up to her team, floating down from the treetops to land in front of them.

Indis rolled her eyes at Zalia. "You are absurd."

"Absurd and floaty," Zalia countered.

The ritual wasn't so much slow-fall as reduced weight, and it meant a lot of good things for her. Her weight wasn't so reduced that it made it hard to run, but she would leave lighter tracks and could move more easily while it was active.

"That was kind of cool," Ember admitted.

"Wanna join me?" Zalia asked, a little excited.

"As much as floating around seems fun, we are kind of out here for a reason," Indis said, stopping them before it got too far.

"Oh, right," Zalia replied, a little chagrined.

"Right, we found some fresh tracks of something smaller further back, or do you want something larger?" Zen asked.

"Something medium?" Zalia suggested.

"Something medium," Indis agreed.

It didn't take long, Zalia was able to easily find a medium-sized creature that they hunted down with skill. The poor Tin rank creature didn't stand a chance as the four Iron ranks descended on it. Zalia felt bad about killing the poor thing, a medium-sized, four-legged creature that looked something like a badger. The unfair fight left a sour taste in her mouth, it wasn't a hunt necessary for their survival but rather for something that might not even work.

It was only a few hours past midday so they still had quite a bit of time. They meandered through the forest to the side of the camp's wall which they knew the creatures to enter through. Following the hard-to-see tracks a little ways away from the wall, Zalia set down her tarp and put the poor hunted animal down on it. Now, it was just going to be a waiting game. The ethereal wolf might not even show up that night or the next but if it did they wanted to be ready.

It was many hours of waiting before something finally happened. Zalia and her team were hidden near the offering, hoping that the creature would arrive. As the sun set and nothing appeared, they began to worry. Darkness overtook the world and still nothing. About an hour after sunset, they saw a dim light moving slowly through the trees towards them. They all got ready, hoping the creature wouldn't just immediately attack or run away. This was the moment of truth.

Out of the trees came a starry wolf, its body ethereal and translucent with small, pinpoint stars glittering within. As it got closer to the camp wall, which was still some few hundred metres away, the wolf was slowly dimming further. The creature finally arrived near to where they had laid down the offering and stopped. They all moved out of hiding, still some ten to fifteen metres away, and the creature bared its teeth as it noticed their appearance.

"Please, we mean you no harm," Zalia said, trying to keep a friendly and calm tone.

It seemed to hesitate for a moment, unwilling to approach any further.

"We wish to make an offering," Zalia added, gesturing to the body they had laid out on the tarp.

It was at that moment that she had an idea. And the ethereal wolf seemed to understand, to some degree, so she continued on.

"We would greatly appreciate it if you could stop taking the food that is stored within our camp." She gestured towards the camp behind her. "I know that you still need to eat, and certainly, taking from us is easier than hunting for yourself. So, I suggest a compromise. Further to the east there are many more camps of soldiers that are guarded much worse. They hold the people responsible for the current imbalance in nature.

We would ask you instead take food from them," Zalia finished, really hoping the creature understood her and she wasn't being a complete fool.

The wolf just stared at her for a moment, sniffing at the air. Zalia looked back at the others, and Indis just shrugged, gesturing for her to continue.

"Um, feel free to take this offering either way," Zalia added.

She was really starting to doubt their whole plan now.

Boreal moved forwards and sat next to Zalia, giving the wolf one single meow.

The creature took another step forwards slowly and bent down to pick up the body laid down for it, raising its head and looking straight into Zalia's eyes. The thought came into her mind not in any language or words but as the imprint of a concept. Acceptance.

CHAPTER FORTY-FIVE

Night Out

Zalia

They watched as the ethereal being walked away, holding the offering in its mouth.

"Well," Zalia started.

"I'm genuinely surprised that worked at all," Indis said.

Zalia frowned. "Why wouldn't it have?" she asked.

"Because our plan was to talk at the glowing star wolf and give it something to eat," Indis explained.

"Flawless, I say," Zalia replied proudly.

Indis refrained from commenting.

"Though, I only got an acceptance from it, so I don't actually know if it's going to come back here or do as I asked," Zalia added.

Indis raised an eyebrow as if to say, "See, my point stands."

"It'll be fine, I'm sure," Ember told her.

"Still, we should wait until after tomorrow night to see if it does come back to take more. If it doesn't, we can tell them we succeeded in stopping the issue," Zalia said.

Boreal was still looking in the direction that the wolf had gone.

"Wanted to make a new friend?" Zalia asked Boreal.

"*Friend*," Boreal said into Zalia's mind.

"You are right, already a friend," Zalia said decisively.

Whenever Boreal spoke into her mind now it came with added emotion or images so that despite the single word sentences, the words carried more meaning.

"Is this speech a result of our bond, or my Druid class?" Zalia wondered.

The Beast Bond description hadn't said they could speak to each other in their minds, and Boreal had spoken to her prior to the bond forming. She had originally thought it an ability of Boreal's but now, having been able to interpret the wolf's message, she reconsidered. It might be that her Druid class advancing was allowing her to interpret, or the advancement of her mental attributes. But she thought the former, since she could understand actual words from Boreal. That part she thought might come from the feline's own basic understanding of the language. That thought gave rise to a question.

"What do you call the language we speak?" Zalia asked.

"What?" Zen asked, as if he hadn't heard correctly.

"Endari," Indis said.

"Probably could have guessed that," Zalia said, feeling a little stupid.

"Better to ask than assume," Indis replied.

"Eloquent as always, Lady Indis. What about other kingdoms or nations, are there any?" Zalia asked.

"Indeed. There are people who live in the desert to the south of Endaria's borders. They live quite a brutal and danger-wrought life due to the inhospitality of the lands they dwell in. The desert is not a good place to go," Indis said.

"Sounds like my kind of place," Zalia replied. She had just told Ember of her plans to go far north after this but maybe, just maybe, the south was an option.

"Further west there is another kingdom, though it is not ruled by a king as we know it. Those lands are owned by the Astar. They are genderless and so don't have a king, but a monarch, one who has ruled for a very, very long time. As far as is known about them, they don't age and die like we do, though higher-ranked people don't age normally either. Not much otherwise is known since they are not so accepting of people entering their lands," Indis continued.

Astar, I wonder what they look like, Zalia thought.

"Then there are the Goblins that live in the mountain, whom you have met, of course," Indis added.

"Those Born of Heat and Stone," Zalia corrected.

"Apologies, yes, the Born of Heat and Stone," Indis replied.

"What about the large humanoid covered in fur that we saw guarding the door at Eztari's little hideout in the town back west?" Zalia asked.

Indis frowned and was about to speak but Ember got there first.

"They are a dying people. They used to live here but the Kingdom of Endaria slaughtered them and took their lands. Now there are very few, scattered across the kingdom," Ember said, a little venom in her voice. It was obviously a touchy subject for some.

"Humans have done very similar things where I come from too," Zalia said, a hint of sadness in her tone.

They reached the gate back around the other side of the camp, one of the large doors opened to let them enter.

"It is a part of history that much of the official documentation and writing has wiped out. We don't know that it was our people who did it," Indis rebuked.

"We stand here on their lands while their people own nothing, fewer and fewer of them alive with each passing year. What more is there to know?" Ember responded, anger now evident in her tone.

Both women fell silent.

Definitely a touchy subject, Zalia thought, regretting bringing it up.

She didn't feel too bad, however, since she had not known. Now she did.

"Rrrright, you all going to go to sleep soon?" Zalia asked, trying to change the subject but only managing it clumsily.

They all gave her an affirmative.

"Boreal and I won't be able to sleep for another six hours or so, so um . . . we're gonna walk around the forest or something," Zalia said.

"See you in the morning," Zen said by way of a farewell, already yawning.

The other two bid her goodbye for the night and Zalia turned to Boreal.

"What do you want to do?" she asked.

Boreal looked like she was considering the question, a little tilt to her head. Zalia could almost see the thought forming.

"And we aren't going hunting again, we already went twice today," Zalia added.

Boreal meowed in protest.

"No! Three times in a day is too many. We don't even need to eat for another two days," Zalia scolded.

Boreal gave a small, sad mew.

"Not today and that's final. We could go for a run through the forest again, though, if you would like," Zalia suggested.

This seemed to interest Boreal as she sat up a little straighter.

"*Run*," Boreal sent to Zalia's mind.

"Alright, a run it is!" Zalia said happily.

The two of them walked calmly through the camp until they reached the gate once more. They were allowed out, but they did receive a few odd glances.

"We'll be back in a few hours," she told the guard.

Boreal meowed at the guard.

"And she says she likes your hat," Zalia added.

"My ha—My helmet?" the guard asked, a little confused.

Boreal gave another meow that sounded like it had a tone of approval to it.

"Ah, she hasn't yet discerned the difference between the two words. She also wants to say it looks like it is a very tough hide and she approves," Zalia told him.

"Thank you?" the guard said, looking down at Boreal.

"You're quite welcome," Zalia said, smiling brightly.

They moved through the open gate and into the forest.

"She is a weird one," Zalia heard the guard say to the other at the door.

"Speaks cat maybe?" the other guard, a woman, questioned.

"Weird ability but possible I guess," the man replied.

The gate slammed shut and Zalia and Boreal looked out into the forest, dark to most but not to them.

Zalia turned to Boreal. "Ready?"

"*Run*," Boreal said.

"Run," Zalia agreed.

They ran for hours, the combination of Iron rank vitality, reduced weight, and Iron rank Mobility giving them both quite a bit of stamina. Zalia wasn't quite sure if Boreal had the Mobility passive or could even get it but assumed the feline must have something like it. She also went easy on the Zephyr, not wanting to run out anytime soon, as she would not have a chance to get more unless she went by Glemp's home. They stopped by a small stream that meandered slowly through the forest and sped up as it dropped a small distance to a beautiful enclosed pond not far beneath.

They trekked slowly around the small ledge and found a safe path down to the pond. Zalia sat on a rock nearby as Boreal went up and began drinking from the cool water. She had gained another level of Mobility from the run, bringing her to Iron sixteen, the ability having advanced extremely quickly compared to her others. Her daily runs were really paying off, and she was excited to learn what the Bronze rank tier would provide. Due to the nature of the passive, it wasn't impossible for it to provide her with a form of flight, but she doubted something like that would come from a general passive.

"Enjoy the drink?" Zalia asked as Boreal walked up to her.

"*Water*," Boreal said.

The thought came with a feeling of contentment.

"Good, want to head back or stay here a while?" she asked, giving the decision to Boreal.

"*Stay*," Boreal replied.

Zalia found a more comfortable spot nearby, using her bag as a rest as she lay next to the pond. She smiled as she relaxed, closing her eyes.

"Not needing to sleep as much is quite relaxing sometimes," Zalia said to Boreal.

The feline didn't respond, instead pouncing on Zalia's foot and freezing it to the ground.

"Hey, stop that," Zalia said, pretending she couldn't free her foot from its icy prison.

Boreal seemed proud of her success in sticking the foot to the ground.

"You, young Boreal, are a menace," Zalia said, looking over her foot at the little devil.

She used her Heat Resistance passive to quickly melt the ice and performed a small Bitterbalm, Zephyr, and Snow-leaf ritual to bind Boreal's legs to the ground with ice and increase her weight. She struggled to break free but was held tight.

Boreal meowed in complaint.

"*Help!*" Boreal said into her mind.

A sensation of freedom and pleading, and an image of Boreal soaring through the treetops accompanied it.

Zalia laughed and Boreal finally broke free, the ritual dissolving as the tiny amount of herbs she used in it were quickly consumed. Boreal gave her a cute little glare, which only made Zalia laugh all the more.

They spent the next hour or so by the pond, playing various games of hide and seek, play-wrestling, and the like.

They returned to the camp soon after, Zalia putting a little mark on her map of the pond's location. It was a really nice place to relax, or so she thought. This time as she returned, she decided to jump the wall with Boreal and sneak in. Mostly just to confuse the guards a little.

The lack of security the camp had against someone like her was concerning for a moment, but she realised that there were probably people like Eztari around, keeping watch for the stealthier people.

She returned to the tent where the rest of her team was currently asleep. As she lay down, Boreal came and curled up beside her, and the two of them finally managed to fall asleep some minutes later. With sweet dreams of ethereal wolves and beautiful ponds, she drifted off into unconsciousness.

CHAPTER FORTY-SIX

Stems and Petals

Zalia

Zalia awoke with a start, heart beating as adrenaline pumped through her body. She looked around quickly, thankfully seeing no immediate danger. She did notice that there was sun shining brightly onto the tent walls, lighting up the inside somewhat. She also noticed that none of her teammates were present, though Boreal was still curled up, only now blinking blearily at her.

Did I sleep in? she wondered.

Ever since her Survivalist passive had reached Iron rank, she needed less and less sleep and she didn't remember the last time she'd slept past sunrise.

"Meow," complained Boreal.

"Oh, don't be a sook," Zalia said, stretching luxuriantly.

Boreal uncurled, stretching in a way that seemed intended to mock her own movements. Zalia gave her a light push, throwing her off balance for only a second before Boreal dipped down, getting ready to pounce.

"Oh no, please, not this early," Zalia complained.

Boreal, of course, didn't listen. She jumped at her, and Zalia caught her midjump, rolling over as she laughed. She held Boreal above her head, the feline giving a small sound of outrage as she struggled to get free.

"No attacking first thing in the morning," Zalia scolded, the smile on her face contradictory to her faked tone.

Boreal meowed at her.

"You have to promise!" Zalia insisted.

There was silence for a moment, Boreal and Zalia holding eye contact. Soon enough, she felt a sensation of acceptance sent from Boreal.

"Wonderful," Zalia said, putting down Boreal and standing up.

She looked around, wondering if her team had left some sort of message, but found nothing. It felt weird to wake up after they had, though it was good to know it was actually possible to sleep longer despite not needing to.

I guess I woke up so suddenly because my body realised I slept much longer than needed, Zalia theorised.

She walked out of the tent, Boreal quickly following, and looked around. It didn't seem like there was any kind of emergency going on, so she accepted her theory and set out to find her team. Her first thought was that they might be out hunting, then she realised they probably wouldn't have bothered and made her way towards the pavilion kitchen.

She found them there, eating at a table near a long line of soldiers waiting to be served. She sat down on the bench next to Zen and looked over at them. Each of them looked at her with various expressions of amusement.

"What?" she asked.

"Good morning," Indis said.

"Good to see you up and about," Zen added.

"I will wake you up early every single day," Zalia threatened.

"Please no," Zen said apologetically, actually looking scared.

The others all returned to their meals, variations of the same thing, and the food looked actually quite nice for mass-produced army food.

"Magic chefs," Zalia murmured, deep in thought.

"What?" Zen asked.

"Do armies have standardised classes?" Zalia asked, ignoring Zen.

"I believe so, yes. Though only those who are permanent members will have such classes, and even of those, only the ones who join from a young age—but yes, they do try," Indis said.

"How do people usually get their classes, is it just up to the person?" Zalia asked.

She hadn't really thought about many things like that, but now she had been in this world for a while she had come to accept that it was now her home and she may as well learn about it.

"Varies by person. Obviously any given person must accept a class before it is applied and the requirements for the class must be met, but how and when they go about receiving one is entirely up to them. Or it is pressured onto them by their parents," Indis explained, adding the last bit with a little bit of resentment in her tone.

"What's considered a normal age?" Zalia asked.

"I only got mine when I was seventeen, which is considered late," Zen said.

"Eleven for me," Ember added.

"That is quite early for most," Indis said, a little surprise in her voice.

"Had no choice about it really," Ember said.

Her tone suggested that was the end of the conversation in this direction.

Zalia knew a little about Ember's past, some tragedy had happened early in her life and she still bore the trauma to this day. Ember hadn't told her exactly what had happened, but she had inferred it had to do with her parents.

"So, no thefts last night?" Zalia asked, changing topics.

"None that we heard of, or that the huntmaster knows of. So, probably not," Zen said.

"Well, that's good news. Shall we explain what happened to them or wait another night?" she asked.

"Might as well tell him now, the other general is scheduled to arrive sometime tomorrow, if I remember correctly, so no point dallying," Indis said.

They had all sensed the distress broaching the topic of Ember's past had caused, but the quick change of subject did seem to relieve some of the tension from her posture.

"Right, let's go then," Zalia said, standing up.

Each of them looked at her, Zen's face holding an expression of pure disbelief.

"We haven't even finished eating yet!" he exclaimed.

"Oh, right. Forgot about that," Zalia said, sitting back down again.

Now that Zalia's enthusiasm to immediately be on the move was dampened, the others were able to finish their meal in peace before they moved to find the huntmaster. In the time it had taken them to eat, the line of soldiers had been served, and for the first time she had seen, the kitchen area was at peace. She assumed the chaos would soon begin again when cleanup needed to be done, but for now they passed easily through the space.

"Huntmaster!" Zalia called as they approached.

"Ah, shades, how may I help you today?" he asked.

"We're here to help you actually," Indis started, trying to be diplomatic.

"We took care of the problem by ritual sacrifice of an animal to the ethereal beings that haunt these woods," Zalia said.

Both the huntmaster and Indis stared at Zalia for a moment, the former in amusement and the latter in disbelief.

"What she means to say," Indis said, turning back to the huntmaster, "is that we have indeed dealt with the problem."

She went on to explain how they had tracked the ethereal beings to where they lived and how they had dealt with the creatures. The huntmaster looked sceptical.

"Are you sure this will work to keep them from coming here again?" he asked dubiously.

"Not entirely," Zalia said. "For my own reasons, I would like to resolve the situation peacefully with the creatures, and they may yet harass your enemies. This way might work out better for the both of you."

"I do like the idea of them dealing with what we've had to for these past weeks," he admitted.

"Exactly, if they do come back, however, we will help you find another resolution to the problem. We know where to find them now, assuming they have not relocated, but would prefer to avoid eradicating them," Indis added.

"Alright, I'll accept it for now. I will let General Faian know of your possible success. Thank you for your assistance, I have a feeling we might be on course to recruit some proper trackers after this, if possible," he said.

"It's a very useful skill, though my opinion on that might be a little biased," Zalia said.

"Your apparent success is evidence enough to put at least a little truth to your opinion," the huntmaster replied.

They left the man there, leaving him to some of the only time he had to relax. As they moved away from the kitchen area, Eztari once more appeared from the shadows.

"Well done," he said.

Zen nearly jumped out of his own boots, obviously not noticing the man had appeared.

"Have you been following us?" Zalia asked, narrowing her eyes.

"I've kept an eye out," Eztari replied.

"That isn't a no," Zalia pointed out.

She really did not like how sneaky this man was. Despite how good her vision was, she just was not able to see him. An idea occurred to her. She used her heat vision and saw that while his form was a bit less apparent than those of her allies, it was still visible. She smiled, tucking away the little piece of knowledge in the back of her mind.

"But it isn't a yes either," he countered.

"Do you bring a message or are you just here to congratulate us?" Indis asked.

Sometimes Zalia thought the woman was too good at keeping conversations on track.

"Just to congratulate you," he replied.

"Got anything else for us to do? We still have the rest of today and no plans," Indis asked.

"No, things are quite well taken care of now," Eztari said.

"Right, nice talking with you. I'm going to go walk around in the forest now," Zalia said.

She looked at her team and saw no annoyance or recrimination at the idea and so she left. They knew her well enough to know she would be alright. For some reason, the beautiful pond was stuck in her mind, and she wanted to go there again.

She left the camp, travelling through the forest with Boreal at her side, and arrived at the little pond once more. She looked around the clearing, trying to figure out why she couldn't stop thinking about this place. She vaguely remembered a dream that had taken place here the night before.

Walking around the pond, she looked into it but saw nothing in the somewhat murky water. She was about to turn away to inspect the rest of the area when a beam of sunlight rose over the trees to hit the water. Where the sun landed, a few thin tendrils of a plant rose to the surface, each unfurling to reveal a small pink flower atop a green pad floating on the water's surface. She looked suspiciously at the plant, thinking it similar to a water lily, but didn't approach just yet. While it had the possibility of being usable with her magic, it also had the possibility of being some kind of plant monster. She slowly walked backwards, looking around to find a long stick before approaching once more.

She poked it. The plant didn't seem to react at all to the touch and she withdrew for a moment.

It's light sensitive, why not heat sensitive too? she thought.

Approaching once more, she used heat manipulation to warm up the stick until it appeared the same as her skin temperature in her heat vision. She once again approached the plant and poked it. Nothing happened.

She felt a little foolish for her unnecessary caution, but she would have felt more so if she had been killed by a plant monster and so didn't feel too bad about it. She threw her stick away and walked up to it, poking the flower with her hand and jumping back just in case. Still, nothing happened, so she began to approach once more before realising she was being a little stupid. With a sigh, she used Preparation to harvest one of the floating flower buds. Paired with Stasis, she was able to immediately store the plant in her spatial storage. She walked away from the pond and pulled it out once more.

Her ability had harvested the stem and petals separately, the stem being of Iron rank and the petals of Bronze rank. She used Flora Identification on both plants and found the petal to be poisonous and helpful, while the stem was helpful and nutritious. Trusting her ability, she made the decision to immediately eat a piece of stem. It had a sweet, almost fruit-like flavour and she savoured the delicious, crunchy stem. Looking back down at the rest of the stem, there was a little more information available.

> **Water Lily Stem (Potent) (Nutritious) (Helpful) - Iron
> rank - Extremely hydrating and slightly nutritious.**

She realised that her ability was spot-on with the description. She could feel something like a cool wave passing through her body as its magic was absorbed. She looked at the petals next and made the smart decision not to eat them.

> **Water Lily Petal (Poisonous)(Helpful) - Bronze rank - Can be used in a ritual to provide an element of Water.**

That could be really useful, Zalia thought.

She had an herb to give her the elements of fire, water, and air so far, amongst others. She just needed to find earth now to be all powerful.

She quietly chuckled at the thought and stored the herb, looking at the other lilies in the pond. She didn't want to destroy the entire ecosystem of lilies but definitely wanted more.

I'll have to plant some when I get back to Endelbyrn.

With that thought, she began carefully harvesting more.

CHAPTER FORTY-SEVEN

The Fall of a King

Zalia

> **Congratulations! Preparation has reached Iron 9.**
> **Congratulations! Stasis has reached Iron 7.**
> **Congratulations! Harvester has reached Iron 10.**
> **Congratulations! Herbalist class has reached Iron 7.**

She didn't harvest too many of the Water Lilies, not wanting to destroy the population of the plants within the pond to the point where they couldn't regrow. She gave it her best estimate, at least; she didn't really know how the plants naturally propagated or if they were even multiple different plants and not a singular one. Either way, she was now well stocked with both stem and petal of the Water Lily plant. She had also taken a few bits that were still in one piece, planning on planting them somewhere closer to home, wherever that was.

While she had started to feel like she belonged in this world, she didn't feel like she belonged to any single part of it as of yet. There wasn't really anywhere she could call home. Endelbyrn had started to feel like that place, but with recent developments and the possibility of Hidey's situation, the feeling of safety the town had given her no longer existed.

She shook herself out of her thoughts and watched as Boreal looked up at her from the edge of the clearing where she had been exploring. Boreal gave her an almost questioning glance with a slight tilt to her head as if asking, "Are you alright?"

She smiled at Boreal before slinging her backpack over her shoulder.

"Ready to go?" she asked.

Boreal ran over and together, the two of them ran into the woods towards camp.

Zalia and Boreal reentered camp, allowed in by the ever-watchful guards. They walked around the camp for a while looking for the others before Zalia decided just to go to their tent, hoping to find them there. She entered and found Zen sitting by himself, holding a small wooden object as he turned it over and over in his hands. He looked to be deep in thought and quickly put the object away as she entered.

"Hey Zen, do you know where the others are?" Zalia asked.

"Hey, um, yeah, they decided to go see if they couldn't make themselves useful around camp," Zen replied, giving her a weak smile.

She considered for a second before sitting down facing the man.

"Are you alright?" she asked.

"I'm . . . not sure," he said.

"Want to talk about it?" she asked.

Generally speaking, she didn't consider herself the best person to talk to about problems, but their small group had grown somewhat close over their months together and she had been worried for Zen for some time now. He'd grown so silent.

"I . . . " Zen started, before pausing.

"You don't have to if you don't want to," Zalia said, not wanting to be pushy about it.

"It's ok, I just, I shouldn't be here. I thought this was the right thing but it isn't," Zen said.

She frowned. "I know it is a hard situation but we all agreed this is the right path to take," Zalia said.

He slowly shook his head as she spoke. "No, you misunderstand. I mean here, as one of the Morning's Shade. At first it was wonderful, an exciting adventure out of my small family farm with all sorts of powerful people all working together to further the kingdom's cause. We destroyed Elementals and packs of Garroi harassing towns and travellers, travelled north to explore unseen lands, and brought back all sorts of exotic objects for people to research. Now though, we are fighting our own people, our own king, and we don't even know for sure if we're doing that for good reason. Even in the small amount of time we've been in this camp, the death and violence we've seen has been horrible. It all really sank in for real when I saw that building filled with the traumatised, their cries and unseeing eyes. I'm not cut out for this," he said, the words pouring out of him like an internal pressure was pushing them out.

She didn't really know how to respond. Of course, she had many similar thoughts but it seemed like Zen had come to this from a more fantastical view of life where she had come to it from a more . . . realistic one.

"What will you do?" she finally asked, after a long pause.

"I don't want to leave you all with this mess but . . . really, I just want to go home and work a trade in peace like my parents did, and their parents before them. I . . . I'm sorry Zalia, I don't want to let you guys down, but I feel like if I continue like this then I'm going to mess up later down the line. Maybe I'll freeze and get one of you killed, or make the wrong decision and cause a catastrophe. I just can't deal with that kind of pressure. I can't deal with the horror that comes with this path in life," he replied, looking towards where the building of traumatised soldiers was, almost as if he could see through the walls of the tents and buildings to where the soldiers sat in their own separate hells.

She stood up and pulled Zen up by his arm and, to his surprise, gave him a hug.

"It's ok, Zen, we all have to do what we need to do for ourselves before we can worry about others, otherwise we'll drown in our own problems before we can help, anyways," Zalia said.

She didn't think she quite worded it properly but hoped the point got across anyway. She pulled back from the hug and saw that he had tears in his eyes.

"Oh, don't cry, you'll get me crying as well and we have a big great general to meet tomorrow. Don't want to be all red-eyed for our important meeting," Zalia said jokingly.

"Thank you for caring, Zalia," Zen said, laughing as well but with a seriousness to his tone.

Zalia shrugged. "Of course I care, I'm just not the best at showing it."

At that moment, Indis and Ember walked into the tent, pushing the flap out of the way. Indis, who was the most socially perceptive of the entire group, immediately spoke.

"What's wrong?" she asked.

Zalia didn't say anything, gesturing supportively for Zen to explain.

"I . . ." he started, looking at Zalia with concern.

Apparently, he dreaded telling the other two more. She nodded in support, waving her hand in a gesture for him to continue; she would have his back.

He took a deep breath, steeling himself before beginning. He explained to the other two what he had told Zalia, managing to better express his thoughts now that he had Zalia's support. The two women stood in silence as he talked, Ember looking more and more sympathetic while, to Zalia's concern, Indis started to look angry.

As soon as Zen finished talking, Ember opened her mouth like she was about to talk, but Indis got there first.

"What!? You're going to abandon us and our cause?" she asked vehemently, tone tinged with anger.

"Indis, stop!" Ember exclaimed. Indis however, was having none of it.

"No, Ember, this isn't some idle matter. Don't you get it, Zen!? If we don't succeed in stopping whoever the *fuck* is performing these rituals, the kingdom is gone. Gone! Our families, our friends, towns, everything! Everything we know will be wiped out and you're just going to go back to your farm because you can't *handle* it?" Indis yelled, practically exploding with anger.

All of them stood stunned like they had just stared at a flashbang. Indis had never yelled, let alone sworn in front of them before. There was a moment of silence as Indis glared at Zen and Zalia. Zen and Ember stared, a little wide-eyed, at Indis.

"How do you know that?" Ember whispered.

A look of guilt flashed over Indis's face but she stood her ground. Zalia realised what Ember meant.

How does she know what is going to happen? Zalia thought.

She could get the answer to that question later, for now she had to try deescalate. She looked at Zen and immediately could feel her blood boil at the expression on his face. She had seen the man steely-eyed in combat, goofy, and a little idiotic otherwise. She had seen him open about his emotions, with difficulty, just a few moments ago. Now, she saw something she hadn't seen in him before. He looked fragile, as if a light push might make him fall and shatter like a thin pane of glass.

"Indis, come with me," Zalia said, trying and mostly succeeding in keeping a calm tone. She walked out of the tent, basically herding Indis in front of her, walking a short distance away. "We are going to talk later about how you know what you just said, but for now, you need to calm the fuck down." Zalia made direct eye contact and held her gaze.

Indis stared right back for a moment before an expression of guilt passed over her face again and she looked away. "None of you know what is at stake, he can't simply walk away from all of this," she replied, still angry but somewhat calmer away from the tent and Zen.

"We haven't found out what the purpose of all the rituals is, how could we know? What do you know that we don't, Indis? What do you know and why have you not told any of us!?" Zalia asked, her own anger now boiling over.

She quieted down her tone again as she noticed some of the nearby soldiers staring at them. Indis looked a little ashamed, her anger now almost all gone, yet she did not say anything.

"It doesn't matter for now. Right now, we're going to go back in there and you're going to apologise to Zen," Zalia said in a quieter tone.

Indis looked indignant and opened her mouth but quickly closed it, schooling her expression into her normal neutrality.

"Yes, I had no right to speak to him that way no matter the situation. I will not back down from my opinion on the matter, however," Indis said.

Zalia nodded. She didn't expect Indis to just forget about it, but she definitely had some explaining to do. All the calm and relaxation that Zalia had experienced over the past couple of days roaming the forest had been lost in an instant, and she had a feeling that it wasn't going to come back any time soon. She took a deep breath and followed Indis into the tent.

When she entered she saw Ember had managed to calm Zen somewhat, which was good.

"Indis! I'm sor—" Zen started.

Indis interrupted him with a raised hand. "No, I am sorry I spoke to you that way, Zen. It was undeserved."

He looked a little stunned but glanced at Ember who raised one eyebrow at him like, "I told you so."

"I am sorry too, for my part. I would say I wish I was like the heroes from the stories of old, but in truth I don't. This is not the life for me," Zen said.

Indis said nothing, pursing her lips with annoyance once more, trying to break through to her usual expression.

"Now that is dealt with. You need to explain yourself, Indis," Ember said in an icy tone.

Ember was not so forgiving as Zen was, it seemed.

"Yes, I suppose I do. Very well," Indis said, pausing to gather her thoughts. "I have lied to all of you about why exactly my family fell from our high station amongst the nobility of the kingdom. I have told you that my family has fallen in status over the past few years, which is true, though I did not tell you why that has happened. I should have done so, considering the relevance to our situation."

She took a deep breath, looking almost in pain, like she was about to reveal her deepest secrets.

"House Indis, not so many years past, was very close to the king and his family. In fact, I share some blood ties with our current king from marriages to some of the minor royal members of my house. I told you that I have once met the current king and did not see any of the malevolence that now exists in him, and that is true. It is not the whole truth, though, as I have met the man on many occasions and even knew him as a friend. This was back before my house fell to its current state and before the man himself became . . . evil. King Alistair of the royal line of Endaria, though he was only prince when I knew him, was once a good man. In his final days of life, Alistair's father, King Horum, began to become addled in the mind. This was a closely guarded secret that not even many of the nobility knew about, let alone any of the army or general population," Indis began, taking a breath to continue.

Zalia interrupted, "Why doesn't Faian know you, then?"

"She did recognise me, in fact we had a conversation regarding my family's status, and just this morning I told her what I'm about to tell you," Indis said.

"That's where you went?" Zen asked.

Indis nodded.

Zalia didn't interrupt again.

"King Horum was a close friend of my father's, and so my father knew many secrets that he otherwise would not have. A few years back the king told my father of a plan he had to access another plane, Cormaine. My father thought it an unwise idea and tried to convince him not to go through with it but had no luck in the matter. He went through with it and seemingly succeeded, but as my father often described, that was the beginning of the end for the king. It was due to that incident that the king slowly became insane, mind-addled, and crazed in his obsession with Cormaine. My father used all the political weight he could muster to obscure what was happening, to hide the king's condition from anyone who could use it to hurt him or the royal family. It was the gold and political favour he spent during those years that brought my house to the fallen state in which it now lies. He did it all to protect the king and the prince who he often treated as his own son. My father would have had me and the prince married one day, I suspect, if things had happened differently. That is no matter now, however," Indis said, looking a little lost in the past as she retold the tale.

"That doesn't explain why you never told us any of this," Ember said, still holding her icy tone and hard expression.

"I'm getting there," Indis said. "Prince Alistair, as I have mentioned, was a good man. He worked with my father and did what he could to help his own father and hide his condition from the kingdom at large. The king often asked his son to come see the experiments he was doing but due to my father's advice, the prince would not. This was often a point of contention between the king and my father, and yet another reason for the fall of my house. One day, the last day of the king's life, the prince finally agreed to see one of these experiments. The king never made him do it, I think deep down he knew what would happen, but eventually, the prince conceded. He went into that room despite all the arguments both my father and I made, and when he came out he was never the same, and the previous king was never seen again. From that point, you know what has happened from the story that Faian told you."

They all stood in silence, Zen next to Ember, and Zalia stood to the side as Indis faced the other two.

"That's why you were always so insistent it was the king who was responsible for the rituals," Zalia realised.

"Yes," Indis said.

She looked miserable and pale, like she had just had her soul ripped out of her.

"Why did you never tell us!" Ember almost yelled.

"Since that time, many minor houses and rich merchants have looked to use me and my family as a stepping stone, to rip us down even further to their own ends. I have learnt the hard way to keep what I know to myself. Even further, during those years we obscured the truth from the public I learnt to bury that knowledge deep and far beneath, and to never speak of it. I never brought this up partly from habit and partly from fear," Indis said, seeming to shrink even further into herself.

Zalia understood now why Indis so often kept up her face of nobility and strength, because if she didn't she would crumble.

"How do you know what will happen with these rituals?" Zalia asked, feeling bad about dragging more out of the woman but needing an answer.

"My father knew, somehow. I don't know how or when he learnt what would happen but after the king's death, he told me. He told me to stop what was coming or the kingdom would fall. My own father has lost his own mind now, whether from seeing his close friend's slow downfall or all the events after, I do not know. I only know I need to stop what is coming or it will be the end for us all," Indis replied.

"And that is why you joined the Morning's Shade?" Zalia asked.

"Yes," Indis replied, "it is."

CHAPTER FORTY-EIGHT

Secrets

Zalia

They all stood in tense silence.

"I still don't understand why you didn't tell us," Ember said angrily, pacing back and forth.

"I have many reasons, none of them are good ones, however," Indis replied, still trying to maintain calm after her earlier outburst.

"We don't even need to meet this other general, we've wasted so much time confirming information you already knew was true!" Ember exclaimed, throwing her hands in the air.

"I . . ." Indis started.

"Did you tell Hidey any of this?" Zalia asked.

Indis shook her head. "The army know who I am, but I have been readying myself to tell both Hidey and you three ever since the Morning's Shade finally became involved in this war. Then, this opportunity came up, and I hoped I would not have to explain my involvement in all of this, that you would be convinced by others," Indis replied, looking a tiny bit ashamed.

"Waste of time," Ember repeated.

"How do we stop it?" Zalia asked.

"I don't know," Indis said quietly.

"How can you not know?" Zalia pushed.

"I don't know! We have to stop the king, we have to . . . we have to kill him. I don't think he will ever stop otherwise," Indis almost yelled, her neutral tone and expression breaking once more.

"Do you know how to heal these corrupted people?" Ember asked.

"No, I've told you everything I know," Indis said, looking just a tiny bit panicked.

"Have you? How can we trust that?" Ember asked, still furiously pacing.

"You just . . . you just have to. Please," Indis whispered, looking small under Ember's glare.

"Guys, stop. This isn't helping," Zen said.

Ember looked at Zen for a moment before she let out a deep breath and sat down, holding her head in her hands.

"What are we going to do now?" Ember said quietly.

"Let's leave," Zen said.

"What!?" Indis asked incredulously.

"Let's leave. Leave the problem to the rebel army and the Morning's Shade. Let the people with all the power handle everything. We can use our link to the Morning's Shade to help the rebellion set up some sort of trap, and then we leave. I'll go back to my farm, Zalia can go back to the wilderness, and you two can go build yourselves lives that don't revolve around your past," Zen explained, gesturing to both Ember and Indis.

They all sat in silence for a while, even Indis, considering Zen's words. Usually Zen was the last person to make a good point but right then . . . he made sense. They weren't some sort of group of powerful heroes, or even powerful people. All they really had was their connections and knowledge. Why not give all that to someone who could use it better?

"I wouldn't be opposed to that. Leaving all this behind and going into the wilds once more does sound . . . tempting," Zalia said tentatively.

"I always thought . . . I always thought I'd be there at the end. I thought I would be the one to finally put an end to his madness, but I guess I don't need to be, do I?" Indis asked, the question almost directed at herself more than them.

Ember remained silent, looking lost in thought, like she had never considered doing anything other than helping others to live a better life than she had.

"So, what do we do then? How do we set a trap?" Zalia asked, looking to Indis.

Despite the woman's lies, she was still the best political thinker out of them all, and she personally knew the king.

"I've thought to some length about how we could accomplish that. I think we simply tell Hidey that the rebellion is aiming to make a large assault on the city; the king should send his army to stop their advance, and then we send our strongest to the capital to kill him. Most of the army must be outside of the capital already, so hopefully such a threat of attack should cause him to amass the armies he has to counter it. The king has some high-ranked royal guards as well, of course, but I know of at least one that has left since his madness. Our job would be to inform the higher-ranked amongst the Morning's Shade without letting Hidey catch wind of the plan. That's all I've got," Indis explained.

"That sounds like a terrible plan," Ember said.

Indis frowned.

"How is that a terrible plan?" she asked indignantly.

"What if the king goes with the army, what if he has stronger guards than you think, what if—"

"Ok, ok, I get it," Indis interrupted.

"We'll work with Faian on something, the help of some good military minds should help," Zalia interjected.

They all fell silent once more.

"I need some fresh air. I'll see you all later today," Zalia finally said, breaking the silence.

None of the others spoke but Zalia didn't mind, leaving with Boreal close behind. She walked off into the camp, letting out a deep breath.

Today had really not gone how she'd been expecting. She thought that after their success in stopping the theft and the imminent arrival of the general, they would relax for a day before things started to really get crazy. As it turned out, crazy didn't wait for anybody.

She thought about leaving right then and there, walking off into the forest and never coming back to the Kingdom of Endaria. She could go back and see Glemp again, then go so far north that not even a kingdom-scale disaster would affect her whatsoever. Thoughts of the north brought her mind back to that first day she had met another human in these lands, Knight Alara of the army of Endaria. The woman hadn't seemed crazed like the soldiers she had seen most recently, nor had her few men. She wondered if Alara was now walking around somewhere in the kingdom, mind lost to whatever madness the ritual would have visited upon her.

She broke out of her thoughts and found herself in front of the building she had first met Faian in. The two guards were no longer there, and she assumed that meant Faian was housed in another of the camp's many buildings today.

"Eztari?" Zalia asked into the air around her.

She spun around as a footstep cracked a stick behind her.

"Yes?" Eztari asked.

"I wish to speak to General Faian," Zalia said.

He raised an eyebrow.

"Alone," Zalia added.

He seemed a little perplexed, which Zalia found reassuring because it might mean that the man wasn't listening in to their every little conversation after all.

"Very well," he said.

He led her through the camp to a replica building that had guards in front of it. He had led her past a few buildings that were also similarly guarded, so she knew you couldn't just find the general by finding the guards.

The guards let her pass as Eztari gestured to them, and Zalia entered the building. It was set up much the same as it was the first time she had met Faian, though neither the advisor nor the commanders were there.

"General," Zalia said by way of greeting.

"Zalia," the general said.

Zalia didn't speak, inspecting the general. Indis had spoken to this woman before she had spoken to her own team about what she knew and had seen. It made sense when Zalia thought about it, but she just did not know how to feel about the whole situation.

"Indis told us about her . . . past, and how it is relevant to the current situation," Zalia said.

"I see," Faian said, gesturing for Zalia to take a seat.

She stayed standing, watching Boreal out of the corner of her eye, making sure the feline made no trouble.

"And?" Faian asked.

"What do you think? Is she telling the truth?" Zalia asked.

Faian raised an eyebrow at her. "You do not trust the word of your own friend and ally?"

"Not so much anymore, trusting easily is something I'm learning might be a little dangerous," Zalia said.

"And yet you trust my opinion on her story?"

"No, I'm just hoping I can learn something from your answer."

"Very well. I believe she tells the truth, and her story does match some oddities in behaviour I now recognise in the late king's last days."

"And?" Zalia asked.

"What makes you think there is an 'and' to that?" Faian questioned.

Zalia didn't respond, waiting for her answer.

"While the story rings true, I do not think it is the whole truth. I believe our Lady Indis is still in love with the prince she once knew. That man no longer lives, of course, but I suspect it is true nonetheless."

Zalia nodded. "I believe you may be right. It does explain in part why she waited so long to tell us of this. She must be torn between the man she once knew, and the man he is today, between love and fear."

"Is that all you wanted?" Faian asked.

"I don't think we can necessarily trust her judgement anymore," Zalia said.

"Quite astute," Faian said.

"We plan to help you. We no longer need the story from the other general with this new information having come to light. We would like to help you set up a trap for the king and remove him from the throne. We've thought of a way to accomplish this, but it definitely needs a general's touch—while accustomed to combat, none of us are great military minds, so to speak," Zalia explained.

"Go on then," Faian urged.

And so Zalia explained the situation revolving around Hidey and his possible weakness, Indis's initial idea for a trap, and the position she and her team were stuck in, in the middle of everything. She didn't know if she was making a mistake but had decided she wanted this over with as soon as possible. She was getting sick of all the confusion, mystery, and politics surrounding the whole situation. Zen was right, she wanted to go back into the wilds once more and forget about all of this. She wasn't about to walk away and so she felt the need to bring it to some kind of resolution.

"I see," Faian said.

"What are your thoughts?" Zalia asked.

The general hadn't reacted as Zalia had talked, but now leaned forwards, looking thoughtful. "We have been making plans for a short time to embark on a final attack soon, this may yet give us a chance at success. I have a feeling that very soon everything shall come to its final stage in this war and I feel the need to move soon. Indis's plan is solid groundwork, but it will need a lot of specifics, backups, and alterations if we are to make it work. I thought you said you were not being so trusting anymore, why trust me with this information?"

"I'm learning, and I do so because you might be one of the only people with enough actual power to stop the king. Keeping it to ourselves will help no one," Zalia said, "you have the supposed intention and means to end this war for the betterment of the people around. It's as simple as that."

"Your reasoning is solid but a little flawed. Nevertheless, I will take what I can get. You and your team may yet have provided us a means of actually winning this war, Zalia. I need to make adjustments to our plans now, if I may have some time to myself?" Faian asked.

"Of course, General, I have only one more thing to say."

"Yes?"

"My team and I will not take part in the assassination. Our part is to provide the deception, and that is all. I am happy to wait nearby to hear of the failure or success of the mission but this is a foe beyond any of us, there is no point throwing away our lives," Zalia told the general.

"Very well, so it shall be," Faian replied.

CHAPTER FORTY-NINE

Starlight

Zalia

Zalia left the building, leaving behind the general and slowly walking through the camp. She felt a little better now that she had put the responsibility of all the information and decision-making onto the general. She probably should have talked to her team first about bringing Faian into the fold, but didn't feel too bad, considering the situation. She knew that Zen, for one, would be happy to be rid of the great weight they had been carrying. Indis would probably be quite upset that she hadn't been included in the conversation, but Zalia didn't care about that considering what the woman had been hiding from them. All they had to do now was their part in Endelbyrn, and one way or another, it would be over.

Zalia thought about what she would do after it was finally over. She didn't really feel like staying with the Morning's Shade at that moment, her only reason to stay being her team, but it didn't seem like they would be staying themselves. Indis would probably leave once her goal had been achieved, looking for more efficient ways to bring her house back to power, and Zen would go back to his farm and family. She didn't know what Ember would do, but Zalia realised she wouldn't mind bringing the woman along in her exploration of the lands outside of Endaria. Not only did Ember have quite a suite of healing and survival abilities, but she was also somewhat introverted like Zalia was. Zalia also knew her to be a good person that she could rely on, though, she had also thought of Indis that way up until recently.

Indis was weighing heavily on Zalia's mind. She didn't know how to feel about recent developments. On one hand, Zalia could see why Indis didn't explain the whole situation to them. Initially, she most likely didn't trust them enough to share it and it seemed like by the time she was ready to share, they were on the path towards opposing the king anyways. After that, well, there were many excuses that could be made.

The other side of her confusion was how betrayed she felt. While she knew people were complex and hard to understand—often very much so, particularly for her—any reason Indis gave for not revealing what she knew couldn't excuse that she'd withheld important information from them. Not only did they waste time confirming things she already knew to be true, but she had also concealed information about her past. If she was willing to lie so easily and withhold information she knew they needed, was she really a friend? Zalia wasn't sure. She didn't know how far Indis would be willing to go to achieve her own goals, what she might sacrifice. When it came to trusting a friend and ally, someone willing to sacrifice anything to achieve their goals was not a prime choice.

She sighed, coming to a stop as she leaned against the stone wall of a building, and placed her hands on her knees.

"Soon, Boreal, soon we can leave this all behind," Zalia whispered.

Boreal looked up with wide eyes, understanding Zalia through her abilities and their bond.

"Mreow?" Boreal asked.

"Yes, we can go back north if you want," Zalia replied.

It seemed Boreal was missing the icy lands of her origin.

"Let's go tell them the news, shall we," Zalia said, pushing off the wall.

She made her towards the tent that held her friends, then hesitated.

"You know what, we can tell them later. Let's go into the woods," Zalia said to Boreal, changing her mind.

She left the camp, making her way towards the beautiful pond for the third time in recent days. This time she didn't run through the woods, choosing instead to watch her surroundings carefully and use the time to mull over the thoughts in her head. She had almost reached the pond when a glimmer in the corner of her sight caught her eye. She turned and found one of the ethereal, starry wolves watching her from the woods. She froze, unsure if the creature was hostile or not but upon seeing her, it slowly walked forwards. Boreal walked up beside Zalia, sitting down and meowing at the wolf. The wolf also stopped and sat.

"Um, hello?" Zalia said, a little worried.

She really thought that the wolves had accepted her idea and left the camp in peace.

The wolf stood and a concept flooded her mind. Images of paths and trails winding through the woods, thoughts of being one amongst many in a pack, all the information forming together to create a single concept within her mind. Follow.

The wolf turned and loped back into the woods, moving quite quickly through the undergrowth.

Zalia looked at Boreal. "Should we follow?"

Boreal responded by purring then running off after the wolf. Zalia hesitated for only a moment before smiling, letting her thoughts drift away and running after the two.

She sprinted through the forest, letting her muscle memory take over as the trees flashed past. They burst out of the woods onto a small plain between two sections of forest, the three of them jumping past or over what looked like an Ironfur rabbit before entering the tree line once more. They dashed through the forest once more, moving ever further from camp.

Zalia let the motion and journey take her mind, her only thought on the next jump, the next sideways adjustment. It felt like only ten minutes had passed before they arrived at a ridge she remembered only too well. Running up and stopping at the top, she recognised the clearing as the sky above went dark by whatever magic rested in this place. A dark pool with a glimmering light in its depths sat in the centre of a clearing. Many more of the ethereal wolves rested there. She paused, hesitant, as the wolf moved down from the ridge.

"Last chance to turn back from whatever this is," Zalia said, looking at Boreal.

Boreal however, didn't seem hesitant whatsoever. She moved down the ridge after the wolf, almost bouncing along.

"*Well, she seems convinced,*" Zalia thought.

Maybe Boreal felt the same way that Zalia initially had about the creatures. They were on the side of nature much as both Boreal and Zalia were. She walked down the ridge after Boreal, following into the clearing as a great number of sets of starlit pinprick eyes turned to observe her. Many of the wolves stayed where they were, sat upon rocky outcroppings with ears pricked in her direction. Others stood up, slowly padding towards where Zalia and Boreal now walked, making their way towards the pool. They reached the pond's edge and began walking around it, still following the wolf that had led them here. As they moved, Zalia began to see a large cave mouth cut into the side of one of the stone outcroppings. The wolves were large, standing at around Zalia's shoulder height, but what she saw within the cave made her stop dead in her tracks. Making its way out of the cave was a wolf twice the size of any of the other wolves. It had an ethereal body, much like the others, but varied in that it grew a thick mane. It also had a crown of stars, the one at the very front larger and shaped like a half-moon.

Zalia stared in awe as the creature approached her and wondered if she should bow to it. The wolf held itself with such nobility as it moved smoothly and silently towards her. As it eventually neared her, it bowed to her, much to Zalia's surprise.

"Greetings, Druid, and welcome to our enclave," a deep and resonant voice sounded in her mind.

Zalia stayed silent for a moment, trying to decide how to address the wolf.

> **? - ? rank.**

That gave her chills, her ability couldn't even decipher what rank the creature was. Many could hide their ranks from her but never had she seen a question mark rank. She decided to be real polite.

"Greetings, Starlit Majesty, thank you for the invitation," Zalia replied, gesturing to the wolf that had led them there.

The wolf seemed amused at the title she had given it.

"Tell me, Druid, how did you come to know of us," the wolf asked, voice resounding once more in her mind.

"I tracked one of your kind here and discovered your enclave. I decided to leave you in peace, yet we needed you to cease stealing from our camp. I hope I have not offended you by my actions," Zalia said, really hoping she hadn't made a huge mistake.

"Offended? No, of course not. It had been a very long time indeed since any have given tribute to us willingly. Not since the Bathar roamed these lands," the wolf assured her.

"The Bathar?" Zalia asked.

"They look much like you, only taller and grow their own fur," the wolf explained.

That must be the race Ember and Indis were talking about, Zalia realised. "I hope my tribute was of worth to you."

"Of course. You must be a Hunter as well as a Druid to track and hunt so well," the wolf said.

"I am, I must say I am significantly better at being a Hunter than a Druid however," Zalia admitted.

"It matters not, you are still young. You will find your way in time. Come, I would give you my blessing, Zalia of the Druids," the wolf told her, walking over to the pool.

"In what way have I earned your blessing?"

"My power has waned much since the days past, not many still revere the old gods. Those of us who remain wish to see nature preserved and you have shown yourself to be someone who would do such. Do I see wrongly, Zalia?"

"I would do what I can within the limits of my power," Zalia said, a storm of different thoughts and emotions rushing through her head.

"And so you shall," the wolf said.

Zalia walked over to the pool next to the great wolf. A god? She did not know.

"Dip your bow into the pool and receive my blessing, young one," the wolf explained.

Zalia summoned her bow, hesitant.

"*Do not be afraid. If I wished you harm, the bow would not save you,*" the wolf said.

Zalia considered the words and realised it was probably true. She knelt down and carefully dipped the bow into the water, holding it there. The glimmer of starlight that she could see deep within the pool slowly grew brighter and brighter. Before long, a beam of light shone from the pool into the sky above, lighting it up from its darkened state. One by one, the wolves around the clearing started howling to the sky, the larger wolf next to her joining in last, its howl deeper than the rest.

> **Congratulations! Your bonded weapon 'Hunter's Bow' has been blessed by a god.**
> **Congratulations! Your bonded weapon 'Druidic Bow, Blessed by Starlight' has become deeply bonded.**
> **'Hunter's Bow (Heirloom) - Bonded Tin rank' has become 'Druidic Bow, Blessed by Starlight (Blessed Heirloom) - Deeply bonded Iron rank.'**
> **Druidic bow, Blessed by Starlight (Blessed Heirloom) - Deeply bonded Iron rank**
> **Tin - Arrows fired from this bow gain a powerful seeking effect.**
> **Iron - When this bow is drawn without an arrow nocked, a Starlight arrow with the 'Starlit' effect will be summoned in its place.**
> **Starlit - Affected weapon passes through non-magical armour and applies Light from Within.**
> **Light from Within - Affected target takes a small amount of damage over time as starlight glows from within.**
> **By becoming deeply bonded, Druidic Bow, Blessed by Starlight is now able to transform into 'Druidic Blade, Blessed by Starlight.'**
> **Druidic Blade, Blessed by Starlight (Blessed Heirloom) - Deeply bonded Iron rank**
> **Tin - Druidic Blade, Blessed by Starlight is magically sharp and remains so permanently.**
> **Iron - When wielded by you, Druidic Blade, Blessed by Starlight gains the 'Starlit' effect.**

Zalia pulled the bow from the pool as the howling stopped, silence blanketing the clearing. She looked down at the transformed weapon in wonder. It looked to be made of a dark wood that had a soft glow emanating from lightly inscribed, flowing lines. The bowstring was ethereal much like the wolves, who were glowing as well. Inscribed amongst the flowing lines was a small feline animal with a frosty paw print trail. She mentally commanded the weapon to transform into its sword shape and found it to be made of a similar material. It had the same flowing lines that were lit from within but it was shaped differently to her old sword. This one was single-edged and slightly shorter, the end tapering to a point on the bladed side. The blunt side didn't taper, simply holding a straight-backed form. The depiction of the feline appeared here too, this time on the blade closer to the hilt. She knew instinctively what it depicted, of course. She knelt down, showing the weapon to Boreal. It seemed the weapon had formed a deep enough magical bond with her to recognise the similar bond she had with Boreal, and shape itself to show that.

"Look, it's you," Zalia whispered, admiring the weapon.

She turned to the wolf, still kneeling.

"Thank you for what you have done for me. I don't know how to repay you for this," Zalia said.

"*No thanks is needed. Go now, protect nature wherever it is found, young Druid. May your path be guided by the starlight,*" the wolf said, turning and moving back to its cave.

Zalia stood, looking around the clearing. All around, the wolves were slowly fading into the nearby forest and rocks, disappearing from sight. The sky above slowly brightened once more, and she was left standing in a seemingly normal clearing.

CHAPTER FIFTY

Internal Conflict

Zalia

Zalia stood in the now empty clearing, dumbfounded by the experience. She'd tried to remain as calm and collected during the experience as possible as to not offend the giant starlight wolf. Her hands were shaking slightly, still gripping her newly transformed weapon, as adrenaline pumped through her body. She looked around, finding Boreal now drinking from the pond as if she expected to be blessed as well. Zalia let out a laugh at the sight, the tension leaving her body. She observed her new blade, swinging it around lightly and finding its weight to be perfectly balanced. She unbuckled her old sword, one she had taken from the first man she'd killed so long ago during the time she had first met Tristan. She meant to replace it quite a while back for something similar to the new sword but had never gotten around to it. She put her old sword into her spatial bag and slung it back onto her shoulders.

Zalia finally felt at peace. It felt like she had something to do in the forests nearby, possibly the reason she had found herself leaving the camp so often. Now though, the forest felt like it was at rest once more and she could move towards the next goal. She began the long walk back to camp, knowing she needed to talk to her team.

Along the way, she thought about the newfound intuition she had developed. She felt that it came from her Druid class though she couldn't be certain. So far, the magical intuition hadn't led her astray and she thought it might be a good idea to learn to trust it.

There you go, giving out trust again, Zalia thought.

She really didn't know much about this world and how it worked. She didn't know if the intuition was the result of some god or powerful creature messing with her mind. However, if she went through life trusting nothing and no one, what kind of life would that be? She silently cursed Indis for betraying her admittedly easily given trust.

Just a few more weeks, Zalia thought.

After that, she would be free from the madness that was the human race. She had thought to see what the people in this world were like and found that she regretted ever leaving the north in the first place.

Zalia arrived back at the camp after about an hour or so of walking. She could probably have run it in a third or less of the time but didn't find herself in a hurry. The reason for that was now before her, as she found Zen still within the tent, the other two nowhere to be seen.

"Hey, Zen," Zalia said, subdued.

"Hey, Zalia," Zen replied, seeming equally lacking in energy.

"Where are the others?"

"Ember went to see if anybody needed healing, and Indis went looking for you."

Zalia sat down next to Zen, bumping him with her shoulder in a friendly way.

"You doing alright?" she asked.

"Yeah, I just didn't expect Indis to blow up like that," he replied.

"I don't think any of us did. She's been keeping a lid on all of that for a long time, the pressure must have gotten to be too much."

Zen shrugged. "She did that to herself, doesn't excuse how she behaved."

"No, no it doesn't," Zalia agreed. There was a moment of silence before Zalia spoke once more. "I told Faian everything."

"Everything?" Zen asked.

"About Hidey, his weakness and everything else we know about the war and the rituals."

Zen let out a deep breath. "Damn, Zalia, Indis is going to be angry about that."

"She doesn't get to be, not after today."

"Fair enough," Zen replied.

"You're not angry?" Zalia asked.

"Nah, kind of relieved actually. It takes a lot of the pressure off us."

"I thought you would say as much. I hope Ember doesn't mind," Zalia said, worry in her tone.

"Oh don't worry, she's more like you. Doesn't care much for politics or the matters of us mere humans," Zen said, trying to comfort her.

She snorted a laugh. "Mere humans? Are you saying I'm not one?"

"Nope, more like an animal of the wilds," Zen said, looking pointedly at Boreal who was busy trying to freeze Zen's shield to the ground.

"Point taken," Zalia conceded.

She summoned her bow, handing it to him.

"Got a shiny new bow, amongst other things," Zalia said in response to his confused expression.

"You were only gone for a couple of hours, how did you get this?" Zen asked, sliding his hand down the length of the weapon in awe.

"Remember those ethereal wolves?"

"Yeah," Zen replied, looking at her warily.

"One of them found me and asked me to follow it. I did, and it turns out the whole pack is led by some giant starlight wolf who may or may not be a god, undecided on that," Zalia explained.

"You're only proving my earlier point."

"Yeah, yeah, I know. Anyways, the wolf wanted to thank me for paying tribute and respecting the wolves by my actions. He? She? They? Blessed my old bow and it transformed into this, a blessed heirloom. It also ranked up to Iron rank, which is handy."

"What does it do?"

"It can conjure arrows for me, which is super nice, though I haven't tried it yet. The arrows pass through non-magical armour and apply some sort of inner burning magic. The final thing it can do is this," Zalia said, mentally commanding the bow to transform.

Zen let out a surprised sound and nearly dropped the weapon as it transformed into its sword form in a flash of light. "Oh wow, that is beautiful," he said, standing and giving it a few test swings.

"Quite the weapon, hey? It has the same effects as the arrows," Zalia explained.

"Kind of shaped like a cross between a machete and a short sword," Zen observed.

"It is an excellent cutting blade."

"And is pretty strong with its ability to ignore armour. One of the biggest weaknesses of cutting blades in combat is how easily armour can stop them. This won't have that problem whatsoever. You'll be able to surprise any too-confident armoured opponent with this," Zen said, handing back the weapon.

"It is quite an upgrade, though I'm more excited to test the possibilities for the bow form," Zalia said, stashing the weapon back in its spatial storage with a thought.

"I'm a little jealous of that weapon storing ability you have," Zen said as he watched the weapon vanish and hefted the giant mace he carried around.

"Do you have any heirloom items?" Zalia asked.

He shook his head. "Nothing that would be useful for this field of work. I have a Gold rank ancestor who left behind some heirloom farming equipment, but nothing much else. We still don't know how he ever managed to get to Gold in the Farmer class, not many people believe us about that, and I'm not sure I believe it myself."

"Heirloom farming equipment," Zalia echoed.

"Odd, I know. I'm the first in my family to ever do anything else as far as we can remember, and look how that turned out."

"It didn't go so badly. You're alive and well, mentally and physically. It's no shame to return to your family and follow your ancestors' path," Zalia told him.

"I suppose not," Zen replied, sounding a little defeated.

"Blood, war, and sleeping in the wilds aren't for everyone."

"Couldn't agree more with that."

They spoke for some time about various topics, staying away from anything sensitive, before one of the other two finally returned. Indis walked in, looking a little out of breath, and stopped when she saw Zalia.

"How long have you been here for?" she asked.

"Past half an hour or so," Zalia said.

"I've been looking everywhere for you," Indis puffed.

"I went out of camp for a bit."

"Should have known." Indis sat down on her bedroll.

"Is something the matter?" Zalia asked.

Indis frowned, obviously picking up on Zalia's not-so-well-hidden tone. Zalia was just trying to be polite because if she wasn't, she might end up yelling at the woman.

"Not at all, I wanted to make sure you were ok," Indis replied.

"I'm alright. Indis, I . . . told Faian everything about Hidey, his weakness, and pretty much everything else we know about the war and rituals," Zalia said, the words rushing out.

Zen looked wary and Indis froze. A complicated expression flitted across the woman's face before she closed her eyes, exhaling deeply.

"I wish you had talked to us about doing that," Indis said calmly.

"I considered it for a short moment," Zalia said.

"And why did you not tell us before making that decision?" Indis asked, a slight bit of irritation making its way into her tone.

"Because rather than comfort and affirm our obviously distressed teammate and friend, you decided to explode and scream at him. I decided to take the stress and pressure off his shoulders so that he can relax for one fucking minute," Zalia explained, clipping off her final words.

"I see," Indis replied coldly.

Zen looked extremely uncomfortable.

"Going forwards, Faian will help us plan a joint attack on the king and his army, the battle of the armies will hopefully be enough of a distraction to assassinate the king before he turns this kingdom into a wasteland. Our part will be to plant information with Hidey, hoping he will bring it to the king, which should give us an advantage. That is all. If you want to go confront the king directly, I won't stop you. None of the rest of us will be, though, assuming Ember doesn't want to throw her life away," Zalia said carefully, trying to maintain a neutral tone.

"So it shall be," Indis said, not quite managing to keep the icy rage from her voice.

Zalia had learnt that if there was one thing Indis hated, it was being in a situation she didn't control in some way. Zalia had just taken all of that control away from her by giving all their information to the general. She didn't particularly care that Indis was upset by that; in fact, if the woman had yelled at her she would have simply left right then and there.

Indis stood up. "I will see you both at our meeting with the second general tomorrow. I shall sleep elsewhere tonight," she said, leaving the tent.

Zalia let out a tense sigh. "I probably shouldn't have aggravated her like that."

"She'll come around," Zen promised, though he didn't sound too certain.

Zalia buried her face into her hands, groaning. Boreal came up and pushed her way onto Zalia's lap, curling up and purring gently. She patted the soft feline, taking comfort in the sensation as a warmth spread from Boreal into Zalia, immediately relaxing her.

"*Is that another magic ability you have, or is it just natural,*" Zalia thought towards Boreal.

She simply looked up at Zalia, blinked once and then curled up again.

"We'll be free of this soon, don't worry," Zalia said, trying to sound upbeat.

"Soon," Zen repeated, though he didn't sound hopeful. Zalia wished she could say she didn't feel the same.

A while later, when Ember arrived back from wherever she had been, Zalia once again explained what she had done. Ember took it much better than Indis had, shrugging it off and saying she trusted Zalia to make the right decision. They didn't speak much for the rest of the day, and night soon arrived with both Zen and Ember falling asleep early. Zalia stayed awake, lost in her own thoughts deep into the night. Indis never returned to the tent that night and finally, Zalia fell asleep in the early hours of the morning.

Zalia woke up before the others, finding it unfair today that she had to be awake for so many more hours. Her opinion on the usefulness of the ability varied, some days she loved it but others she wished she could turn it off and sleep through the morning. Sighing, she got up and left the tent, bringing nothing but her simple clothes. She decided it was a good idea to start the day with her usual routine, running to the gate and taking her morning sprint through the forest. She travelled in a large loop to the pond and took a short bath before arriving back in the camp, looking to find someone to spar with. A few early risers turned down her offer, but luckily, one younger man wanted to test himself against a member of the Morning's Shade and accepted. Zalia didn't use her new sword, knowing it would be much too dangerous. Instead, she had to use a practice sword that felt much too unwieldy in comparison.

Before long, the young lad called off the spar as she whacked him across the side for the eighth time in as many bouts. She had quickly picked up on the weakness in his defence on the right side and had thoroughly taken advantage of it, unfairly taking out her frustration on the man's body. She healed him in recompense, ensuring he wouldn't have any bruises or sores from the bouts. She thanked him and he left, still rubbing his arm despite the healing she had provided.

Zalia made her way back to the tent, knowing that the other general would be arriving at some point today. She wished they could call off the meeting, but it would be quite rude to do so after asking him to come here. Besides, they could bring him up to speed and get his assistance with forming a plan that would work. She pushed aside the tent flaps and made her way, loudly, into the space. Ember groaned, muttering something that sounded like an insult that Zalia couldn't quite make out.

"Come on, you two, we have work to do," Zalia announced loudly.

"O away," Ember said into her pillow.

"Maybe another time, up you get!" Zalia said, pulling her blanket off.

This was possibly Zalia's favourite part of her morning routine.

CHAPTER FIFTY-ONE

War Council

Zalia

Zalia, Zen, and Ember stood near the entrance of the camp. With them were Eztari, General Faian, her advisor, both commanders, and a host of other camp officials. Indis was also there, near to Zalia, Zen, and Ember but not standing with them. A scout had been sent ahead of the soon-to-arrive reinforcements, bringing word of their arrival. They were expecting a few hundred soldiers along with various army logistics workers. This included cooks, healers, and builders, amongst other necessary roles.

Behind the first row of higher-ranked camp officials stood the currently camped army, in formation and at attention. The tents had been cleared specifically for this occasion as Faian wanted to make a good impression for the new recruits. While it had seemed like there had been a lot of soldiers within the camp when they were spread out, it was an entirely different view with them gathered. Whilst definitely impressive, the number of soldiers there couldn't compare to how many were under the command of the kingdom, especially with the recent draft that had swept through the towns within the last few weeks. They weren't a huge force but they represented some of the best and longest-serving soldiers of the kingdom, now fighting against a corrupt king for the benefit of the common folk. Theirs would be the advantage of experience and discipline whereas the enemy had numbers but not the training, and their minds would be clouded by madness.

"Think they have a chance?" Zalia asked Zen and Ember.

Zen shrugged. "I'm no military genius, we don't even truly know how many soldiers the kingdom has."

"I wonder if the madness that has been inflicted upon our enemies can be cured," Ember said, thinking out loud.

"With magic, I'm sure there is a way. Maybe, if things go well, you could be the one to find out how. There will be many in need after this is all done," Zalia said, trying to comfort her.

That seemed to bring energy into her posture, like the idea brought some direction to her future. Normally, that wouldn't be comforting to someone whatsoever, but Ember was all about helping others in need. It wasn't comfort in the fact that there would be much loss in the coming weeks, it was comfort in the fact she could help those who had lost something.

A horn resounded through the camp as one of the watchmen on the tall guard posts blew into their horn. One deep, long sound signalling the arrival of allies.

The gates swung open, and making their way out of the forest, a column of soldiers came forth, the land in front of them transforming as they moved into a clear and flat path. At the forefront of the column rode a contingent of knights on horseback, clad in shining armour. Following closely behind were foot soldiers, armoured only with breastplate, greaves, arm guards, and a helm much like Zalia's own armour but made entirely of metal. Each foot soldier held a shield and spear, a sword sheathed at their side, and a large pack slung over their shoulders. Behind them came a variety of people dressed in various garb, from work clothes to more official clothes. At each side of the column, more foot soldiers marched, keeping a perimeter around the less combat-oriented members of their party. Following the more logistical members of the arriving party was a contingent of archers in only light leather armour. The next section was what looked to be battle mages; various different elements and types of combat magic could be seen as passive effects altered the appearance of the wielders. The final segment was another group of foot soldiers, but Zalia didn't look too closely as the knights at the front finally arrived at the gates.

Zalia could now see that some unarmoured people rode amongst the knights, possibly these were the ones responsible for the terrain transforming to better allow travel. Amongst the less armoured of the first arrivals, Zalia could immediately identify the general. Though the man wasn't particularly tall, he was so broad Zalia was surprised his horse could hold the weight. He wore the uniform of a general much as Faian did, though his held fewer adornments.

He raised a fist and yelled "HALT," as the column came to a stop at his command.

He jumped down from his mount, passing the reins off to a nearby attendant and approached on his own. General Faian also moved away from her own entourage, walking to meet the man in the middle. As they stood face-to-face, they each saluted the other. The salute was a closed fist over the heart, then they lowered their heads till their faces looked to the ground and raised the back of their hand to their foreheads, fists still clenched. It was a gesture that she thought might indicate great respect, though she hadn't seen any of the other soldiers doing the same over the past few days.

"What's that gesture mean?" Zalia whispered to Ember.

Ember looked oddly at Zalia for a second before realisation dawned in her eyes.

"I forget you're not from around here sometimes. It's a gesture of great respect between two very close individuals. Pretty much the only people who will ever use it have grown up together or have gone through some trauma together," Ember whispered back.

"I heard that those two fought in the last war with the Astar," Zalia heard a man somewhere behind her whisper.

The Astar, the people to the east? I haven't heard of a war with them. Might ask Indis about it later. But she immediately regretted the thought, turning her mind away from that avenue. She had grown so used to being able to ask the well-educated Indis her more difficult or obscure questions.

Faian and the other general held their gesture for a short moment before standing up straight and embracing.

"May my soldiers and I enter your camp, General Faian?" the man asked formally.

"Of course, General Ballast, you and yours are always welcome," Faian replied.

At that declaration, a host of people wearing formal clothing moved across the distance to each other, talking quickly and quietly, some passing around pieces of parchment. Very soon, the column of soldiers was on the move once more, filtering into the camp where various officials directed different groups of people to the right places. All in all, the merging of the two forces happened extremely quickly and efficiently, enough so that Zalia was thoroughly impressed. She should have expected it, of course, this was a meeting of two well-respected generals and their properly hired and trained retinues, after all.

General Faian approached Zalia, Ember, and Zen, bringing General Ballast with her. Indis appeared from the crowd, standing next to them with a stiff posture. She was obviously still not over their most recent argument.

"General Ballast, these are our guests from the Morning's Shade, Zen, Ember, Zalia, and Lady Indis. Representatives, this is General Ballast of the southern division," General Faian said in introduction.

Zalia still didn't know how to properly greet a general in these lands, if there was even a proper way, so decided to use the method from her own home. She squared her feet with her shoulders and brought her hand to the side of her temple, held flat with the palm pointed outwards, the military salute from her home country. It was probably a poor imitation of the real thing but they wouldn't have known it anyways.

"General," Zalia greeted.

"Shade," Ballast replied.

He looked to approve of Zalia's attempt at being formal.

"A pleasure to meet you," Indis said, giving a light bow.

In response to that, the general just grunted. He seemed straightforward with a no-nonsense attitude, and Zalia was liking the man already.

Both Zen and Ember gave a similar bow as Indis had, though definitely less refined.

"Let's get to business then, shall we?" General Ballast asked.

"Certainly, right this way," General Faian said, leading them into the camp.

Zalia picked up Boreal, not wanting her to be caught up in the amount of movement happening throughout the space. Boreal didn't seem too impressed by the move, but Zalia knew it would be for the best. Zalia noticed that quite a few people were following them, some she recognised: Advisor Ryn, Commanders Gurz and Lynette. Some, she didn't recognise. She assumed by their uniforms that they were the counterparts of Ryn, Gurz, and Lynette amongst General Ballast's own army.

They all arrived at a bigger structure that Zalia hadn't seen before. With the amount of powerful magic wielders compressed into this one camp, she wouldn't have been surprised if the structure had been conjured by someone that very day. They all settled around a table, larger than the usual one Faian sat at with a map that stretched across the entire battlefront, as well as the centre of the kingdom. There was a lot of information carefully written or shown in detail, with miniatures marking known or suspected troop placements.

"We have a few key points to touch on today. Our first point will be General Ballast retelling his story of the events that led to this war. The second point will be an explanation of some new information that has come to light that may give us a chance, provided by our guests from the Morning's Shade. Once that is done, we will discuss additional war plans for the near future. Everyone ready?" General Faian explained once everyone seemed seated and settled.

There was a chorus of affirmatives and nodded heads so General Faian gestured to General Ballast, who began retelling his version of the story. It was very similar to the story that Faian told, differing only in that it appeared he had realised what was happening a bit later than she had. Zalia had already decided on helping the rebellion but paid particular attention to his every word, trying to find discrepancies in their stories. When she found none, it was finally settled in her mind that she would do what she could to help them. It was no longer a question of if, but how.

It seemed like the others all had come to the same decision as well, Indis obviously already having decided long ago.

"Any questions?" General Faian asked, once General Ballast had finished speaking.

"None whatsoever," Indis said.

"No," Zalia replied as well.

Zen and Ember shook their heads.

"Very well, on to our second point of information for today," General Faian said.

She then explained the situation concerning the Morning's Shade, Hidey, and all the information Zalia had given over to them. They corrected or added information where asked or needed, bringing Ballast and his retinue up to speed. Once Faian was done speaking, she locked eyes with Ballast for a moment, seeming to have a silent conversation. Ballast nodded and she continued.

"Very well, now we need to make some decisions as soon as possible. From everything we have gathered, we don't have a lot of time to move before whatever the king is up to is finished. We believe he has brought in the Morning's Shade in a last ditch attempt to push us as hard as he can with his army to buy as much time as he can. This leads us to believe he isn't really worried about either the Morning's Shade discovering the truth, or our eventual victory against his army. That puts us in a delicate position. We have to make an aggressive and possibly dangerous move to put an end to this," General Faian began.

She paused for a moment, one hand leaning on the table while she held her chin with the other, thinking.

"It could be a feint to draw us into doing exactly this but it would be a foolhardy and dangerous feint for him to make if he didn't have some sort of backup," Faian finished. She looked around the table and the discussion began.

Zalia didn't take part very much, barely even managing to keep her mind focused on what they were speaking about. There was a lot of talk revolving around logistics, a few more people were brought in, people in charge of various supplies or organising groups of people. Each point was heavily discussed to cover issues and possible solutions as they slowly but surely formed an in-depth plan as to how to respond to each possible issue that could crop up.

As a hunter, Zalia was no stranger to thorough planning of traps, escapes, and methods of taking down big game. This though, was an entirely different scale. They were talking about the movement of an incredible amount of supplies, troops across an entire battlefront moving in a coordinated push to gather into one large army that would assault the capital. They would give up each and every defensible position they held, leaving only a skeleton garrison, to make a hopefully final push towards victory. It was a desperate plan that held many dangers: possible ambush or unknown forces could cause a domino effect of failure across the whole board. Misplaced or mishandled supplies could cause an entire division to lose cohesion or starve, requiring assistance from nearby towns or allies. It was a logistical nightmare, but Faian and Ballast along with their logistics officers broke the entire thing down into tiny parts, solving each issue as they moved. They had one of the strange devices Zalia had first seen when she had arrived in camp, a form of long-range communication that allowed them to include other generals and officers from across the battlefront.

After a few hours, Faian called a break to the discussion and each included party retired to speak amongst themselves for a short time.

"I am not made for this," Zalia said as soon as they were out of earshot.

"I don't know how they can possibly even remember all of that information," Ember replied, nodding in agreement.

"They are quite good at what they do. I'm sure they have some magical abilities that help in this regard," Indis added, still stiff and formal.

She had decided to come with them rather than stay behind.

Zalia avoided looking at the woman, not wanting to cause more issues. She felt like it would create another argument if she spoke to her.

"Boreal is a bit restless, we might go for a quick run. I'll see you all here soon," Zalia said, making to move away.

"Zalia," Indis called.

Zalia stopped, feeling a tiny bit of dread, but turned around.

"Yes?" she asked.

"I'm sorry for how I have acted. You did the right thing," Indis said.

Zalia watched Indis for a short time, not trusting herself to speak. In the end, she simply gave her a nod before turning around and leaving.

CHAPTER FIFTY-TWO

Talks and Travel

Zalia

They went through three days straight of planning and discussion, endlessly going over and over every little detail until everyone was satisfied with the plan. All across the battlefront, other generals and local armies were doing the exact same thing for their specific sections, though many used the long-range communication device to ask Faian or Ballast a question if they got stuck. From what Zalia picked up through the course of the discussions, there were three main encampments along the length of the border they held. Faian's was the furthest north with another south, and one more even further south of that. The camp that was furthest south was officially where Ballast and his soldiers were stationed but they had taken on the role of roaming reinforcements, travelling to wherever was needed. Only a token force was left in that southernmost camp, the majority of the war taking place more centrally towards where the capital of Endaria was.

At the end of the three days, a plan was set. All of the rebellion's forces would make their way towards the capital, avoiding enemy soldiers where possible and fighting through when necessary. Certain sections would group up with others at set locations until they arrived as one singular large force. One of the main issues, and the largest point of contention between the generals with this stage of the plan, would be that they were leaving enemy soldiers behind that could harass or even form into a larger fighting unit to flank them. It was definitely a weak point in the plan, but Faian thought the risk was necessary. They would then assault the capital and hopefully take it within short order. One of the reasons that the generals thought this would be possible was the most recent change within the kingdom's armies. When they got the Morning's Shade involved to take care of the Elemental issues, the majority of the soldiers who were kept behind within the kingdom's borders to deal with that issue were moved outwards to the battle-front. This meant that there weren't nearly as many people defending the capital, and an organised and efficient push through to reach it may yet succeed.

The reasons that convinced the final general holding out about the plan were the strange actions of the king. His most recent decisions would lead to a definite loss in the war in the long-term whilst giving him a strong front in the short-term. While losing the war, the king could slowly move back forces in a defensive retreat to delay his loss as long as possible. Instead, attacks on the camps were more prolific than ever, the most recent a good example. This would naturally lead to a more defensive stance from the rebellion, allowing the king's armies to dash themselves against their well-set defensive positions. The only reason they could deduce that would cause that kind of behaviour is if he expected some reinforcements or realised a new method by which he could shortly win the war. The constant discovery of more ritual sites and the further agitation of Elementals across the lands only added to the theory that something big was coming, soon. This meant that they would need to act unexpectedly and push straight to the capital and stop whatever it is the king planned. After they had captured the capital they would be able to use its own defences to recapture the kingdom from a central point. So, they agreed it was the right plan and made ready to begin. Of course, it could all be a trap set by the king to get them to do exactly this, but they didn't have much choice.

Zalia and her team had a slightly less explicitly dangerous task. They would go back to the Morning's Shade and convince them that they believed it to be the rebels who were the cause of all the ritual sites. They would tell Hidey that they had managed to deceive the rebels into thinking they would be on their side and had learnt of their plans. They would have to convince Hidey that the rebels were already moving all their forces far south to push through the weak defences there, and that they planned to strike out at a large town a week's distance from the capital. If they were correct about Hidey's hidden controller being the king, he would learn of the plans through Hidey and react accordingly, sending his armies down to counter the attack. Hopefully that would give the rebellion a little bit of leeway and some extra time in their own actions. There were, of course, many more specifics to each and every part of the plan on the rebellion's side but Zalia and her team's goal was thankfully simple and specific. After they had accomplished their own part of the plan, they could either leave to wherever they wanted to go or stay to see if the plan worked.

If possible, they were also meant to convince some of the stronger members of the Morning's Shade to head to the capital to confront the king. This was a very risky idea, however, and they were only to do it if they thought it absolutely would not get back to Hidey. After all, they weren't high ranking members of the organisation and most would not trust their word over the word of Hidey himself.

It was the morning of the fourth day that Zalia and her team departed. They were given a small stone object that when cracked would send a signal to the rebellion that their part of the task was done. They now trekked through the forests as they made their way back towards Endelbyrn.

"I think this could work," Ember said.

"I definitely feel a lot better for not being the only ones that know so much. Our part is so much simpler now, it's quite freeing," Zalia replied.

"Like the weight of the world has been lifted off our shoulders," Zen added.

Indis was walking some ten metres in front of them, not taking part in the conversation. Zalia glanced towards the woman for the hundredth time since they had left the camp; her emotions surrounding Indis's actions were still a confused mess.

"What are you going to do once we are done with all this?" Zalia asked Ember.

None of them had specifically said it, but they were each leaving the Morning's Shade once this was all said and done. Either way, there would be no place for them there.

"Well, I think I'm going to try and help all the people who will be in need after the war, like you suggested," Ember replied.

"I think I'm going to go south, see the desert lands and the people who live there. Maybe further north than we ever went. I also really want to see what is further east, where the Astar live. I know Indis said that they don't accept humans within their lands but I want to try anyway. You'd always be welcome to join me if you wanted," Zalia offered.

"I'll keep it in mind," Ember promised.

Zalia knew Ember wouldn't come with her, the woman just wouldn't be able to leave behind people in need. She hadn't really expected otherwise but thought it worth a try.

"I'm going to work the fields with my family, relax in the sun, and live peacefully for the rest of my days," Zen said dreamily.

Zalia did have to admit, it sounded pretty nice. She glanced once more at Indis walking ahead and decided to try and make a peace offering.

"What about you, Indis, what are you going to do once this is over?" Zalia called out.

Indis looked back, seeming a little shocked that Zalia had asked her, but quickly fell back to answer.

"I don't really know, I haven't thought much about it. This is kind of my whole life, my family, my friends. I don't know if I'll even have any of those once this is over," she replied.

There was a short awkward silence but Zen quickly broke it.

"You could help the rebellion with leading the country. There will be a lot of confusion once this is over, the people won't know what to think or believe. Someone who was a close member to the royal family might be a hope to grasp on to for many," he suggested.

"That's . . . not so bad of an idea. Thank you, Zen," Indis replied.

More and more recently, Zen had seemed to have grown out of his fantastical thinking. He had definitely become more sobered and thoughtful in his actions and words as of late.

"Are we going to go straight to Endelbyrn, or are there any stops we want to make along the way?" Ember asked.

Zalia thought it over for a moment. "I might have an idea that can help, and it shouldn't be too far out of the way. Why don't we try to convince Glemp and their people to help us?" Zalia asked in turn.

"It's a bit late to be making changes in the plan, besides, why would they?" Indis asked.

Zalia thought it over. She did remember there had been conflict in the past between Glemp's people and the humans.

"You're probably right, just a thought. We go straight to Endelbyrn then, unless you two have an idea," Zalia said, looking to Indis and Zen.

Both shook their heads.

With the decision made, they continued onwards.

Almost two weeks later as they were travelling, Zen stopped at a fork of the road. They were nearing Endelbyrn, and the closer they got the more stressed they all were. The moment of truth would soon come, whether they would be able to pull off a successful lie and help bring the downfall of the king. It was a terrible situation for all of them for different reasons, yet they still each dreaded it equally. A lot could go wrong depending on what happened with them now, and though their task was simple it might be able to sway the course of the war in either direction. Initially they had revelled at the lessened burden since the rebellion had taking on the role of those who would have to invade the capital and attack the king. Now though, the stress had returned.

"Are you alright, Zen?" Zalia asked.

"If I go down this road instead, it will take me home," Zen replied, looking off into the distance.

"I wouldn't stop you," Zalia said, realising what he wanted to do.

Indis looked like she was about to protest, but Ember gave her a glare.

"No, I said I would help you see this to its end. We only have to do one last thing, I can survive until afterwards," Zen said, turning away from that other road and firmly stepping in the direction of Endelbyrn once more.

They all followed after, Zalia reading through her latest messages from the past two weeks. They hadn't been idle during that time, often hunting beasts they passed by, and Zalia continued training particularly hard. She had almost six extra hours each day, after all.

> **Congratulations! Kill Shot has reached Iron 8.**
> **Congratulations! Hunter's Sight has reached Iron 10.**
> **Congratulations! Survivalist and associated skills have reached Iron 13.**
> **Congratulations! Hunter class has reached Iron 8.**
> **Congratulations! Flora Identification has reached Iron 8.**
> **Congratulations! Stasis has reached Iron 8.**
> **Congratulations! Herbalist class has reached Iron 8.**
> **Congratulations! Nature's Wrath has reached Iron 6.**
> **Congratulations! Druid class has reached Iron 6.**
> **Congratulations! Low Light Vision has gained**
> **three levels, reaching Tin 20.**
> **Congratulations! Low Light Vision has reached Iron 1.**
> **Low Light Vision - passive**
> **Tin - You see better in low light areas.**
> **Iron - Your vision is able to pierce magical darkness**
> **of the same rank or lower of this ability.**
> **Congratulations! Aura Observation has gained**
> **three levels, reaching Tin 19.**
> **Congratulations! Mobility has reached Iron 17.**
> **Congratulations! Teaching has reached Iron 7.**
> **Congratulations! Bow - Weapon Proficiency has reached Iron 15.**
> **Congratulations! Sword - Weapon Proficiency**
> **has gained two levels, reaching Iron 8.**
> **Congratulations! Throwing knives - Weapon Proficiency**
> **has gained six levels, reaching Tin 17.**

It was steady progress, the new ability from Low Light Vision being the most interesting upgrade. She hadn't encountered any magical darkness yet, as far as she knew, but thought it a handy skill all the same.

It was evening when they finally arrived back in Endelbyrn, looking in at the fortress-like city with the glittering reflective walls and dark, light-absorbing spires in the centre, giving the impression of a dark castle within a halo of light.

"I don't think I'll ever get tired of that sight, even in these dark days," Ember said.

Zalia grunted in agreement, the other two nodding as well. They all stood there, almost as if none of them wanted to move any further. When they stepped into those walls they would have to play a role, lie to those they worked with and for. Once they were in those walls, one slip up could spell disaster for a lot of people. They had discussed and discussed again what exactly their story would be, what they would tell Hidey, how they would answer certain questions. Now it was time to play the part.

With a sigh, Zalia took the first step forwards, Boreal following. "Might as well get it over with," she muttered.

The others soon followed and they walked down the slight decline towards the city.

All seemed normal as they passed through the gates, showing the guards their little badges designed after the very view they had just witnessed. They walked through the streets of the city proper, surrounded by people going about their days as normal, completely unaware that the kingdom may soon fall. Before long the inner wall of the Morning's Shade's keep appeared and there too they were granted entrance. They stepped into the main spire's grand entrance and began making their way through the winding stairs and passages towards where they knew Hidey's office was.

They came to a stop at his door. Zalia knocked.

"Come in," the muffled voice replied from beyond.

Zalia gave her team one last glance before grabbing the handle, pushing it down, and swinging the door open.

CHAPTER FIFTY-THREE

Lies

Zalia

A few expressions passed over Hidey's face as they entered the room. The first was surprise, quickly followed by what Zalia swore was a frown in her direction, and lastly a broad smile.

"You're back!" Hidey exclaimed, standing from his seat.

"Hey!" Zalia greeted, using her leg to block Boreal's approach towards the bookshelf at the back of the room.

"*Oh no, you don't,*" she said to Boreal through their bond.

"Please, sit, sit," Hidey said, gesturing to a couple of chairs stacked in a corner.

They each pulled out a seat and placed themselves in front of his desk.

"I'm sure it must have been an arduous journey, but as you know the situation is dire. Are you up for telling me what you have learnt?" Hidey asked.

Zalia's heart skipped a beat. This was it.

"Of course," Indis replied, face as neutral as ever.

Indis looked to them as if asking if one of them wanted to start, but Ember quickly gestured for her to begin.

"Well, we met with the spy as planned and made our way to one of the rebellion's military camps. Everything seemed fine at first and their general, Faian, told a compelling story that nearly convinced us of their side in the war. We asked to meet another of their generals, firstly to provide another version of the story for us to pick at, but also to buy time to do a little looking around for ourselves. Whilst the general told a convincing tale, we wanted to be sure," Indis started.

Ember quickly interjected. "Soon, we found a building filled with madmen.

Some were unresponsive, some muttering to themselves, others clawing at the walls. We couldn't help but draw a parallel between the men and the corrupted man Zalia found near to Ostoss. This was . . . the first of the red flags."

Ember looked to Zalia and she started speaking.

"They were having a supply issue, something was stealing and destroying supplies leading to increased costs for the army. We offered to help with the problem while we waited for the other general to arrive, and they reluctantly agreed. We discovered the issue was a group of Elementals that they couldn't quite track. I managed to do so and we resolved the issue for them, gaining a little trust. Something struck me as odd about it, and after talking we realised that the only other times we had seen Elementals causing so much trouble was around ritual sites. At this point the evidence was telling us that they definitely had something to do with the rituals," she said, keeping to their planned story.

"The final straw was when they told us their plan," Zen continued. "They want to invade the kingdom from the south with a large force, push through to the capital and destroy the king. They played it off as being the good guys, and taking down the evil king who's using sacrificial rituals to destroy the lands, but we didn't buy into it. We soon left, knowing we needed to get this information to you as soon as possible so that we can do something to help. We can't let this happen, we must at least warn him!" Zen finished, actually sounding the most convincing of them all. He managed to put emotion behind the words so that whilst the others sounded like they were giving a report, he sounded like he was genuinely worried.

Hidey looked them all over and gave an exhausted sigh, looking troubled. "This is terrible news you bring, though it is good to know of this plan before it takes place. You are right, we must warn the king."

The story was mostly the work of Indis. Unsurprisingly, the woman knew the best way to spin a tale that you wanted someone to believe. The best way was to use as much truth as you could get away with, twisting it to suit your purpose. When they had been coming up with what to say and Indis had suggested this, they all thought the same thing though none spoke it: it was exactly what Indis had done with them, spinning her story to suit the purpose she needed in the moment.

"Any news of what is happening here?" Zalia asked, changing the subject now that their task was done.

"Things are not good. Elemental awakenings have increased in number and we are struggling to keep up. Teams are still working on destroying the Gold rank Elementals that awaken near ritual sites but work is slow. It seems like they are slowly getting stronger, and we even had to deal with a single Emerald rank Elemental. It took all of the Gold rank members to deal with that one. Even then it was a close call," Hidey replied.

"Emerald?" she asked.

"The rank above Gold," Indis told her.

Just another thing I forgot to learn about. "What are the other ranks?" she asked.

"Diamond then Mythical. There are some who say there is another rank above that, Ascendant, but rumours of such occasions are few and far between. It's hard to confirm such things, and no one of that rank has been kind enough to come tell us it is true," Indis replied.

"A little off-topic guys," Ember interrupted.

"Sorry," Zalia said.

"No matter, I believe we should start gathering our people back in preparation to act. Thank you for a job well done, team, the rest of the day is yours. I must discuss this with Matthias and Hildebrandt, and we will make an announcement tomorrow morning," Hidey finished, dismissing them.

They left the room, making their way down out of the building. They didn't speak of the conversation or their apparent success, and they wouldn't until everything was over. The chance of being overheard was not worth the risk. They entered a hallway that should have led to an exit, but ahead of them there was nothing but darkness.

"What is that?" Ember asked, trying to see through.

"I don't know, I can't see in," Indis replied.

Zen lifted his shield off his back, hefting his mace in the other hand.

Zalia though, could see. Within the darkness was a figure, a humanoid, a shade. Within the darkness was the Hidden.

"He knows," Zalia whispered.

"What?" Indis asked.

Ember understood and drew her weapons too, but it was too late.

The darkness spread through the corridor faster than they could react, sending them all into a pitch black void. Zalia could see as Indis tried to spark lightning off her body, but it simply fizzled within the shade. Zen lifted his shield towards where the Hidden had been, trying to block any incoming attacks. Ember was spinning her head around, desperately trying to catch sound or sight of their enemy. Zalia summoned her weapon into its sword form and waited.

"*So that's why I couldn't detect the bow anymore,*" the Hidden whispered, his voice coming from all around.

"Why are you doing this?" Zalia asked, still trying to feign innocence.

"*I'm sorry, child,*" the disembodied voice replied, almost sounding sad.

Arms began reaching from the walls, floor, and ceiling, each grabbing onto limbs, clothes, and armour. Indis was immediately restrained against the wall and Zalia desperately slashed at the shadow limbs, trying to cut her free. She managed to destroy two of the arms before she had to leave Indis and cut at the limbs grabbing her. Failing to destroy them all, she tried to activate her Nature's Wrath and Protection of the Wilds abilities, but neither of them activated. Her magic felt dull and withdrawn, as if it was being crushed by another force. Despite all the training and effort Zalia had put into getting stronger, it wasn't enough. One by one they were each restrained and as they were smothered, the deep darkness of unconsciousness eventually overtook them.

Zalia blinked her eyes.

What happened? she thought.

Then the memories came back in a rush and she jumped to her feet, summoning her weapon as adrenaline rushed through her body. She quickly inspected her surroundings, finding that she was in a dark cell along with Zen, Ember, Indis, and Boreal. The others had been stripped of their armour and weapons, Zalia found her own armour was missing as well. Luckily, it didn't seem that the Hidden had been able to take her bonded weapon.

She was the first to awaken and tried cutting at the bars with her magically reinforced and sharpened blade but found it to be of no use. She considered trying to use some of the herbs she had stored within her spatial storage but thought better of it, deciding to keep them as a secret weapon. At least, she didn't think the Hidden knew about it.

She walked over and picked up Boreal's still unconscious form, hugging the feline close and sitting on one of the stone benches.

We failed, she thought.

She played back their conversation over and over in her head, trying to figure out what they had said, what they had given away that had ruined the carefully prepared lie. How had he known?

"*So that's why I couldn't detect the bow anymore.*"

Maybe that was why?

Zalia shook her head and pushed the thoughts to the back of her mind. Right now they had to find a way out, find a way to warn the rebellion. They hadn't cracked the stone that Faian had given them, would they now change their plans? Would the rebellion know they had failed?

Bringing herself back to the current situation, Zalia started focusing her Healing Aura onto Ember, hoping to wake the woman so she could help heal and wake the others quicker. Soon, Ember stirred and Zalia gently placed Boreal down so she could shake Ember's shoulders.

"Wake up," she said gently.

She didn't wake.

"Wake up," Zalia said, shaking her a bit rougher.

Ember finally woke up, reacting in a similar way to Zalia, immediately trying to attack her.

Zalia jumped away quickly, holding her hands up in a peaceful gesture. "Hey,

hey, just me. Help me wake the others." Zalia then focused her healing equally between the other three.

Ember walked over and began working her own healing spells on them as well.

Soon enough, they were all awake. They all stood or sat, trying to figure out what to do. It had been a few hours and they were still each trying out their own ways of breaking down the bars that now held them. Outside the bars was a hallway that led both left and right, though all they could see was the bench opposite the cell and the torch glowing dimly above it. Boreal had even tried to slip between the bars but some shield had fizzled to life where she walked, blocking her exit.

"At least we aren't dead," Zen said, trying to sound upbeat and not entirely succeeding.

"Yippee, now they can torture us for the information we didn't tell them," Zalia said dryly.

Zen seemed to go pale at that.

"Oh, don't worry about her, I'm sure it won't come to that," Ember said comfortingly, giving Zalia a glare.

"Sorry," Zalia said apologetically.

They heard footsteps coming down the hallway beyond and all stood, facing the bars defensively.

They all recognised the man that walked around the corner. The Hidden.

"I'm truly sorry for this," he said, looking miserable for his part.

"Yet here we are," Zalia replied.

"The choice was not mine to make, unfortunately," the Hidden said.

"Yeah, we know," Indis said sadly.

"No, I don't think you do," the Hidden replied.

They heard another set of footsteps and Juniper came into view.

"Juniper?" Zalia asked, confused.

"I'm sorry, dear, I couldn't let you interfere with what comes next," Juniper said, taking a seat on the bench opposite their cell.

"I don't understand," Zalia said numbly.

What part did Juniper have in this?

"Oh, dear, you wouldn't. I've worked too many years to get him back, and I won't be stopped because they brought in an interloper. It just won't do," Juniper said, almost looking through them into the walls of the cell.

"What are you talking about?" Ember asked angrily.

"Oh, nothing for you to worry about now. Soon it will be over and you'll be free, one way or the other," Juniper replied, dropping two pieces of stone to the floor.

Zalia hadn't noticed the object the woman was holding but now immediately recognised it. It was the stone that, when broken, would send a message to the rebellion that their part of the plan had been accomplished.

Oh no. "Why are you even here?" Zalia asked in frustration.

Juniper frowned. "I guess I felt bad for deceiving you. I am sorry for the way this had to go, but years of preparation won't be wasted for your comfort. I must be off now, the timing is very important and I must be ready. Goodbye, Zalia," Juniper said as she stood and walked off.

The Hidden gave them a sad smile before he too left.

CHAPTER FIFTY-FOUR

Rituals

Zalia

Zalia stared at the hallway where Juniper and the Hidden had just walked out of sight. She could vaguely hear the sound of Indis and Ember arguing behind her as she watched the stone wall in shock.

Did she really trust too easily? Was she just gullible?

Of all the people to betray and lie to her, Juniper would have been the very last person she would have expected that from. She'd been one of the first people she truly thought of as a friend in this world. Would Glemp betray her as well?

From the very start, Juniper had been so friendly and kind. She'd given Zalia the bow she now wielded. She had given her advice, direction, and information. Zalia had helped the woman with a problem for no other compensation than a few coins barely worth the work. Had that problem been a lie as well? Had she only given her these things to gain the trust she so ruthlessly wielded now?

"I won't be stopped because they brought in an interloper. It just won't do," Juniper had said.

Was she the interloper? If so, who had brought her here? Maybe the strange portal that had brought her to this world hadn't been so much of an accident or natural occurrence as she had thought. Had the woman known from the very start how and why Zalia had been brought to this world?

There were so many questions running through her head and she was having trouble answering each one as the next shoved its way to the forefront of her mind. She managed to move past the misery that hounded her and considered the woman's other words. She had said, "I've worked too many years to get him back."

Was Juniper referring to Zayes? If so, how could she get him back?

Then she remembered the very first time she had heard of Cormaine, from the Hidden, of all people. He had said that some believe those who die move on to Cormaine, their very beings reincarnated within the other realm. Was that what Juniper was trying to accomplish, bringing Zayes back from the dead?

There were so many emotions fighting within her body, so much so that her very skin just felt . . . raw.

"We need to get out of here," Ember was saying, trying to pull at the bars of the cell. She wasn't able to even wrap her hands around them as the magical field stopped her fingers.

"We have tried every way possible, we simply can't," Indis snapped at her. She was sitting on the floor in the corner, arms propped on her knees.

"I refuse to believe there is nothing we can do!" Ember yelled, spinning around to face Indis.

She was met with a frustrated gaze from Indis, Zen's sad eyes, and a shell-shocked expression from Zalia. Boreal was weaving between Zalia's legs, brushing against her in an effort to provide some comfort.

"So that's it!?" Ember asked angrily, meeting each of their eyes.

"We can't get out, Ember," Zen replied sadly.

He looked lost, far off in thought and Zalia knew where his mind was. He was back at that crossroad, looking down the path that would have led him to his parents and home as he stepped firmly past it.

"Maybe the rebellion will succeed anyway, they can't possibly know the entire plan right?" Zalia offered weakly.

"He seemed to figure out we were lying pretty quick," Ember retorted, turning back to the cell bars and angrily slamming her palms into them.

"They might," Indis said, though she didn't look convinced.

Ember put her back to the cell bars and slid down to the floor, now mimicking Indis's posture. "There must be something we can do," she mumbled, her anger quickly fading to hopelessness. "There must be something."

The rest of that day passed in a drag, all of them barely speaking a word as they stared hopelessly at the walls and bars that now held them. The depressed mood seemed to infect even Boreal, who curled up next to Zalia in a tight ball. Towards the end of the day, a guard arrived and pushed food on a metal tray under a small cutout in the door designed for that very purpose. It was only after the man left that Zalia realised where she recognised him from. He was one of the two guards that had been at the doors to the Morning's Shade's spires when she had first arrived.

Ignoring the food, Ember quickly started poking and prodding at the small section that had allowed the food to pass through, hoping to find some sort of weakness, but ultimately failing. After the attempt she sat back against the wall with a dull thud, staring at the platter that sat untouched on the floor.

As she thought day faded to night outside, each of Zalia's companions slowly fell to sleep, curling up on the cold stone floor. While they were all pretty much immune to normal cold at this point, the darkness and hopelessness of their situation seemed to instil a chill within their bodies anyways.

Zalia sat awake, staring at the walls without hope as her mind turned over the day's events. Thoughts of every kind smile and gesture she had been given from the old farmer Juniper passed through her mind, each a lie, each a ploy to gain her trust. There was so much frustrated energy within her body making her want to act whilst simultaneously making her so tired. Despite that, she still could not find sleep.

Much later, her companions started waking again, and yet Zalia still sat awake in the same position as she had been. The shell shock, frustration, and emotional pain she'd been experiencing was slowly turning to anger. Anger at the human race for their tendency towards horror and pain, anger at Juniper for her lies, and anger at herself, for her own naivety. Since she had arrived she had given her trust out easily to those she met, hoping beyond hope that maybe the people here were more like her. Practical, upfront, and honest.

Maybe she was more like Zen than she thought, living in her own fantasy only to be brought out rudely by the real world.

"*Wolf of the stars, please help us,*" Zalia prayed, trying to project her thoughts. She had no idea if the creature really was a god but it was worth a try. Right?

"Do you think they've started marching yet?" Zen asked.

"Probably," Indis replied.

She knew what Zen was hoping for. He was hoping that the rebellion would somehow find out about their fate and rescue them. Realistically, that wouldn't happen. Nobody even knew they were here, some members of the Morning's Shade might have seen them arrive, but what would they think about their disappearance? They hadn't ever stayed around long before this either.

Even then, they knew that at least one of the members was under Hidey's control or had given him their loyalty since the guard didn't seem surprised by their presence. Maybe the man bringing them food didn't know why they were here, though she doubted convincing him to break them free would be possible.

When the guard did come by to deliver their food for the day, Ember tried to do exactly that. Zalia didn't know what he'd been told, but he simply did not acknowledge Ember or her words, passing the food through unceremoniously. After he didn't respond to her words, Ember tried to grab at him through the slit as he pushed the platter in, yet despite the fact that it did not prevent the metal tray from entering, the field still stopped Ember's hand cold. She finally resorted to banging on the cell bars as he walked away, yelling insults at him.

She let out one final yell of frustration as he moved out of sight. "Damn it!"

Zalia moved forwards and took a plate off the tray and tried pushing it back through the bars. Oddly, it worked.

"We might be able to use that," Ember said, her frustration quickly turning to interest as she started thinking almost visibly.

Feeling like an idiot, Zalia summoned her sword and tried to push that through the bars. Unfortunately, it didn't work.

"Damn," Zalia said.

She had really hoped that would work.

After everyone had finished eating, Ember collected all the plates as if she planned on using them as weapons. Zalia didn't eat, giving her food to the others since she wouldn't need to eat much on any given day.

Soon enough, the others fell asleep once more, and Zalia and Boreal were the only ones left awake. Before long though, Zalia too fell asleep, not having slept at all the night before. She drifted off fitfully.

She woke again barely two hours later, somehow feeling rested yet exhausted. It was like her body was perfectly rested yet her mind was taxed in a way that sleep would not help.

That day passed much as the one previous did, consisting mostly of sitting against the wall trying to think of anything they could do to escape or accomplish anything.

Once more, the guard came with food and slid the platter beneath the door. As he did however, a deep rumble could be felt in the ground and walls around them. As it settled, the man smirked at them and spoke for the first time.

"Not long now," he crowed.

His smile instantly turned to shock as in a flash of movement, he was slammed backwards into the wall, cracking his head. Standing over his limp body as he fell unconscious to the floor was a woman that Zalia recognised.

"Larel?" she asked.

"Quiet," the woman whispered, moving over to the cell and grabbing the door.

She strained as she pulled and after a tense moment, the door gave way to her Gold rank strength. Zalia was surprised at how difficult it looked for her to rip the door off its hinges, especially after having seen her strength not so long ago against a Gold rank Elemental.

"What's happening?" Zalia asked.

Larel gave her a pointed look, holding her pointer finger over her lips in a shushing gesture.

She motioned for them to follow, moving away and through the long hallway. They could now see the end where a set of stairs led upwards, hopefully towards the open sky. It hadn't been long and Zalia was already feeling claustrophobic and craving open air and land once more. She had thought being in a city was bad; being stuck in a cell was unimaginably worse.

They moved up the flight of stairs, and Larel put her ear to the door before opening it slightly and peeking through. She closed the door once more and turned back to them.

"What are you all doing down here in a cell?" she asked in a whisper.

Zalia frowned.

"You don't know why?" Indis asked quietly.

"No, someone left a note in my goddamn room saying you had been imprisoned wrongfully. I thought it must have been someone fucking with me but I asked around and discovered you had entered the city but not yet left. I asked Hildebrandt if she knew where you all were and she thought you were still out of town. I snuck down here after I saw that guy entering the cells. These cells haven't been used in years so I knew something was up with a guard coming down here. I figure there must be something wrong if Hildebrandt doesn't know about it, so I'm breaking you out. Now, why are you here?" she repeated once more.

"Long story," Ember said, moving as if to push past.

"Make it a short one, or you're going back in the cell," Larel said firmly, holding out an arm.

Zalia considered explaining for only a moment but the most recent betrayal of her trust made her change her mind. She thought Larel was a good person but wasn't ready to risk that. Luckily, Indis was.

"Hidey and Juniper are both responsible in part for the rituals. They're working with the king to perform some kind of huge-scale ritual that is meant to happen soon and we need to stop it," Indis explained.

Larel looked at her intensely, searching her face for a lie. She looked at Zalia.

"It's true," she confirmed.

"How can that be true?" Larel asked.

Another rumble passed through the building.

"What the hell is that?" Zen mumbled.

Indis quickly summarised what they knew about the entire situation to Larel, ending with their report to the Hidden and eventual capture by his hand.

"I don't really trust what you are saying. We will bring this to Matthias and Hildebrandt and ask them what they know of the situation. In either case, you should not have been imprisoned without the agreement of all three of them. Come," Larel said, opening the door once more.

She stepped out and immediately froze.

"What the hell is that?" she said, looking up into the sky.

The cause of the rumbling was now apparent. A bright beam of light was shooting up into the sky, originating at the top of the tallest spire. The centre of the beam was a pure white with red and purple lights swirling around it ever up into the sky. The ritual had begun.

"Please, Larel, we need to stop that RIGHT now," Zalia pleaded.

"While I don't trust you fully on your story, that much we agree on," Larel replied, sprinting off into a building.

They all ran after her, none of them able to keep up, but their destination was clear. Ember took the lead as the best at navigating the spires.

They ran for a few minutes, arriving on the small, flat rooftop of the tallest spire. Kneeling before the giant beam of light was Juniper, her hands cradled in her lap, bleeding from long gashes. The ground around her was splattered with blood and body parts that looked to be from one, maybe two people. Guarding her kneeling form were two more people with curved blades atop large wooden polearms. Standing even closer, Larel was confronting Hidey.

"What is happening here, Hidden?" Larel was yelling.

"You should not be here, Larel, leave," the Hidden replied.

"We shall see what else you have to say when Hildebrandt and Matthias join us," Larel said, taking on a defensive stance, both hands raised.

"They will not be joining us today," the Hidden replied with a sombre smile.

Zalia and her team stood behind Larel, ready to fight. Zalia was the only one with a weapon, her bow summoned and held at the ready, starlight arrow nocked.

"Bastard," Larel snarled, launching into an attack.

"Can you do something about that ritual?" Indis asked Zalia.

She was the only one with any kind of ritual knowledge on their team.

"I can try," she replied.

"We'll distract those two, hurry!" Indis yelled, running around the Gold rank and Hidden as they fought. Ember and Zen quickly overtook her, taking defensive stances in front of Indis, hoping to protect her from the two approaching guards.

Zalia sprinted around the other side, followed by Boreal. One of the guards briefly looked to her and was about to move to intercept but he turned away as his attention shifted to Ember, who made a feint dash forwards.

Zalia sprinted past, firing an arrow into the man as she ran. He held his side in pain; the arrow ignored his heavy armour completely, a distraction that allowed Ember able to tackle him. Zen and Indis were keeping the other man busy, so Zalia turned away and focused on her task.

"Juniper!" she yelled, her voice and the sounds of battle behind her drowned out by the rumbling sound coming from the ritual. She could see similar, though significantly smaller beams blasting into the sky all across the land behind her.

"What have you done!?" she yelled.

This time Juniper heard her, turning in surprise. The woman looked ghastly, like the life had been drained from her.

"I did . . . I did what I had to," Juniper sputtered out between coughs.

Zalia ran past the obviously spent woman and managed to push through the winds surrounding the beam to see the ritual. She tried to cut at the runes and lines but didn't manage to even scratch them.

"How do I stop it!?" she yelled at Juniper.

"You can't, Zalia, it is over," Juniper said weakly.

Zalia stared desperately at the runes.

She looked back over Juniper's head just as Zen was run through by the guard's blade.

"NO!" she screamed.

Zen grabbed the blade impaling him and Indis blasted the guard with a bolt of lightning as a primal sound, a mix of a scream and a yell, escaped her mouth.

"STOP THE RITUAL," Indis screamed at Zalia.

Zalia turned away as tears formed in the corners of her eyes. She started focusing her Healing Presence on Zen, hoping he would survive while she broke the ritual.

As she looked at the ritual, only a single idea entered her mind. The process she had repeated many times over when she was trying to deal with rituals she didn't quite understand but wanted to enhance or change their effects.

She started quickly overlaying the entire thing with Bitterbalm. The herb had a description that said it would add an element of curse to a ritual, but through her instinctive knowledge she knew that wasn't quite accurate. It more accurately reversed the ritual's intended effect.

Juniper tried to rise to stop her but only managed to get to one knee, still weak from whatever she'd done to start the ritual in the first place. Zalia finished her work and the ritual activated. She didn't know what was about to happen but held out hope all the same.

The Bitterbalm started glowing. Juniper made a sound of protest as she collapsed. Zalia turned towards her friends, watching helplessly as Larel and the Hidden fell over the side of the spire with their fight.

With a sucking sound, the beam instantly reversed and smashed back into the tower, ripping Zalia into it. Eerily similar to another event she had recently experienced, she saw vivid colours, and closed her eyes as she begin to feel nauseated. She heard the sound of a water drop hitting a still pond, only magnified a hundredfold.

Zalia opened her eyes as the tear on her cheek finally fell to the ground.

About the Author

Leif Roder is the author of the Hunting and Herbalism series, originally released on Royal Road. A one-time engineering student, he ultimately dropped out of school and proceeded to bounce around, pursuing a hundred different interests and career paths, before finally arriving at writing. An Australian, Roder currently resides in New Zealand.

Podium

DISCOVER MORE

STORIES
UNBOUND